THIS
IS MY
TRUTH

ALSO BY YASMIN RAHMAN

All the Things We Never Said

THIS IS MY TRUTH

YASMIN RAHMAN

HOT
KEY
BOOKS

First published in Great Britain in 2021 by
HOT KEY BOOKS
80–81 Wimpole St, London W1G 9RE
Owned by Bonnier Books
Sveavägen 56, Stockholm, Sweden
www.hotkeybooks.com

A CIP catalogue record for this book is available from the British Library.

ISBN: 978-1-4714-1052-9
Also available as an ebook and in audio

1

This book is typeset using Atomik ePublisher
Printed and bound in Great Britain by Clays Ltd, Elcograf S.p.A.

Hot Key Books is an imprint of Bonnier Books UK
www.bonnierbooks.co.uk

PLEASE NOTE: This book deals with domestic abuse, both emotional and physical. Please read with caution and turn to page 381 for a list of support resources, should you need it.

For anyone whose life has been affected by domestic violence

1

There are plenty of theories about the best way to wake up in the morning. Some go for a gradually brightening light alarm, waking up gently as they adjust to the fake sunrise. Others opt for loud noises that immediately strike fear in their heart. I, on the other hand, put forward that the most effective way to get someone out of bed is having their five-year-old brother sit on their head.

'Oh my God, Ismail, GET OFF!' I yell, my voice muffled by his body.

Ismail giggles as he wiggles around on my face. I can't help but laugh too as I push him off. He flops onto the mattress, cackling maniacally. I take my chance, reach over and start tickling him under the arms; as expected, he screams happily.

'Shhhhh,' I say, covering his mouth and watching the door. 'We'll get told off.'

Ismail's grin slowly melts against my palm.

'Why are you up so early?' I ask, reaching for my phone to check the time. The screen doesn't light up. I tap it again. Nothing. I press the power button and my stomach drops when I see the dead battery sign. I check my charger lead and find that it's been disconnected from the plug adapter all night.

'Oh crap,' I say, jumping out of bed. I check the clock on

the wall. 'We are *so* late,' I tell Ismail. His slightly too long black hair is standing up in haywire tufts, and his Spiderman pyjamas are all crinkled from the tickle fight. Ammi normally wakes him up and gets him ready; I don't understand what's happened today. I need to shower. Now I guess I'll need to get Ismail ready too. And give him breakfast. And, oh God, I was supposed to wake up early to revise for my biology practice exam! Crap, crap, crap.

'Where's Ammi?' I ask. I'm angry at her. My phone died during the night, but what's her excuse? She's meant to be up first. It's her job to do all this. Ismail is usually eating breakfast when I wake up.

'She's sleeping,' he tells me, casually stretching out across my bed. 'I tried waking her but she won't get up.'

She must be having an off day. She has these sometimes, where she can't get out of bed. I'll come home from school and she'll only just be eating breakfast. On days like this, things are super scattered, and it makes me anxious and flustered. Normally I'm up on time and can take over.

'OK, right,' I say, trying to gather myself. 'Right, yes . . . let's . . . We can do this. First things first, you need to get into your uniform.'

Ismail looks right at me and blows a raspberry, before dissolving into laughter again.

Oh God, this is going to be hard.

'I don't wanna eat Shreddies! I want pancakes!' Ismail says, knocking over the box of cereal so brown squares scatter across the table. I pick one up and pop it into my mouth, partly because they're delicious, and partly to stop myself from yelling, like I so want to. I don't know how Ammi does this every day; Ismail can be really annoying when you're stressed.

'We're already late – there's no time for pancakes,' I tell him, picking up the box and fixing the mess he's made. 'We don't even have time for breakfast, but I know you'll just end up cranky and your teacher will tell Ammi off again. Just eat your cereal. Here, I'll even put some sugar on it for you.' I go to sprinkle some sugar in his bowl, but he knocks the spoon out of my hand and starts giggling again.

'Ismail!' I yell. 'This isn't funny. We're *so* late. Can you just eat. Please?'

'No Shreddies! I want pancakes!'

Ughhhhhh. This boy, I swear to God. Sometimes he acts like he's three years old, not five. I look at the clock and panic again. I should've just given him a banana and forced him out of the door. I look down at his grinning face, those mischievous brown eyes, and realise I need to play dirty if I'm gonna get anywhere with him.

'Fine, you know what? You don't have to go to school today. At all,' I say.

His eyes light up and he sits up straight. 'For real?'

I nod, cleaning up the spilled sugar on the table. 'Yeah, you can just stay at home. Ammi's not well, so she'll be in bed all day. It'll just be you and Abbu when he gets back from work. I don't think he's gonna be happy about you skiving though.'

That does it. His smile drops. I almost feel bad, but I force myself to act normal. Calm. Like Ammi. I hand him the cereal spoon again. He takes it this time.

'Can I watch a video?' he asks, his mouth still empty. 'One of yours?'

I shouldn't let him; I know that it's a bad habit. But I also know the best thing to do right now is let him have his way. My phone's still on charge, so I grab Ammi's iPad, load up my YouTube channel and pass the device over.

Making videos is my biggest hobby. I make all kinds of weird things – remakes of movie scenes (mostly Disney films) using toys or household items, videos of Ismail being goofy, and sometimes stop-motion shorts. Ismail helps with a lot of them, which is probably why he's so into them. I usually save watching them as a treat for him, but like I say, this is an extreme case.

He *finally* starts eating, and I busy myself making cheese sandwiches for his lunch. God, I can't believe we woke up *this* late. As I spread mayonnaise, I imagine what will happen when I get into school. Miss Kirtley in reception is always a bitch to anyone who's late – 'You'll get nowhere in life if you turn up late, Amani,' she'll say. And then there's the whole thing of having to walk into class while everyone's already working. I'm tempted to skive, but like Ismail, the thought of being around Abbu all day while Ammi's upstairs resting is a bit much.

As if I've willed him into existence, I hear Abbu's voice. My heart spikes, thinking he's going to go ballistic, seeing Ismail and me still at home, seeing me making sandwiches while Ammi's asleep upstairs. I turn around, the butter knife almost dropping from my hand, but then I realise that Ismail has just switched over to the live TV app on the iPad. And there's Abbu on the screen, smile plastered across his face. You'd think I'd be used to this by now – Abbu's been a presenter on a kids' TV show about vets and animals, *Creature Clinic*, for years, though I haven't watched it myself in ages. Today he's on adult TV though. Some breakfast show, trying to promote the next series of *Creature Clinic*.

'Look, Maani, it's Abbu!' Ismail says, his voice full of glee (and, thankfully, Shreddies).

We both watch the screen, watch this version of Abbu that we never see at home. I get that he has to become this personality for his job, but it's honestly like a completely different person is in front of me. He even has banter with the presenters as he sits on the sofa, stroking a cat. The presenters are also holding small animals. They're laughing as if they've never heard someone funnier than Abbu. It makes me smile – seeing that he's so good at his job.

Abbu was a proper vet for years, when I was younger, and then he got offered the *Creature Clinic* gig, which paid a lot more. He often does these live TV appearances to promote the show – he'll go on and entertain people with some cute animals and weird facts.

I focus on putting extra mayonnaise on Ismail's sandwiches because I know he likes them soggy. I'm just cutting the crusts off when I hear yelling from the iPad. I turn to find chaos on the screen. Everyone is up off the sofa now. There's a . . . a cat attached to Abbu's beard. He tries to shake it off, but it's got a death grip on him. The blonde female presenter screams as his movements make the cat swing back and forth. Next thing I know, the other animals have gone berserk too. There's a lizard tangled in the blonde lady's long hair, with the same death grip, and a guinea pig runs into the audience.

'Get this fucking piece of shit off me!' Abbu yells, as the woman continues to scream.

He stumbles and falls backwards over the sofa. There's a loud crash and then all you can see is his legs sticking up behind the red sofa.

The screen *finally* cuts to the weather.

I am mortified. Ismail, however, is cackling. Milk-running-from-the-corners-of-his-mouth, danger-of-choking-type cackling.

'Did you see that, Maani?' He turns to me, tears in his eyes. 'Abbu had a cat on his face! He fell over!' He begins cackling again.

Oh God, this is bad. So bad. Fear courses through my body. Abbu is going to feel . . . humiliated.

'Ismail, come on,' I say, more fiercely than ever. 'We have to go. Now.' I snatch up the half-finished bowl of cereal and drop it in the sink.

'Hey, my Shreddies!'

'Oh, *now* you want them?' I shove his sandwiches into his lunch bag.

'I want Ammi,' he says, a slight whine in his voice.

I don't reply, just focus on filling his water bottle.

'Why is she still sleeping?' he asks. 'Isn't she gonna walk me to school?'

'Nope, it's gonna be me today.'

We need to leave. Need to get away from here as soon as possible. I keep seeing Abbu falling backwards over the sofa, the cat attached to his beard.

'Get your shoes on.'

'But Ammi *always* walks me to school,' he says, still at the table. 'She's walked me before when she's sick. Why not today?' He's talking in that soft vulnerable voice that says he's about to start crying. Oh God, it's breaking my heart.

'Hey, it'll be fun. Just us two. We can blow dandelions on the way. Sound good?' Ismail loves doing this in the garden.

'Will Ammi pick me up?' he asks, looking up at me.

'What, I'm not good enough for you?' I joke.

'I want Ammi to take me.'

I can hear the tears crawling further into his voice. No no no! It's at times like this I wish Ismail could suddenly be five years older. I love him to bits, but he can be a handful to look after, even more so when I'm already stressed about being late, about my biology practice exam, about Abbu, and Ammi, and just everything. I *need* to get to school. There's something about school that calms me. Even though I'm not the best student, I like being there. At school, I know what's happening. I know what classes I'm supposed to be in, where I have to go next. I know what we're going to be learning about, and the names of everyone in my class. There's structure, and certainty. Ten times ten is always one hundred. But at home . . .

'Hey, c'mon, don't be sad,' I tell Ismail, immediately cringing because I know this will make it worse. As expected, the tears start falling.

'Wanna know something *super fun* we can do?' I ask him, desperately trying to both distract and cheer him up. 'I can take you the super-secret way to school. No one knows about this way. Not even Ammi.'

'Really?' he sniffles. 'But Ammi knows everything.'

'Not this. This is a secret only I know. It's the big-kid way.

And today I'll let you in on it, but you have to promise not to tell anyone. I can trust you, right?'

He nods eagerly.

'Good, OK, now hurry up and put your shoes on – otherwise we won't have time to go the secret way.'

He scrambles into the hallway. Thank God.

Now I just have to think up some secret way to walk to school.

2

School passes in a weird rush. Maybe that's what happens when you're late (and trying to forget the image of your dad being humiliated on live TV). Homework is doled out in most lessons, we're reminded about coursework due in others. Biology was fifth period and my brain is still hurting from the practice exam as I walk towards the gates after school. There's a big notice board right in the middle of the quad. It's usually filled with posters about discos, parent–teacher evenings and upcoming school trips. That's all been replaced now with a countdown. One just for us Year Elevens.

22 DAYS TO GO

Twenty-two days left until exams start. Until the end of school. Of course there's still sixth form, but that doesn't seem the same. It's the end of an era. And every time I think about it, my stomach churns. It feels like I'm in a car speeding towards an unfinished bridge. The ones that only appear in bad action movies, or cartoons. Except I don't have the skills to avoid the inevitable crash – I don't even know how to drive the car I'm in. That's why I usually avoid walking through the quad. I don't need any more reminders about the terrifying future ahead of me.

I put my head down and walk faster. Past the board, past the horrible visions of the future, and towards the art block, where Huda is waiting for me. She's talking to a boy in our year. Ezra Fitzgerald. Huda's that person who knows EVERYONE; we'll be walking around and every other person will give her a nod, a high five, even a hug. I didn't realise she was friendly with Ezra though. Our year is separated into two halves – the X band and the Y band. Each band has three classes. The separation is just for registration – our actual lessons are a mix of all students. But even so, there's a sort of unspoken rivalry. The X band thinks all the Y band are losers, and the Y band (which includes me and Huda) thinks the X band are troublemakers. Which is why I'm shocked to see Huda with Ezra. He's like the most popular boy in the X band. Also a dickhead. Back in Year Nine, he once called me a towelhead, and I've never forgiven him. Huda, on the other hand, doesn't seem to remember any of that, considering how she's laughing with him. I'm too far away to hear what they're talking about. I try to remember whether he's in any of her classes, but no – Huda is in top set for everything, and Ezra . . . well, Ezra is in the X band for a reason.

'It's gonna be epic!' he says as I get within earshot.

Huda notices me finally, and smiles. 'Talk to you later, yeah?' she says to him before walking towards me.

Ezra turns and our eyes meet. I swear his smile drops. His focus goes to my headscarf, and I instinctively reach up to adjust it. Which is stupid, because he was all laughs and jokes with Headscarved Huda just a second ago. Why doesn't he look at her like this, with the scorn he's giving me?

Actually, I can answer that. Huda just fits in. With everyone, everywhere. She is one of those people everyone loves, and trusts. Which is ironic, considering how many foster homes she's been in. OK, that was a bit harsh. But I'm ashamed to admit, I really am jealous of her ability to fit in. What I would give to be able to join any group and not feel like a sore thumb. It's effortless for Huda, and she doesn't even notice it.

'What was that about?' I ask her as soon as Ezra's behind us. I can't help the tinge of annoyance in my voice.

'What was *what* about?' she asks nonchalantly. The thing is, I don't think she's doing it on purpose; she probably genuinely doesn't understand why it's weird for her to be talking to Ezra.

'Since when are you two such good friends?'

'Jealous, are we?' she teases, nudging me off the path with her elbow, then pulling me back into a one-armed hug. 'Ah, no one can replace you, Amani – thought you'd know that after all these years. I love you, bestie.'

I shrug her off. 'I didn't say you were besties. It's just . . . It's *Ezra*. What does he even talk about besides how often he goes to the gym?'

'How many protein shakes he has,' Huda replies.

I can't stop the snort that comes out. 'How many packs he's got. Because a six-pack isn't enough nowadays.'

'I hear he's up to sixteen. If he gets to eighteen, it'll be a world record.'

I laugh as we walk out of the gates onto the main road.

'Seriously though, what did he want? Was he giving you grief?' I think back to his stupid comment from years ago.

'Ezra? Nah, as if. We were just talking about the prank war.'

'Oh God, is that starting already?'

Blithe Academy has a longstanding tradition for Year Elevens. The last few weeks of school are always filled with ridiculous, stupid pranks. It usually starts off as another way to enhance the rivalry between the bands, and then somehow everyone comes together to pull increasingly wild stunts. I don't know how long this has been going on for – as long as I've been at this school, that's for sure. It's reached the point now where the last few years they've started study leave early. Last year they suddenly took all the Year Elevens out of class three days before the countdown was due to finish, to a special emergency assembly – I remember hearing that some people thought there'd been a terrorist attack or a school shooter or something. They got everyone in the hall and told them that school was over. That was it. They were escorted off the campus. Like, no going back to pack up the classroom or anything – a girl I know was halfway through doing a sculpture for her art coursework and wasn't even allowed back in to wash her hands. Teachers have just become so scared of what students will do – they're trying anything they can to get the upper hand. And to be fair, I don't blame them. There have been some crazy pranks. One time everyone brought in hundreds of small alarm clocks and hid them around the school – in the assembly hall, in classrooms, even in the toilets. The alarms went off randomly and everyone was frantically trying to find and stop them.

'I tried to get Ezra to spill what they were planning, but he's giving nothing up,' Huda explains sadly.

'Tell me you're not getting involved with all that,' I say, surprised.

'I wish,' she says. 'Like literally. I *wish*. I thought that if I tried to mole out some details from the other side, they'd let me be part of things.'

'Why would Ezra tell you anything though? Doesn't that defeat the whole point of a prank *war*?'

'I pretended it was for the end. Y'know, when everyone gets together. I so wanna know what they're planning. It's gotta be huge, don't you think, to beat the clock thing?'

I shrug. 'I'm not really that fussed. I'd rather not bother with any of this; it's distracting.'

Huda scoffs. 'But this is what we'll remember! When we're old soggy grandmas, living next door to each other, ignoring our grandkids to sit in the garden eating samosas together, this is what we'll be talking about. The best times of our lives.'

'You really think this is as good as it gets?' I raise an eyebrow. 'You think in seventy, eighty years, nothing will beat some alarm clocks going off at our old school? I'd like to think I'd have had a few more adventures.'

She shrugs. 'I guess. It just feels like *a lot*, y'know? There's so many lasts – it feels like we need to recognise and celebrate them all.'

I want to tell her there's not much to celebrate. That the future is scary as hell. That I feel like the end of school signifies the end of my freedom in a way. Speeding down a career path I'm not entirely comfortable with.

I'm planning to become a vet like Abbu. But the truth is that I don't think I'm going to be any good at it. Actually, I *know* I won't be. The number of times Mr Cavanaugh rolls his eyes at me during lessons is frankly quite insulting. I'm barely passing at the moment, and I need at least 7s in biology, chemistry and physics to do them for A level. I have this weird vision of me being the thickest student in sixth form – everyone laughing at me for not being able to identify an element or something. It's inevitable though. Regardless of how shit the situation is. Of how shit I am. I have no choice but to carry on.

'How did your biology test go?' Huda asks, proving that best friends really can read each other's minds.

I groan. 'Oh God, don't.' I theatrically throw my head back and feel a raindrop on my face. 'I am *so* going to fail.'

'It can't have been *that* bad.'

'You would say that. You're just naturally perfect at everything. Tell me your secret, please.'

She laughs. 'How about I help you study?'

'Oh God, yes please. Thanks, Huda. You're the best.'

'What was that?' she asks, cupping a hand around her ear.

I laugh; this is peak Huda. 'You're the best!' I shout. 'HUDA FARQUHAR IS THE BEST IN THE WORLD!' I scream it out loud, with her full name, because I know she won't stop until she gets me to that point.

'And don't you f—'

Huda is cut off by a voice behind us.

'Oh, look, girls, Amani is publicly declaring her love for her girlfriend. Isn't that cute?'

I turn around, but there's no mistaking that voice. I'd know it anywhere. Cleo Walters. She's surrounded by her two minions – Suzie Babble and Imogen O'Donnell. Those three are inseparable. You know those teen films where the mean girls make everyone's lives hell? That's them. Huda and I call them The Coven behind their backs. Well, Huda says it to their faces too actually.

'Don't be jealous just because you'll never have someone say they love you,' Huda retorts, without even batting an eyelid.

Here's another thing I'm insanely jealous of Huda about. She always has the perfect comeback. The wittiest remark – the best response – to *anybody*. Regardless of what they've said to her. Nothing fazes her. Me, on the other hand, I'm already filled with anxiety, wanting Cleo and her sidekicks to just move on, to go as far away from us as possible, because it's legit making me feel on edge just being *near* them.

Cleo rolls her eyes at Huda, then turns her sights back onto me. It's like she has night vision, but instead of seeing in the dark, hers pinpoints the weakest link. And that's always me.

'Saw that video of your dad, Amani,' she says, a smirk tugging at her mouth. Her groupies giggle.

'What video?' It slips out.

'God, I know your people are from a different land, but surely they have social media there?' She gets her phone out and taps away on it. After a few seconds, she turns it around to show me, and there's Abbu. His TV appearance from this morning. My heart stops and my vision blurs with tears, but I can still hear Abbu's voice screaming, 'Get this fucking piece of shit off me!'

'My favourite part is when the cat gets stuck to his chin,' Suzie laughs. 'Everyone's calling him cat beard, you know.'

Huda moves in front of me and pushes Cleo's hand away. She glares at Suzie. 'Better than being called Boozie Blabbermouth, which is what everyone calls you behind your back.'

Suzie says nothing back. I think she's scowling, but I can't tell. My vision has gone funny. Everyone was at school when Abbu was on air – how did they find this video?

'Oh, like you can talk,' Cleo says to Huda. 'You're so ugly that your own parents couldn't stand to keep you.'

'Right, yeah,' Huda says. 'Your parents kept *you*, the pretty baby, and look at the witch they're stuck with. They probably *wish* they'd given you up as a baby.'

Cleo starts to respond, but Huda cuts her off.

'C'mon, Amani, let's get away from these bitches. Oops, I mean witches. No, wait, bitches is also true.' She grabs my arm and drags me away.

I don't know if Cleo and her friends say anything else as we walk off. I'm not paying attention any more. All I can think of is that video. How on earth did Cleo find it? And how many more people have seen it? I pull out my own phone from my pocket as Huda moans about what a bitch Cleo is. My phone barely charged this morning, so I've been avoiding using it all day. There's only five per cent battery left now. My screen is filled with notifications. Twitter, Instagram, even Facebook. You know it's big when people are using Facebook. I flick through my notification screen quickly, just to make sure

16

there's nothing important I've missed. I try not to focus on any comment in particular, but I catch the odd word – 'omg' and 'lol' and of course 'your dad'. There's no way I can just skim this. I open Twitter first, but instead of pressing the notification icon, I accidentally click on 'Trending Topics'. A photo appears with the top trending story and . . . Holy shit, it's Abbu.

Abbu is trending on Twitter. There's a photo of him at the top, the cat clutching on to his beard. My thumb hovers over the hashtag – #CatBeard – as I try to decide whether it's better for me to see what they're saying about him, or ignore it all, pretend none of this is happening. I wonder if I can report this to Twitter for bullying. If Abbu catches wind of how big it's got, hears that people are making fun of me for it, he'll go ballistic.

Luckily – or maybe unluckily – the decision is made for me, as my phone runs completely out of battery. The screen turns black, blocking out Abbu's face, his humiliation, taking away all the people making fun of him. It's all gone.

'Did you know?' I ask Huda. We sat together at lunch today, and even in third period. She hasn't said a word to me about it. But she's constantly on Twitter, so she must have seen it, right?

'Know about what?' she asks, all innocent. 'I know about a lot of things. Like, did you know that to stop hiccups, you just need to press a finger to your –'

'About my dad,' I say, cutting her off. 'About the video.'

She doesn't reply straight away, which says it all. 'I didn't know if you'd seen it,' she says softly. 'I just . . . I didn't want you to feel . . . well, like you do now, I guess.'

'I saw it live,' I tell her. 'This morning, when we were running late, Ismail was watching on the iPad.'

'Have you spoken to your dad since?'

I shake my head. I can't think about talking to Abbu about this. Or seeing him. He's probably home right now, sitting in the living room, seething. Abbu in a bad mood is not something anyone wants to encounter.

We've reached the fork in the road where Huda and I split. The rain is coming down a bit heavier now. Huda's put her blazer over her head.

'Were you serious about the tutoring?' I ask her quickly. 'Can you do right now?'

'Uh, yeah, I guess so. I can come over –'

'No, no, let's just . . . Can we go to yours?' I stare at her intently, trying not to seem *too* desperate, but desperate enough that she feels she can't say no to me.

It works.

'Sure, let's go.'

3

Huda's foster mum, Nafisah, is nowhere to be seen. She's left a sticky note on the fridge saying '*Popped out to get some baked beans – having cravings! Will get you some Reese's cups! x*'. I smile when I see it – Huda's foster parents are the absolute cutest. If you met them, you'd think they were right out of a picture book – that's how well they treat Huda. And if you saw them together, you'd think they were part of some cheesy rom-com – that's how much they love each other. And they're not afraid to show it. I remember the first time they kissed in front of me. It was just a peck, but I was so shocked. No one's parents had done anything like that in front of me before – well, no Asian parents anyway.

Huda reads the note, rolls her eyes and scrunches it up into a ball before dropping it into the bin. She turns to me, and her sour look has been replaced by a smile. I don't think she knows I saw her reaction.

'Crisps and hummus?' she asks.

'Only if you've got the good stuff,' I tell her. 'None of that weird beetroot crap you had last time.'

'Oh God, that was Ali's fault. He wouldn't know good hummus if it hit him in the face.'

'When's he back from work? He's not gonna mind if I'm here, right? I know you usually check . . .'

'Don't be silly. Him and Nafisah love you. You're basically like the furniture here. Just a bit less scuffed.' She takes a couple of cans of Sprite from the fridge and throws them to me, then grabs the big tub of hummus and closes the fridge. She gets out a giant bag of Kettle Chips from the cupboard and heads towards the stairs. I follow.

I stick my phone on charge as soon as I get into Huda's room. I sit cross-legged on her floor, take off my blazer and lean back against her bed, waiting for the Apple logo to come up on the screen. Huda busies herself opening the crisps and starting up a Spotify playlist on her laptop. When I finally get onto the internet, I feel sick. Abbu has gone proper viral. Like that guy whose cute kid came dancing into the room when he was on the news. *Everyone* is talking about him. UNILAD has the video up on there, the *Metro* too. There's so many edits of it all over Twitter, YouTube. So many comments, so many laughing-face emojis.

'I feel sick,' I say. I thought I'd muttered it, but Huda hears and ambles over.

She snatches the phone out of my hand and replaces it with the large packet of crisps – she's already made a decent dent in them. How long was I even looking at my phone?

'None of that crap,' Huda tells me. 'Eat this crap instead.' With one hand she holds out the pot of hummus for me to dip, while closing down all the social-media pages on my phone with the other.

I take a crisp and submerge it completely in the dip before bringing it out and sticking it whole in my mouth.

'It'll pass,' she says. 'This stuff always does. There'll be something new to talk about tomorrow.'

'Today's news, tomorrow's chip paper,' I mumble, repeating something my media studies teacher says a lot.

'Huh?' Huda asks.

I shake my head. It's not really the reactions of strangers I'm worried about. Just Abbu's. How's he going to react to people laughing at him, telling him he's an embarrassment to TV, that he should just quit his job? One person even went so far as saying he should . . . kill himself. God, people on the internet are cruel.

'How about I distract you with something?' Huda says, all mischievous-like.

I raise an eyebrow at her.

'Something *fascinating* and *exciting* . . .' she teases like a circus entertainer.

'I swear to God, if you say science . . .'

'Not just *any* kind of science . . . cell biology!'

I roll my eyes. 'You have the same sense of fun as a forty-year-old teacher.'

She grabs a cushion from behind her (her bed is covered in them – literally like ten cushions just sitting there for show) and knocks me over the head with it. 'Do you wanna pass your science GCSEs or not?'

'Yes, miss.'

'Good. So make sure you pay attention. You won't get to be a vet if you don't know about cell biology.'

I don't reply. I just dunk another crisp in the hummus. It breaks as I go to pull it out.

* * *

Huda and I do our prayers together before settling down to study. An hour or so later, the front door opens.

'Huda?' Nafisah calls from downstairs. 'Can you come and help with the bags?'

Huda huffs a little. She hands me the pad she's been neatly writing notes for me on and stretches before grabbing her headscarf and leaving the room. I've been sitting down for so long my bum has gone numb, so I decide to go and help out too.

When I get downstairs, the front door is open and there's a cool breeze coming through. There's no sign of Ali, but Nafisah is standing in the kitchen opening a tin of baked beans.

'Salaam, Nafisah,' I say.

She looks up from her tin and gives me the biggest smile. 'Salaam, sweetie. How are you?'

'Yeah, good, thanks. Uh . . . want any help?'

She turns back to her beans, spinning the tin opener with ease. 'Huda and Ali are just getting the shopping. You can help put things away if you want.' The lid snaps off and Nafisah stares down into the tin with such adoration it makes me smile.

'Cravings still going strong then?' I ask.

She laughs. 'Oh, Amani, it's ridiculous. This baby, I swear.' She pauses to rub her very large bump. 'The other night, at 3 a.m., I was desperate for biryani. To the extent that I got progressively more nauseous the longer I went without biryani in my mouth. And so what could I do?'

'You got up and made biryani at three in the morning?' I exclaim.

22

'Um, no,' Ali says as he comes in through the door, arms loaded with shopping bags. '*I* had to get up and make biryani at three in the morning.'

Huda traipses in behind him with a few more bags.

'Baby wanted him to make it,' Nafisah explains with a smirk.

'Baby wants, baby gets,' Huda says.

'Exactly!' Ali enthuses. 'Only the best for my lil bump-erina.' He walks from the pile of bags he's dumped by the door over to Nafisah and gives her a hug from behind, caressing her bump. She smiles big and raises a hand to stroke his cheek.

I feel a blush rising up my face, watching them be so openly PDA. Affection, especially in public, is not something my family does. It's not something I've grown up with. When I was a kid, I used to assume my adult relatives just didn't get on very well with their spouses. I thought that's what marriage was – not being happy. As if Bengali people weren't allowed to be happy with their relationships, or not in public anyway. And then I came across Ali and Nafisah. They're so not the usual Bengali parents. They're quite young, for starters. Nafisah wears her scarf turban-style, adding jewellery to make it pop. They're so laid-back too – Huda has it so easy with them. And like I said, they're *very* touchy-feely. It was such a strange sight at first, but of course completely and perfectly normal – why shouldn't they show their affection for each other? I just hope they never do it in front of my parents, because I think they'd die from shock.

And then there's the name thing. Ammi and Nafisah are best friends, even though Ammi is a lot older, and I always hesitate to call Nafisah by her name when they're together, even though she insists. Calling someone Auntie or Uncle is a sign of respect in our culture. It's weird to come across people who reject that.

I think what strikes me most about Ali and Nafisah though is just . . . how normal they are. They don't ever seem to fight, or hold grudges, or have big secrets. They just get on with it, with huge smiles on their faces at all times. It's like they've come straight out of some kids' TV programme. They make me realise that it's possible to have this. That one day, I could have this. Because God knows my own parents have not been setting the same example.

A cupboard door clatters loudly as Huda starts putting away the shopping. Everyone turns to look at her, thinking she was doing it on purpose, but she doesn't even apologise, just continues packing stuff away. I grab a bag and help her. I come here often enough that I actually know where most of the food goes.

'How's Shirin?' Nafisah asks me. 'We're meant to be going to town tomorrow, and I've texted her to confirm a few times, but she hasn't replied.'

'Yeah, Ammi's fine,' I say, putting away a box of cereal. 'She's just . . . picked up a few more shifts at work. Everyone's having barbecues cos of the weather, so it's been busy at the shop.'

'Ah, well, remind her she needs to finish the mural in the nursery,' Nafisah says before spooning some baked beans into her mouth.

'Are you just eating those straight out of the tin?' Huda exclaims.

'What, you want me to put them on a plate?' Nafisah asks, her voice muffled. 'Ain't nobody got time for that.'

Huda just stares in shock, a look of disgust on her face. 'You're eating them *cold*?!'

'They're nice! Here, have some.' Nafisah holds the spoon out to her, but Huda recoils.

'Huda, are you *scared* of cold baked beans?' Ali teases. He takes the spoon out of Nafisah's hand and begins chasing Huda, shouting, 'OooooOoooOOoO cold beans are gonna get you.'

Huda squeals and runs away from him. They're all laughing now, and I'm just standing at the edge of the room looking on, wishing that this could be *my* family. I take out my phone and start filming the scene. I find myself doing this a lot – just filming random things that strike me. My media studies teacher, Mr Voake, says it's because I have an 'artist's attention span'.

Ali turns to me, and I lower my phone. He puts out his arms all zombie-like and starts walking towards me, spoon of precariously stacked beans inching towards me.

'How about Amani? Is she scared of the dubiously cold beans that look like guts?' He approaches me and I just smile and stay in place, unlike Huda. I even open my mouth, and he sticks the spoon in.

'Guts do taste good,' I say, realising cold beans actually aren't that bad.

Ali smiles and Nafisah laughs.

'Can I have my spoon back now? The tin's still half full.'

Ali turns and walks back to Nafisah, handing her the spoon. She tucks right back in.

'Save some for dinner,' he reminds her, starting to unpack the next shopping bag. 'I thought you wanted a beanie bake?'

'No need. Baby just wants this.'

'Well, either way, we've bought all the stuff now. So baby is getting beanie bake.'

'Oop!' Nafisah squeaks, putting her hand on her stomach. 'Baby does not like you disagreeing with it like that.' She laughs.

Ali laughs too, as he bends over so his face is level with Nafisah's bump. 'Whatcha gonna do, eh?' Ali asks. 'You're in there, and I'm out here, and I'm gonna make all the beanie bake I –'

'It's kicking loads!' Nafisah laughs.

'Well, baby better –'

'Do you wanna stay for dinner?' Huda asks me suddenly, loudly.

I turn to look at her. Ali turns to look at her. Nafisah turns to look at her. Everyone's confused at her outburst. Huda herself has a weird look on her face: a mix of sadness and anger and desperation. It's a look I've not seen on her before. But I get that she needs me to answer. I just can't decide *how* she wants me to answer. It's not like I have much of a choice though.

'Thanks,' I say. 'But I should get back home.'

4

'Thanks for the lift,' I tell Ali as I open the door super slowly, trying to prolong the amount of time I spend out of my house. 'You really didn't have to.'

'Don't be silly,' he replies. 'Anything to get me away from the angry pregnant lady.'

I laugh. 'Serves you right for dropping her beans.'

'It was an accident!'

We sink into silence. I sort of want him to offer to walk me to my door, just to give me another minute of normality, of ignorance, but I know that's a dangerous idea.

So instead I say goodbye and get out of the car. Ali drives off immediately.

I look towards my house. The living-room light is on. Abbu and probably Ammi are in there. I stand outside the front door and listen. When I hear nothing, I slip my key into the lock as slowly and quietly as I can, and turn it.

The door to the living room is shut. And as I take my shoes off in the hall, there doesn't appear to be any noise coming from in there. I'm tempted to go in and say salaam to Abbu. But there's something stopping me. If I don't go in, I don't have to know the truth. I can pretend. Maybe Abbu hasn't seen any of the stuff online. Maybe . . . just maybe, he's laughing it all off. Maybe he's over it. Maybe . . . he's had a complete personality transplant.

I go up to my room, change out of my uniform and do my last prayers for the day. I know I should go over the notes Huda made for me, but I'm suddenly hit by the smell of dinner. Not just any dinner. Lamb pilau. Ammi is making Abbu's favourite. (And mine, but I'm assuming she's not doing this for my benefit.) Could it be her way of trying to cheer him up? Or distract him.

I go downstairs to the kitchen. Ammi turns to look at me. I'm worried she'll tell me off for choosing today to go to Huda's house, but she smiles.

'The smell brought you home then?' she asks, turning back to the stove. Wow, she's making samosas too. We only ever get that combination when we have guests.

I walk over to her. 'You know how much I love your lamb pilau. Is it done yet?'

'Almost,' she replies, lifting the lid of the pot and looking in.

I stand by the samosa pan and start ladling hot oil over the frying snacks – a trick Ammi taught me when I was younger. I try to assess her out of the corner of my eye. She seems normal. Maybe Abbu really is in an OK mood. But if he was, she wouldn't be making pilau. At the very least, Ammi knows what happened. She's either seen it herself or heard from Abbu.

'Nafisah says hi, by the way,' I say, just to break the silence. 'She said to call her.'

Ammi smiles. 'I will. We're going to town together tomorrow – do you need anything?'

'Can you get some sand? I wanted to recreate a scene from

Moana for a video. I was going to ask you – can you paint me a background like you did for the *Inside Out* one? That was amazing.'

Ammi frowns. 'Shouldn't you give the videos a rest now? Focus on your studies. You know what your abbu will say if he sees you with your camera again.'

I do know what Abbu will say, and none of it will be good. He caught me making a YouTube video with Ismail a few months back and completely lost his shit. He told me that film-making is a hobby for people who have no skills, that I should be aiming higher, using my time more wisely. He trashed the scene I had set up – Ammi had spent ages making some cardboard trees. Ismail cried. I did too, but not till I was alone in bed that night.

I tried to stop making the videos then, but there's something in me that won't let it go. I've just learned to hide it from Abbu. Ammi still helps me out with arty stuff on the sly, which is nice. She's amazing at making scenery and props. Ammi, Ismail and I make a great team actually.

I want to tell her I *can't* give up film-making. It's practically the only thing that brings me joy. Instead of saying anything though, I just continue cooking the samosas, like the meek little pushover I am.

Dinner starts off awkwardly. Abbu's shaved off his beard entirely. It's so weird to see him without one. It makes his expressions more obvious. His face is downcast, moody, stern. I'm scared of something setting him off.

'We played a new game today,' Ismail says as he eats. 'It's

called Stuck in the Mud. You do eeny meeny miny mo to choose the person who's *it*, and they have to chase everyone around, and if they touch you, you can't move. You have to stand there like this.' He pulls a strained face and sticks his arms out to the side. 'And you have to jiggle your way down to the ground like a wriggly ghost. The other people running around come and touch you and then you're unstuck and you can run again. *But!* If you get all the way down to the floor, then you have to sit down and you're out. We were playing at lunch and I was stuck for *ever*. I wriggled really slowly so I wouldn't have to be out and Sachin kept running near me but he wouldn't unstick me. He just ignored me all the time. It was so mean.'

Ammi smiles at Ismail as she repositions his napkin. 'What else did you play today, locki?'

'Forget playing,' Abbu butts in. 'What did you *learn* today?' He says it in his normal voice, but there's a dark undertone that makes my ears prick up a little. I can tell Ammi hears it too.

'Um . . . I learned . . . that . . .' Ismail scrunches up his face and looks to the ceiling, thinking. 'I learned that . . . Sachin is rubbish at Stuck in the Mud. Oh! And Alex is a bully. She pushed Pooja over while she was stuck. That's totally against the rules. Pooja fell over into the grass and got hurt. Oh! Just like you this morning, Abbu.'

I suck in a breath. Ammi goes still, and Abbu's head snaps up.

Ismail is oblivious. 'Abbu, that was so funny when you fell over. And with the cat. Is that why you cut your beard? I was telling Rahul and he said –'

'ENOUGH!' Abbu shouts, slamming his palm down on the

table. 'I told you to tell me what you *learned* at school, not these rubbish games you waste your time on, and the stupid things you talk to your stupid little friends about.'

Ismail's tearing up next to me already and I want to tell Abbu to just stop it. To give the little five-year-old some slack. But I feel almost paralysed.

'B-bu-but . . .' Ismail whimpers. 'I was just saying it was funny . . .'

'I said, *ENOUGH*!' Abbu roars.

Ismail begins crying quietly, but not quietly enough. I put one arm around him and pull him in close. I want to soothe him, tell him to ignore Abbu. But Abbu is not in the mood to be hearing that right now. I have to make do with a half-cuddle and rubbing Ismail's arm a little. His crying gets a little louder.

'OK, that's it. Go upstairs to your room! If you can't sit and eat dinner with us nicely, then you shouldn't be here at all.'

I snap my gaze to Ammi, who's just sitting there, as torn as I am. She knows she should stick up for Ismail, but also knows that would make Abbu even angrier.

'Come on, be a good boy and eat your food,' I say while Ammi remains silent. 'Look, you're almost d—'

'I said . . . *upstairs*,' Abbu growls. He's looking at Ammi now, not Ismail. Not even at me, who dared to be a voice against him. His tone vibrates through me. I find myself holding my breath, trying with all my might to stop time, right here and now, to stop things from getting worse. To stop them going exactly where I know they're going to go.

Abbu's words do something to Ammi. I'd say it's magical, but that suggests it's a good thing. It's not. This is all my fault. I shouldn't have said anything. He hates people undermining him. Stupid, stupid Amani.

Ammi places her fork quietly on her plate and turns her attention to Ismail, who's still crying into my shoulder. I'm gripping him so tightly, it might be adding to his tears. But there's nothing else I can do. I'm responsible for this – the least I can do is comfort the poor kid.

'Come on, Ismail. I'll take you up,' Ammi says, almost robotically. She's gone into the version of Ammi she becomes when Abbu is angry. Self-preservation mode, protection mode. She knows not even to call Ismail a pet name – moyna or locki – as she normally would. She knows this would tip Abbu over the edge. She walks up to Ismail, holding her hand out for him to take. I let go of him without another word. He looks up at me, face all red and wet, mouth turned down in the biggest sad face. It tugs at my heart.

'Ismail,' Ammi says more forcefully.

'Just go,' I tell him quietly. *Please*, I add in my head. *Just get past this moment. Please please please . . .*

Ismail slips out of his chair as if the life has been drained out of him, grabs onto Ammi's hand and lets her lead him away. I hear him sobbing all the way up the stairs.

Now it's just me and Abbu at the table. He continues eating like nothing just happened. While all I can do is sit there, feeling sick just at the sight of the food in front of me. The sight of *his* favourite food, that Ammi made to improve *his* mood. I want to leave. Just get up and go upstairs. I look over at Ismail's plate and see that he didn't even get to finish eating. I wonder if I could sneak into the kitchen, grab him a snack and take it up to him without Abbu noticing.

'How was your biology exam today?' Abbu asks suddenly, interrupting my fantasy of me going all *Mission: Impossible*, trying to snake-crawl up the stairs and into Ismail's room with a packet of biscuits.

That's the thing about Abbu. He's a good father. He always asks how school is going, asks if I need any help with anything, even gets concerned when my grades slip. He used to take Ismail and me out on the weekends – to the funfair, cinema, roller skating, etc. Always without Ammi. And Ismail and I would love it. I always felt torn though. I felt bad for going out and enjoying myself with Abbu, while Ammi was stuck at home. Never bad enough to actually say anything though.

Abbu looks at me expectantly. To be honest, I'd forgotten all about the practice exam. Also forgotten that I stupidly mentioned it to Abbu. He's really into my studies. Well, my studies in science. He's infatuated with the idea of me following in his footsteps to study veterinary medicine at university. I don't know that I ever actually agreed to it, but somehow it's become a given that I'm going to become a vet, like he used to be, before the TV show.

'It was OK,' I tell him. It's not the truth, obviously. My revision session with Huda pointed out so many mistakes I'd made. It's the first time I've really panicked about the possibility of failing the subject. Not just getting a bad grade, but flat out failing. Abbu won't accept that. He doesn't accept my answer

33

either. He just looks at me, cocking an eyebrow slightly. *I need more*, the eyebrow says.

'It went well,' I amend. 'I was talking to a few friends afterwards, and they said they all got stuck on a question about cell biology – but I know I got that one right.'

I hate the words coming out of my mouth. The lies coming out (sorry, Allah). But it's the only way forward. It's the only way to prevent Abbu from freaking out. And frankly, it's the only answer he will accept.

'Excellent!' he says, genuinely happy. 'I'm proud of you, futh. You'll be top of the class, I know it.'

Anything less is unacceptable, his expression says.

'And then I can call up some of my old colleagues and get you a job straight away. I need to call Joseph actually. He was telling me about . . .'

He keeps talking, but I no longer listen. I can't hear this. I can't hear the expectations he has of me. They weigh down on me. The images flash in my head – me in a sterile room, a sick animal in front of me, depending on me, and me not having a clue how to save it.

Abbu says that he's proud of me a lot. And every time, something fires up inside me. A warm fuzzy feeling spreads. Because, despite everything, despite all of Abbu's flaws, I want to make him proud. It makes me feel good to make him proud. And if what it takes is following this route, then I'll do it.

'I'm done with my dinner,' I announce as Ammi comes back into the room. I take my plate over to the sink. 'I'm going up to my room. I've got homework.'

'OK, moyna,' Abbu says. He smiles at me before returning to his food.

He *smiles*.

Ammi notices too. She shoots me a grateful look before sitting down at the table.

5

I'm woken in the middle of the night by the sound of my door clicking open. In my half-asleep state, I of course assume it's a burglar coming to stab me, so I push myself back against my headboard, heart already pounding. But then I hear it. Hear the noise that's dominated the nights in our home for so many years now. Abbu's deep baritone rumbles up the stairs and through the walls.

There's a shadow at the door. Ismail.

I guess Abbu's good mood from earlier about my fake upcoming good grades could only last so long.

'YOU THINK IT'S FUNNY, DO YOU?!' I hear booming from the living room.

Ismail actually quivers as he stands in the doorway. Poor kid – I'd have thought he'd be used to it by now too, but I keep forgetting how young he is. He doesn't ask if he can come into my bed, but he doesn't need to any more. It's sort of become our ritual on the Bad Nights. I'm ashamed to say I probably would have slept through this argument if it weren't for Ismail.

I put on a reassuring smile and flip down the corner of the duvet as an invitation. He starts to approach but suddenly stops halfway. Before I can ask him what's wrong, he turns around to go and close the door, to close out the shouting. Well, to an extent. You can still hear it, but it's muffled. It's dark in the room now, so our senses are tuned to listen to the noise.

'YOU'RE A FUCKING IDIOT!'

Ismail still hasn't moved from the door, so I grab my phone and turn the torch on so he can use it as a lighthouse, to find his way to safety. He shuffles across the carpet and climbs in. I wrap the duvet over us and cuddle him close to me, turning my phone torch off. It's just us in the darkness now. Us against the fighting. These rows at night put me on edge. It's like I'm waiting for it to reach boiling point, to hear the sound of Abbu's fists on Ammi's face, or her body, and I'm just desperately trying to bury Ismail's and my heads in the sand. If we don't hear it, it's not happening.

There's one teeny tiny little silver lining in all this though. Ismail is never as free with his cuddles as he is on Bad Nights. It's horrible of me to even think that, isn't it? Poor kid's terrified. But at least I'm here for him. I'm here to look after him. I'm here to distract him.

'Wanna watch a video?' I ask him, forcing some semblance of cheer into my voice. I think he buys it, because he nods vigorously.

I pull over my phone, attach two sets of headphones to the splitter and plug it into my phone. This is part of our ritual too. Our Bad Night Ritual. I open YouTube and click over to my channel.

I started uploading things online just over a year ago, and there are already over seventy videos there. Videos I've made alone, ones Ismail and I have made together, and some that

I've made with Huda. They're silly videos mostly. Ismail's really into Disney films so we usually recreate his favourite scenes using toys and random objects. I load up a video we made where a My Little Pony doll plays Aladdin. Ismail puts in his headphones and leans in closer; I can practically feel the smile that's spreading across his face. We lie intertwined, my phone raised above us, the volume up high, watching as his Fluttershy doll steals a brioche loaf ten times its size. I can practically feel the tension leaving Ismail's body, feel the sleep entering his mind. And it makes me feel teary. Not about the fact that neither Ismail nor I should have to be going through this, having to live through all this arguing and fighting and being on edge *all the time*. But teary for a different reason, a . . . good reason. I'm teary because I'm a bit glad. Glad we have this. We have each other. Our sibling bond is something that cannot be broken. When Ismail most needs a distraction or cheering up, I'm there for him. And so are these videos I make. I'm glad there's *something* that can make him feel less stressed, less upset. And I'm glad I can be the one to give him that.

I remember when Ismail was born I was sad that he wasn't a girl. I'd been fantasising about having a little sister to treat like a human doll – one I could dress up in my old clothes and whose hair I could plait. But I think Ismail's turned out to be way better. He's one of a kind, and I'd protect him with my life. I keep telling Huda about this bond – well, trying to. I tell her how much fun she's going to have with her new sibling, and try to get her to come up with baby names, or look at onesies, but she refuses. It's like she doesn't want to acknowledge that she's going to be a big sister. At least Huda and her sibling won't have to go through what Ismail and I have to go through at home. I wouldn't wish this on anyone.

I can hear Ismail's breaths getting deeper and slower. When I know he's properly asleep, I take off both of our headphones. There's silence in the room now, so the shouting from downstairs comes through clearly. I have my own Bad Night Ritual, which takes place only when I'm alone or Ismail's asleep. I open up the camera on my phone and turn it on selfie mode. I let the screen illuminate my face as I record about twenty seconds of video. Just my face, staring into the camera, as Abbu's voice rises and rises in the background. I see myself flinch when I hear him hit her.

I started doing this a few years ago, just filming randomly every time I'm awake and something like this is happening with my parents. I can't explain why. Maybe just to . . . document it? To acknowledge it's happening? To know it's not all in my head. To know that, even though both my parents will pretend nothing is wrong, something is. I can't explain it. It's become a habit I can't get out of. I don't look at the videos after I film them and I definitely don't upload them. I just keep them in a folder on my phone.

When I'm done, I swap over to Spotify, put my earbuds back in and beg Taylor Swift to sing me to sleep.

6

No alarm mishaps today. I come down the stairs, putting my tie on, and stop short when I hear the TV in the living room and see Abbu sitting in his armchair in front of it. He doesn't turn to look at me, but I can see his face clearly. I can't describe his expression. Not happy, not sad. Not even angry. Just . . . defeated, maybe?

Seeing him throws me. I'd forgotten he'd finished filming the latest series of *Creature Clinic*. His schedule had been predictable for the past few weeks; he'd always be out of the house by the time we were getting ready for school and come home quite late. But now things are going to be up in the air again. There's usually a gap between filming, and Abbu tends to do random freelance jobs in that time. This means that there's no way of knowing when he's going to be around.

Morning Afters are always weird. Abbu is always overly cheerful, helping out with house stuff, being nice to Ammi, asking her about her day. But not asking how she feels. He never mentions the night before. No one ever does. When it's a weekend, I keep Ismail occupied with me in my room, to avoid having to deal with it, and partly hoping that giving my parents privacy will help them . . . fix things. But now that I've been accidentally faced with it, I don't know what to do. I can't go into the kitchen and see Ammi, can't go in and try not to let her notice me examining her body for new bruises, can't see that look on her face that says she'd rather be anywhere but here. I can't. I can't. I can't.

I grab my backpack, quietly open the door and sneak out. No breakfast, no packed lunch. Anything to get away as quickly as possible.

I text Huda as I rush down my street, asking if she can leave any earlier because I 'just happen to be ready really early'. I cross my fingers she buys the excuse, and luckily she texts back saying she's been up for ages anyway and can leave right away. I wait for her at our usual spot.

'Did you see the stuff online yesterday?' she asks in lieu of a hello.

My chest constricts. She's been looking up the stuff about Abbu. She's seen all the memes, knows that the video of him has over 100,000 views. She knows how much people are laughing at him.

'Someone's put the school up for sale,' she says, her face alight with amusement. 'As a prank. And what's funnier, someone's actually bid on it!'

Oh. So she wasn't fixating on Abbu. I repeat her words from yesterday. It'll pass. Today, no one will remember. They have better things to focus on. Like this prank war.

'Surely eBay would have realised it's fake?' I ask. 'And isn't that illegal?'

'Oh my God, Amani, chill.' Huda laughs. 'No one's going to

jail over a silly prank. Gotta admit, it's pretty hilarious though, right? Backpack is gonna be so pissed.'

Backpack is what we call our headteacher, Mr Bach. The nickname started when he was new to the school and came in every day wearing a backpack. He's stopped doing that now, obviously.

'I dunno,' I say. 'It sounds pretty lame.'

Huda swings her head round and gawps at me. Her expression makes me laugh.

'I just think it's a bit superficial. No real impact.'

'Oh, just you wait till we get to school and you see all the teachers freaking. I hope someone puts up one of those "For Sale" signs at the front gates. That would be amazing.'

Unfortunately, there's no sign when we get to the gates. There is, however, a sour-faced Backpack himself. Although, to be fair, he's constantly sour-faced. Huda squeezes my arm and begs me to hang out around the gates in case there's some drama.

'Get to class, girls,' Mr Bach says when he notices us loitering. 'Now.'

I don't need to be told twice. I drag Huda away.

'Make sure you keep an ear out about prank stuff,' she reminds me as we split to go to our form rooms.

I just roll my eyes as I walk off to registration. Maggie Chan is sitting at our usual table, saving the chair next to her with her bag even though everyone knows that's my seat. Her jet-black hair is up in a very messy bun today, her eyeliner already a bit smudged, as if she went to sleep wearing it. She's slouched over the table, ready for a nap. I don't think I've ever seen her sit upright.

'Wassup?' she says, moving her bag so I can sit down. She yawns right after.

'Not much, how 'bout you?' I ask.

'I miss my bed.'

'Nothing new then,' I say with a laugh.

'Twenty-one more days and then I can just stay in bed all I want.'

There's a twinge in my chest. Three weeks exactly. The panic that comes over me every time I think about exams, and what comes after, has returned. You'd think by now I'd have come up with a better way to deal with it than denial, but there's a reason why people say ignorance is bliss.

The rest of the form starts trickling in, and I get out my biology textbook to try to do some revision. I keep my head down.

Just because I don't see them come in doesn't mean I can't hear them. Cleo and her coven. They're giggling, as usual. There's something about their giggling, or just giggling teenagers in general, that makes the hairs on my neck rise up. As if they're talking about me. They *must* be talking about me. Saying bad things, making fun of me. That's what they love to do. It's just my shitty luck that they're all in my form and Huda isn't. I force my eyes to focus on my textbook.

Cleo and her coven normally sit at the back corner of the room. Almost diagonally opposite to me (I didn't choose this seat at random), but for some bizarre reason today they're breaking the socially established seating plan and walk right past their normal desk. Girls like them get to do that, break the rules. I watch from the corner of my eye as they walk between the tables and choose their seats . . . right behind me.

Oh shit.

They sit down with rustles of their bags and, of course, muted giggles. I turn to Maggie, to see if she finds this as weird as I do, but she's got her head on the table, using her blazer as a pillow, and is maybe genuinely asleep. Panic bubbles inside me, but I keep my head down. If I ignore them, they can't hurt me. I focus on revision.

Cell wall. Enzymes. Chloroplasts.

'Miss,' Suzie pipes up in the fake sweet voice she reserves for teachers, 'can you come and help me with this? I don't understand.'

Miss Hoover gets up and comes over. I relax a little. They can't do anything if a teacher is here. I don't hear what Suzie asks Miss Hoover for help with, but I hear a chair scrape and Cleo says, 'Here, miss, take my seat. I just need to get something from the cupboard.'

I tense up as Cleo brushes past me. I don't know if it's on purpose or legit just an accident, but she knocks my pen off the desk with her hip. I wait until she's over at the cupboard by Miss Hoover's desk before I bend over to pick it up.

I keep repeating the mantra in my head. Registration is only fifteen minutes long. Just ignore them for fifteen minutes and it'll be over. Maybe they've forgotten about yesterday, or maybe they'll remember how Huda always makes them look stupid when they insult me. Maybe just the threat of her could be my protection. As pathetic as it is, I sort of hope they think that if they try anything in registration, I'll go to Huda and she'll get back at them. Like I said, pathetic. But it's what gets me through.

I remind myself that registration is almost over and go back to struggling with biology.

Photosynthesis. Cellulose. Flagella.

A small giggle moves its way through the rest of the class, and my cheeks heat up. I look up and see Cleo fiddling with Miss Hoover's laptop. Probably going to change one of her grades or something. It's bold trying something like that with Miss Hoover in the room. I just roll my eyes and get back to my book. The giggling intensifies, and I'm surprised Miss Hoover's attention is still on Suzie. I raise my head a smidge and see Cleo run from behind Miss Hoover's desk over to the chair next to Katya Jackson (who she's probably never spoken to in her life). A second later, music starts playing around the classroom. Loud music. It's the melody that's played in comedies when people are being chased – a piss-take type of tune. I look up at the whiteboard, which is connected to the laptop, and . . .

It's Abbu.

The viral video Cleo showed me after school yesterday. The video I was hoping no one else would have seen, or at least they'd all have forgotten about. But no. It's right there in front of me. In front of *everyone*!

This is a nightmare.

The video plays out, the music running in the background.

The bit when Abbu falls over the sofa is on loop. Over and over and over.

The class erupts into laughter. I sit staring at the screen, mouth open. Not able to believe that this is happening. That Cleo is this cruel. What am I talking about? Of course she is. This is the girl who took photos of me when I once had a piece of loo roll stuck to my shoe, and plastered them all over the internet. She's still sitting over with Katya, acting all shocked and surprised, as if everyone (except Miss Hoover) didn't just see her fiddling with the laptop.

Everyone's looking at me. They're laughing at me. Not just laughing; cackling. My ears are ringing, heart racing, head pounding. Everything is closing in; I feel the desperate need to be anywhere but here.

'What's going on?' Miss Hoover asks, standing up. 'Who did this?' She rushes over to her laptop.

The video continues. On and on and on. Miss Hoover faffs. I pick up my bag and race towards the door, as the laughter gets deafening.

7

I spend the morning not saying a word. No one even notices. Except Huda. Huda always notices. I told her everything at break, couldn't say it without crying. She was so pissed. She wanted to find Cleo and attack her. But I persuaded her that wouldn't make a difference. Cleo would probably get her revenge or get Huda in trouble in return.

Luckily Huda's been in the rest of my classes for the day. Unluckily, now we have maths – one of the few classes where we're with Cleo too. And of course she has once again chosen to sit right behind me. I've been coiled tight for the last fifty minutes, waiting for her to do something.

'Are you getting any of this?' I ask Huda. I've had a headache ever since Mr Hawthorne started talking about Pythagoras two minutes into the class. Although that could be another Cleo effect.

Huda turns and looks at me as if I'm crazy. 'It's all revision – we've been studying this for *weeks*,' she says. Maybe a bit condescendingly.

'Not my fault I'm not a brainbox like you,' I say, a little spitefully. This is one thing about Huda that bugs me. She's so clever, it's as if she was born knowing everything, and what she doesn't already know, she grasps straight away. But she doesn't get that not everyone is the same as her. In fact, *most* people aren't the same as her. We're both in top set, but I am hanging on by a thread. Part of me wishes they would just move me down, all the way down to foundation level; at least that way I'd have half a chance of passing my maths GCSE, but a bigger part of me enjoys being in this class, enjoys people thinking I'm on the same level as Huda at something.

'It's simple,' Huda says. 'Pythagoras's theorem is just saying that with any right-angled triangle, the square of the hypotenuse is equal to the sum of the squares on the other two sides.'

I stare at her. 'I did not understand a word you just said.'

She sighs a little. 'OK, think of it like this. If you draw a square on each side of a triangle, the square along the longest side always has the same area as the two smaller ones added up.'

I frown at her. 'Was that you trying to dumb it down for me? Because, if anything, that was a worse explanation.'

Huda groans. 'Argh! Forget it. Just do what you can for now. I'll help you study later.' She starts scribbling on the worksheet we've been given. The one that looks like it could be in hieroglyphics.

Screw Huda and her condescension. I'll show her. I'm going to get all the answers right on this sheet and beat her score. I put my head down and start with the easier questions.

There's a loud giggle behind me. Cleo and Imogen are whispering, but I catch the odd word.

'Can you believe . . . headscarf . . . ?'

My ears grow hot. Without thinking, I reach up and adjust my scarf to make sure it's covering my hair fully. As I do, they

48

let out another round of giggles. Louder this time. It makes me want to curl up and disappear completely.

Huda's heard it too now. She lifts her head and looks at me. I begged her earlier to leave Cleo alone, to not retaliate. I've always thought that if you ignore bullies for long enough, they'll eventually get fed up and move on. I give Huda a look, telling her to leave it. But she doesn't listen. She turns around in her chair and looks right at Cleo and Imogen. I want to turn around and look too, just to see what Huda is about to do, but I also want to hide away, knowing that this isn't going to help things at all.

'I know it must be hard to not laugh when you look at each other's stupid faces,' Huda says at full volume. 'But keep the hyena noises down, yeah? Some of us actually have a chance of passing our GCSEs.'

The whole class titters. I still don't turn around, even though I'm dying to see how that's put Cleo and Imogen in their places – whether they're feeling as red and hot as I do when they laugh at me.

I wish I could be like Huda, have that confidence. I've never known Cleo to pick on Huda (unless it's a comeback). She's never made comments about *her* headscarf. Why is it just me? Because I'm the weak one. The easy target. I'd love to show them that I'm more than that. That I can rise above their taunts. A part of me just wants to fast-forward five, maybe ten years. To show them that what they're saying now will have no effect in the future. That their words mean nothing.

Sticks and stones may break my bones, but words will never hurt me.

Yeah, right.

'Are you quite done there, ladies?' Mr Hawthorne asks.

I elbow Huda as she turns around. 'Why'd you do that?' I whisper, much quieter than when Cleo and Imogen whisper. I keep an eye on Mr Hawthorne, though he's gone back to his laptop.

Huda looks at me, confused. 'What? They were being dicks.'

'Yeah, but they're *always* dicks,' I explain. As if that makes anything better.

'You might be fine with them talking shit about you, but I won't let them get away with it. No one gets to say mean things about you except me.'

My phone vibrates in my blazer pocket. A split second later there are a couple of chirps around the room. I look up to check if Mr Hawthorne has noticed, but he's still looking at something on his laptop. I slide my phone out of my pocket and check the screen in my lap. Whenever I get a text during school hours, part of me freaks out, thinking it's Ammi. That she's ended up in hospital or something. Or that something has happened to Ismail.

It's not Ammi though.

Cleo Walters would like to share a photo with you.

There's a preview of the image. It's small, but I recognise it immediately. I've seen the video it comes from so many times now. Seen that specific moment repeated over and over. I don't even need to accept the picture to know it's of Abbu. From that video. There's something written over it in a bright yellow scrawl. Part of me wants to open it, to see what she's written, but judging by the snickering coming from my classmates, it's better I don't know.

Sean O'Reilly, who sits in front of me, turns around, looks right at me and laughs. Being mindful enough to cover his mouth though.

It's happening again. A repeat of this morning. The way my ears are heating up, the way my heart is pounding. The way my legs want to get up and run out of the room.

Huda gets out her phone as I start to get up off my chair. I can't deal with this. I can't. I need to get out. I look towards the door and plan my exit route. I'll have to squeeze past a few people, but it'll be worth it. Before I can fully stand up, Huda grabs my arm and pulls me back into my seat. She does it so forcefully I know she's pissed.

'Sir!' she says, sticking her hand up. 'Cleo's being a bitch.'

I snap my head towards her. 'What the hell are you doing?!' I hiss, just as Mr Hawthorne looks up.

'Language, Huda,' he says lazily.

'Sir, you need to see this,' Huda continues, ignoring me completely. 'Cleo is sending out bullying material.'

My head automatically swivels towards Cleo. She's sitting there open-mouthed. She's as shocked as I am, as everyone is. You don't grass. Especially not in public. Everyone knows that. I can't believe Huda is doing this.

'Huda, stop, please,' I say desperately, quietly.

Instead she lifts her phone in the air. 'Sir,' she repeats.

Mr Hawthorne reluctantly gets up and comes over with a sigh. 'Watch your language, Huda,' he says half-heartedly. He takes the phone from her.

51

'She's bullying Amani by sharing slanderous memes about her dad.'

Kill me now. Honestly. This is so fucking embarrassing.

Mr Hawthorne looks at the photo, then at me. His face is red too. I see a flash of pity there, alongside helplessness. 'Um . . . I . . . This . . .' he stutters.

'Well, aren't you going to do something?' Huda asks.

'I didn't do shit!' Cleo says from behind us.

'Language, Cleo,' Mr Hawthorne says. It really is just automatic for him. He looks up from the phone, to Cleo, to Huda, to me. Imogen's just sitting there, speechless. She's probably worried about getting in trouble too.

Is this it? The moment someone puts a stop to Cleo's reign of terror?

The bell rings for the end of class. For the end of school. Everyone around us starts packing up their stuff. But the five of us stay still.

'I didn't do nothing, sir!' Cleo proclaims. 'They're making this up. There's no proof!'

'He's literally just seen what you AirDropped to half the class, you fucking moron,' Huda says.

'Huda! Language!' Mr Hawthorne says. 'I won't tell you again.'

'This is what she does,' Cleo jumps in. '*She's* the bully. She's always blaming me for things I never did.'

Even I'm shocked at what she's pulling now.

'Are you fucking kidding me?' Huda says, exasperated.

'Huda!' Mr Hawthorne says again. 'Don't make me give you detention.'

'Are you for real?' Huda finally snaps. 'You're gonna punish *me*, when *she's* the one making fun of . . .' She turns and looks at me, probably for the first time during this whole discussion. I don't know what my face is saying, but her expression softens a little.

'Can we go now, please?' Imogen chirps. 'We're going to miss our bus.'

'You don't even take the bus!' Huda almost screams.

'Yes, girls, you can go,' Mr Hawthorne tells Cleo and Imogen. 'As for you, Huda, I think we need to have to have a serious conversation about your language.'

'*That's* what you're taking away from this?' she says tightly. 'I tell you she's been bullying a student, and your reaction is to tell me off for my language?'

'This is just a photo on your phone, Huda. Can you prove Cleo sent it?'

Huda sits there, gobsmacked. As do I. I can't believe what's happening right now. An actual teacher fobbing us off like this. He's right though. Cleo will always be one step ahead of me. She'll always win.

'She sent it!' Huda screeches. 'Ask anyone else – they got it too. Amani, c'mon, back me up!'

'I'm just saying –' Mr Hawthorne starts, trying to defend himself.

'Huda, c'mon, let's just go,' I say urgently, tugging on her sleeve.

'If you want to make a serious complaint about bullying, that's what your form tutor is there for,' Mr Hawthorne says. 'I'm just –'

'A fucking waste of space, that's what you are,' Huda says before storming out.

I don't give Mr Hawthorne another glance before following her, tears beginning to leak from my eyes.

8

Huda storms out of the school gates, and I meekly follow. I'm annoyed at her for making a scene, for pissing Cleo off like that, which is guaranteed to have made her more likely to retaliate. Part of me wants to just leave Huda to walk alone. But then . . . it's Huda. I could never ditch her. I know what she did was because she was sticking up for me.

We walk home side by side, not saying a word. It's only when we're near the fork in the road where we split up that I start to panic. Abbu was home this morning. He'll probably still be there now. And he's probably going to still be in a terrible mood. I don't want to be around that. Especially not with the way I'm feeling after Cleo's attacks today.

'Can I come to yours?' I ask Huda quickly. 'You said you'd help me with maths, right?'

I'm scared she's going to say no. That she's too annoyed at me for being a pushover to help me study.

'We're *always* at mine,' she says. 'Can't we go to yours? I haven't seen Ismail in ages.'

My heart jumps into my throat. 'There's a reason we're *always* at yours,' I say. 'Your house has better snacks.'

Huda laughs, and I relax a little.

'True,' she says. 'But your brother is better than any snack in the world.' She hooks her arm through mine and drags me down the street towards my house. 'C'mon, I've missed him so much.'

I try to think up excuses in my head, but nothing sounds good enough. 'But . . . everything is such a mess . . . Ammi won't . . . She doesn't like having people over unexpected.'

'It's only me, she won't mind. I don't care about mess; you've seen my room. Why are you walking so slow? C'mon!' There's a renewed sense of enthusiasm in her at the prospect of seeing Ismail. While that's nice, I'm too filled with panic to appreciate it. All too soon, and before I can think of a better excuse, we're outside my house. I breathe the biggest sigh of relief when I see that Abbu's car isn't in the driveway. Maybe he had a job starting a bit later.

Suddenly I'm excited to have Huda over. She's right, it's been ages. Ismail freaking loves her. She's like the fun big sister who spoils him, whereas I'm the one who shouts at him when he doesn't tidy his toys away. I can just picture how his face is going to light up when he sees her. I open the door and walk in. There's a tiny part of me that worries Abbu really *is* home, and that something's happened to his car – stolen, broken down somewhere. But no, luckily his shoes aren't by the door either. I should be able to relax, but now I'm wondering when he'll be back. Although . . . he's usually on his best behaviour when he's in public. He's never so much as raised his voice at Ammi when we've got guests. So maybe Huda being here will end up being a good thing. Maybe I should start bringing her round more often.

'Ammi?' I call out, as I always do when I get in from school.

It's partly to let her know I'm home, and partly because I want to make sure she's OK.

'In the kitchen!' she calls back.

'Maaaaani!' Ismail calls from the kitchen too. I hear a chair scrape and next thing I know he's bounding down the hallway towards me.

'Maani, we made biscuits at school!' he yells.

He comes to a stop when he sees Huda standing next to me. 'Huda!' he squeals, voice full of glee. He races over and envelops her.

'Hey, you!' Huda says, a giant smile on her face.

OK, yeah, this was definitely worth it.

'What, no hug for me?' I tease.

Ismail tries to move from Huda over to me, but she grabs him.

'No. No hugs for Amani. She always gets your hugs. I'm gonna steal *all* your hugs today.' She holds Ismail under the armpits and lifts him up into her arms, cuddling him tighter.

He laps it up, giggling away.

'Not fair.' I pout. I start fake crying. 'I'm going to tell Ammi. Ammiiiii!' I wail, running into the kitchen.

'Let's get her!' Huda exclaims, swivelling Ismail around onto her back. She holds on to his legs and gallops after me like a horse.

Ammi jumps as we barge into the kitchen. She drops the bowl she was holding and presses back against the worktop, her face stretched to a panicked expression.

Shit.

'Sorry!' I say. 'We didn't mean to scare you . . .'

I feel awful. Ammi is cornered, looking terrified. The plastic bowl rolls around on the floor.

'Ammi, look who's here!' Ismail says, kicking his heels into Huda's sides to make her be his horse again.

'Salaam, Auntie,' Huda says, galloping on the spot.

'Huda, it's so lovely to see you,' Ammi says, switching from vulnerable to the face she puts on for everyone else. Her public face. 'It's been too long.'

'Huda, will you help me and Maani make a video?' Ismail asks as Ammi picks up the bowl. I notice her wince slightly as she bends. 'We're gonna do my *fave* scene from *Frozen*. I'm gonna be Olaf!'

Damn. I forgot I'd promised to do that with him today. He's gonna be upset if I choose studying with Huda over playing with him.

'Really?' Huda asks, switching into her kid-friendly amazement voice. She drops Ismail to the ground. 'That sounds super fun. Can I be Kristoff? I do a really good reindeer impression.' She demonstrates.

I always find this transition in Huda amazing. Normally she's feisty, no-nonsense. But when it comes to little kids, she's a whole other person. I think it's from having such a muddled childhood.

'Kristoff's not the reindeer. That's Sven!' Ismail dissolves into a fit of giggles.

'Huda's come over to study,' I tell Ammi. I feel the need to explain, because I can guess that although she loves Huda, she's not over the moon to have company.

'That sounds like a good plan. How are you finding all the

exam stress, Huda?' Ammi asks. 'I hear you're planning on taking *four* A levels.'

Huda smiles and shrugs. 'I just can't choose between all the subjects I like best, and I haven't got a clue what I'm gonna do after. Thought I might as well enjoy what I'm studying, rather than pushing myself into something I'm not sure about. You know what I mean?'

Ammi laughs a little. 'That sounds very wise.'

This is another thing about Huda that I admire: how she can remain calm, not needing to map out her entire future, while I'm scared shitless by all the lectures telling us that whether we succeed or fail in life comes down to our GCSEs.

'C'mon!' Ismail says, tugging on Huda's arm. 'We need to go make the video!'

'Go on up,' Ammi says. 'But only half an hour. You two have got serious studying to do, and Ismail needs to learn his spellings.'

'Why don't you come with us?' I ask Ammi. 'We'll need some snow monsters, if you can think of a way to make some.'

Ammi considers it, but then looks back at the bowl on the counter. 'Your dad'll be back from meeting his boss soon . . . I need to make dinner.'

'Half an hour. That's all. I promise.' I know how much fun she has when we do this. I want to see that smile on her face again.

'C'mon, Auntie, please!' Huda begs. 'I want the full Akhtar-family film-making experience.' She smiles at me, and everything feels right again. Like nothing happened at school today. Like she's not angry at me for being a pushover, and

I'm not angry at her for making things worse with Cleo. It's like *us* again.

Ammi laughs. 'Oh, all right then.'

Filming with Huda, Ammi and Ismail is honestly the most fun I've had in forever. Ammi makes snow monsters out of cotton wool and toothpicks, and Ismail draws scary faces on them and gives them deep voices as they attack Sven the reindeer, as voiced by Huda playing with Ismail's Rainbow Dash doll. It's nothing like the actual scene from *Frozen*, and I'm laughing so hard that the camera shakes, but it's the perfect filming session. Ammi enforces the half-hour thing though, and drags a crying Ismail away from my room as Huda and I tidy up and get our textbooks out. We spend the next hour sitting on the floor and studying. Huda explains Pythagoras to me three times before I start to get it. After that, I can actually complete some of the questions on our homework sheet.

'God, Huda, you're a miracle worker. I might actually pass maths now, thanks to you. Seriously, why aren't you going into teaching?'

She rolls her eyes at me.

'Have you thought any more about it?' I ask. 'What you wanna do after A levels.'

She shrugs, turning away from me. 'That's two years away. I don't plan that far ahead.'

'I know, but they keep asking at school, don't they? Have you had your pastoral meeting yet? Mrs Farook grilled me for ages about what I wanted to do, how I was going to get there, what subjects I needed to do at A level. It was intense.'

'How did you decide?' Huda asks. 'That being a vet was what you wanted to do. Like, how did it become . . . so . . . fixed . . . in your head?'

I panic a little. The teachers always ask *how* you're going to get there, but they don't ask *why* you want to go there. Or even if that's really what you want. Say something with enough conviction and anyone will believe you.

'I dunno,' I say, fiddling with the edge of my hijab. 'It's just always been in my head, I guess.' Planted, and nurtured, by Abbu of course. 'I guess my dad had a lot to do with it.' I don't tell her the full truth. That I'm terrified about this being my future. That I feel trapped. I can't tell anyone that.

'Why?' I ask, to divert attention from myself. 'Are you worried about your meeting?'

She sighs a little. 'I'm worried about my *life*, Maani.' She drops the textbook on the floor and leans her head back so it hits the bed. 'Everyone else seems to just . . . *know* . . . what they want to do with their life. You've got your vet shit, Sarah has acting, there's Kim with her police-officer dream. Everyone seems to be able to see the future clearly. But for me, it's just . . . blank.'

'Blank?' I ask. 'I thought you were OK with that? What you said downstairs to Ammi, about having the time to figure stuff –'

'It was all bullshit. It's the stuff I keep saying to myself, to other people, hoping I'll start to believe it. But I'm freaking out, Maani. I had my pastoral meeting the other day. And she was *not* happy with me saying I had no fucking clue what I want to do with my life.'

'But . . . I mean, it's not really a big deal . . .' I say lamely.

61

'You've got . . . You're so good at so many things. You can make a career out of something you enjoy doing?'

'Like watching Netflix?' She gives me a sad smirk.

'No, come on, we can work this out. Let's do like that episode of *Friends* – make a list of jobs and see which one you like.'

She shakes her head. 'I did that with Mrs Farook. She gave up because nothing seemed right to me.'

I want to tell her that I'm feeling the same. That I've locked in this future for myself, knowing it's wrong. Like a puzzle piece that I've hammered into place. But maybe there's something else I'd be better at doing. Maybe something like . . . making videos.

'I wouldn't care,' Huda continues sadly, 'but it just emphasises the fact that there's something wrong with me.'

'Wait, what?' I ask.

'*Everyone* else knows, Amani. Everyone else can picture their future. I grew up moving between homes, never sure how long each place would last, always being yanked away just as I got comfortable. I learned not to expect anything. Not to make long-term plans. Once, one of the carers I was living with promised to take me to Thorpe Park in the summer holidays. I looked forward to that for *months*. And then one of her own kids got really sick, and I got moved homes. I asked the new lady if we could go, but she didn't give a shit.'

'Huda, God . . . I don't . . .' *I don't know what to say*, is what I want to say. But you can't say that, can you? When someone's baring their soul, when they're looking for reassurance, help, sympathy.

'It's different with Ali and Nafisah though, right?' I say.

'You've been with them for four *years* now. They've taken you on holiday and you've met their family and stuff. They're hardly gonna make you move, are they?'

Huda laughs once, harshly. 'Of course they are,' she says bitterly. 'They've got their own kid coming now. They're not gonna have time, or space, for me. What even am I to them? Just a monthly cheque.' She goes all quiet and still, and her words have tugged at me so much that I shuffle over and wrap her into a hug.

'Oh, Huda, don't be silly. It's not like that at all. Ali and Nafisah freaking *love* you. Nothing will change that,' I say, clinging on to her.

Something in her switches, and she pulls away from me. 'Oh God, look at me being all soppy,' she says in a tone that's trying to be a laugh but shows her discomfort. 'Ignore me, I'm just being stupid. Let's get back to work.' She shuffles back against the bed and picks up the book from the floor. In her shuffling, she accidentally hits her elbow against my bedside table and knocks over the framed family photo I keep on there.

'Shit, sorry!' She picks it up. 'Phew, not broken,' she says, turning the frame over in her hand and looking at it.

It's a photo of all of us: Ammi, Abbu, Ismail and me. Taken a few months ago. We have a tradition where we take a family photo every year. Get all dressed up and go to a studio. Abbu's idea. He always buys a big framed one and hangs them on the wall going up the stairs. They start at the bottom with the earliest photo – where Ismail is just a baby and I'm grinning in a bright pink dress I wouldn't be seen dead in now – and go up the years with each step. This year there was an offer, so Abbu bought a bunch of smaller copies, and I thought I'd keep one beside me. Ismail is pulling the biggest grin in the photo, and every time I see it, it makes me smile. Huda's smiling too, as she looks at it. But there's a sadness in her eyes too.

'You guys are like the perfect family,' she says quietly. 'Two parents in love, with their own kids – one boy, one girl. I mean, isn't that the dream?'

'It's not real,' I blurt.

She looks up at me, confused, and I stutter for an answer. I'm shocked by my own outburst, shocked at how much I *want* to tell her the truth right now. But I know I can't. Not ever.

'I mean, like, that's a posed photo. It's not real,' I backtrack quickly. 'It . . . it doesn't show the huge fight that happened just before we left the house that day, where Ismail didn't want to wear a tie but Abbu *really* wanted them to match. It's not . . . it's not perfect. *We're* not perfect. Anyway, you have Ali and Nafisah; they love each other, they love *you*. And you're getting a sibling soon, so you'll be just like –'

Huda laughs bitterly. 'You don't *get it*, Amani. Your family . . . you have this history. You've got a whole staircase of memories. You've got baby books, and blankets and childhood toys. You've got . . . you've got blood. You can't compare our situations, it's not the same.'

A rush of heat hits my face. 'I'm not saying that,' I say defensively. 'I'm just saying that you can't judge perfection based on photos, or surface-level things. We're not as idyllic as you think.'

Huda groans. 'You don't appreciate what you have, Amani. It really winds me up. Do you know what I'd give to have what you have? To have the permanence you have? To know that no matter how much I screw up, there are people who will always love me and accept me? You have no idea what it's like, living with this fear that any day things could come crashing down. That Ali and Nafisah could simply say they don't want me any more, and that's it. And what about when I turn eighteen? Even if they keep me that long, they can get rid of me and not feel bad, because I'm supposed to be able to support myself by then. Sure, the government will still help me for a bit, but that's not the same, is it?' She takes a breath, pierces me with her eyes. 'I have literally no clue about what my future holds, Amani. But you, you'll always have your parents. You'll always have a home.'

'You can't get mad at me for that. It's not my fault –' I cut myself off before I say anything I can't take back.

'It's not your fault my own parents didn't want me,' she spits. 'You can say it.'

'Huda, that's not . . .'

'Ugh! It's fine, Amani.' She shakes her body, shrugging off the conversation, and puts the photo back on my bedside table. 'I just wish . . . just, please appreciate what you have more.'

'Me?!' She has no idea. *No* idea what my life is like. How dare she paint it as idyllic? '*You're* the one who doesn't appreciate what you have. Ali and Nafisah are, like, the best parents ever. I've seen the way they talk to you, talk *about* you. Trust me – not everyone has such a loving household. You think *I'm* the one who's ungrateful? Take a look at yourself.'

I'm breathing hard now, and there's something coursing through me. Anger, yes. But also anxiety. Huda and I have never fought like this. We've never really fought at all. But this is serious. And she's being stupid. I'm on the verge of telling her about Abbu, about how our family is the opposite of perfect, but she's just sitting there, seething, and I know that if I reveal the truth during an argument, I'll regret it.

It's silent in the room; all I can hear is the pounding in my ears. Huda opens her mouth to say something, but just at that moment there's a shout from downstairs.

'IT'S ALL YOUR FAULT.'

Shit. Abbu's home. And he's angry. Oh God. No no no, not now. Please, God, not right now. What can I do? Huda can't hear this. How do I get her away from it? We can't leave the house – that would mean going downstairs, past Ammi and Abbu. God, why hasn't Ammi told him that Huda is here? He wouldn't be doing this if he knew, or at least he wouldn't be so loud. Why does he have to be so loud?

I pull out my phone. 'Let's put some music on!' I say quickly. Far too quickly. I get up and rush over to my desk, where my iPhone dock is, and start scrambling around, trying to find the lead.

'I ONLY TOOK THAT STUPID, EMBARRASSING JOB TO SUPPORT YOU AND YOUR SPENDING HABITS.'

Where's the plug? Why isn't this plugged in? It's always plugged in. We need loud music *now*.

'AND SO I'VE HAD TO QUIT. ARE YOU HAPPY NOW?'

'Maani . . .' Huda says slowly.

'It's fine!' I say. 'I just need to find this plug. It's fine, it'll be fine. Maybe, uh . . . maybe you could help me look for it?

Yeah, come here. Come away from the door.' I go over and almost yank her arm out of its socket so she'll come to the far end of the room.

'What the hell are you doing?!' she says, snatching her arm away from me. She doesn't get it. I can't have her hear. I can't make it stop, so I need to mask the noise.

'WHERE IS THIS STUPID PLUG?!' I shout. I get down on my hands and knees and crawl under the table in a panic. Everything has become so tangled, and I'm annoyed at myself for being such a slob and not tidying this up earlier. It's my fault. All my fault.

'Amani, you're being . . .' Huda doesn't finish her sentence. But I know what she means. I'm being stupid. I'm being weird. I'm being pathetic.

I finally find the plug and push it into the extension cord. I jump up from the floor and jam my iPhone into the dock. I'm so close to starting the music, when the resounding sound of a slap echoes across the house, up the stairs and through the door to my room. The door that's somehow now open.

I look over and see Ismail standing there, on the verge of tears.

I look back at Huda, and see so much written on her face. Confusion, concern, anger. I look back to the door. Where the sounds of Ammi whimpering and Abbu continuing to shout come through loud and clear.

It's over.

My family's deepest darkest secret is out.

9

Ismail scampers into my room, towards Huda. He leaves the door wide open, so I rush over to shut it as Huda wraps him in a hug. Thankfully he's not crying. Yet. I look into Huda's eyes again. She's heard. She knows everything. The secret I've been desperate to hide from the world for so long. The secret that could split my family apart. If she tells anyone, then that's it. They'll break my parents up, take Ismail away. I can't have that. I can't. I stand with my back pressed against the door, hoping I can somehow push away any remnants of noise that are still coming up.

'Ismail, c'mere,' I say, strangled.

He rushes over dutifully. He goes in for a hug, but I don't let him. I bend over and put my hands on his shoulders. I force a smile onto my face, hoping it'll convince him there's nothing to be upset about.

'You wanna watch a video on my iPad? It's over on the bed.'

He hesitates a second, and I'm scared he's going to say no. Go into a full-blown crying tantrum. I send him another smile, encouraging him to listen to me. I say in my head, *Please please please* . . . He goes over to my bed and sits there cross-legged while he fiddles with my iPad.

'Use the headphones, please,' I tell him. 'Huda and I are studying.'

He listens. Thank God, he listens.

I look again at Huda; she's standing in the middle of the room, gawping at me. I need to act normal. If I act normal, she won't make a thing of it. I go over to the desk again and open up Spotify on my phone.

'I found the best playlist. You'll love it.' I scroll through the app, trying to find it as quickly as possible, while also trying to stop my hand from shaking. 'Where is it?' I mutter to myself. 'I swear I saved it.' I laugh a little, but it comes out like a squeak. 'Argh, forget it.' I just put on my Favourites and let it play out across the room. I adjust the volume so it's loud enough to cover up what's happening downstairs, but quiet enough that Abbu won't hear it and get mad.

'Should we go down?' Huda asks quietly. 'See what's happening?'

I avoid eye contact as I walk back over and sit down on the floor with the textbook again. 'No, no. There's no need for that. It's fine. Everything is fine. Let's get back to maths.' I look up at her, but she doesn't move, so I pull on her hand until she drops down.

'Maani, I really think we should go and check on your mum. She sounded –'

'No, no, it's fine, Huda, honestly. It'll be fine. She'll be OK. She always is.'

Oh, crap. I shouldn't have said that. Stupid Amani. Stupid, stupid, stupid.

'What do you mean "always"?' Huda asks before I manage to distract her again.

I ignore her question, trying to focus on the book, but it all looks like hieroglyphics again.

'How . . . often does this happen?'

She says this so slowly that I can tell she's trying to piece it all together. I need to stop it. Stop her from figuring it out.

'Oh, it doesn't,' I assure her in my most confident voice. 'He's not always like this. It's just –'

'Just what?' she says sharply, cutting me off. 'You're trying to tell me what we just heard was *normal*?'

'No!' I tell her, flicking through the textbook. 'You're making a big deal out of nothing.'

She sits down next to me, *finally*, but facing me instead of leaning against the bed. Thank God, she's buying it. I just need to keep this up for a bit and then I can get her out of the house, and we can move on. I knew I shouldn't have let her come over.

'Maybe we should do these practice questions,' I say, showing her a page of the book.

She's staring daggers at me. 'Amani, talk to me. You can't just brush this off. What we heard – your dad shouting at your mum, him . . . hitting her. How can you not want to go down there?'

'It's nothing, I told you,' I say. 'You're imagining things.'

'So now you're saying it didn't happen?'

'What didn't happen?' I look at her with a blank face. Maybe I can convince her like this instead.

'Amani, come on. Stop being weird. Talk to me, *please*. You can't say that was nothing. The way you're acting, the way Ismail came in here all upset . . .'

I force a laugh out. 'You and your overactive imagination again, Huda. Miss Cuthew was right when she said you're talented in the storytelling department.'

I can't have her telling anyone. She wouldn't, would she? I stare at her sternly.

'OK, fine,' she says. 'How about I go and see for myself?' She raises an eyebrow – a challenge. My heart's thumping again, but I just stare back. If I win this stare-off, she'll get that there's nothing worth looking into.

Believe me.

Don't believe me.

Don't go downstairs.

Go downstairs.

End this.

What feels like a whole minute passes, with us just staring at each other. And then suddenly she stands up.

I grab her wrist again. 'No, don't!' I plead. I stand up too and hold her so tight that it must be painful, but she doesn't say anything. She's just staring again. Full realisation has hit her now, and she's looking at me with the pity eyes. The ones I can't stand. The ones I wanted to avoid. Especially from my best friend. All of this suddenly gets to me, and I start to cry.

'Huda, please . . . you can't . . . You can't tell . . . You can't go . . .' My words are coming out in little hiccups, as if I can't catch a breath, can't finish a sentence.

'Hey, hey, calm down.' She puts her hands on my arms, pins them to my sides firmly but gently. She's restraining me, keeping me rooted to the spot, keeping me grounded, as if I'm going to explode, or take off like a rocket. It feels weirdly comforting.

'You . . . you can't . . . Please.' I look right in her eyes, begging.

'Amani, this . . . this isn't right,' she says.

'Huda, please . . . *promise* me you won't tell anyone. You can't say a word. They're gonna . . . If anyone finds out, they'll break up my family, everything will fall apart. PLEASE, Huda.'

'God, Amani, you're shaking. Here, sit down.' She sits down on the edge of the bed and pulls me down next to her. Ismail sits behind us, happily glued to the iPad, music blaring out of his headphones, thankfully. He'd be so freaked out if he heard me like this. I have to remember that this is all for him – to keep him safe, and with me. I wipe my eyes.

'Huda, they'll . . . If anyone finds out, they'll split us all up. They'll take Ismail away. Don't you understand? *No one* can know.'

'Amani, that's not . . . that's not how it works. No one is going to split you up. You can't . . . you can't just ignore this, let it go on, just because of this fear. It's not right.'

'I know,' I wail. 'You think I like it? You think I like hearing him . . . do that? You think I like hiding in my room pretending not to hear her cries? I hate it, Huda. I hate it so much.' My snotty cries start up again as Spotify flips over to an advert. A montage runs through my mind of all the times it's been happening downstairs and I've hidden in my room. All the times Ammi's cried out in pain and I could have gone down and maybe helped by just being there, but didn't because I was too scared.

'It's all my fault,' I whimper. 'I could have stopped it. All those times . . . He never does anything when there are people around.'

'It's *not* your fault,' Huda says firmly. She holds my hands, which are in my lap, and squeezes them tightly. 'Not your mum's fault either. It's not on either of you to stop it. But you *can* get help.'

'No!' I snatch my hands away. 'You don't understand! Just please. Pretend you didn't hear anything. Just pretend this never happened.'

'Like you have been?' she snarks.

I snap my head up. 'You have no idea!'

'So tell me,' she says, quietly, calmly, kindly. 'Tell me about it.'

Her words stir something inside me, a yearning to talk to someone about all of this. I've kept the truth locked inside for so many years, pressed it down. *If I don't talk about it, it's not happening.* But Huda's right here. She's heard. She *knows*. She would understand. Huda's probably the only person in the world who has my back, no matter what. Surely she's the best person to talk to about this.

And so I do . . .

I tell her about the first time I knew it was happening, how I had convinced myself it was a one-off, that Abbu was stressed. How I heard him apologising profusely the next day, and believed every word of it. I tell her about conversations I've overheard at family gatherings, where aunties and grandparents have flat out stated that this kind of thing is acceptable in our culture – some of them going so far as to blame the woman, as if she'd asked for it, as if she deserved it, as if it's her responsibility to change the man or put up with him. I tell Huda how backwards it all is, and how much it's been stressing me out. I tell her that if any of our family found out, they'd treat Ammi the same way, as a pariah, as if it was her fault.

I tell Huda everything, and end up feeling weirdly so much lighter.

'Amani,' she says when I'm finished. She takes my hand and squeezes it again. I look at her, to find she's got tears in her eyes too. 'I can't believe you've been hiding that from me all this time. You could have told me, you know? There's nothing you can't tell me.'

I shake my head. She doesn't understand how hard it is being so open with her, how hard it's been being so closed off from everyone. 'Everything's going to fall apart,' I say quietly. 'I don't want that.'

'That doesn't have to be the case. C'mon, Amani, even *you* must realise that this isn't going to get better if you keep it hidden away. What does your mum say about it?'

'We don't discuss it. I tried at the beginning. Over and over. But she just excuses him. Blames herself. She used to get so angry when I asked her about it. Said I was being disrespectful to Abbu. Told me I was being a bad daughter. And so . . . I stopped.' I shrug, before pinning Huda with my gaze again. 'But it'll be worse, so much worse, if other people find out. You know what Asian aunties are like. They'd destroy Ammi. They'd take his side. She'd be humiliated. And then if it reaches anyone official –'

'Amani, you can't just let this go on. It's wrong. We can ask Ali and Nafisah for help. Nafisah will know what to do – she's worked with some women's charities before.'

'No, Huda! You can't tell her about this. I told you, you can't tell anyone!' There's panic coursing inside me now. The truth is so close to becoming public, and I need to do anything I can

74

to stop it. There's no way I can have everyone knowing. People already make fun of me for who I am – imagine if Cleo and her coven got hold of this.

'I'll do *anything*,' I beg her. 'Huda, please. Just this once, please listen to me. I'll do anything, anything you want. You just . . . You *have* to keep this secret, PLEASE, Huda.' I'm full-on sobbing now, my body shaking again. What was I thinking, telling her everything? This is all my fault. She's going to tell Nafisah, she's going to put this out into the world. Everyone is going to know. People will judge. Cleo's going to continue making my life hell. Social services are gonna take Ismail away.

'Huda, *please*, I am literally begging you.' There's snot all over my face, tears streaming down my chin. My face is a hot wet mess.

'OK, OK, shhh, Maani, calm down,' she says, checking to make sure Ismail isn't looking. 'Stop crying, please. I can't stand it when you cry.'

I sniff, trying to quell my tears. 'Promise me,' I beg.

She pauses, looking at me. I can't gauge what her reaction is going to be – can't tell whether or not she's going to listen to me. After what feels like an age, she reaches up and wipes away the tears on my cheek.

'OK,' she says softly. 'I won't say anything. But . . . on one condition. You need to do something for me.'

10

I look at Huda, not knowing what to expect. I promised her I'd do anything, so I guess I can't say no to whatever she's about to ask me. And it's true, I'll do whatever it takes to keep this secret.

'What is it?' I ask.

She looks shy and uncomfortable. 'OK, so I feel bad for asking. And look, I'd keep this secret anyway. I want you to know that. I shouldn't have said "on one condition", like I'm blackmailing you or whatever. I'm not. OK? But . . . but I would like your help with something.'

I nod. 'Name it. Anything.'

She stares at me; I can see her brain ticking, trying to formulate the words. She bites her lip, like she always does when she has something big to say but doesn't know how to start.

I grab her hand again, squeeze it. 'Hey, it's me. You can ask me for anything, you know that.'

She smiles. 'It's a bit . . . weird. And God, I feel so terrible asking right now. Maybe we should wait. Do you wanna talk more about –'

'Huda, c'mon. Tell me. Please. I could do with being

76

distracted.' I strain my ears as the Spotify track comes to an end, trying to hear any sounds from downstairs. But with the door closed, and Ismail's thumping music playing in the background, the few seconds' pause between tracks isn't long enough to tell for sure what's going on.

'OK.' She sighs. 'Look, I want your help. I *need* your help. Out of the two of us, hell, out of everyone I know, you've always been the shiny perfect one. You've been the good girl, the one who never gets in trouble, the one everyone loves. The one every parent wishes was their child. I want you to . . . to teach me how to do that. I want you to teach me how to be the perfect daughter.'

'What?' I ask, flummoxed. 'None of that is true. No one thinks I'm . . . perfect.'

'I do.' She says this with no hesitation in her voice.

'You don't really think I can help you be *perfect*?' I ask. 'Huda, you're . . . you're amazing the way you are. You don't need to become more like me. In fact, *don't* become more like me. You'd be changing all the things I like about you, the things everyone else likes about you.'

She shakes her head. 'It doesn't matter. It's not good enough. *I'm* not good enough. Ali and Nafisah . . . I want to become the kind of daughter they can be proud of. Not the one who can't keep her mouth shut and is always getting into arguments. I want to be someone they can . . . love. For real.'

It's weird to see Huda so . . . open and emotional. I never knew she was filled with such anxieties, that she thought such negative things about herself. I've always seen her as the strong one in our friendship, the one who can go up against anything and win. But right now she seems so resigned, so defeated, so . . . like me.

'It's weird, I know,' she continues, all fast. 'But ever since the baby . . . God, I know it sounds pathetic. But I just . . . I'm scared. This baby – it's their own flesh and blood, y'know? Not just someone they took in out of pity. They're gonna love the baby so much more than me. And that's fine. Like, of course, it'll be their kid. But I need to . . . I need to rise up to that level, y'know? I figure if I'm the best version of me I can be, if I can make myself the perfect daughter, then they won't get rid of me. I'll be enough for them. They're the best carers I've ever had, Maani. I can't lose them.' She sighs sadly, before looking up at me with the biggest, widest, wateriest puppy-dog eyes I've ever seen on anyone.

I want to say something meaningful to her, something that'll make her see sense, see that her fears are unnecessary. That she could never be not enough, that this baby will never take her place. But once again, she cuts in before I manage to get my words together properly.

'Please, Amani. Teach me how to be perfect.'

11

She's late. Huda's always here at 8.10 on the dot. She's usually the one waiting for me. But I've been standing on the street for a whole two minutes. My foot has been tapping non-stop, partly because it's cold and partly because I'm nervous. I'm nervous Huda will go back on her word. That she'll tell someone about Abbu. Maybe that's why she's late, maybe she's gone to school early to tell a teacher, or she's told Ali and Nafisah. Maybe she's avoiding me? When she left mine last night, we didn't really say goodbye properly. It was awkward, and she was obviously feeling so vulnerable, I didn't want to push her. I thought we had an understanding, but now I'm wondering . . .

'Hey,' Huda says, so suddenly that it makes me jump. My heart jolts, sending adrenaline spiking through my body.

'Crap, you scared me,' I say.

'Sorry,' she says quietly. She gives me a tight smile before looking down at her feet. It's weird. Normally we'd already be talking away, speaking over each other, about whatever we did last night, things we saw on the internet. I'm scared that she'll bring up my parents, and am about to distract her, but then she starts speaking again – seriously, it's like she's psychic all of a sudden.

'How was your mum? What happened after I left yesterday?'

'Nothing,' I reply as quick as I can. 'She's fine. Everything's fine.'

I know it's stupid. I know that now it's no longer a secret, I should be able to talk to Huda about it. I know I *can* talk to her about it, and that she will listen, and isn't that exactly what I've been wanting for so long? I could tell her how awkward dinner was last night, that I couldn't stop staring at the red mark on Ammi's face, wondering where else on her body there were bruises. I could tell her that everything went back to normal this morning; Abbu went out to meet some of his old vet buddies, Ammi made us breakfast as normal. I could tell Huda how nervous I was all morning, waiting for someone to come knocking on the door to take Ismail away, to break up my family. But if I talk about it, that makes it real. I'd much rather push it to the back of my mind. Which means pushing something to the front.

'So, come on then, tell me – how am I going to turn you into a Perfect Daughter?' I ask, forcing a smirk into my voice.

She looks at me for a second, and I can tell she knows what I'm doing, knows that I'm deliberately changing the subject. And I just say in my head, *Please please please* . . .

And thankfully, like the good friend she is, she smiles at me a little and plays along.

'I'm not sure of the details yet,' she says.

'You know I think it's a stupid plan, right?' I ask.

'Yes, yes, I know,' she says, rolling her eyes.

'You don't need to change yourself. Ali and Nafisah love you as you are. You think they'd let someone they don't like live with them? For four years?'

'For the right money, sure.'

'Huda. C'mon . . .'

'I know, I know what you're gonna say, Amani. But it's not . . . You just don't get it. OK? You *can't* get it. You could tell me a million times that I don't need to do this, but it's not gonna convince me. Anyway, you already agreed to it, so no backsies.' She sing-songs the last line, which means we're definitely past the awkwardness.

I laugh. 'OK, OK. Amani the Daughter Whisperer at your service.' I salute her. 'Awaiting your instructions.' It's obvious she's not going to take no for an answer, and if it makes her feel better, why not?

She laughs. 'Excellent. Although Daughter Whisperer sounds pervy. We can think up a better title for you. How about for now you just sort of . . . watch me? And let me know anything I do that seems wrong. Basically, let's go with WWAD – What Would Amani Do?'

'Ha, well, Amani would totally buy her best friend breakfast when she gets to school. A fried-egg sandwich sounds good.'

'It's a shame Amani's best friend doesn't like egg,' Huda says, scrunching her nose.

'Hmm, you're right, chocolate is much better.'

My phone vibrates in my pocket and I pull it out. Someone has tagged me in a post on Instagram. The preview is small, but it's a photo. And it looks very familiar. I know I shouldn't, but I open up the post and look at the new meme of Abbu. The photo is of the moment the cat grabbed his beard. The text below reads 'How to get all the PUSSY!'

It's weird – I had completely forgotten that people were

making fun of him, were making fun of *me* for it. I guess there are more important things going on. Still though, it stings. Seeing this stupid, yet hurtful, meme that Struan Dunn, a boy I've barely said three words to in my whole life, has decided it's OK to tag me in.

'Rude much?' Huda says. 'I'm talking to you and you're just gawping at your phone.'

'This is what Perfect Daughters do, duh,' I say, putting away my phone. The sting of the meme is overshadowed by the fact Huda and I seem to be back to normal. It's nice. Normal is good. It means I can relax a little.

'No criticising. That's your first note for improvement.'

'What?' she squeaks. 'I wasn't criticising, I was just pointing out that you were being super rude. That's more a bad thing about *you* than me!'

'Oof – saying mean things about your best friend, that's another note for you.'

'Shut up,' Huda laughs. She nudges me with her elbow so that I lose my balance.

'Oh, again, right there!' I exclaim, stepping back in line with her. 'Endangering someone's life. That's major points taken off.'

'Endangering life?!' she screeches. 'It was a nudge!' She's laughing though, and so am I.

'You know what?' I say, trying to contain my laughter. I spin my backpack round to the front and pull out a small notepad. It has a pen slotted in the wire loops at the top. I take the pen out and flip the notepad open to a blank page. 'I'm going to start making actual notes. So, first you insult me, and then you try and kill me –'

'Kill you how? You're the one with the terrible balance. If you die by stumbling off a flat pavement, that's on you, boo.'

'Called me boo,' I say slowly, writing it down in the notepad. 'That's an offence too.'

'*You're* an offence,' she laughs. She snatches the pad out of my hand, and I reach to get it back, but she's always had longer arms.

'You want your nerd notebook?' she asks. 'Come get it!' She takes off, sprinting down the street with my notebook raised in her hand.

'You're being the opposite of perfect right now!' I yell as I set off after her. 'I'm so putting this on the list!'

12

We debrief at break time. Huda and I meet at our usual bench by the field and I take my notepad out of my bag with a flourish. Huda rolls her eyes.

'Adding that to the list,' I say with a smirk.

'Oh my God, stop,' she whines, throwing her head back. 'This is unbearable!'

I laugh. 'You're the one who asked for it.'

'I know, I know,' she says. 'OK, hit me. What's on there?'

I decide to go all theatrical again. I'm enjoying this a bit too much. I exaggerate my movements as I lick my thumb, like old people do, and then reach over to turn the page.

'Weeeeell,' I say, dragging the word out. 'Let's have a look-see.' I'm giggling so much, I can't even get the words out.

'C'mon, be serious, please,' Huda says quietly.

'Sorry, sorry,' I say, composing myself. 'OK, so from the top: you shouted at five different people on the way to school today. Four of them you swore at.'

'They all deserved that!' she cries. 'Stacey Lineham's just a general bitch who was taking up the entire pavement. I was basically doing my duty as a citizen telling her to get out of the way. And those boys . . . You can't say *that* wasn't justified. They were trying to take a photo up that girl's skirt. I should've kicked them all in the balls for that. Worse, even.'

'OK, yeah, point taken about the boys. Though you could have dealt with it better.'

'How would you have handled it then? What's the Perfect Daughter method?'

I shrug. 'Not threatening to cut their dicks off, that's for sure. These things are best dealt with by adults. Tell a teacher.'

'You think a teacher is gonna do shit?' she asks. 'Do you not remember Mr Hawthorne yesterday? Completely ignoring Cleo's cyberbullying and telling me off for swearing instead?'

'The police then. I mean, upskirting *is* actually a crime.'

She shakes her head. 'Oh, Amani, you so don't understand the way the world works. You can't put your trust in anyone official. They don't care.'

'You're wrong – that's what they're there for. It's literally their job to help.'

'Would you go to the police about your dad?'

This is so unexpected that it makes my heart stop. I turn to look right at her, and she's got this neutral expression on her face. How can she think it's something she can just talk so casually about? Something that can be solved so easily?

'That's . . . It's not the same,' I tell her.

'Why not? Why wouldn't you go to them? They'd be on your *side*, isn't that just what you said? That it's their *job* to help?'

'This,' I tell her firmly. 'This is another thing you do. You don't let things drop when the other person *clearly* doesn't wanna talk about it.'

'OK, fine, noted,' she concedes. 'Although I still think you should tell *someone* about what's happening at yours. Your mum – at least you should talk to her.'

'OK, fine, noted,' I parrot. Although inside we both know that's never going to happen.

I flick the page of my notepad.

'You also spat on the ground. Twice. It's gross. Especially when you did it during PE. People fell in the grass playing hockey. Someone could have fallen in your spit. What if they'd landed face first?'

Huda snickers, which makes me roll my eyes.

'You're the one who asked me for help. If you're really serious about changing, then you need to pay attention.'

She says nothing for a few seconds, then sighs loudly. 'I just . . . I didn't realise there was so much. I'm scared I'm too broken to fix.'

'Hey, don't be silly. There's nothing broken about you. I still think this is a stupid idea. These are the things that make you *you*, the things I love about you. Except maybe the spitting, and the constant swearing. Telling creeps off though – I'm totally on board with that. I know it's coming from a good place.'

'Like you say though, I need to find better ways of going about it.' She sits completely still for a second, gazing out to the field. There's not much of break left, and the boys are getting all het up, trying to win the football game they're playing. Out of the corner of my eye I see Cleo and her coven walking towards us. Well, I'm hoping they're going to the humanities block behind us. I'm hit with a wave of anxiety, remembering the video played in registration yesterday, the meme from this morning.

'Hey, Amani,' Cleo says in a sickly-sweet tone, stopping in front of us.

I wait for her to say something about Abbu, or to show me a new remix video of his TV fail, or maybe she's here to just show me the same meme I got sent this morning.

'I just wanted to say I really like the way you wear your headscarf,' she says.

What? I frown. Her words seem . . . nice. Has she . . . ? Has she maybe turned a corner? Maybe all of the times Huda shouted at her for being mean have finally worked and she's now trying to make friends with me.

'Yeah,' she continues, her tone turning nasty, her face lighting up. 'It really does wonders for your big fat head.'

Her friends giggle.

Suzie pipes up. 'Yeah, but, like, you sit in front of me for English, so can you keep your head down a bit? I can't see the board because it's so fat.'

'You'd think you'd be used to looking at fat things by now,' Huda pipes up. 'Considering you have to look at your fat nose all day long. What happened? Did you get stung by a bee there or something? Or did you Botox it to match your fat arse?' She says this all so quickly and seamlessly that I go very quickly from worrying about the size of my head to being impressed with her comeback speed.

'Oh, fuck off, Huda,' Imogen says. 'Why are you always the one speaking up for her? Is she your girlfriend or something?'

'Nope,' Huda replies, quick as a flash. 'That position is currently vacant – are you interested?'

'Not even if you paid me,' Cleo says with an air of disgust.

'Oh no, really?' Huda asks, putting on a sad voice. 'But it's the thing I want most in the world, Cleo. For you to love me. Why won't you love me? Your badly drawn-on eyebrows are the biggest turn-on.'

I snigger, and Cleo shoots daggers at me, while raising a hand to her forehead. I stop myself immediately. She scoffs, and opens her mouth to say something, but thankfully the bell rings.

'Come on, girls, time for class!' Miss Cuthew calls out to us as she walks towards the humanities block. She lifts up a bundle of papers in her hands. 'We're doing blackout poetry today! Eek!' She actually says 'Eek'.

I can't help smiling at her enthusiasm, but Cleo and her coven mutter about how stupid and childlike she is. I want to say something back to them – the impulse is stronger than when they say mean things about *me*, that's how much I love Miss Cuthew. We were supposed to be revising *Macbeth* today, but apparently now we're doing blackout poetry. I don't even know what that is, but it sounds really interesting.

Cleo and her coven thankfully leave without saying anything else.

Huda gives me a look as she gets up from the bench. 'Let me guess, you have notes.'

I smile. 'I mean, I enjoyed watching that, for sure. And yeah, OK, they probably deserved it. But I think something you do a lot is just speak without thinking. You're always so defensive and aggressive. I didn't say a single thing while they were talking shit to me. They would have just walked off eventually.'

'Yeah, once they'd made you cry, probably,' she says as we push open the doors to the humanities block. There's a huge huddle of students crowding around, trying to get up the stairs. Huda and I join the jumble. 'Plus it feels good to talk back. To take a stand. It shows bullies they're not in control. You should try it sometime.'

'You need to stop questioning my suggestions too,' I tell her. 'That defeats the point. You're supposed to just say, "Yes, Perfect Daughter Amani, I'll stop taunting the bullies by saying mean things."'

She sighs melodramatically. 'Yes, Perfect Daughter Amani, I'll stop . . . doing whatever you just said. There were too many words for me to remember.'

I hear giggling behind me. Familiar giggling. Huda and I both turn around to find that somehow Cleo and her coven are right behind us, even though they came into the building before us. That can't be coincidental, can it?

They stop giggling when they see us looking, and put on over-the-top smiles.

'I think you sat in something on the bench outside,' Cleo says, all sickly sweet. 'There's *something* on your trousers.'

I immediately crane my neck and twist my body to look at my butt and legs, but there's nothing there. Not that I can see anyway. Maybe it's something you only notice when looking up. Oh God, this is so embarrassing.

'I think you shat yourself,' Imogen says, so loudly that

people around us turn to stare. A few giggles ripple out through the crowd.

My face burns. So hot it must be visible to everyone. Just like the shit stain lookalike on my trousers. I turn to face the front again.

We're halfway up the stairs now, and people behind are getting impatient. I look at Huda – her brow is furrowed, thunder in her eyes. She goes to say something, but then locks eyes with me and closes her mouth. We move forward up the stairs.

I should be impressed at Huda's restraint, but my brain is just focused on the fact that Cleo and her coven are laughing at me *again*. I keep telling Huda to ignore them, and I make out like it's easy for me to do this, but it cuts at me. Every. Single. Time. Each mean comment chips away at my heart, at my soul. It takes away a piece of me, and if things go on like this, there'll be nothing left.

We continue up the stairs. Cleo and her friends giggle again, and I feel something like a foot brush against my leg. Instinct says to turn around and see what they're doing, but I won't give them the satisfaction. I speed up, trying to get to the classroom as fast as possible. Only that won't help. They sit behind me there too. I'll never be able to escape them.

All of a sudden, Huda stops in her tracks. Cleo and Imogen bump into the back of her. They must have been trying to take a photo of whatever they've spread across my trousers, because as they crash into Huda, they both drop their phones, which skitter through the gaps in the stairs and fall down at least one flight.

I turn to Huda.

'What?' she asks.

She surveys the scene – Cleo and Imogen pushing against the tide of people to get downstairs and grab their phones – then looks back at me, smirking. 'I didn't *say* anything, did I?'

13

Media studies is by far my favourite subject. It's the one GCSE I know I'll not just pass, but do well in. I'm genuinely a bit devastated that I haven't chosen it for A level. Or, well, that Abbu wouldn't let me choose it, since it doesn't fit in with the whole training-to-be-a-vet thing. Mr Voake is seriously the best teacher ever; he gives us free rein on our coursework. Other teachers set the strictest guidelines for what we can and can't submit, but I guess the perks of creative subjects are that as long as you can back yourself, anything goes. For my final project, I've done a trailer for a horror film I made up about the apocalypse. It all stemmed from Ismail dressing up as a zombie for some school event. Ammi did such amazing make-up on him that it seemed a shame to let it go to waste. I've basically finished editing the trailer now, so I work on my reflective commentary during class. I'm even enjoying this essay part; I get to explain how much thought I've put into my style, my selection of angles, my editing choices.

I try not to think about how much I'm going to miss this. Getting to work on things I'm truly passionate about. Sure, I'll always have my YouTube videos, but it's not the same. It's nice to be in a class full of people with the same interests, where I don't have to hide who I really am.

The bell rings for lunch and everyone starts packing up happily. I reluctantly save my work and gather up my things.

'You coming to the canteen?' Maggie asks, eyes on her phone, like they have been basically all lesson, though at least she wasn't napping.

'Nah,' I reply. 'Gonna try and get some revision done in the computer suite.'

'Nerrrrrrd,' she says playfully before leaving.

Huda follows me to the computer suite (OK, I beg her to come). There's a no-food rule in here, but that's not going to stop Huda. She lifts an apple slice to her mouth, hand moving at a snail's pace. Her eyes flit around the room before she puts the end of the apple slice between her teeth and presses down, as quietly as she can, which, again, means as slowly as she can. It's hilarious watching her try to eat her entire lunch like this, and I can barely contain my laughter as I log into the student portal. Usually no one pays attention to the no-food rule, but Ms Powrie, one of the PE teachers, is in here, doing something on a computer herself. Huda reckons she comes here to watch porn, so she can blame it on a student if anyone ever tracks her web activity.

Huda finishes her apple slices and tries to extract a bag of Wotsits from her bag without making it rustle. She employs the slow-as-a-snail technique again, which *really* doesn't work with crisps. I ignore her and load up Mr Cavanaugh's notes from last week. I was hoping bringing Huda here would make her feel bored enough to help me out – she is honestly a master tutor. But she's too busy pecking on her lunch and browsing Twitter on her phone.

Cleo and her coven walk through the door. It seems as if they're *everywhere* I go recently, and I can't tell whether it's just coincidence or a concerted effort to make my life hell. They don't seem to notice me though, just sit down a few rows in front of us, which makes me feel safer; it's much better to have the bullies in front of you than whispering and giggling behind your back. They're far away enough for me to feel relaxed. Well, minus the rising panic about how I'm ever going to pass my biology GCSE, considering Mr Cavanaugh's notes are worse than the ones I take in class myself.

An email alert pops up in the corner of my screen. It's from someone who's labelled themselves 'ANONYMOUS', and the subject title is 'Blithe Academy Burn Blog'.

'What's a burn blog?' I ask Huda.

'Hmmf?' she says, lifting her head from her phone, her mouth stuffed with Wotsits.

'I just got an email with the subject line: "Blithe Academy Burn Blog".' I open the message. Huda cranes her neck to see.

Dear Blithe Academy student,

Wanna know a secret?
Trust me, you do.

Click this link to unveil the truth.

'What does this even mean?' I ask.

'Ooh, I wanna know a secret!' Huda leans in to get a better look. 'Click the link!'

'No way, it's probably a virus. Don't you remember when this happened in Year Nine? Someone opened a weird email and it infected the whole school? Oh God, what if I've already done it just by opening the email?' I race the mouse around the screen looking for the quickest way to delete the email, but Huda pins my hand down with hers.

'No, no, stop,' she says. 'It's probably something to do with the prank war. Just open it. If the computer hasn't exploded yet, you're probably good.'

'Probably?' I repeat. 'I can't be dealing with *probably*. Maybe I should ask Ms Powrie to have a look? She'll know –'

'Oh God, just open it, Amani,' Huda says. 'Leave Powrie to her foot fetish porn. C'mon, this looks juicy.'

Huda takes control of the mouse and I let her. I know she's not going to let it go. She clicks the link. A black screen loads and I'm scared this is one of those websites where something jumps out to scare you, like that maze she made me play once and a scary lady's face suddenly appeared. It took me weeks to forgive her for that – during which time she kept jumping out from behind things and laughing to make even more fun of me.

Nothing jumps out though.

I look properly at the page. The title is in big red fiery letters at the top.

BLITHE ACADEMY BURN BLOG

FAO: Year 11s (anyone else can fuck off)

We've been together 5 years now. 5 years of fun, frolicking and laughter.

Lol.

Do any of us even like each other?

Sure, everyone has friends, but other than that.

I bet there's someone in our year that you hate.

Flat out hate.

More than one person, probably.

I personally hate all of you.

But who am I?

We'll get to that soon.

But first, let's play a game.

How well do you know your classmates?

Why don't I fill you in?

Let's see if you can guess who I'm talking about . . .

Anyone remember Hanneke Tooke's house party last term?

Of course you do.

That was the night someone
shat
in Hanneke's little sister's toy box.
And left their dirty knickers there too.

The poor kid was traumatised
the next day when she went to get her Barbie.

Everyone's heard that story.
Everyone's laughed at that story.
But no one knew who it was,
until today . . .

Drumroll, please . . .

It was . . .
the one and only
bitch extraordinaire . . .
Cleo Walters.

I'm sure Pampers will be in touch
with a sponsorship deal soon, Cleo.

14

'Holy shit!' Huda hisses. There's excitement laced through her words, like she's fizzing from it, ready to burst.

We're both an inch away from the computer screen, our eyes glued to the words.

'This can't be real, can it?' I ask, finally tearing my gaze away and looking at Huda. She has the biggest grin on her face.

'Why would someone make this up? Oh my God, I can't believe it!'

Her phone vibrates on the desk, and my eyes are drawn to it. The email notification pops up on her screen.

'Did you get the same message?' I ask.

Huda swipes her screen, the smile still on her face as she rereads the email. 'Yep, same one. Holy shit.'

There's a ping from another phone at the front of the room. Oh my God! If everyone's being sent the email, Cleo's going to get it too!

'Look!' I whisper to Huda, clutching her arm tight. We both peer over the screens to the row two in front of us, where Cleo and her friends are all looking down at their phones. There's no one else from our year in this room, and it seems like they still haven't noticed Huda and me, considering they haven't said a thing to us. We've got front-row seats to their unfiltered reaction. We both wait for them to read, for the chaos to start. There's a weird buzzing feeling in my stomach – part nausea, part excitement. I know I shouldn't be enjoying this rumour being spread about a classmate, but c'mon, when that classmate is Cleo . . . I don't wanna say she asked for it, or that she deserves it . . . but if it's going to happen to *someone*, then she's a pretty good target. I can't tell if that makes me a bad person.

Cleo makes a noise. A strangled type of gasp. Her head snaps up from her phone and she looks at Suzie. Huda and I instinctively duck our heads to make sure she doesn't see us, even though she's looking in the opposite direction.

'You *told* someone?!' Cleo hisses at Suzie.

Holy crap, so it's true! I can't help the grin that spreads across my face; it's hard trying to keep the laughter in.

'Who did you tell?' Cleo asks quickly. 'You *swore*.'

'I didn't!' Suzie pipes up. 'I promise I didn't tell anyone.'

'Wait, it's true?' Imogen asks. 'Why would you tell *her* and not me?'

Watching this is like watching *Keeping Up with the Kardashians* or *Jeremy Kyle*. It's terrible, like a car crash, but I literally cannot tear my eyes away. The three of them start arguing. I don't think I've ever seen Suzie or Imogen speak up against Cleo, say even a single bad word about her, let alone to her face.

'I can't believe you'd do something like that,' Imogen says. 'In a kid's toy box?! That's so gross.'

'Shut up, Imogen,' Cleo says. 'I had food poisoning. It's not like I *chose* to do it.'

'But in a *toy box*?'

'There was someone in the bathroom! What else was I meant to do?' Cleo's voice is filled with tears now. I've never heard her sound desperate before.

'God, Hanneke's sister really didn't notice?' Suzie asks, looking down at her phone. 'Before, like, putting her hand in there?' She shudders.

Cleo snaps her head round to her. '*You* can shut the fuck up, you traitor.'

'I didn't tell anyone!' Suzie whines.

'Probably blurted it out when you were shit-faced,' Imogen says with a snarl. 'You did the same thing last year about . . . about what happened at the Christmas disco, *Boozie Blabbermouth*.'

Cleo starts to say something, but her phone goes off with a succession of pings. 'Oh God, everyone got the email!' She's definitely crying now. 'Who's doing this? Why would *anyone* do this to *me*?'

Her friends remain silent.

I can't take my eyes off the three of them. They've even attracted the attention of the other students in here – some Year Nines and a couple of Year Seven girls. A tiny, terrible part of me hopes the email has been sent to every student in the school, not just our year.

'Do you think the teachers got it?' I whisper, half hopeful.

Beside me, Huda laughs. 'I'm sure they'll see it soon enough. This shit is gonna spread like wildfire.'

'No pun intended?' I ask.

We dissolve into a fit of giggles. At some point Cleo notices us, and when I look up, I see her glaring right at us, right at me.

There's a spike of anxiety in my heart and I freeze, but then the image of her squatting over a toy box comes into my mind and makes the laughter rise again, and it comes out in a snort.

'Oh, fuck right off!' Cleo shouts. If she'd said this to me at any other time, I'd feel a wave of total fear rush over me, but now . . . she seems like the least scary thing ever.

Huda and I just collapse on top of each other, crying with laughter.

It's only now that Ms Powrie looks up. She just looks at us and says, 'Girls!' in that bossy PE-teacher voice. Huda and I try to compose ourselves, wiping our tears, hiding our mouths with our hands.

Cleo looks to Ms Powrie, probably hoping she'll do something more, but she's gone back to her computer screen. When nothing further happens, and Huda and I are just silent giggling, Cleo storms out of the computer suite. Imogen and Suzie stay still for a few seconds before deciding to follow.

'Probably off to buy some nappies,' Huda manages to get out between laughs.

It's a lame joke, and I know I shouldn't encourage her, but we've got the giggles, and everything is so hilarious that I literally fall out of my chair laughing. Huda howls, and Ms Powrie tells us to get out because we're disturbing everyone.

It's so worth it.

15

Huda tells me about all the reactions to the blog post the whole way home. Cleo herself seems to have disappeared. No one's seen her since she legged it out of the computer suite earlier. She hasn't posted anything online either, which genuinely surprises me. I legit expected her to take to Snapchat to defend herself – to call whoever wrote that blog a liar. But nothing. No one knows who made the blog either. It's obviously part of the prank war, but neither band is taking responsibility, or credit. Huda is desperate to find out who it was, so she can thank them.

Cleo's coven has been suspiciously quiet too. Judging by Imogen's reaction to being left out of the original secret, I thought she might go rogue, blow up online and make things worse, but she just sat there on her own in maths, not answering when anyone asked her questions about Cleo.

When I walk up the drive to my house, I'm in a weirdly good mood. The blog has cheered me up. I know it's terrible to get joy from someone's misery, but c'mon, it's Cleo. It's good to see her on the receiving end for a change. Also, thankfully, this has taken the heat off me and that video of Abbu. I scroll through Twitter as I walk in, reading what everyone's posted about the blog. I'm so distracted I don't notice Abbu standing in the doorway to the living room, watching me as I take my shoes off, until I look up and we lock eyes.

'Oh, God!' I say, jumping from the shock.

Abbu's just staring at me. It's still weird to see him without a beard.

'Sorry,' I say automatically. 'I didn't see you there.'

He remains silent, and the hot, itchy feeling rises inside me. I want to leave, to get away from his emotionless stare, but I can't just leave abruptly. I often wonder what it would be like to have a normal dad. Would he hug me hello when I came home? Be excited to see me? I mean, there was a time when he was exactly that. Or at least, I thought he was. I can even remember when I wasn't scared of him, when his presence in the room didn't suck all the air out, didn't put me completely on edge. I do have memories of those times, when I'd get home from primary school and run right into his arms, desperate to tell him every little thing that had happened. When he'd surprise me at the school gates, letting me get an ice cream for the walk home, the way he still does with Ismail every Tuesday. The good times existed. They were real. It just seems to be getting harder and harder to remember them.

'How was school?' he asks. I know where this is heading.

'It was fine,' I tell him. 'I haven't got my biology result yet.'

He nods, once. Best to get straight to the point, right?

Although maybe I'm being the hypocrite; I say I want a better relationship with him, but I'm not putting any effort in myself.

'How was . . . *your* day?' I ask tentatively.

Something crosses his face; he's surprised by the question, and why shouldn't he be? I've never asked him this before. Never made any small talk. We don't go beyond the necessary basics and things about school. A tiny smile grows on his face, and the sight of it makes my heart skip.

I made him smile.

I made a difference.

I made him . . . change.

'It was good,' he says.

And then there's silence again. The smile is gone from his face, and with it that brief promise of change.

'Do some revision before dinner,' he tells me, the lightness completely evaporated. 'And pay no attention to your brother's whining. He's grounded. Don't let him out of his room.'

'Grounded?' My parents have never grounded either of us. Ever. Also, Ismail is five. He'd probably *want* to stay in his room all evening. 'What did he do?' I can't help but ask.

'I've had my ear chewed off by his teacher for his misbehaviour. That boy needs to learn some manners.'

His voice has risen again. Not to the scary level, but on its way there. There's a constriction in my chest at the thought of it getting worse. But also at the idea that Ismail is in trouble. That Abbu's shouted at him. He must be sitting in his room terrified, probably crying his eyes out.

'OK,' I say quietly. 'I'll make sure he stays in there. I'm going to . . . go and study now.'

Abbu nods, and I quickly move away from him and up the stairs. I wait till I hear the door to the living room close before tiptoeing across the landing to Ismail's bedroom. I open his door as quietly as I can.

Ismail's not playing with his toys, even though his room is filled with them. Abbu must have really had a go at him. He's just sitting on the edge of his bed, uniform still on, hands in his lap, head down.

'Hey, you,' I say softly as I walk in.

He doesn't even look up, just starts sobbing lightly. I rush over, sit on the bed and put my arm around him. He snuggles up to me immediately, his crying becoming louder.

'Shh, it's OK,' I tell him, partly to soothe, but mostly to stop Abbu from overhearing. 'What happened?'

'A-Abbu shouted at m-me.'

'He said your teacher was angry at you. Is that true?'

'It w-wasn't my f-f-fault!' he wails.

'OK, OK, calm down, Ismail. Shh, otherwise Abbu will hear.' That reduces him to light sniffling again.

I wipe his eyes and raise his chin with my hand so he's looking right at me. 'Tell me what happened.'

'Miss Harvey told Abbu I got into a fight.'

'A fight?!' I exclaim. This can't be true. Not him, not Ismail too.

'I . . . I only pushed Sam because he hit Maisie first. I was trying to get him away from her. She was real sad, but he wouldn't leave her alone. I was just . . . I was only doing it because he was naughty first. It's not . . . it's not my fault!'

My heart clenches. 'Did you tell your teacher this? That Sam was being mean to Maisie?'

He nods super fast. 'She said I still shouldn't have hit him. That I should have told her instead.'

'Well, she's right. Why didn't you go to her?'

'Because it would've been too late. Maisie was already crying. He was being really mean. Why am I in trouble when I was just being nice?' He's clenching his fists now, his face a mess of snot and tears. 'Abbu shouted so much, Maani. He's really mad.'

I take his hand. 'Abbu won't be mad forever. You're right, you were doing a good thing, but you know that fighting isn't the answer, right? Just because Sam was being rough doesn't mean you can be.'

He looks up at me. 'It's not fair. Why can some people get away with hitting and I can't?'

Oh God, is he expecting me to answer that? How do I tell him the truth, that the world isn't fair? How can Ismail be expected to learn violence is wrong with our father as a role model?

I can hear Abbu moving around downstairs, the TV on. He's a bloody hypocrite, punishing Ismail when this behaviour has probably come from Abbu's example.

I give Ismail an extra-big cuddle. There's a part of me that wants to tell him he probably did the right thing. Showing Maisie that there are some men in the world who will stick up for her. That the world isn't full of Abbus or Sams. Ismail could very easily have been Sam in this situation. They say kids pick up on things, and there's a chance he could have thought that doing what Abbu does is acceptable. I'm relieved he's learned the opposite lesson.

'Hey, look – listen to me,' I say to him as I slip off the bed and kneel in front of him. 'Hitting people is bad. Always.'

I make sure to keep my voice stern so he understands how serious this is. 'If anything like this happens again, use your words. Tell Sam to stop. Tell him you're going to get a teacher. Never hit. OK?'

He nods, his sniffling almost completely gone now.

'But . . . I'm proud of you.'

His head snaps up.

'It's good that you wanted to defend Maisie. I'm proud of you for that.'

He smiles a little.

'But that doesn't make it OK . . . And you have to do Abbu's punishment. OK?'

'OK,' he mumbles.

I give him one last hug before I leave his room quietly.

Dinner starts off super awkward. Abbu's still mad at Ismail, so makes him finish his dinner at lightning speed and then sends him straight up to bed. It's so weird sitting at the table with just my parents. Although Abbu seems to be in an OK mood now that Ismail isn't here. He and Ammi are chatting like a normal couple. She doesn't seem on edge at all, which in turn makes me relax.

'How did your meeting go this morning with your old colleague?' she asks him.

He smiles, actually smiles. 'Good. He said he knows of a job going and will recommend me for it.'

'That's great!' Ammi says. There's delight in her voice, a sense of pride too.

'Is it for another show?' I ask. It sort of slips out, as my words often do when Abbu is in a normal mood.

He shakes his head. 'Not TV. I'm going back to being a vet. I quit *Creature Clinic*. Just have to do the interviews and appearances I'm booked in for, and then I'm done.' He looks at me and smiles. At least, tries to – it looks forced, stretched. I'm assuming this job hop is to avoid the backlash of his TV blunder. 'So I'll be ready to take you under my wing as soon as you finish your studies.'

'Oh.' I try to hide the fear that's creeping in at the thought of us working together. 'That's exciting!'

He smiles more naturally before returning to his food.

'*So* exciting,' Ammi enthuses. 'Imagine. You two working together. Helping poor animals –' She gesticulates with her hand and accidentally knocks over a glass of water. It spills all over the table and some pours onto Abbu's lap. I suck in a breath as he jumps up with a shout.

'For fuck's sake!' he bellows, arms waving in the air as if it's hot oil.

Ammi jumps out of her seat with her napkin and quickly starts trying to wipe the water off him. 'I'm sorry,' she says quickly. 'I wasn't looking. I'm sorry. Sorry.'

'Of course you weren't paying attention. Too busy yapping away, like always,' Abbu says.

Ammi doesn't reply.

Please stop. Please please please . . .

'Look, you've ruined my dinner.'

Ammi concentrates on wiping Abbu's trousers. She's kneeling on the floor now, scrubbing furiously at his thigh.

'I said, *look*!' Abbu reaches down and grabs her chin, forcing her to look at the table where his dinner is floating in a puddle of water. I can see from Ammi's pained expression how hard he's squeezing her. I can see from the wideness of her eyes how scared she is. Her gaze connects with mine and I realise I'm just sitting there, frozen. Watching this. I can't . . . I literally can't move. Can't do anything but watch this play out.

'I'm sorry,' Ammi repeats. Her voice is strangled and distorted since Abbu's fingers are now squeezing her mouth.

'Sorry isn't going to bring my dinner back, is it?' he asks. 'You're so fucking clumsy sometimes, I swear to God. It's a wonder I put up with you.'

Ammi doesn't reply. She's still kneeling there, tears leaking out of her eyes, waiting for this to be over. The silence seems to anger Abbu further though, and I find myself squeezing my fork so hard that it digs into my skin.

'You think this shit is edible now?' he asks. 'Let's see how you like it.' With his free hand, he takes his plate and . . . tips the contents into Ammi's face.

She gasps a little, which makes some of the food fall into her mouth, causing her to splutter.

'Not nice, is it?' Abbu asks. I swear there's a tinge of enjoyment in his voice.

Once again Ammi doesn't reply. Generally that's the best approach. She'll stay silent and he'll run out of steam. But apparently not today.

'*Look*, you little bitch,' he says, pulling her by her mouth until she's forced to her feet. His fingers move to her neck and now she's gasping for breath.

Ammi's eyes connect with mine again and the desperation in them kicks me into action.

'STOP IT!' I shout, standing up so fast the chair falls behind me.

The suddenness of this gets to Abbu. He probably forgot I was even here. He immediately turns to look at me and loosens his grip. Ammi stumbles back, grabbing her neck, coughing.

Abbu's glaring at me, fire in his eyes. In this moment, I hate him. I really do. I'm also terrified he's about to come after me.

'Just . . . stop it, please,' I find myself saying again. Quieter though. Meeker.

We stand there staring icily at each other until finally . . . *finally* he lets out a groan of frustration. He hurls the plate still in his hand to the floor so it smashes. I gasp and recoil, tensing up in case he's going to transfer his anger to me.

'Clean this up,' he says to Ammi as he leaves the room.

As soon as I hear the front door close behind him, I scramble over to Ammi and wrap her into a hug. She weeps into my shoulder.

16

Ammi works silently, scrubbing the wooden floor as I pick up the shards of broken china that have splintered all around the room. I look up at her every few seconds, wanting to say something, but not knowing what. Her face is blank. There's food in her hair, and down the front of her clothes. She's tried to cover herself up with her scarf, but she looks . . . dishevelled, beaten, resigned. We both know that tonight was different. He's never ever done anything like that in front of me or Ismail before. In front of *anyone*. He's starting to have no boundaries. It was easy for me to pretend nothing was happening when it was literally behind closed doors, but seeing that today, seeing the sense of power he got from her humiliation, seeing how Ammi was shaking, the fear in her eyes as he choked her . . . I can't . . . I can't ignore this any more.

I put down the dustpan and brush. 'Why do you put up with it?' I blurt.

Her eyes snap to mine, and she pauses scrubbing. She stares at me for a few seconds before dropping her head and returning to her task.

'Ammi,' I say, reaching over and taking hold of her wrist to stop her.

She flinches at the touch and I remove my hand immediately. I can feel tears pricking in the corner of my eyes.

'Why don't you . . . ? Why don't you tell someone about what he does? Why don't you . . . tell him to stop?'

'Amani, please. Just . . . Let's do this and then you go up to study, OK?'

'You can't keep ignoring it, Ammi. It's not going to get any better. The opposite, rather. You need to . . . I don't know, stand up to him, tell someone, you need to –'

'Amani, you don't understand these things. What it takes to make a marriage work.'

'You're the one not seeing sense. You need to get out while . . . while you still can.'

'You're making mountains out of a molehill again. It's nothing like that. Your dad . . . he's just . . .'

'A wife beater?' It's the first time I've said it out loud.

'Amani, stop! You cannot talk about him like that – he's your father.'

'Some father he is. Look at what he's doing to you. And you know what? It's not just you, Ammi. You need to realise this. This affects me and Ismail too. Did you know Ismail comes into my bed at night when you're fighting?'

She looks up at me again. Her face falls.

'He climbs into my bed and he's shaking like a leaf. What if he'd been at the table just now? Do you think this is the kind of behaviour you should be teaching him? Teaching me? You realise you're basically telling me it's OK to stay in an abusive relationship, right?'

'That's not . . . He's not . . .' she stammers.

'Ammi, you can end this, OK? You can get free. Let's just pack up. You, me, Ismail. We can . . . move away. Just . . . we can . . . we can leave.' A tingle runs through my body at the mere suggestion, at the thought that's been in my head so much recently but that I've never before dared to voice.

She shakes her head slightly. 'You're just a child,' she whispers. 'You don't understand. It's not as easy as that.'

'It can be as easy as you make it. If you're worried about Ismail and me, don't be,' I tell her. 'We'll be fine. Better even, without him.'

'You think I haven't tried leaving?' she whispers. 'You think I like enduring . . . this? I've tried to leave so many times, Amani. Remember a few years ago when we went to stay at your nani's for the summer holidays? I swore that would be the last time, that I wasn't coming back.'

I remember that holiday. I was about twelve and so excited for a whole summer at Nani's. Ismail was tiny then, and no fun to play with, while at Nani's all my cousins came to visit every other day. That was all I thought about that summer: how nice it was to have people to play with. I thought Ammi had taken us all there for that reason – so I'd have company. What a self-centred brat I was.

'What happened?' I ask softly. 'Why did you come back?'

She shakes her head a little. 'He begged me, like he always does. Told me it would stop, that he'd go to anger-management classes. All that stuff. And your nani . . .' She sighs. 'Well, you know what she's like. She told me I should come back, for you, for Ismail. She told me I . . . shouldn't complain. That people go through worse. She told me I could change

113

him. That it was my *duty* to change him.'

I gasp. 'That's crap! You shouldn't have to put up with this, Ammi, *no one* should.'

She sighs, her whole body sagging. 'It doesn't work like that in our culture. Your nani, your aunties, uncles, they're all . . . they'd never . . . understand. They'd blame me, no matter what. It's part of what's kept me coming back – I don't want to let your nani down. Every time I think about leaving, or actually try to, I just can't help but feel like I'm doing something wrong, that I'm being weak, that I should just –'

'Ammi, no.' I take her hand in mine again. 'You can't let that stop you. Who are they to stand in your way? It's not them living this hell. I see it, Ammi, I see you every day, how he's taken so much away from you, how much he hurts you. And it's getting worse. You need to put a stop to it. Before it's too late.'

She stares at me for a few seconds and I think she's got it, that she's going to agree, but instead she snatches her hand away and goes back to scrubbing. Her manner changes instantly. 'Wrap the plate shards in newspaper and put them in the bin. Then go upstairs.'

'Ammi –'

'Upstairs. Amani. We're not talking about this any more.'

I want to keep trying to make her see sense, but the blankness has returned to her expression. This conversation really is over.

I do as she says and go up to my room, where I do my usual Bad Night Ritual: film myself crying as Ammi clatters around in the kitchen. I'm on edge, listening out for Abbu, but I'm asleep before he returns.

17

There are flowers on the dining table. Bright, colourful, expensive flowers. They take pride of place in a sparkling glass vase. There's also a waft of cinnamon coming from the kitchen, where Abbu is making pancakes. This is the ritual of our family. The Morning After Ritual. The Apology Ritual. Ammi's not at the table, as expected; she's still in bed. Sleeping or hiding, who knows? Abbu must have gone out super early to buy those flowers. He usually likes a lie-in on Saturdays.

On mornings like this, I usually busy myself taking charge of Ismail. I help him get dressed, make sure he's washed his face and brushed his teeth – basically do all the things Ammi would do on a normal day.

Ismail's face lights up at the smell of pancakes, and he runs into the kitchen to see if Abbu will let him help. I hover at the opposite side of the kitchen, finding menial tasks to keep me occupied. I take a cloth and start wiping the already clean counter. Abbu notices me but doesn't mention anything about last night. Just, once again, carries on as if nothing happened. But then, aren't I doing the same?

'Can I flip? Pleeeeeeease,' I hear Ismail ask.

Abbu laughs. 'Sure, I'll help you.'

I watch them for a bit – watch how Abbu goes behind Ismail, holds his hands to help him flip a pancake, watch Ismail beam at his accomplishment.

Abbu turns and smiles at me. 'Nutella and bananas for you?'

His words tug at my heart, and I involuntarily smile, and nod. Days like this mess with my brain. I'm mad at Abbu. So angry at him for yesterday, for the days before yesterday. And I know, in my heart, I *know* that this side of him, the pancake-making, smiling, playing with Ismail when he was so angry at him just last night, I know it's not real. I know it's temporary, because I've seen it time and time again.

But . . .

But somehow, every single time, my head starts to wonder . . . Maybe this is it. Maybe this is the moment of change. Ammi said he's promised to change. Maybe he means it, and yesterday . . . last night . . . maybe that was his rock bottom – doing that to her in front of me. Maybe now that he knows I know, he'll change . . .

'Maani!' Ismail calls from over by the stove. 'Watch me flip!' He grabs the pan and my heart lurches, thinking he's going to burn himself, but then Abbu steps forward and puts his hands over Ismail's, all gentle like, and they flip together. The pancake lands halfway out of the pan.

'Wow,' I say, laughing. 'That was great. Who's that one for?'

'Hmm,' Ismail says, looking between me and the pan. He's got a look of pure struggle on his face, and it makes me laugh.

'It's OK,' I tell him. 'You did the hard work; you can eat that one.'

'Thanks, Maani!' Ismail says. Within seconds, the pancake is stuffed inside his cheeks.

'You want a try?' Abbu asks me.

I shake my head. 'No, looks like you two have got it covered.'

Abbu smirks. 'Oh, look, Ismail, your sister's scared that she can't flip a pancake as high as us.'

Ismail giggles, his laughter muffled by the pancake.

I don't know whether it's that sound, or the playful look on Abbu's face, the way he seems like a completely different person, but his challenge brings a smile to my face.

'OK, you're on,' I say, stepping up to the stove.

Abbu ladles in a scoop of pancake batter and steps back, giving me free rein. He stands with Ismail in front of him, hands on his shoulders, like the picture-perfect dad.

'Amaaaaaaaani,' Abbu chants.

I turn to him and he quickly looks up at the ceiling, a smile all over his face.

'Maaaaaaani,' Ismail copies Abbu's sing-song, trying to put me off.

I can't help but laugh. But I keep my concentration. The first side of the pancake is cooked.

'OK, you ready?' I ask Ismail and Abbu. They both take a step back, and Abbu whispers something to Ismail, probably trying to distract me. I brace myself, like a sportsperson. Both hands on the handle, hips square, shoulders set. I don't know why I'm so desperate to get this to work, to prove myself to Abbu, even if it's only in a jokey way.

I lift up the pan and flip just as Abbu and Ismail both shout, 'BOO!' As intended, the sound startles me, causing me to yelp and miss the pancake as it falls back down. It lands with

117

a flop on the counter. Ismail and Abbu crack up. I should be angry, or at least irritated, but just one look at them . . . makes everything else disappear.

'Not fair!' I fake whine.

Ismail begins cackling.

'Not our fault the pancake-flipping gene didn't get to you. Maybe it's only in the men in the family. Right, Ismail?'

'Yeah!' Ismail shouts, even though I'm sure he doesn't even know what genes are.

'I want a rematch!' I declare.

Abbu laughs. 'Fine. You practise while I make a lemon-and-blueberry batter for your mum.' He goes off to the fridge, while Ismail sneakily starts eating the collapsed pancake on the counter.

Why can't it always be like this? Why can't every day be a Morning After? Why can't Abbu always be like this? I look through to the dining room and the flowers on the table as I hear the shower start in the bathroom upstairs.

Maybe, like these flowers, something new is blooming in our house.

Maybe, just maybe, this is the beginning of the change.

I know I've felt like this before, but last night was different, so maybe today is different. If anyone were to look through our window, they'd see the idyllic family. Like Huda saw in our photos. And if we can be that, even just for a morning, what's to say we can't we stay like this forever?

Last night, Abbu stopped because I stood up. Because I spoke out. Yesterday, *I* made the effort to ask about his day, and he responded. That's the key. I just need to try harder.

'What are your plans for today?' Abbu asks, his head buried in the fridge.

I was supposed to be meeting Huda for another Perfect Daughter lesson. But I think today I'm the one who needs to try to be perfect. Maybe it's what will make the difference.

'Nothing,' I reply, pouring another dollop of pancake mix into the pan. 'I was just going to hang at home, do some revision.'

'Good,' Abbu replies, emerging from the fridge with some lemons and a tub of blueberries. 'We can have a family day then.'

'Can we go to the zoo?' Ismail asks desperately.

'Hmm, let's see what your mum thinks of that. You know she's scared of elephants.'

Abbu smiles at Ismail, smiles at me, then starts preparing the batter for Ammi's favourite pancakes.

This is different.
It is.
This is when everything changes.
I can make it happen.

18

We're at a wedding. Ammi's second cousin's daughter is having her reception tonight. It's in some fancy hall – chandeliers and centrepieces. There's even a candy-floss machine and a photobooth. Ammi, Abbu, Ismail and I are sitting at a table together. Ismail's diving into the tiny bags of sweets they've left as party favours. Everyone's been in really good spirits all weekend. Abbu's still being . . . normal. Yesterday, on our 'family day', we ended up just taking a walk in the park (Ismail kept bugging Abbu to take us to the zoo – Ammi obviously backed Abbu's idea of a walk, and that settled it. Ismail was *not* happy). In the evening we watched a film together, in silence. It was . . . awkward. I kept thinking, as we all sat and watched *Frozen*, that maybe this was OK. Maybe this was what counted as normal. Not 'good', but just 'fine'.

I try to shake off all these thoughts and enjoy the wedding. Because I am a huge fan of weddings. It's the one time Ammi and Abbu are guaranteed to be the best versions of themselves. There's no tension between them, or at least it's really well hidden. Like how Ammi has draped her scarf in a way that covers the bruises on her arms. It's even better than the 'normal day' we had yesterday. Because there is absolutely no risk of things kicking off in front of all these people. I imagine that, for Ammi, weddings are like a date night – when Abbu's on his best behaviour. And when it's like this, like this whole weekend has been, it's easy to think it's *always* like this, to forget the nights where the shouting pierces the walls and the thuds reverberate around the house, to forget the bruises and the wincing and the broken plates. When it's like this, I start to think that I catastrophise those nights. Make them more than they are, in my head. Sometimes I doubt they even happened. And then I remember the folder of videos I have on my phone – the ones of me crying my eyes out as Abbu abuses Ammi in the background.

But the thing is – the Morning After, when Abbu apologises, or tries to make it up to her with flowers and pancakes, I truly believe, start to hope again, that he has changed. Until the next bruise appears. The next fight happens. And we're back to square one. I know this is the pattern, and yet this weekend has given me more hope than I've had in a while. I just wish, with all my heart, that my parents could always behave as they are right now. But that's just it, isn't it? They're putting on a show. Only the four of us at this table know the behind-the-scenes details.

The food comes and we eat under the watchful eyes of the cameramen. Then Ismail runs off to get some candy floss and I go to sit with my closest cousins, Sofia and Jaz.

'I can't believe Sabrina's *married*,' Jaz says. 'Like, *married* married. Crazy, innit?'

Sofia laughs. 'What's crazy about getting married?'

'I mean, she's only twenty-one. *Twenty-one*,' Jaz expands. She loves emphasising things. 'That's only five years older than us. There's no way I'm gonna be ready to get *married* in five years.'

'I dunno,' Sofia says. 'I guess it depends on the person. If they're the one, why not?'

I roll my eyes. 'You really believe in *The One*?'

'God created us in pairs, Amani.' Sofia references the Quran, in a sing-songy voice.

I laugh and roll my eyes again.

'Do you think you could actually achieve everything you wanted in five years?' Jaz asks. 'There's so much I wanna do before settling down.'

'Being married doesn't stop you from doing things,' Sofia argues.

I raise an eyebrow. 'Really? You think there's no pressure on you to give a piece of yourself up to your husband and his family?' I stop myself from saying any more, from blurting out that I think marriage sucks out the life of you. I don't tell them that I don't see myself getting married any time soon, or maybe ever.

'Not necessarily,' Sofia says. 'Loads of girls keep their jobs, get to go out with their friends and whatever. It doesn't have to be such a big change.'

'Then what's the point?' I counter. 'It's more hassle than it's worth. I'd rather just stay single.'

'Yes, exactly!' Jaz says, suddenly enthusiastic. She raises a hand for a high five and I give her one. 'I mean, I am not busting my butt this hard to pass my GCSEs, do my A levels, get into uni and then do an MA just to waste my time picking up some lazy boy's socks.'

'You're gonna do an MA?' I ask, genuinely shocked. 'I mean, you've thought that far ahead?'

'Of course,' Jaz replies, eyebrow cocked. 'It's hard getting into screenwriting. Competitive as hell. Having an MA lifts you above the pack. What about you, Amani?'

'Oh, you know,' I reply, flustered. 'Veterinary medicine. My dad has some contacts he says can help me get work, so that's good. Taking all the sciences at A level to get in.'

'Ugh, you're so lucky,' Jaz says. 'If my parents knew I was trying to get into screenwriting, they'd freak out.' She puts on a voice I assume is supposed to be her parents. 'That's no job for girls. What will people say? Why can't you get a decent job like a lawyer, or an accountant? Or become a doctor like your cousin Sofia?' She rolls her eyes.

Sofia laughs. 'Vet school though, Amani. I've heard it's more competitive than actual medicine. I'm so scared about getting in. I completely bombed my biology mock. I got my one and only 7.'

Her one and only 7. That's what she counts as bombing?! I don't think I've ever gotten as high as a 7, except in media studies.

Jaz and Sofia start comparing grades, going through each of their subjects, and even talking about the topics they hope will come up in the exams. I start to feel heat rising in my body. They're so . . . calm, about everything. About their exams, about their careers, their future. They seem to have everything mapped out, and are happy with it. I guess it really is just me who feels this lost. The only one who freaks out when they think about what comes after GCSEs, after A levels. The only one who's freaking out about what life has in store for her. Jaz seems so set on being a screenwriter, even though she knows her parents won't approve. If she can do that, why can't I tell my parents I don't want to be a vet? Why can't I pluck up the courage to say that I don't want to be like Abbu? In any way.

'Do you want to go to the photobooth?' I ask suddenly, cutting off Jaz recounting the questions from her latest French practice exam. Weddings are supposed to be fun, an escape. All their talk about exams and the future is flooding my body with so much anxiety that I might combust.

'Sofia!' Someone, an old lady, calls from a few tables down. 'Come here!'

'Ugh, looks like Nani is trying to brag about the fact I'm going to be a doctor again. I swear, she tells *everyone*. I haven't even got my GCSEs yet, and she's practically telling people I'm qualified. God.'

Jaz and I laugh as Sofia leaves.

'I'm gonna pop to the loo,' Jaz tells me. 'You coming?'

'To hear you pee? No, thanks.'

'Who said it was a number one?' She winks at me.

'Gross.' I laugh.

I wander back over to the table where Ammi and Abbu are still sitting. Ammi's sister, Auntie Kameela, has joined them. She's got a plate of food in front of her, although she's not paying it much attention. Her chair is turned so she's facing Ammi. Her hands flap, and she's leaning in so far it looks like she's about to fall off her chair. She's got some good gossip, by the looks of it. Ammi, on the other hand, is just sitting there, not really engaging. There's a strange look on her face that I can't decipher. Her lips are pursed, her body tight. I look to Abbu, and he's looking down at his phone, though his fingers don't move. He's got a stern expression. I sit down at the table, opposite them. They're all too preoccupied to notice me.

'Everyone's shocked,' Auntie Kameela says. 'She can't do that. There's rules. Can you believe the audacity? To just take the children and leave. In the middle of the night too.'

Ammi doesn't respond. This doesn't stop Auntie Kameela, obviously.

'I spoke to her mother, to get her to talk some sense into her. But she's just embarrassed. She's ruined. Everyone's gossiping about her and her daughter. Imagine! Imagine if your daughter grew up, got married and then left her husband all over some silly row. Does Aisha not realise how much shame she's bringing to her poor parents?'

She pauses, waiting for Ammi to give her something, but Ammi remains tight-lipped. She tends not to indulge Auntie Kameela in her gossip, although she is usually a bit more encouraging than this.

'And over what?' Auntie Kameela continues, oblivious. 'A little slap? These girls nowadays, I tell you, Shirin, they don't understand what it takes to maintain a marriage. They run at the first sign of trouble.'

My heart skips a little, and now I understand Ammi's reaction.

'Her mother's in bits, she is. I told her to try to get Aisha to give him another chance. OK, so he's not perfect, but what man is?'

'It's none of our business really,' Ammi says quickly, as if on cue.

Abbu's phone is still out, but he's not paying any attention to it any more. He's staring at Ammi, relying on her to change the subject.

'Everyone's just looking out for her,' Auntie Kameela carries on. 'The best thing for her is to stay with her husband. It's common sense. They've got kids, after all. Those poor children shouldn't have to live in a broken home just because their mother can't handle it.'

'That's not fair!' I blurt. 'You can't put all the blame on Aisha.'

'Amani!' Abbu barks immediately.

I jump in my seat, causing a glass to clatter against the plate. I shouldn't have said that. I shouldn't have said *anything*. Stupid Amani. Stupid, stupid, stupid.

'Don't you dare talk back to your elders,' Abbu growls, his dark eyes piercing me. I feel sick. I'm going to be sick. Right here. Right now. The way he's looking at me . . . He's only ever looked at Ammi like that before.

'Go back to your cousins,' Ammi says, quickly, decisively. 'Now.'

I practically jump out of my chair and scuttle away. My heart's still racing, the image of Abbu's stare seared into my eyelids.

I don't go back to Jaz and Sofia. I go to the dessert buffet instead. I need sugar to calm me down. My favourite dessert is this pudding called firni. It's a sort of ground rice pudding, usually served in small individual containers, and thankfully there are loads of them on the table. I grab myself one and tuck in, feeling the sugar rush through my body. I stand by the table, secretly watching my parents and Auntie Kameela, and can't help but get mad.

People have such high expectations of women in our culture – it's bullshit. Wives are expected to put everyone before themselves, to completely lose their sense of self and give their everything to their husband. I know it, Ammi knows it, and Abbu feeds off it – the fact that Ammi is effectively trapped. If she tried to speak out, the gossip would destroy her. Auntie Kameela, her own sister, would say it was Ammi's duty to change Abbu, that she should just put up with it, like she's saying about Aisha. Then there'd be someone who tries to link it back to religion – as if it says in the Quran that women are obligated to stay with their husbands even if . . . even if. I know it's till death do us part, but what if the marriage itself turns out to be the cause of that death? Is that part of the vows? If so, I can't see why anyone would get married.

19

Mondays are probably my favourite day of the week as it marks the longest period I can go before another full day at home. There's some of the usual Monday-morning joy within me as I get dressed for school, but there's also a large pit of nervousness and anxiety. This weekend has been . . . weird. Not in a bad way. The opposite, I guess. I thought Abbu would kick off after the wedding yesterday, after hearing Auntie Kameela's comments about Aisha, after he told me off for speaking up. But he was fine afterwards, even when we got back home. I was remembering that look he gave me, still a bit scared, but then he showed me that he'd hidden some pots of firni in his jacket pockets, just for me, and I couldn't help but smile. Other than that one moment yesterday, he's been so much calmer . . . so much nicer, this weekend. It's been lovely.

But that's what's causing the anxiety. I'm scared. I'm scared a new week will take that away. That everything is about to crumble again. I'm scared that I've gotten my hopes up for nothing. That this will be like all the other times Abbu was normal for a little while.

There's a clatter upstairs in Ismail's room – something

dropped on the floor. Ammi's voice rises and says something to Ismail in a disapproving, though not angry, tone. I look out of the window as I eat my crumpet in the kitchen, loving the feeling of melted butter on my fingertips.

Oh, crap. Abbu's car.

It's still in the drive.

I'd forgotten he doesn't have a regular schedule any more. I try to remember if he's mentioned any plans for today. If he's on edge because of having to promote a show he's leaving soon, the slightest thing could set him off. Something tiny like an object dropping in Ismail's room . . .

This weekend has been so good, I have to keep reminding myself, making myself hope, that it's going to stick. That Abbu really will try to change, like he keeps promising Ammi. I don't want anything to spoil the memory of this weekend. I can't be here to see if things go downhill again.

I shove the rest of the crumpet in my mouth, wipe my buttery fingers on my blazer and grab my bag from the foot of the stairs. I'm out of the house within seconds.

There's too much nervous energy in me to wait for Huda. I text her to meet me at school then start walking

When I get to school, I decide to spend the time until Huda appears in the library. Maybe I can do some research for her Perfect Daughter plan. I wonder if there are any resources online on what makes a Perfect Daughter. Maybe I can get some tips myself. I walk towards the library and find myself in front of the notice board in the quad. I swear this thing is going to haunt my dreams. Today, the number 17 stands tall and proud.

Seriously, who even changes the numbers on this? Which sad teacher gets in to school extra early just to change the card? Does anyone other than me even pay it any attention? I think I'm going to wreck it. On the last day, just before they chuck us off campus, I'm going to come here with a sledgehammer and bash this stupid notice board to pieces.

'You got that?' I mutter to the board. 'I'm going to wreck you. Bash you once for each time you've taunted me.'

I glare at the board before walking off.

Not before giving it a little kick.

Huda texts to say she's running late, so I don't even see her before registration. With all the family stuff over the weekend, I had forgotten about the prank war and the Burn Blog. It doesn't seem like anyone else forgot though; it's all they're talking about. 'Can you believe it?' 'I wonder what she'll do.' We sit in registration, waiting for Cleo to show up, waiting to see how she deals with it. A couple of boys, Dylan and Khalil, walk into the room chuckling and nudging each other, their hands hidden behind their back. They walk over to the far corner where Cleo and her coven usually sit. The boys go right up to the desk, glancing at Miss Hoover every few seconds to make sure she's not looking. When I finally catch sight of their hands, I see that they're each carrying a pile of mud in their hands. They must have got some soil from outside and wet it, because there's been no proper rain in weeks. They take the mud and spread it all over the chair Cleo normally sits on, giggling like toddlers as they do. Everyone else in the room starts snickering too, but not loud enough for Miss Hoover to notice. She normally uses registration period to catch up on her marking.

The boys finish their masterpiece by placing a couple of mud-covered dolls on the chair, just as Suzie and Imogen walk in. The entire room goes silent, eyes on the door, waiting to see if Cleo is behind her friends. The girls look awkwardly around the room before scuttling off towards the back, towards the messed-up chair.

Cleo isn't with them though.

The realisation of this lands on everyone at the same time. I think I'm the only one who's relieved. Even with the blog, and everyone making fun of Cleo, there's a part of me that worries that if she *had* come in today, she'd be able to brush it off, to just reclaim her position of power, like she always does. And then she'd set her sights on me again, but more so, because she'd be desperate to get the attention off her. But she's not here. I can relax. I can smile (and roll my eyes) at the display on the chair, and the way Imogen and Suzie stare at it, dumbfounded. Dylan and Khalil burst into laughter, and someone else pulls out their phone to film their reactions, thinking that they're the next best thing. Suzie and Imogen stare at the chair for a second then look at each other, before sitting down on the two clean chairs next to it.

'Where's Poopypants?' Khalil asks them, trying to get the mud off his hands.

A titter goes around the classroom.

'Grow up,' Suzie retorts.

'She's not in today,' Imogen says. There's a sharpness to her voice that tells me she's still not over being kept out of the loop, not knowing this secret beforehand.

'Let me guess,' Dylan pipes up, wiping his hands on his trousers. 'At home with diarrhoea?'

'Or out buying toy boxes?' Khalil suggests.

The bell rings, saving the girls from having to reply. Miss Hoover shoos everyone out of the room. My phone vibrates in my pocket and I pull it out. It's a text from Huda.

OH MY GOD. You HAVE to see this. Come to the science block NOWWW!!!

It takes a lot to excite Huda this much, so it must be something big. I would text her back, but I know that if she hasn't told me now, that means it's something she wants me to see myself. Luckily I have biology first thing, so I'm going there anyway.

There's a crowd at the entrance when I get there. Mostly from Year Eleven. Mostly *not* in my biology class. I get up on my tiptoes to see.

'Amani!' Huda screams from inside. I look for her, but don't spot her anywhere. Next thing I know, I'm being dragged by the arm right through the crowd.

'Huda!' I say, when we're finally out of the crowd. She pulls me close. We're just inside the building. I look to see what the fuss is all about.

And . . .

Holy shit.

There's a long blue tarp along the floor of the narrow corridor, covered in water and soap.

'It's a freaking slip 'n' slide!' Huda squeals. At the same time, someone next to us takes a run-up and then flops stomach first onto the tarp, with what looks like plastic trays from the canteen taped all over their body. There's a crack-smash sound as the trays connect with the tarp and she slides down the corridor, whooping as she goes. Everyone around us cheers too.

'Oh my God,' I laugh. 'How . . . ? How on earth did someone set this up without being caught?'

Huda shrugs. 'Fuck knows. It was like this when I got here. You gonna have a go?'

'You're kidding, right?'

'Why not?' she asks seriously.

'Wait, *you're* gonna have a go?'

'Well, *duh*. This is way too epic not to be a part of! I've been waiting, like, five minutes for a turn.'

I stare at her, flabbergasted. 'But . . . but . . .' There's too many things I want to say to her; I don't know how to make her see how stupid this is. Surely she should *realise* how stupid this is. 'Backpack is gonna go crazy,' I tell her. 'He already found out that it was Ezra Fitzgerald who did the whole eBay thing. I heard he was in isolation on Friday. There's no way they'll let this go. Especially considering people are gonna miss class. I'm already late for biology.'

'Oh God, loosen up, Amani,' Huda says, rolling her eyes. 'It's the last few weeks of school. What better time to do stuff like this?'

'What happened to wanting to be better?' I ask her. 'The Perfect Daughter plan?'

She looks at me for a second, expressionless, quiet. I've finally got to her.

'Huda, c'mon, you're up next!' a boy behind her, someone from the X band, calls impatiently.

Huda looks at him, and then back at me. I can see the indecision in her face.

'When are we ever going to get the chance to go on a slip 'n' slide in a school corridor again?' she asks me.

'Why do you even *want* to? Your clothes are gonna get soaked.'

'Oh nah, don't worry, we got that covered,' the boy says. He rummages through a bag on the floor, pulls out a rolled-up white bundle and presents it to me proudly. I stare at him, confused. He unrolls the bundle and holds it out in its full form. It's a white jumpsuit, the kind exterminators or forensics people wear. A full-body overall.

'Genius, innit?' Huda says. She takes off her blazer and starts putting the jumpsuit on.

'Huda, c'mon . . .' I try. I don't even know why I'm so bothered. It's not like *I'm* going to get in trouble. But something about the idea of Huda getting detention, or worse, makes me anxious. I think it might be because of everything she said to me the other day, how she's worried about Ali and Nafisah not loving her as much if she's not the Perfect Daughter. I didn't believe the idea of it when she told me, and I still don't believe it now. But I saw how much *she* believed it, how much *she* wanted to change, to become the image of this

Perfect Daughter she's conjured in her head. And I also know Huda – how self-destructive she can be.

I have to convince her it's worth it.

'Huda, c'mon! You're holding everyone up. We gotta get through all these people before Backpack comes,' the boy says.

I open my mouth to pour my heart out to Huda like I had planned. But she just launches herself onto the tarp.

'WHAT IS GOING ON IN HERE?' a deep booming teacher voice roars over the heads of the crowd, as Huda's halfway down the tarp. Everyone shrieks and starts jostling around. I can't see Huda any more. Can't see how far she got. I should wait for her. I should stand by and stick up for her while she gets punished for taking part in this.

But I don't.

I follow my class down the hall in the opposite direction, to biology.

20

In class, the slip 'n' slide is all anyone can talk about. You can tell Mr Cavanaugh is at his wits' end. He's shouted 'BE QUIET!' around fifteen times already, no lie. I've been keeping an eye on my phone, waiting for Huda to text me, to tell me she's been suspended, or sent to Mr Bach's office. But nothing comes. I can't tell if that means she got away with it, or whether she's just mad at me for being a spoilsport earlier.

I try to concentrate on what Mr Cavanaugh is writing on the board, but there's a giant distracting feeling of nausea in my stomach. I can see the pile of papers on his desk. The practice exams from last week. The ones that have been graded and will indicate how the real exam we're due to take in three weeks is likely to go. The grade that will decide my future. I've been waiting for him to give them out for thirty minutes. With the previous tests we've done, he's given them out at the beginning of the lesson, let us read over them and ask questions, then we went over the things people got wrong. But today . . . he's in a bad mood. Someone said he slipped on the water from the slip 'n' slide. I heard someone else say he was going to sue. Who knows what's true? The only thing I know is that I'm freaking out about the grade that's on my paper.

Mr Cavanaugh tries to control the class, but even he knows when to admit defeat. I've noticed a change in atmosphere recently. More people have become like Huda was this morning. They've gone all rebellious, just because school is ending. Surely it should be the opposite – this should be the time we buckle down. It's the last chance to make a difference. I guess that's the thing though, isn't it? Everyone but me has everything figured out. They're all clever enough to get good grades without really trying. I don't remember the last time Huda sat down and revised for herself, rather than just to help me or keep me company. Me, on the other hand – I've had to cram in hours and hours of revision each day, just to try to keep up. I feel like my whole life is studying. Studying at school, going home to study, and then a few hours' sleep before waking up to do it all over again. I'm hoping praying wishing that I'll scrape through. I just need to get decent enough grades to get into A levels. Next year it will be easier. There won't be so many subjects. I can really focus. It'll be better.

Finally, twenty minutes before the lesson ends, Mr Cavanaugh begins handing out the papers. He calls everyone up one by one, sits them down at his desk and has a conversation with them. Oh God, I thought he was just going to hand them back and let us get on with it. I can't sit there and talk to him about why I suck so bad at science.

I watch as student after student goes up to collect their paper. Trevor Equiano sits and chats with him for nearly five whole minutes, while Max Murray gets a smile and a 'well done' before returning to his seat. He so got a 9. I can see it in his smug smile. I watch everyone's faces as they go up; no one seems nearly as terrified as I am. No one returns with a sad face. Maybe he marked generously. Stacey Lineham, who sits next to me, is trying to get me to talk to her. To gossip with her. She wants to know what I think about the blog, about Cleo. Stacey is generally a chatterbox, so this isn't new, but she's really grating on me today. Huda says her voice sounds like a crying puppy and I can totally hear it now.

And then Mr Cavanaugh calls my name. I stand up without even realising my body is moving. Stacey is still trying to talk to me, but I'm focused on the front desk. Mr Cavanaugh is looking at me, but when I make eye contact, he looks down at the paper in his hand. At my paper.

Uh-oh.

I sit down opposite him and become acutely aware that anyone trying to listen to our conversation could eavesdrop easily.

'OK, so, Amani, here's your test back.' He hands me the papers. There's a big red 3 on the front.

Shit.

'Did you study at *all*?' he asks in the most condescending tone ever.

'Yes!' I say, desperately, the reality of this grade sinking in. 'I studied *so much*.' Tears prick at the corners of my eyes and I feel so pathetic.

Mr Cavanaugh sighs. 'We had a conversation at the start of the year, didn't we?' he asks. 'Where you said you were hoping to go on to be a vet. Is that still the case?'

I nod meekly.

He sighs again, looks at his watch. 'Judging from this

practice paper, and the others we've done, as well as looking at your mocks . . . Amani, I think you need to seriously reconsider your future plans. You'd need top grades in your biology and chemistry A levels, and I don't see how that can happen if you're barely scraping by now. I'm sorry to be blunt, but I don't want you to waste your time.'

His words rattle in my head. It's basically my worst fear come true. How is Abbu going to react when he finds out? Even if I don't tell him about this, he's going to know when I'm not allowed to take any of the sciences at A level. Could I lie to him about it? And also, God, a 3. If I can't pass the subject I've studied most for, then what chance do I have with the rest of my GCSEs?

This was bound to happen. I know I should have said something when the idea of me following in Abbu's footsteps first came up. Even if it felt like I had no choice, I should have *forced* myself to speak out. I can't help but wonder what things would be like, what life would be like, if I had just said no to Abbu back then.

There's a tiny voice in my head saying, 'Imagine what it would have been like if you'd pursued film-making, like you *really* wanted to. Like you still want to.' Would I be happy now? Would this 3 be a 9 instead? But most importantly, how would that have affected Abbu? I might have been happy in that alternative universe, but how would he have been?

'Is there anything I can do?' I ask Mr Cavanaugh desperately. 'I can get a tutor? Can't you just tell me what topics are gonna come up on the actual exam? If I focus *really* hard on those, I can do it. I know I can do it. Please, Mr Cavanaugh, I *need* to

139

pass this subject. I can't . . . If I don't . . .' I run out of steam, run out of words, because I can't even verbalise that. If I don't pass science . . . If Abbu finds out . . .

'I'm sorry, Amani. You know I can't give you information like that. I myself don't know what's going to be on that paper. And cheating isn't the way forward.'

'So what are you saying?' I ask, the tears so close to falling now. I have to remind myself that I'm in class. 'I should give up?'

He sighs again. 'I'm just saying you need to have a serious think about what you want to do with the rest of your life. You *could* continue this path, sure, but it won't be easy. If you're so keen to work with animals, maybe a veterinary nurse would be an option. I suggest you book a meeting at the guidance centre. Plus there's the careers fair this week. Maybe you'll get some ideas there. I just don't want you to get your hopes up and be sorely disappointed when you get your results.'

God, does he have to be so *harsh*? It's only my dreams he's crushing here. Well, Abbu's dreams.

'Now, go back to your desk, Amani. I still have loads of these to get through.'

I don't want to get up. I want to just sit here and wallow. Beg Mr Cavanaugh to give me a different grade. Wait for him to realise that this has been a mistake, or maybe he mixed up the papers. Something that will prove this isn't real. But I can sense his agitation. I can basically hear the clock ticking, and the impatience radiating off my classmates behind me. I take my red marked paper and retreat to my desk.

'What did you get?' Stacey asks when I sit back down. She tries to look at my paper, but I slam it face down on the table.

'That bad, huh?' she says, less interested now. 'Don't worry. Can't be as bad as I did. I know I bombed. I spent the last fifteen minutes literally just staring at the empty lines. I didn't have a clue what to write.'

'Stacey?' Mr Cavanaugh calls from the front.

'Pray for me,' she jokes before walking up.

I don't try to listen to their conversation, don't crane my neck to see the big red number on the front of her page. I just sit immobile in my chair, feeling my world crashing down around me.

Someone's phone chirps on the other side of the room. Normally Mr Cavanaugh would confiscate it, but he's busy with Stacey. Someone else's phone chirps. Then another. My phone vibrates in my pocket. It's only the fact that everyone else is doing it that forces me to make my arms take out my phone. The simple movement makes my body ache.

I light up my screen.

There's a new post on the Burn Blog.

BLITHE ACADEMY BURN BLOG

C'mon guys, you didn't think last week was a one-off,
did you?
Of course not!
You'll be seeing much more of me . . .
And everyone will be seeing a lot more of YOUR
secrets . . .

There's only 17 days left of school.
Only 17 more days we have to spend around each other.
Before FREEDOM.
(For those of us clever enough to pass our exams –
here's looking at you, Ezra Fitzgerald)
And so why not make those last days the
BEST WE CAN!

And what better way to do that,
than to get to know each other better?

Today is a special edition of the
Blithe Academy Burn Blog.

Two for the price of one.

Last week you got a very
intimate
look at Miss Popular,
Shit Pants Walters herself.
Now let's move on to her two most loyal subjects.

Suzie Babble
and
Imogen O'Donnell

I wonder,
do they even have a life outside of Cleo?
What have they been doing since their leader has
been off school buying new underwear?

There's a reason I've grouped Suzie and Imogen
together today.
Because that's what Ezra Fitzgerald has been doing.
Having it off with them both.
Not together, obvs.
(He wishes!)

I know best friends like sharing things,
but normally they both know about it.

Might wanna get yourselves tested, girls.
Who knows where else Ezra's dick has been?
(Probably in a jar of peanut butter.)

As for the rest of you,
keep an eye on your inbox, because
I'll be back.
(Please read that in an Arnie voice.)

I wonder
WHO
my next target will be?

21

We're at Huda's house. I've spent most of the day in a bit of a haze after the talk with Mr Cavanaugh – trying to ignore it, but failing. Huda apologised to me profusely at lunchtime, and I had to stop her mid-speech to ask what she was apologising for.

'You were right,' she told me. 'I shouldn't have gone on the slip 'n' slide. It's going against everything I wanted to do with the Perfect Daughter plan.'

She didn't get in trouble, as it turns out. She managed to hide in the loos as Mr Bach chewed everyone else out. I don't think anyone got in any *real* trouble.

She practically dragged me to her house after school. She's suddenly desperate to get this Perfect Daughter plan running properly. I didn't argue. Anything that keeps me out of my house is good. Anything that keeps me out of my house while I've got a biology paper with a big fat 3 written on it is even better.

Huda really wanted to cook Ali and Nafisah dinner. She found a recipe online for biryani, which is currently one of Nafisah's constant cravings, and wouldn't let me do a thing to help her. I had to stand on the sidelines and force myself not to jump in to stop her adding so much salt. It's hard being a spectator. The biryani's keeping warm in the oven now, and so we've moved on to cleaning. She spent a whole fifteen minutes going through and understanding each cycle on the washing machine, learning what the buttons do. I would laugh, but she's taking it so seriously it's endearing. You can tell she really thinks this will work. She's even been taking notes. Like, real life, written-in-pen notes. In a notepad. It's adorable.

'OK, so do I just cover everything in washing-up liquid now?' she asks, looking into the dishwasher she's just loaded.

'I can't tell if you're joking . . .'

She pauses for a second. 'Um . . . course I am. Ha! Gotcha . . . Dishwasher tablet, right? Where does that go?'

I point to the little hatch for the tablet and she puts one in, closing it with a click. I give her a light round of applause.

'Oh, fuck off,' she laughs, rolling her eyes.

The dishwasher starts with a gurgle and she comes to sit on the bar stool next to me.

'God, I'm knackered,' she says. 'It's a tough gig being a Perfect Daughter, innit?'

I wouldn't know, I want to say. I smile instead. 'If you think loading the dishwasher is hard, you're in for a shock when you start actual cleaning. That turmeric you spilled all over the counter is going to take some scrubbing.'

'Ughhhhhhhhhh,' Huda whines, tilting her head back dramatically. 'This better be worth it.'

'You know they'll still love you without all this, right?' I say. 'Like, how well you can load a dishwasher doesn't mean anything.' I put as much emotion behind these words as possible.

She sighs. 'Yeah, you said. Over and over. It's not gonna hurt

146

though, is it? Like, it'll be one less reason for them to want rid.' She puts on a gruff voice I assume is meant to be Ali's. 'Might not love her as much as the new baby, but the girl sure can cook and clean. Worth keeping just for a good meal.'

'I thought you wanted to be a Perfect Daughter, not a servant,' I say, digging my elbow into her side.

She doesn't reply. I can tell she's slipped into her melancholy self. I need to bear in mind how much this means to her. This isn't the time for jokes.

'Have you thought about talking to them about this?' I ask.

'It's not as easy as that,' she says quietly after a few moments. 'It's such a . . . weird thing to bring up. So heavy, y'know?'

She sounds hesitant, which shows me there's a chance I might get through to her. I jump on it. 'Yeah, but it's like ripping off a plaster. Just endure the pain of *one conversation* and everything will be so much better. They'll understand, I promise you.'

She shakes her head. 'I just don't want them to hate me. For ruining what we've got. The situation works so perfectly for us all.'

'Well, it's not perfect if you're feeling like this,' I point out. 'So insecure, so scared. So . . . prepared to wash dishes.'

She doesn't laugh, or make a joke, like I expect her to. She just starts talking faster. 'You really think I should talk to them?' she asks. 'Tell them how everything is getting to me. How unhappy I am.'

'Yes! Absolutely.'

'Should I tell them, Amani? Should I open up that conversation? You really think that *talking* through everything is the best answer?'

'I do. I really do. I don't think anything bad can ever come from talking through your problems. And Ali and Nafisah are so –'

'You're not getting it, are you?' She sounds frustrated. She turns to look at me and all I can do is stare because I have no clue what she's talking about, what caused her mood to turn.

'You should take your own advice,' she tells me. 'Talk to *your* parents about everything.'

I turn my head away from her, look down at my fingers in my lap. I can't believe she'd bring that up, now. Use that against me.

'You promised you wouldn't say anything,' I mumble.

'I won't, you know I won't. But you're the one harping on about *talking about your worries*. You can't tell me that's the best thing to do and not do it yourself. That makes you a hypocrite.'

'It's not the same at all,' I say, anger rising inside me. 'Me talking to my parents, or anyone, about anything could make my entire family fall apart –'

'Right, same,' she cuts in.

'It's not . . . that's not . . . You can't be saying our situations are the same?'

There's no way she's comparing her loving, caring foster parents to my abusive father.

'Of course I'm not,' she says softly. 'I would never. Ugh, I know I'm being a brat, getting so frustrated by my situation when yours is so . . .'

'So much worse, you can say it,' I say jokingly, trying to lighten the mood again.

'No, but it is,' she says. 'But you can . . . you can change it.'

'Let's not,' I say, cutting her off once and for all. 'Please let's not.'

'Amani, I –'

'Hey, did you see the blog post today?' I ask quickly, knowing it'll distract her. 'So crazy about Ezra, Suzie and Imogen, right? Did you catch their reactions or anything?'

'I know what you're doing.' She pauses, and I look around for the fastest route to the door, because I will straight up run out of here if she brings Abbu up again. 'But I'll go along with it,' she finishes with a smile. 'I didn't get to see the witches' reaction. I so wish I had. It would've been epic. Hopefully someone filmed it.'

'First Cleo, now them. It's weird, no?' I ask, relaxing now that the danger of heavy conversation is over. 'I wonder who's behind it. Someone who hates that group, I'm sure.'

'I asked all the prank people and no one has a clue. Plus, pretty much everyone hates them, so that's no help. They're trash people.'

'Huda . . .'

'The blog itself was a shit one today though, don'tcha think?' she says quickly, stopping me from telling her not to be so mean about Cleo and her coven. I don't know why my instinct is to stop her bad-mouthing them.

'I was really hoping for something hilarious and embarrassing like Cleo's. I hope whoever's writing it steps it up a notch soon. Ooh, speaking of . . . Do you think they've updated their relationship statuses?' Huda pulls out her phone and starts swiping away.

I laugh. 'You mean on Facebook? Does anyone even use that any more?'

'Hmm, you're right. I wonder if they've done one of those "no one understands me" Snaps, to get everyone to reply "you OK hun?" and "you're better off without him".'

'I mean, they *are* better off without him. I can't believe he was going out with them both. Best friends are never a good idea.'

'Good to know you'll never go after anyone I'm with,' she says, still swiping and tapping away.

'Find anything?' I ask. I hate that I'm curious, but whatever came over me when Cleo's secret was revealed has resurfaced.

'Nah, not on theirs. Ezra's posted a snap with one of those tongue-out crazy emojis though.'

'It sucks that he's getting off so lightly here,' I say. 'I mean, *he's* the one who's been cheating. And while they're being slut-shamed, he's probably getting high fives from his mates. God, I hope the blog gets him again, but with something worse.'

'Oh, look at you, Miss "I don't care about this blog",' Huda laughs.

I roll my eyes. 'You got me caught up in it. Anyway, look, those lovely yellow gloves and that bottle of Flash are calling you. Get to it, Huda-rella.'

'Ugh, fine.' Huda pulls the gloves on and grabs the bottle of cleaning spray, holding it like a gun, with both hands. 'Turmeric spills are no match for Perfect Daughter,' she declares in a deep voice. She aims the nozzle at the counter and squeezes.

* * *

Huda spends the next half an hour furiously scrubbing every surface in the kitchen. She even wipes the ceiling. *The ceiling!* I watch from the breakfast bar. We chat about everything and nothing. I even make up some fake cheerleading chants to motivate her.

'Thanks for today,' Huda says when she finally sits down.

I know it should be me that's saying thanks. Helping Huda has been the best distraction. Although . . . maybe that's a bad thing. Should I be ashamed of escaping the house at any opportunity I can get? Oh God, what if this is making it worse for Ammi? Maybe me being home helps. Stops Abbu from . . .

I'm distracted from my thoughts by the front door opening.

'I'm hooooooooome,' Nafisah sing-songs. There's the sound of her wiping her feet on the mat before the door closes, and her keys jangle as she drops them on the table. The entrance is in direct sight of the door to the kitchen, so when Nafisah takes her coat off and looks up, she sees us standing staring at her.

'Salaam, girls, you OK?' she asks. 'It has been a *long* day at work, I am desperate for some –' She breaks off and starts sniffing the air. 'Is that . . . biryani I smell?' She walks into the kitchen, still sniffing, and finally notices the yellow rubber gloves on Huda's hands. 'What . . . ? What is going on in here?' The confusion in her voice is hilarious.

'Ta . . . dah?' Huda says slowly, doing some jazz hands. The gloves flap noisily and Huda takes them off.

'You're . . . cleaning?!' Nafisah asks. She looks around the kitchen, her eyes opening wider and wider as she takes it all in.

I expect Huda to make some sort of joke, to brag about her

151

efforts, or *something*. But she's just standing there silently. It's weird. I look at her and her gaze is locked on Nafisah. Her desperation to please Nafisah tugs at my heart.

'Yes, that *is* biryani you smell,' I tell Nafisah. 'Made from scratch by Huda. She wouldn't even let me chop anything. She's put the dishwasher on too. And a load of washing. She's been working since we got home from school.' Huda shoots me a quick glance, as if she's annoyed. But I'm not going to apologise for sticking up for her, being proud of her. Showing Nafisah that she should be too. I don't need to show her though; she already is. I can tell.

'You . . . you cooked biryani?'

'I know how much you've been craving it,' Huda says quietly. 'I don't know if it'll be any good or whatever . . . I think I added too much –'

'You made biryani just for *me*?' Nafisah asks, her voice catching.

'Yeah, I did,' Huda says slowly.

Nafisah lets out a little yelp/sob and lunges towards Huda, wrapping her into a big hug. 'Oh my God, Huda, you are the *best!* I can't believe you went to all this trouble.'

I watch as Huda's face adjusts to the situation. Her expression relaxes from surprise into a smile. She lets herself hug Nafisah back. The sight makes me tear up. As much as I think this was all unnecessary, that this love between them would exist without biryani, it's lovely to see Huda feeling good. Feeling loved. I have to blink to keep the tears away.

'Are you just extra hormonal today?' Huda laughs as Nafisah pulls away, revealing her face soaked with tears.

Nafisah laughs a little and wipes her nose with the back of her hand. 'It's just so . . .' She pauses. '*Biryani*, Huda. I can't believe you went to all that trouble.' She looks around the room. 'This place is freaking spotless. Have we unlocked a new talent?' She looks at Huda and smiles mischievously. 'Rookie mistake, Huds – you're gonna be in charge of cleaning the kitchen now, you know that, right? Hang on . . . Did you clean the ceiling?!'

Huda laughs once. 'I was . . . happy to,' she says quietly.

Nafisah takes another sniff. 'Oh God, that smell is making me salivate. Can we eat it now?' She walks over to the oven and opens the door, taking another great big sniff. 'Huda, this smells amazing. I didn't know you could cook! You're only telling us this now? Sneaky!'

Huda's smile drops a little.

Nafisah takes the dish out of the oven with the oven gloves and places it on the stove.

'Geez, if I knew you were this crazy over biryani, I would have made it ages ago.' Huda pauses, watching Nafisah. 'Are you . . . are you crying? What is it? Does it look gross? Oh God, I did add too much salt, didn't I?' Huda rushes over, gets out a fork to taste it, but Nafisah grabs her hand instead.

'No, no, it's nothing like that,' she says, full-on sobbing now. 'It's just . . . just . . .' She holds Huda's hand and pulls it to her chest, looking at Huda's face concentratedly. 'We really got lucky with you, didn't we?' she says softly.

Surprise blooms on Huda's face.

'I've had such a tiring day and . . . to come back to this . . . I just . . . I love you, Huda . . .' Nafisah tries to carry on but she's overcome with emotion.

Huda pulls her into another big hug, cuddling her as close as the baby bump will let her.

'You're crazy,' Huda says, a laugh and tears mixed into her words. 'This baby is making you soppy.'

Nafisah laughs too. I stand at the side of the room with my phone out, filming the scene, feeling emotional myself. I'm so glad that Nafisah gave Huda the recognition she so needs. I can tell that just those few words, from an overly emotional pregnant lady, mean the world to Huda (and she will deny that it made her cry, but I have video proof). There's something else rising within me though. A bitter feeling. Watching Huda and Nafisah makes me . . . sad. I can't remember the last time Ammi got so happy over anything, let alone something small like biryani and a clean kitchen. Even when we're doing things she seems to enjoy, like filming videos or playing a new nonsense game Ismail's created, her joy is always fleeting. Her smile always fades, replaced by worry. Nafisah has the biggest grin on her face, pure joy in her voice. When was the last time Ammi was as happy as this? More importantly, when was the last time *I* did something to make her smile? Huda roped me into this scheme to teach her to be a Perfect Daughter, but have I even been a GOOD daughter lately?

22

Nafisah forces me to stay for dinner, to enjoy Huda's hard work. It's a really lovely experience actually. To sit and watch Nafisah and Ali gush over Huda, to see Huda quip back self-deprecating remarks when I know inside she's glowing. She's glowing on the outside too – her smile is gigantic. They all bend over backwards to make me feel welcome but I feel like I'm invading an intimate family moment. I make my excuses as soon as I've cleared my plate. I pretend Ammi has texted me to get home to help her with something. As I tell that lie, I see a flash from dinner from the other night. When Abbu attacked her in front of me. What if something like that is happening at home right now? I feel sick. I'm such a bad daughter. A bad sister. I can't believe I've left Ismail to deal with that.

'Tell your mum to call me!' Nafisah says as she waves me out of the door. 'And that she owes me for bailing on our coffee date the other day!'

I smile and wave back, knowing I won't relay the message. Abbu doesn't hide the fact that he doesn't like Nafisah. Ammi manages to meet up with her every now and then, but she's wary about phone calls at home, in case Abbu hears. I'm guessing their cancelled meet-up had something to do with Abbu too. As Ali drives me home, I form a plan in my head. I'm determined to make Ammi smile, to make her happy. I need to bring some joy into her life, in whatever way I can. I'm going to cheer her up. I'm going to make a difference. I *can* make a difference.

I slot my key into the door and turn, planning to go straight to Ammi and offer to make her a cup of tea. She always says I make the best tea, not that I do it very often any more. Dammit, I should have asked Ali to stop at the shops on the way home so I could buy her some bourbon biscuits. Maybe I can just spread some Nutella on a plain biscuit; she used to love when I made her those when I was a kid. It's going to work. It's going to be better. If Huda can become a Perfect Daughter, then so can I.

I push the door open and step in. Before I can even get my shoes off, I hear it. The shouting. Abbu's voice booming. They're in the living room. The door is closed, yet it seems like he's standing right in front of me.

'I MAKE SO MANY FUCKING SACRIFICES FOR THIS FAMILY, AND HERE YOU ARE, BEING A SELFISH BITCH.'

I'm rooted to the spot. Paralysed. His words keep coming and coming. Ammi's voice is there too. Quiet and unintelligible, but there. Her tone is pleading, begging. Trying to calm Abbu down, get him to stop.

'WHY DO YOU EVEN WANT TO DO AN ART COURSE? IT'S NOT LIKE YOU'VE GOT ANY TALENT.'

Ammi wants to do an art course? I thought that was just a hobby, not something she'd like to take further. Although

I'm sure she would think the same about my film-making . . .

'I DON'T CARE IF IT'S FREE. YOU'RE NOT FUCKING DOING IT!' He's louder now.

Stop.

He needs to stop.

I think back to the other night. Abbu squeezing Ammi's cheeks hard, her neck, almost choking her.

Until I told him to stop.

Until I stood up and did something to help.

'DON'T YOU THINK ABOUT ANYONE ELSE BUT YOURSELF?'

If I want to be the Perfect Daughter, or even just a decent human being, I should open that door, step in and tell him to stop. He'll stop. He will. It's worked in the past. It will work again. I have the power here. Not him.

So . . . I should just go in there.

Just step in and say the words.

Maybe even just my presence will stop it.

Just step inside, Amani.

Open the door.

I can't move.

OPEN THE DOOR, AMANI.

I can't move.

YOU CAN STOP THIS.

I CAN'T MOVE.

I'm scared. I'm scared of Abbu. Of what I might find when I walk in there.

But . . .

He's only shouting right now. I can't hear anything that suggests he's . . . doing anything worse. It's just words. I can cope with words.

I can do this.

Just take a few steps. Just say a few words.

A few words can make a world of difference.

I can do it.

I can help Ammi.

I reach out towards the door handle of the living room . . . and notice that my hand is shaking.

'Maani?' a voice whispers.

I almost let out a yelp as I jump away from the door. My heart's pounding, my breathing shaky. I look around and see Ismail standing at the top of the stairs. His eyes are wide, his arms wrapped around himself.

'Ismail,' I breathe. I rush up the stairs and scoop him into a hug. 'Hey, what's wrong? Why are you crying?'

He pulls me against him as tight as he can and buries his head in my shoulder, staying there silent and still. There's a thud downstairs in the living room. A familiar thud. Followed by a familiar cry. A cry for help. I could have stopped that. If I'd stepped in right away, it wouldn't have gone this far. I could have . . .

'Maani, I'm scared,' Ismail says against my neck.

I can't help Ammi right now, but I can definitely help Ismail. I lift him up and carry him into my room. I shut the door with my hip and take him over to my bed. As soon as I put him down, he scrambles under the covers. He knows the drill. The Bad Night Ritual. I take out our headphones, plug us in to my phone and start up a video we made together, based on *Finding Nemo*. I'll do my own Bad Night video when he's asleep.

23

There aren't any flowers on the dining table today. No smell of pancakes wafting through the house. But there is a box. A cardboard box with a photo advertising the bread maker Ammi has been wanting ever since Nafisah got one months ago. Next to the box is Abbu, with ribbon wound around his hands, a pair of scissors and a roll of tape on the table in front of him. I watch from the kitchen as he struggles with the ribbon – it gets tangled between his fingers as he tries to make a bow. I can see him muttering under his breath, concentration written all over his face.

I look back at that box. It's the exact brand Ammi wanted. I remember she marked the page in a Lakeland catalogue, even circled it in pen. I thought it was to remind herself for later, but I guess it was a hint. A hint that Abbu's picked up on. When Ammi's obsession with fresh bread started, he would tell her to just walk down the street to the Co-op and buy some. He told her there was no point her even trying to make bread because she would fail. He reminded her of the time she used the wrong ingredients and made a bitter cake for Ismail's birthday.

But now . . . He knew how happy this would make her, so he went out to buy it. Or maybe he ordered it months ago, when she first hinted, and it's only just arrived. Bread makers are pretty in demand; it was probably sold out. I don't even entertain the idea that he's just doing this as part of the Morning After Ritual.

I hear soft footsteps. Ammi's. She's approaching the dining room from the other direction. For some reason, I panic and press myself against the wall, so neither of them can see me. I need to get a textbook I left on the dining table, but I don't want to disrupt this moment.

'Oh!' Ammi says when she walks in, surprised.

'Ah, you caught me! I'm not finished yet!' Abbu says, almost giddily. 'You weren't supposed to see it until it was fully wrapped. Ribbons are hard.' He lets out a little chuckle.

'When did you buy this?' Ammi says after a pause. She's so quiet I barely hear her, but she sounds a bit . . . annoyed? Why would she be annoyed? She's been wanting this bread maker for ages.

'Is it . . . not the one you wanted?' Abbu asks shyly.

Ammi doesn't reply. I move closer to the doorway, strain my ears, and hear her footsteps, then a cupboard opening. She sucks in a breath as she pulls out a mug with a clink.

'Do you . . . do you want some help?' Abbu asks hesitantly.

She doesn't reply. The kettle clicks on and then she opens a tin, probably getting a teabag. My heart's pounding as I fight the urge to look around the corner and watch them. I want to see their faces. See the look on Ammi's face. She must be smiling at least, right? It's such a big gift. Definitely the biggest he's bought her in ages.

After a few seconds of silence, Abbu sighs. 'Shirin . . .' he says slowly. 'I'm . . . I'm sorry about last night. I didn't mean to hurt you, but sometimes you make me so angry.'

Oh

my

God.

He . . . he apologised. He . . . actually acknowledged what happened last night. He *never* talks about the abuse. None of us do. It's an unwritten rule of our family. And it's not just empty words, either. He actually *sounds* sorry. His voice is low, with a sort of nervousness and vulnerability about it.

He's trying. He really is.

The glimmer of hope that comes with every Morning After returns. But bigger this time. I've never heard him like this, never heard him actually say the word 'sorry', acknowledge what happened. I swear his voice has never been so full of regret. It makes me feel like this time really could be the start of something new. That this could be the day, the moment, that everything starts to change.

Abbu starts to apologise further, but the rising whistle of the kettle blocks it out. I feel the urge to peek around the corner, to see if I can hear what he's saying, but . . . it's probably best not to, right? This should be a moment between them. I shouldn't eavesdrop.

I sneak out of the kitchen through the other door, grab my backpack and leave for school. But there's one thought blossoming in my head.

He's changing. He's really, truly changing.

24

Huda is two steps ahead of me on the way to school. She doesn't notice the distance, or that I'm not listening to a word she's saying. I'm imagining what must be happening at home. Abbu continuing to genuinely apologise, promising to change, and actually meaning it. Ammi forgiving him. Them both making plans for the future. It's the only thing on my mind right now. Suddenly, I find myself bumping into the back of Huda as she stops abruptly in the middle of the path.

'Ouch!' I step back and rub my nose.

'Thought that would get your attention,' she says with a smirk.

'Sorry,' I say. 'I was daydreaming. Carry on.'

Normally she would ask me what I was daydreaming about, but today she simply picks up where she left off.

'I honestly can't believe it,' she says. 'How well the plan is working. Nafisah was so . . . just wow, y'know? I mean, you saw – you saw how emosh she got about the food, right?'

I nod, trying to stay in this conversation, in this moment. Not thinking about whether Ammi's already started making bread, whether she'll make something that Abbu would like.

'Can we have another session today?' Huda asks. 'I really

think we're on a roll. I don't know what we could do next though – can you think of anything?'

It's going to be different from now on. I know it. It has to be. He's never apologised so sincerely. Well, not that I've heard. He means it. All of it. He must.

Next thing I know, I'm bumping into Huda's back again.

'OK, c'mon, spill,' she says, turning to look at me. We're stopped in the middle of the pavement again. 'What's up with you? You haven't been listening to a word I've said.'

'Nothing, sorry,' I say.

'C'mon, Maani, I know when something's up with you. What is it?' She stares at me with such intensity that I have to look away.

'Just . . . y'know. Revision and stuff, the yoozh.'

Huda starts walking again, but backwards so she's still facing me, so that she can stare me down.

'The "yoozh"?' she asks, cocking an eyebrow. 'You have never used that word before in your life. Now I *know* you're keeping something from me. What's going on?'

I could tell her. Huda already knows. She heard what happened the other day. There's no point hiding it any more. She should be pleased, anyway, to hear that things are improving.

I take a deep breath. 'It's just . . . Abbu. Stuff at home,' I admit.

She's walking beside me now. 'Oh shit. Did something happen?' she asks right away. Her immediate reaction placates me, in a way. I thought it would be awkward, that she'd want to avoid talking about it, like part of me does. But she cares. I can hear it in her voice.

'Last night was . . . it wasn't good,' I say. 'But then today, this morning . . . it was different,' I add quickly, before Huda can say anything. 'Like more different than ever. He apologised, Huda. He apologised so sincerely. He's bought Ammi a bread maker like Nafisah's – she's wanted one for ages. And he just . . . seemed different. Like he was trying. I can tell he's really trying.'

'Trying to bribe her?' Huda asks heartlessly.

Anger flares within me. 'No, of course not. That's not what it is. He's being . . . he's being *nice*, Huda. What's wrong with that?'

'He thinks he can just buy a fancy gadget and . . . what? That makes it OK?'

I clench my fists. 'He apologised, Huda. The gift was in addition to that.'

'Why can't he just stop doing it instead?'

'You don't . . . you don't get it,' I say through clenched teeth.

She pauses for a second, probably thinking of some more bad stuff to say about him, but then she surprises me. 'OK, right, so *talk* to me about it. Tell me about it. Tell me anything, everything,' she says. 'I promise not to . . . I'm gonna shut up and listen because I don't know the right thing to say. Is that OK?'

I smile a little. This is it. This is what I need. I just need her to listen. Not for her to butt in, telling me she thinks Abbu's giving fake apologies, or that he's lying about changing. Not for her to judge. For her to just listen. I need to get this off my chest, and she is the only person in the world who will actually listen.

'That's perfect,' I say. 'Thank you.'

And so I tell her. I tell her about the Morning After Ritual, and how each time I feel as if things are going to change. I tell her what a nice weekend we had, how it felt to be a normal family. I also tell her about dinner the other night, how it felt to actually see it happening for the first time, and how I managed to get Abbu to stop with just a few words. How I can't get the image of him holding her by the throat out of my head.

'I keep wondering if I need to start my own Perfect Daughter plan,' I say as we approach the school gates. 'I managed to stop him that time, so maybe I can help make him change. Things are getting better, I just need to help it carry on. Maybe if I just . . . was around more? Talked to him more. Maybe that would help.' I pause, waiting for Huda to reply, to give an answer, a suggestion. I turn to her.

'Oh, do you actually want me to say what I think now?' she asks.

I nod.

'Amani, I am going to be honest, yeah? This . . . this isn't right. You shouldn't feel responsible for his actions. You need to know that you're NOT responsible for his actions. Neither is your mum. What he does isn't on you. It's on him. And you . . . you can't put it on yourself, or on your mum, to try and stop him, or not set him off. He has to do that himself. And I know you don't want to hear it, but he's probably apologised like that tons of times before.' She pauses for a second, notices my shocked expression. 'Fuck, I don't know . . . I just don't know what the right thing to say is. I'm sorry, OK? I'm trying.'

'I know,' I say quietly.

'Amani, I think it's time to tell someone.'

'I can't, Huda.'

'Do you want *me* to?' She's serious.

I snap my head up and now I'm the one that comes to a stop, right in the middle of the quad. 'What? You said you wouldn't . . . You *promised* you wouldn't tell anyone. You can't go back on that. Huda, it's not fair. You can't . . .' I feel breathless, like I'm about to hyperventilate.

'Whoa whoa whoa, calm down,' she says, putting a hand on my arm.

I shrug her off. 'You *promised*.'

She sighs a little. 'I know, I know. But I meant . . . if you wanted to but didn't have the guts, I'd do it for you. But if you don't want me to . . . I won't say a word, I still promise. I would never go against that. But you . . .' She makes a frustrated little sound. 'You've got to realise that is the *only* way out. The only way you and your mum can get help. You need to tell someone. Even if it's just for advice.'

'I thought that's what *friends* were for,' I say, putting as much venom into my voice as I can.

'But you won't listen to a thing I say!' she proclaims, gesturing wildly.

'Because you're saying . . .' I realise my voice is so loud people could hear us, and lower it. 'Because you're saying . . . terrible things about my dad. I'm not going to listen to you talk shit about him.'

'Look, I'm sorry, OK? I don't want to make you sad, or angry. And I'm not shitting on your dad. But I'm not gonna pretend

I'm OK with what he does. And I'm obviously gonna speak up when *you're* feeling responsible for him.'

'But it's not that simple though. To just "speak up". The way our family is, the way our culture is. You've been lucky with Ali and Nafisah. They're not like everyone else. The way my aunties gossip about people, tear women down for any minor thing, never accepting that men can do wrong. You just . . . you don't get it, Huda. You *can't* get it. Yeah, you may be Bengali too, but you haven't grown up in a family so steeped in Bengali culture. It's the worst.'

Huda opens her mouth, but just then the bell rings.

'I'm going to registration,' I mumble, starting to walk off.

'Wait!' she calls.

My mind races, wondering what she's going to say. Whether she's suddenly understood everything that's going on in my mind and has come up with some amazing advice.

'It's Tuesday,' she says. 'We've got assembly.'

I look around and see that most of our year is in the quad, waiting to be let into the hall. And there, right in front of me, is the notice board again, taunting me with the countdown. Just over two weeks now. And I'm still no closer to feeling secure about any aspect of my life. I want to kick it again. Want to take out my frustration and anger after that conversation with Huda by giving the stupid notice board a great big kick. But of course, I can't. Everyone would think I'm crazy. So instead I join the crowd as we file in.

Huda is still by my side. 'Amani, we're OK, right?' she asks, almost desperately. She does this every time we have a fight, however small. After a lifetime of people bailing on her, I think

I've become her constant. She doesn't want to lose me. And I don't want to lose her. She's been my best friend since we were twelve. There's no breaking us up.

'We're good,' I tell her. I nudge her in the side with my elbow – our thing. And we *are* good. But I've realised something. I can't talk to her about this stuff at home. She doesn't get it. I'm just going to have to keep dealing with this alone.

Huda can't help me.

I don't think anyone can.

25

Huda and I find seats almost slap bang in the centre of the hall. She hooks her arm through mine and rests her head on my shoulder. This is another thing she does to make sure we're 'OK'. She won't stop until she's got me laughing, I know it. And it's working. I can feel the anger from our disagreement dissipating. Taking it further, Huda rearranges herself so her head is in my lap. This makes me laugh out loud.

'Oh my God, stop,' I laugh whisper. 'Your arse is, like, right in Maggie's face.'

'Oh shit,' Huda says, shuffling her body again. She turns to Maggie Chan, who's sitting on the other side of her. 'Sorry, dude.'

'No worries,' Maggie says through a yawn. 'Did I catch you two in the middle of something?' She wiggles her eyebrows suggestively.

'Why, you jealous?' Huda asks, hooking her arm through mine and resting her head on my shoulder.

'Soz to disappoint, but I've got a pact with my girlfriend that I can only cheat if it's with a celebrity,' Maggie says. She sits up in her seat suddenly. 'Oh my God, what about Ezra and Suzie and Imogen? Crazy shit, right?'

'You mean the blog posts?' I ask.

'I'm *obsessed*,' Maggie says. 'I keep checking the website in case there's something extra on there that they haven't emailed about.'

'Me too!' Huda chimes in. 'It's so good to see those bitches being taken down, though, right?'

'Oh, for sure!' Maggie replies. 'Cleo's the one who started that petition to get separate changing rooms for straights after I came out. Fuck her entirely.'

'Is she in today?' I ask, looking around.

'Dunno,' Huda replies. 'Don't think anyone's seen her since the first blog.'

'I guess that's proof that it was true, right?' Maggie asks. 'You wouldn't disappear if it wasn't. If someone made up shit about me, I'd be making sure everyone knows it's not true.'

Huda snorts. 'Cleo doesn't need anyone making up shit about her. She makes her own shit. I hear it goes everywhere.'

Maggie starts cackling, and I just roll my eyes.

'What about her two groupies?' Maggie asks, craning her neck around the room. 'Anyone seen them today? I hope there's a bitch fight! I can't believe Ezra was sleeping with both of them. Crazy, right?'

'Er, I dunno,' Huda replies. 'You didn't think it was a crap secret? Compared to Cleo's?'

'No way!' Maggie says. 'Those two have been besties forever. This is, like, the ultimate betrayal. There's going to be a huge fallout, and you know I live for that drama.'

I find myself scanning the room for Imogen and Suzie, eager to know whether the fallout has happened.

'They're not sitting together,' I say quietly. Part of me hates myself for joining in, but I can't help it. 'Imogen's over there by the door and Suzie's all the way on the other side of the hall.'

'Where's lover boy?' Huda asks, craning her neck. 'I wonder who he's chosen?'

I spot Ezra sitting a few rows in front of us, and to the left. He's looking at his phone, laughing with his friends. 'I hate the double standard,' I say. 'He's probably being crowned a legend by his mates. They're probably begging him for tips on how he got them both. It's gross. Guys get away with so much.'

Huda gives me a pointed stare. I start to feel hot under her gaze. I know I'm blushing.

'Amen,' Maggie says, thankfully moving the moment on. 'Guys like him make me glad to be gay.'

Mr Bach walks onto the stage, towards the lectern that's in front of the projector screen. The screen is off, but lowered, which must mean he's got a slideshow or something planned.

'OK, everyone, settle down,' Mr Bach says, even though everyone is already settled. 'I had planned to give you all a motivational assembly today. Considering there's not long left before study leave, I thought it would be beneficial to get your brains pumping, thinking about the future, where you're going to go from here, what you're going to use your GCSEs for in the real world. I had a very nice speech all prepared. But that's not going to happen today.'

I turn to Huda and pull a surprised face; she pulls a silly one back. This is another one of our things that we do every time Mr Bach, or any teacher, makes a cliffhanger comment like that.

'Instead, I'm having to lecture you all, and you know how much I hate that.'

Huda and I roll our eyes at each other.

'I know it's the end of year, and everyone's excited about summer, and freedom, and festivals and whatever it is you all get up to these days. But that does not excuse the behaviour that Year Eleven has been exhibiting for the past week or so. I've had several complaints from teachers about the disruption that these so-called pranks that have been going on have caused.'

Huda and I look at each other again. She grins maniacally. I was going to roll my eyes again, but seeing her expression makes me burst out laughing, which I have to disguise as a cough. I elbow her in the side as I cover my mouth.

'Now don't think I don't know about the "prank war" that takes place this time every year,' Mr Bach continues, 'but also don't think that just because it's existed in the past that it has been *accepted* in the past. We had a zero-tolerance policy on end-of-year pranks last year, and it will be the same for you. Henceforth, anyone found taking part in any of these *pranks*, anyone found to be planning anything, will be given three days' detention and isolation. At the very least. And possibly even suspended.'

I turn to Huda, but she's actually paying attention.

'Look, I get that you want to have fun.' Mr Bach's voice loosens. 'And that the end-of-the-year atmosphere can be intoxicating. But there's only two weeks left. And those days really should be spent revising. Doing practice papers. Paying attention to your teachers. Because at the end of the day, that's what you're here for: to pass your exams, to get the best start in life that you can. The reputation of Blithe Academy is in your hands and . . .'

He keeps talking, but a whirring noise has started up, murmuring beneath his lecture. From the way his eyes wander, I can tell he's trying to figure out the source without drawing attention to it. It's not working though; everyone starts looking around. Suddenly the projector screen behind Mr Bach comes to life – the light flashes on and the screen goes from grey to white. The light shines directly onto his face, so harsh that he brings his arm up to his face and moves to the side. The projector screen is now in perfect view. A video starts playing. First there's an image of Mr Bach, his usual teacher photo. And then a song starts playing.

'*I like backpacks, they are my life,*' a male voice raps in the style of 'Baby Got Back'.

'What's going on?!' I ask Huda. She's too transfixed on the screen to reply – there's a look of wonder and amusement on her face.

'*All the other bags are just shite,*' the song carries on. The tune is so catchy, I know it's going to be stuck in my head for the rest of the day.

The image on the screen changes, like a PowerPoint presentation. It switches to a photo of a backpack. An animation starts up, and Mr Bach's staff photo gets placed onto the backpack, so his face is the design of the bag. Everyone in the room cackles as the song carries on with backpack-related lyrics that fit perfectly to the tune.

The screen zooms out so next to the bag is another photo of Mr Bach – a full-length one of him turned to the side. The animation kicks back in and the backpack with Mr Bach's face floats across the screen and attaches itself to the back of the full-length photo of him. Mr Bach is now wearing a Mr Bach backpack. The whole thing is so immature and badly done, yet at the same time, with the song and everything, it's completely hilarious. I find myself crying from laughing so hard. Huda and Maggie are in a similar state.

Mr Bach starts going crazy on stage, trying to block the screen while screaming, 'Who's doing this? Make it stop! How do I stop it?' Which just makes it even funnier and I legit almost fall out of my chair.

The teachers scatter – some rushing backstage to fiddle with the controls. And then a few seconds later, the video lets out a last, '*I like backpacks, they are my life!*' The screen returns to grey.

'Everyone, quiet!' Mr Bach shouts, his voice louder and harsher than I've ever heard. We all have a hard time controlling ourselves. The laughter just won't go away. Every time I feel myself calming, the song loops in my head and I get the giggles again.

'Who's responsible for this?' Mr Bach bellows into the crowd.

No one replies, obviously. There's still some shuffling going on around the hall. I see someone two rows in front take out their phone, look at the screen and nudge the person next to them. Someone else does the same. And then I feel my phone vibrating in my pocket.

BLITHE ACADEMY BURN BLOG

Welcome back to the Blithe Academy Burn Blog,
guys, gals and non-binary pals.
Hope you've been enjoying the REVELATIONS
I've been providing.
It's an honour to be of service, truly.

Though if you don't nominate me for student of the
year in the yearbook, you're all dead to me.
Anyway, another one for you.

You all should really stop having such dirty secrets
(or at least keep them better hidden.
You're making it too easy for me).

Stacey Lineham.

You've always been a bitch.
We've been stuck with your stuck-up self
for five years now.
And we've had enough.

I think your parents have too.
Oops sorry – parent. Singular.

Your mum's so fed up of you that she's turned into a
raging alcoholic.

Don't think we didn't all see her on parents' evening,
slurring like an addict,
smelling like she'd showered in wine.

Do your mum a favour,
do *us* a favour,
and stop being such a bitch, Stacey.

You'll drive us all to alcoholism too.

As for the rest of you . . .
Yep, you guessed it,
I'll be back
with some more juicy revelations.

I wonder
WHO
my next target will be?

26

Maggie and I walk to media studies together. She's on her phone, watching all the tweets and Instagram posts and Snaps coming in about Stacey. I didn't tell Maggie or Huda how I'm feeling about this new post. And they didn't ask; they just assumed I was as amused as they were. But I'm not. The truth is that I'm mad. This is so out of order, and no one seems to see it. Today's blog seems different. More of a personal attack. Well, I guess all of them have been personal. But to make it about someone's parent? That's crossing the line. Especially when it's exposing a real illness.

'I knew it!' Maggie says for maybe the fifteenth time since we left assembly. 'I knew there was something up with her mum at parents' evening. Did you see her knock over the Christmas tree? That was hilarious.'

I bite my tongue. Maggie and I aren't really close enough for me to show my truth, for me to go against what she and pretty much everyone else in the year is enjoying. But inside I'm bubbling with rage. At the person who's posting these blogs, for thinking it's OK to do this, that it's *funny* to do this. I'm angry at everyone else for going along with it. I'm even angry at myself, because I'm being a hypocrite. I didn't mind

178

when it was Cleo, or Suzie or Imogen; a part of me thought they *deserved* it, so what right do I have to be angry about Stacey – just because I have no problem with her?

'Do you think there's a pattern?' I say. 'I mean, how does whoever's doing the blog decide who they're gonna . . . target?'

'Hmm, I dunno,' Maggie replies. 'Cleo was obvious. She's the biggest bitch in our year. And then of course her little groupies. Stacey's a bit left field, innit? I've never had any beef with her, though she can be annoying. I wonder who's got it in for her?'

'Whoever wrote it sounded like they hated her,' I say. '*Really* hated her.'

I wonder if there's anyone who feels that strongly about me. I try my best to be a decent person, but now I can't help but run over everything in my head, wondering if I've pissed anyone off in years gone by. I try to think if there's anyone who would want to write such things about me. Because if today's shown me anything, it's that the blog could go after anyone. And worse, if they have no problem going after people's parents, then I'm in real trouble. What if they somehow find out about Abbu? Would Maggie be this excited about the gossip? Would my classmates be this eager to make fun of me if the truth about my family came out?

But of course it can't. It won't. I've been so careful. Only Huda knows, and she's promised not to tell. I just hope Ismail hasn't said anything. If he's mentioned it to a friend, it could get to their older siblings, who could be someone in my year. Oh God, the possibilities are endless, and all so terrifying.

'Who do you think's doing it?' I ask. Maybe Maggie has an idea. Like Huda, she knows most people in our year. She might know if anyone was acting shifty, or maybe she's heard something.

'My bet's on Ezra,' she replies.

'But he was *in* the blog,' I say.

'Mind tricks, innit!' she says, excited. 'Throwing people off the scent. Plus, the blog basically bigged him up. He's doing all those other pranks so it makes sense, no?'

I shake my head. 'Ezra's not clever enough to think like that,' I say. 'It must be someone who knows a lot of secrets. Someone who's maybe friendly with a lot of people?'

'Hmm, I guess you're right,' Maggie says as we reach the humanities block. 'Like, you'd have to trust someone a lot to tell any secret like these. I'd only really tell my girlfriend about things with my parents. I mean, if there *was* anything.'

'Exactly!' I say. 'Don't you think it's wrong? You trust someone to keep your secrets, and then they go and do something like this. It's betrayal, kinda. No?'

Maggie doesn't reply right away. She's still scrolling through her phone as we climb the stairs. Oh no. Have I gone too deep? Our friendship is sort of surface level, and it feels like I've made myself a pariah by showing that I don't find this blog fun.

'It's probably just someone who's a big snoop,' Maggie suggests eventually. 'Maybe they're just always in the right place at the right time and find these things out somehow.'

'Hmm, maybe.'

'Oh my God! Look!' Maggie says, suddenly jerking her head up. She holds her phone out.

'You found out who it is?' I ask, my heart spiking. I lean over to look at her screen. But it's not a confession, or an accusation, like I had expected. Just an Instagram post. Someone has Photoshopped the words 'Blithe Academy Burn Blog' onto a photo of the Burn Book from the film *Mean Girls*. Underneath, there's a caption asking people to submit secrets for the blog.

'It's from Ravi Singh's account,' Maggie says. 'So obvs not the legit blog, else it'd be anonymous, but I am living for the memes. Did you see the one someone did of Cleo with a toy box?'

Something heavy drops in my stomach, a new worry growing the same way the popularity of this blog is. 'Do you think . . . they're gonna go after *everyone*?' I ask.

'I hope so!' she says joyfully. 'Fingers crossed they get that bitch Rachel Huxley next.'

'Aren't you scared?' I ask. 'That, y'know . . . something could come out about you?'

'What are they gonna say?' she says with a laugh as we reach our classroom. '"Maggie Chan is gay?" Or that I really like naps? Pretty sure everyone knows that already.' She swings her bag off her shoulder and sits down. 'I haven't got any secrets. I'm an open book.'

'I'm not,' I mutter to myself as I take the seat next to her. God, what if I'm next?

27

The rest of the day passes without any more disruption. After the prank at assembly, the teachers have been watching us closely. Not that anyone cares. At break I overheard some of the boys saying that they were going to order actual backpacks with Mr Bach's face on them. I saw Stacey Lineham too. She was crying. Her friends all had their arms around her, maybe trying to hide her from everyone, maybe just comforting her. It didn't stop idiots like Ezra making cracks about *needing* a drink. It's ridiculous that nothing's being directed at him. All the girls are getting flack, and he's strutting around like he owns the place. Maybe Maggie was right about him being part of it.

There's some teacher training thing going on, so we get the afternoon off. Huda begs me the entire way home to come round and do more Perfect Daughter stuff. I can't say no to her. I never can. She hasn't brought up our fight from this morning again, which I'm glad about. But all this blog business has been playing on my mind. I can't help but think about someone out there sitting with a bunch of secrets that don't belong to them, just deciding when and how to leak the next one. Huda doesn't have the same anxieties though, obviously.

'Did you see what Suzie posted on Twitter?' she asks as she pours me a drink in her kitchen. 'She put up this whole essay about how you can't trust anyone, everyone's a snake, etc., etc. It's like, hello, we all know you're talking about your best friend.'

I say nothing, but that doesn't stop Huda.

'I had a nosy, and she's unfollowed Imogen too. Taken all the photos of them together off Instagram. I so wish I could hack into their DMs – I'm sure there's shit going down there.'

I sip the drink Huda hands me.

'I can't believe they haven't had a bust-up at school though,' she continues, making herself a weird cocktail of lemonade and some purple syrup. 'They sit next to each other in almost every lesson – that must be awkward as hell. Have they moved seats? Hey, you're in their form. What's the sitch?'

She looks at me, and I just raise an eyebrow.

'What?' she asks.

'You're gossiping,' I say. 'I thought we agreed that wasn't very *Perfect Daughter*?'

Huda rolls her eyes. 'It's not *gossiping*,' she clarifies. 'It's just . . . talking. A discussion. Between friends. It's not . . . malicious.'

'You're enjoying their misery.'

'Only because they deserve it! You can't deny that. Especially with how they've always treated you. I just wish Cleo would show her face again so she could be humiliated too. Can't believe she's getting away with being off for so long.'

'Do you think Stacey deserved it too?'

'Well, yeah. Don't you remember all that stuff she said to me in Year Seven? About how Nafisah and Ali only fostered me because they're broke? Guess now she knows how it feels when someone talks shit about your parents.'

There's anger rising in me now. I want to tell her it's all bullshit. That this blog is getting out of hand and needs to be stopped. I want to tell her that I'm terrified whoever's writing it will find out *my* secret. But I know if I do, it'll result in another argument. And I've realised that even though Huda can't be my person, someone I can talk to about Abbu, about how I feel about the future, about how terrified I am constantly, she's still my best friend. I love having her on my side, in my life. I *need* her in my life.

'Whatever,' I say, mentally wiping away all the anger and sadness. 'Anyway, aren't we supposed to be focusing on you? I've come up with the best Perfect Daughter lesson for today.'

'Oh yeah?' Huda smirks. She doesn't notice the turmoil inside me, and that hurts more than anything.

'Yeah,' I reply. 'The ultimate one. It's gonna be hard.'

'I'm up for a challenge.' She raises her chin defiantly.

I take another sip of my drink, enjoying the feeling of making her wait for it. She's staring at me expectantly, and the whole situation makes me laugh into the glass, causing me to dribble.

'You're such a child,' Huda says, grabbing a tissue and offering it to me.

I cough-laugh as I start patting the parts of my scarf that are now sprinkled with lemonade. 'Interesting you should say that.'

Huda cocks an eyebrow at me.

'OK, so . . .' I say, 'I've realised the one thing that would mean the most to Ali and Nafisah, the thing you can do that'll make them the happiest.'

'What is it?' Huda asks, her eyes widening.

'Accept the baby.'

It takes her a few seconds to get it. Realisation dawns on her face, before being replaced by a frown.

'I know you're feeling anxious about it,' I say. 'It's a scary thing, I get it. But like it or not, that baby is gonna be a big part of their lives. And the best way to move forward is to get on board with it. Even though you're scared of the baby taking your place, you have to . . . you just have to show them that, even with the baby, there's a place for you. You have to make them understand that there's room for both of you. You have to show them you can be not just a Perfect Daughter, but a Perfect Big Sister.'

Huda's silent for a few seconds. She fiddles with her fingers, looking down. I can't tell whether I need to explain it more to make her understand, or whether she just needs a bit of silence to process it.

'It's weird,' she says finally. 'I've literally never even considered it – that I could be the baby's big sister.' She smiles a little.

'You're gonna love being a big sister,' I tell her. 'You can play games, have fun, be best friends when you feel like it. It's sort of nice to just have . . . someone look up to you.' I pause for a few seconds, consumed by memories of Ismail – the way he comes to me when he's confused or needs something, the tickle fights we have, the way he hugs just my legs sometimes. I can't wait for Huda to have that.

'The baby is going to love you, Huda. It's gonna be so much better for having you in its life. Just like I am. Ha! You're basically my sister already.'

Huda laughs. 'Let's hope the baby's less annoying as a sibling than you are.'

'Oi!' I screw up my tissue and chuck it at her.

'You make it sound like . . . like everything is always sunshine and flowers. It's not going to be like that though, is it?'

'Well, no . . .'

'There'll always be a difference between how they view me and the baby,' she continues solemnly. 'It's nature, innit? I'm just some rando they get paid to have live here, while the baby is their actual literal –'

'You're not some *rando*,' I butt in. 'Sure, money might have played a part in the beginning, but they've *chosen* to keep you for *four* bloody *years*! The money can't be *that* good to put up with you if they didn't want to.'

'But . . .' She trails off.

'Look, Huda . . . you put me in charge of making you the Perfect Daughter, right? Well, that means you don't get to question anything I say. And I say that this baby won't change anything, at least not for the worse. But only if you do your part. This baby is innocent, Huda. Your fears about Ali and Nafisah are your thing. And I understand where it's coming from. God, I really do. But the best way forward is to get excited. You're going to have a little brother or sister! If Ali and Nafisah see that you *want* to be in the baby's life, that you *want* to help out with things, then your position in the family is fixed. OK?'

Huda just stares, a slight smirk on her face. 'Nice TED Talk there, Amani.'

I roll my eyes. 'Let's hope it got through your thick skull. Now, c'mon, let's go.'

'Go where?'

'We're gonna sort the nursery.'

28

The nursery isn't as big a mess as I remember. There's boxes of stuff everywhere, like when I last saw it a month ago, but now there's actually a gap in the middle, where I sit and assemble the changing table. Huda suggested we build the cot, but I thought that was maybe something Ali had been looking forward to doing himself. Men and their weird egos. Ammi was supposed to be doing a wildlife mural for the main wall, but all she's managed so far is a pencil sketch. We leave that wall free and put a decal with a cheesy quote about love on the opposite one. We rearrange the room, putting the cot box in the corner for Ali for later, and build all the furniture we can. Huda lays out the rug in the middle of the room, and I line up the stuffed toys on the windowsill. We chat as we clean and organise, and after a few hours the room almost looks like a finished nursery.

'I'm beat,' Huda says, lying down on the rug in a star shape.

'No time to rest – we've still gotta get rid of all this packaging.' I kick her leg lightly, but she doesn't move. Instead she closes her eyes.

'Huda, c'mon,' I say. I give her another nudge.

She just rolls over onto her side, still pretending to sleep.

Or maybe actually falling asleep. I'm about to give up and lie down next to her when the email alert on my phone goes off.

'Ooh, is it another blog?' Huda squeals, sitting up with a jolt.

'Who needs alarms when you can wake people up with email alerts, eh?' I say, sitting down next to her and taking out my phone. She leans over to look.

It's not another post. Just a notification to say I have a new YouTube subscriber.

'Aw, man,' Huda says, deflating. 'I got all excited.' She gets out her phone and starts swiping away. 'I'm gonna check the website, just in case.'

'Do you think this whole blog could be fake?' I ask casually. 'Like, do you think the person writing it has a vendetta against certain people and this is their way of getting revenge? Just making stuff up?'

Huda shakes her head. 'Nah, I don't think so. Even if the people were chosen for a reason – which I guess is possible, because so far they've all been pricks – I don't think the secrets are lies. No one's defended themselves yet, have they?'

She has a point. No one's denied any of the rumours. Not even Cleo, and that alone shocks me. I guess now she's lost her coven, she's got no one to do her dirty work for her, no one to spread the message that she's innocent.

'It's starting to scare me now,' I admit. 'Whoever's writing it doesn't seem to care what it does to people's lives. You can't just . . . make accusations without any proof. This type of thing could have . . . real consequences.'

'You weren't complaining when it was Cleo and her coven,' Huda points out, finally looking up from her phone.

I know she's right. And that's the thought I've been having since this all started – questioning whether I'm a terrible person because I enjoyed Cleo's humiliation but feel bad for everyone else, but this is . . . it's different.

'That's not the same,' I tell Huda. 'It's getting too *personal* now. Exposing a family secret like Stacey's mum . . . what's next?' I pause before continuing, unsure how she'll take this. 'This blog is . . . It's too much, Huda. Whoever's writing it is ruining people's lives. They need to be stopped. They deserve to be punished.'

'What are you on about?' Huda asks. 'The blog's doing a service, getting revenge on people who've been dicks. *They're* the ones who need to be punished. And the blog is doing that. It's basically karma. You can't argue with karma.'

'And what about when they get to you?' I ask. 'You've said some horrible things to people. You think it's gonna be fun when this blog spills one of your deepest, darkest secrets?'

She whips her gaze to me, stabs me with her stare.

'I don't have any deep, dark secrets.'

I give her a look but don't say anything. I want to though. I want to remind her that there's so much of her life she refuses to share with anyone. She never mentions anything about her life before Ali and Nafisah fostered her when she was twelve. Never mentions anything about her birth parents, or even whether she knows anything about them. Her whole childhood is shrouded in mystery. There's no way she doesn't have secrets.

There's a weird atmosphere between us now. I know I can't make her see things from my angle, and that she won't budge on her standpoint. That's another thing about Huda – she's stubborn as hell. Part of me wants to tell her that's something we need to focus on in her Perfect Daughter lessons, but most of me is too scared of the fallout that would come. Another thing about Huda is that she has a temper.

The front door opens. Our heads snap towards the noise, then back to each other, and then around the room.

'Shit, they're back,' Huda says, hopping up.

I get up too. There's still rubbish all over the floor, and we need to push the changing table back into place.

'I'll finish off in here, you go bring them up.'

She nods before leaving the room. I hear her thunder down the stairs, then muffled voices. I quickly pick up all the rubbish, stuff it in the bin then push the changing table into the corner of the room. It takes a lot more strength than I'd anticipated, and by the time Huda brings Nafisah and Ali up to the room, both with their hands over their eyes, I'm out of breath.

'Don't peek!' Huda says with a laugh. 'I mean you, Ali.'

'How dare you accuse me of such a heinous crime?' Ali asks, fake offended.

Nafisah reaches out with one hand in front of her as she walks – her other hand is on her bump. 'Y'know, Huda, it's really not a great idea to make a heavily pregnant woman walk around with her eyes closed.'

'She's right,' Ali adds as they shuffle forward. 'Her belly's a mile wide. It'll knock things over before you know it.'

Nafisah gives Ali a shove, and he laughs.

'Almost there,' Huda says.

'Please let it be a new jacuzzi,' Ali mutters.

'Sorry to disappoint,' Huda says with a laugh. There's a tinge of nervousness in her voice, which makes me smile. This moment means so much to her. I can't wait to see her face when they say they love it, which they will. They'd be monsters to not love what she's done.

Nafisah and Ali are both at the doorway to the nursery. I take out my phone to film the moment.

'OK, you can look . . . now!' Huda announces.

'Ta-dah!' I exclaim as they open their eyes.

Nafisah smiles at me, opens her mouth to say something, probably a joke about how me being here isn't a surprise, but then her eyes drift beyond me to the rest of the room, and her words never come.

'Oh my God,' Ali says. 'Did you guys do this alone?'

'It was mostly Huda,' I say.

She flicks her eyes to me for a second, uncertain, before looking at Ali and Nafisah, who both have huge smiles on their faces.

'Huda,' Nafisah says quietly. She breaks down into tears and wraps Huda into a huge hug. 'This is so wonderful. I can't . . . I can't believe you'd . . .'

'It's no jacuzzi,' Ali says. 'But it's . . . wow. Yeah. You built that changing table by yourselves?' He looks over to Huda, who's still being squashed by a weeping Nafisah. Huda raises her head above Nafisah's arm and nods.

'We were going to do the cot too, but Amani thought that's something . . . you would want to do,' Huda explains.

'Oh my God, I can't with the cuteness,' Nafisah wails, wrapping Huda into an even tighter hug. Huda's smiling so wide, it's infectious.

'That's . . . that's really sweet of you,' Ali says. His voice is cracking.

'Ali's gonna cry,' I tease.

'Well, I'm not dead inside, am I?' he says with a laugh, wiping his eyes.

It's such a beautiful moment to witness. Ali and Nafisah are both so overwhelmed, but in a good way. They're all so . . . happy. Watching this scene, seeing the smile on Huda's face, it's like . . . like watching a picture-perfect moment of what a family *should* be. It makes me confident that Huda has no reason to worry; there's no way Ali and Nafisah would give up on her. There's too much love there.

I end the video and Huda drags them both over to show off the details – the decal we've put on the wall, how we've organised the toys, and even suggesting where to put the cot once it's been built. I step to the side and let them have this moment together. Watching them makes me feel all warm inside. I feel tears rising too, and at first I think it's because of the emotion in the room, at how adorable and heart-warming this situation is. But then I realise . . . this whole scene, this is exactly what I want. I want my family to be like this. I want my parents to be like this. It strikes me then, the irony of it all. This whole time I've supposedly been teaching *her* how to become perfect, but Huda's already perfect. This whole family is. The jealousy rising within me is so unfair, so unexpected, but also so present.

I want this.

More than anything, I want this moment to be recreated with my family.

29

The bittersweet warmth of the scene at Huda's house lasts the whole journey home. Ali drops me off, passing on some more heartfelt thanks before he drives away. I make sure to tell him it was all Huda's idea. He hasn't stopped grinning. I try to push away the bad thoughts in my head. The ones that yearn for Abbu to be more like Ali. I counter those thoughts with memories of when Abbu *has* been like Ali. The times he made a fort in the living room out of duvets and cushions for me and Ismail. How he got us Nerf guns and we had a battle. The time when he told me I was going to be a big sister, the way he smiled at Ammi, how he doted on her through her pregnancy, held her hand to help her out of cars, and wouldn't let her carry the shopping. Those were truly perfect family moments. We *have* had them, and I'm convinced we will have more. We can be a perfect family too.

Ammi and Abbu are in the living room when I get in. I stand and wait by the door, listening, trying to assess the mood, see the state of things. The TV is on, as always. But there are voices above it too. I strain my ears, trying to determine their tone, and thankfully things are light-hearted. I even hear Ammi laugh at something Abbu says. I guess his heartfelt apology from earlier really did do the trick. I go upstairs, change out of my uniform and do my prayers. Afterwards I sit at my desk and finish editing the *Frozen* video I made with Ammi, Ismail and Huda the other day. After I've uploaded it to YouTube, I work on my media studies coursework – my fake apocalypse film trailer. I still need to finish writing the commentary. I open up the project but . . . but my heart isn't in it. For some reason my heart is tugging me towards the folder of videos I've got saved from all the Bad Nights. The videos I take of myself while it's happening. I don't know if it's the fear of whoever's writing the blog getting hold of them, or what, but I suddenly have the urge to watch them all. I plug in my phone to the laptop and start transferring the videos. There are 262 clips. That's 262 nights when Abbu has been shouting at, or hurting, Ammi. And those are just the times I had the chance to film. My laptop says it's going to take twenty minutes to download all the videos, so I lock the screen and go downstairs for a snack.

Ammi and Abbu have moved into the kitchen. I don't really want to go in while they're both there – I like having the image of them laughing together in my head, and I'm worried things will have changed already, but I legit think I might faint from hunger if I don't.

'Hey, moyna,' Abbu says as I walk in.

My entire body relaxes. I look over to him, standing in the doorway to the dining room, and he's smiling. He's got some papers in his hands.

I smile back. 'I was just gonna get a snack.'

'Dinner will be ready soon,' Ammi says. I try to examine her voice, but I can't quite judge what mood she is in by her tone. Her words are neutral too. She's so used to hiding her feelings.

My stomach rumbles so loud, the noise basically echoes around the room.

Abbu laughs. 'I guess there's no point telling you to wait, is there?'

'Just a snack, I promise,' I tell Ammi. I see she's placed her new bread maker front and centre on the worktop, where the toaster used to be. I smile as I open the cupboard beneath it for a snack.

'So, did you figure it out yet?' Abbu asks.

I raise my head, thinking he's talking to me, but he's looking at Ammi.

'I told you, I don't remember.'

'How can you not remember?' he asks, looking at the papers in his hand. 'You took a hundred pounds out. You must remember what you spent it on.'

'I don't,' she says quietly. 'Not all of it anyway. I just used it for bits and pieces. Nothing special.'

'Then why bother getting cash out?' he asks. 'Everywhere accepts cards these days. There must have been *some* reason you got cash out of the account.'

'Maybe I thought it was my account,' she says, a bit flustered. 'I probably didn't realise it was the joint one.'

Abbu huffs a little. 'I still don't see why you need your own account. Why can't you put your wages into this account? Or better yet, quit your job altogether.'

Oh God. It's starting. The goodness from this morning is fading already. This subject is always one that sets off a fight between them. Abbu really wants Ammi to leave her job as a cashier at Morrisons, but it's one of the only things she stubbornly refuses to do. Luckily Abbu doesn't go . . . that far . . . on the topic. Normally, anyway.

'We've been over this,' Ammi says, her voice steeling a little. 'I enjoy my job. I like getting out of the house. We agreed that as long as it doesn't get in the way of anything, it's fine.'

Abbu doesn't answer, just shuffles the papers in his hands. Silence engulfs the room again, but not in a good way. Now that the topic of Ammi's job has been brought up, the air is crackling with tension. I have a feeling things are only going to get worse. I need to neutralise. I close the cupboard door, having only taken a single biscuit to nibble on.

'Um, I think some of that money was for me,' I tell Abbu. I take a bite of the biscuit so my speech becomes garbled, just in case he pulls apart the lie I'm about to tell; I can say he misheard. 'I needed some money for school, for, um, the . . . prom. Yeah, I left it too late to pay by card, so I had to ask Ammi for some cash. I'm really sorry. I should have asked you, but I thought you might . . . I mean, I didn't want to disappoint you. It was my fault. I'm sorry.'

I wait. Ammi waits. I don't look at her. I know she'll play along. We both know this is the only way to end this argument. Abbu would never get mad if it's something for school. I mentally kick myself for not pretending it was to do with something academic, rather than social, but hopefully he won't ask too many follow-up questions.

He looks up, settling his gaze on me. I feel myself starting to sweat. I try to look as genuinely apologetic as possible.

Eventually he sighs and folds up the papers. 'Next time ask me instead, OK?'

I nod. 'Sorry, Abbu.'

'And Shirin,' he adds, turning to Ammi, 'if you ever need money for anything, come to me. It's what I'm here for. I really think it's best to close that sole account of yours. We'll be able to keep track of our finances better if it's just one account.'

'I'll look into it,' Ammi basically whispers.

Abbu beams, slaps the folded-up pile of papers in one palm and then moves from leaning against the door frame to standing up straight. His entire posture, his entire demeanour has been transformed by Ammi's vague promise. 'Great!' he says. 'I'm going to watch TV. Dinner smells good – can't wait. You know how much I love your aubergine curry.'

I look over at Ammi bent over the sink, washing some rice, and watch the smile bloom on her face from his compliment.

30

I'm running late for registration – Huda spent the whole walk
to school telling me how happy Ali and Nafisah were about
the nursery. They're planning to build the cot together tonight.
Her words made me smile, but, man, that girl can chat. I have
to jog, and get to my form room just as the bell rings. As I open
the door, someone bumps right into me. I instantly apologise,
even though they were in the wrong. But then I look up.

It's Cleo.

She's back.

She looks at me, fury on her face.

'Sorry,' I say again. Quieter this time. My heart's pounding,
just being in her presence. My brain can't help but relive all
the times I've been in a similar situation. Standing in front of
Cleo Walters, waiting for her to unleash some horrible words,
to make fun of me for . . . anything, waiting for her to make
me feel like crap. My ears start burning, knowing that the rest
of the form are probably watching us, waiting for the drama
to begin. God, why can't she just get it over with?

'Going to the loo, Cleo?' someone shouts from the corner.
'Hope you make it in time!'

Cleo's face heats up, the red spreading across her cheeks. She takes another look at me, and I expect her to say something. Anything. But she just . . . turns around and walks to her seat at the back of the room, with her head down.

What just happened? Not once has she missed an opportunity to make a dig. It only hits me then. Is her reign of terror over? Just because of a blog post? I glance at her as I walk to my own seat. Her whole demeanour has changed. Before, she used to walk around with her head up, defying anyone to even look at her wrong; she's now cowering. Walking like . . . like I do when I'm around her.

'Cleo's back!' Maggie whispers excitedly as I drop my bag onto the floor under our desk. I've never seen her this animated this early. She's actually sitting up in her chair, rather than slouching, or slumped over the table sleeping.

'I saw,' I reply.

'She walked in literally twenty seconds ago and the guys have already made, like, five poo jokes.'

I don't respond, just sit down and get my chemistry revision book out.

'Also,' Maggie half whispers, half shouts as she leans in close, 'did you hear about Ezra?' She cranes her neck to look to the back of the room, where Cleo, Imogen and Suzie normally sit together. But today they're not. Cleo sits hunched in a chair at her usual desk, but she's alone. Imogen too is sitting alone at another desk, not looking at Cleo or acknowledging her presence. Suzie is three tables away. The coven has officially broken up.

'Apparently Ezra's chosen Imogen as his *one and only*.' Maggie sniggers. 'And that's not even all. Suzie went batshit when he told her. She went to his house and egged it. She was so drunk she even put it on Snapchat.'

I roll my eyes, but Maggie's too preoccupied watching the others to notice. It's getting to me now. All the gossip. Everyone's obsession with other people's secrets and their downfalls. I don't expect us all to be best friends, but what's the harm in letting people just get on with their lives?

'It's not nice to talk about people behind their backs,' I say, aware that I sound like a toddler. 'We don't even know if any of this stuff is *true*. That blog could be making up shit about people, for all we know.'

I think back to what Huda said yesterday, about how no one's denied any of the accusations so they must be true. I can't bring myself to believe that. Just because you don't deny something doesn't make it true – that seems like such childish thinking.

'Duh,' Maggie replies. 'Of course it's all true. Who would bother making up such stupid lies? They're probably having all the lols, while we watch on.'

'I can think of much better things to watch,' I say.

'Like your media studies coursework?' she asks, slouching down in her chair again, realising there won't be any more drama. 'How's it going anyway? Can I see the final edit?'

We chat a bit about our coursework. Though I love having her to discuss this stuff with, Maggie's always vague about her project. The only thing I know is that it's about her sister. Her voice goes all soft when she talks about it. It makes me wonder whether I should be doing something more personal for my coursework. Is that the way to get better grades? I've been considering changing things up for my YouTube channel – as

201

much as I love making Disney re-enactment videos for Ismail, I'd like to diversify, in terms of both content and technique. I know I'm cutting it fine, but maybe this coursework is the place to experiment. After all, this project is basically the last big thing I'll be able to do before I'm resigned to only studying science, and careening down the path to becoming a vet.

31

I swear to God, I'm going to destroy that countdown. The number 15 taunts me as Huda and I walk to the library for a careers fair that's been put on for all the Year Elevens. I give the notice board a kick as Huda peers into the library.

'Can we just skip?' Huda asks, turning to me.

I stand up straight, as if I wasn't just kicking a piece of wood.

'I mean, no one's gonna be taking register,' she adds.

I stare towards the building; there are posters on the windows shouting 'CAREERS FAIR', with clip-art smiley cartoons carrying briefcases or wearing lab coats or fixing taps below.

'Oh, come on,' I tell her. 'It'll be . . . fun?' Our PSHCE teacher told us there'd be tests to see what careers we're suited to. That part intrigued me.

She cocks an eyebrow. 'You have a warped sense of *fun*.'

I roll my eyes. 'Think of this as a Perfect Daughter lesson. You've admitted you're worried about the fact you don't know what to do after school. Maybe this careers fair will help you figure that out. Didn't you say you wanted to show Ali and Nafisah that you have ambition and whatever?'

'Ugh, I hate it when you throw my own words back at me,' Huda groans.

'Also when I'm right,' I add. I link arms with her and drag her along.

The library has been transformed – there are stations focusing on various types of jobs, tables with guest speakers standing by to tell us about different career pathways, piles and piles of leaflets that'll end up in the bin within hours. So much information, so much choice, just buzzing around the room. I don't need the choice though. I already have a plan. Nothing can change that. No matter how much I wish something would.

'Do you think I'm the only one?' Huda asks as she picks up a leaflet about the army, telling her to 'Be the Best'. 'Who doesn't have a clue. I mean, you've got your vet stuff, a bunch of people in my English class already know they wanna be journalists or authors. Everyone seems to have their shit figured out. How do you get there? How can *I* get there?'

I want to tell Huda I'm almost as lost as she is, but I can't. If I actually say the truth out loud, that I don't want to be a vet, that really I want to get into film-making . . . I feel like everything will fall apart. Everything in my life is already so precarious, I can't rock the boat. So instead I grab Huda by the arm again and pull her along, ignoring her question. 'Come on, let's go try those career tests. Maybe that'll help you.'

I drag her past the table with information about Jobcentre Plus, the one about jobs in the NHS and a display all about the different roles in the police force. We walk past a woman with a clipboard giving out free branded stress balls in return for people's personal information. At the back of the library, there's a bank of computers reserved for an online career test that takes into account your strengths and interests and spits out the perfect career for you. I tell Huda I'll do the test to keep her company, because even though I'm set in my path, there's still a part of me that's really curious about what my result will be.

We sit down next to each other. The tests are already loaded on the screen, and Ms Powrie is watching over everyone. I wonder if she always wanted to be a PE teacher, or whether she was pushed into it. How many teachers actually *want* to become teachers?

'Ready to discover your future?' I ask Huda in a spooky voice.

'Someone once told me you can't count on the future,' she says. 'The present's all you've got.'

'Well, at this present moment, your task is to work out your future,' I say. 'Why are you having such a hard time with this? All the other Perfect Daughter lessons worked out for you, didn't they? You were happy to build a changing table, but God forbid you take a simple test that might actually help you.'

'It's not that.' Huda shakes her head. 'I just . . . I can't put my finger on it. Where the frustration is coming from. I just . . . I'm not used to the future being fixed, y'know? I think part of me feels like if I make a plan, follow a specific path, then I'll just be a bit devastated when it doesn't work out. When I fuck it up.'

I pinch her arm. 'You're not gonna fuck it up.'

'Language!' Ms Powrie snaps from a few rows away. Supersonic hearing must be a requirement to be a teacher.

'Just go with your saying then,' I whisper. 'Focus on the

205

present. Focus on you *wanting* to create a future. Don't think about how you're going to get there, or all the things that could go wrong. Just focus on the fact that you *want* this.'

Huda just stares blankly at the computer screen.

'Oh for God's sake, just do the test, else I'll do it for you. And with my luck, your future career will turn out to be, like, old-lady back scratcher.'

Huda laughs, and finally puts her hand on the mouse.

We spend the next ten minutes answering questions like whether we want to work alone or as part of a team (we both say team), whether we like working with visuals or words (I pick visual, Huda picks words), whether we want to help other people (I'm neutral, Huda strongly agrees). We compare our answers and call each other out on bullshit – like when Huda says she hates kids, I remind her of all the times she's been with Ismail and enjoyed it. And then, after what feels like hundreds and hundreds of questions, there's a big green button down at the bottom of the screen. Huda presses hers first. We wait anxiously for a few seconds while the wheel spins.

'I bet you get something to do with writing,' I tell her. 'Journalism maybe.' She's been working on the yearbook, and taking things way too seriously. She'd be brilliant working on a real publication.

'I'm sort of hoping for old-lady back scratcher, now you've mentioned it.'

I give her another pinch. She laughs and twists away from me. Her page refreshes.

'A dog breeder?!' she exclaims.

'What?!' I say, leaning forward to see her screen better.

Huda points at the list of ten careers. Dog breeder is indeed number one. I scan the list, looking for something that sounds even slightly like something she might enjoy.

'Oh, there, look – counsellor. You'd be good at that. God knows you sort my life out enough.'

'That's number four,' she points out. 'Way down on the list. Apparently I'd make a better *dog breeder*.'

'Well . . . I mean . . .' I stutter. 'Maybe you'll breed the best dog ever?' I mean it as a joke, but I cringe as soon as the words come out.

'I don't even LIKE dogs! God, I knew this would be a waste of time,' Huda huffs. She angrily force-powers the computer off. 'What about you then? What kind of animals are *you* going to breed?'

I click on my green button and we wait. 'I hope it's peacocks,' I say, trying to add some lightness to the situation. I can tell Huda is really disappointed by the lack of clarity given by the test. I want to reassure her, to console her, but I also know Huda. She's not in the mood to be consoled. If I even try to make something good out of this result, she'll just get angry, and I can't diss the test, because I *forced* her to take it.

My screen loads.

Number one career suggestion: photographer/videographer.

A shiver of something runs through my body. Excitement? Pleasure? Fear?

'Huh, yours wasn't close either,' Huda says. 'Unless you wanna take videos of sick animals.'

It's there. Number one. The thing I'm apparently most

suited to becoming. What my skills are geared towards. It's . . .
reachable.

'Although I guess yours was better than mine,' Huda says,
picking up her bag off the floor. 'At least you like doing that
shit in your spare time. Could be a good hobby to go with
your actual job.'

She stands up. I'm supposed to stand up too, but I can't stop
looking at that top entry. I can't pinpoint what's making me
feel like this. I've never really dared to dream that it could be
possible. That I could make this into a career. That I could do
what *I* wanted, instead of following in Abbu's footsteps. But
this . . . this makes it seem . . . achievable.

But no. Of course not. There's no point getting my hopes up.

'This test is stupid,' I tell Huda. I quickly close down my
page too, although the words are seared onto my eyelids. 'You
were right, we should have just skipped. I mean, there's still
time,' I say quietly, making sure Ms Powrie isn't looking.

'That test pissed you off enough to skive?' Huda laughs
quietly. 'Damn, you must really want to be a vet.'

I stand up, grab my bag and start walking off. Huda follows.
We pretend to be going to one of the stalls, and then, when
no one's looking, we slip out of the doors.

32

We practically run out of school and down the street, taking off our ties and blazers to blend in. I never do this – skip school, I mean. Precisely because of the anxiety that's currently bubbling away in my stomach. It's the easier alternative though. There's no way I was going to hang around school, take part in that stupid careers fair, being reminded that I have literally no choice over what my future holds. I kind of envy Huda in a way, that she doesn't know what's coming. It seems like there are infinite possibilities for her.

Nafisah's working from home today, so the only option is to go to mine. Which isn't ideal, but at least I know Ammi's at work, and she usually goes to town before she has to pick Ismail up. Abbu said he's got an interview today, for a vet job. It's been nagging at the back of my mind since he mentioned it this morning. I know that if it doesn't go well, it'll be tense at home tonight. I'm just really hoping he gets the job – it'll make things much easier if he has steady, predictable work.

I slip the key into the front door quietly and turn it. We take our shoes off, and I make sure to hide them in the shoe drawer.

'You got any good snacks?' Huda asks, walking into the kitchen. 'I'm craving Pringles.'

'We've only got the barbecue flavour. You hate those.'

'Ugh, why does your family have such bad taste?' She opens the cupboard and pokes around. I like this about our friendship, that she can feel this at home at mine, even though she rarely comes here.

'Blame Ismail,' I tell her. 'He's the one who –'

I'm interrupted by a sound at the front door. The sound of keys.

'Shit shit shit,' I whisper, closing the cupboard Huda's opened. I stare at her, wide-eyed. 'If my parents catch us, I'm dead.'

'Can we get upstairs in time?'

I shake my head, as the front door opens and voices become audible – it's both Ammi and Abbu. I quickly push Huda over to the corner of the kitchen. There's a bit of space between the fridge and the wall that we can both squeeze into and hide. If Ammi and Abbu go into the living room, then we can probably sneak upstairs, or maybe out of the back door into the garden. God, if Abbu catches me skiving, there'll be hell to pay. I push Huda against the wall as far as I can. She makes an 'oof' noise as I squeeze in after her. I peer around the edge of the fridge. Their voices are distinct now. They're coming this way. Crap.

'I've told you a million times we should sell that piece of junk,' Abbu says. His voice is at mid-level. I can tell they've been arguing for a while already.

'I need it for work,' Ammi says quietly. She grabs a pan, fills it with water and sets it on the stove. 'I know it's not the best car, but it does the job.'

I take a sneak peek and see it's her chai pan. She's trying to soothe him. She opens the cupboard, thankfully on the other

210

side of the room, and takes out some spices. Crap, that means they're gonna be in here for a while.

'It does the job?' Abbu asks in a mocking tone. 'Is that why I've just had to pick you up? What if you had called when I was in the middle of my interview?'

'I'll get it sorted,' Ammi says quietly. 'I'll call a mechanic.'

'And what about the next time?' he asks. 'What about when I'm not able to rescue you? What would you have done without me today? How would you have come back from your perfect little job?'

Ammi mumbles something I don't quite hear, as she stirs the chai with a spoon. I feel Huda move and suddenly I'm terrified. This fight is going to escalate, I can feel it. God, why didn't we just go straight upstairs or, better yet, stay at school? We could have been far away from this. I could be somewhere where I'm not terrified that Huda is about to witness Abbu at his worst.

'Answer me,' he growls.

I hear a small squeal and I'm guessing he's grabbed Ammi. I feel Huda flinch next to me, with an intake of breath too. I go entirely still. I need them to stop. Oh God, please stop. I can't, I can't watch this. Not again. Worse than that, I can't have Huda witness this.

'I'm sorry,' Ammi whimpers. 'I didn't . . . I didn't . . .'

Stop. Stop. Stop. Dear God, please make this stop right now.

'It's your fault, you know that, right?' he says. 'That car was working fine last time I drove it. And then *you* get in and it just stops working? You ruin everything.'

'The . . . the engine light's been on –'

'Shut up,' Abbu demands. Harsh. Brutal. Absolute. 'Things always go wrong with you around. If I don't get this job, it'll be your fault. We won't be able to pay the mortgage. Everything will fall apart, because of you.'

She doesn't answer, just sniffles quietly.

'I'm right, aren't I?' he insists. 'Say it.' He must squeeze Ammi harder because she cries out in pain.

'You . . . you're right . . .' she weeps.

'About what?' he presses, his voice deep and growly.

'You're . . . you're right about . . . everything,' she says, sobbing throughout.

'And that stupid job, the one that's responsible for your car breaking down,' he says, his voice somehow turning more menacing, 'are you finally ready to quit that?'

'W-what?' she asks. 'What's that . . . got to do with anything?'

I peer with one eye around the corner of the fridge again. The chai is boiling now, and there's steam rising, but through it I see Abbu twist Ammi's wrist. She lets out a yelp. I suck in a breath. In the tiny space we're hiding in, somehow Huda finds my hand.

'The car wouldn't have broken down if you hadn't driven it to work.'

'I . . . I drive it to work all the time . . . Nothing –'

'Shut up!' he shouts.

'I . . . I just –'

The sound of the slap reverberates around the room. Huda gasps, and I feel her angling her body to try to see what's

212

happening. I can't have her see. I can't have her *actually* see what it's like. Last time she just heard the shouting from upstairs. If she actually sees Abbu put his hands on Ammi . . . I can't . . . THIS CAN'T HAPPEN. I need it to stop. I need to MAKE it stop.

'Don't you dare talk back to me!' Abbu bellows. He twists Ammi's arm again so that it's behind her back, and pushes her up against the counter. She's crying hard now, her sobs mixed with cries of pain.

'Please . . .' she begs.

Hearing Ammi like this, so helpless, so defeated – I can't just stand here and watch. The other day, at dinner, Abbu stopped when I told him to. When I reminded him I was there. He heard me. Maybe I can do the same again.

'Do you know how much it's going to cost to fix that car?' he growls. 'Huh? And whose pocket is it going to come out of? Are you going to pay for it, with the pitiful amount you earn sitting on your arse at a till?'

I see his arm move, and another yelp comes out of Ammi.

'I . . . I can pay for it . . .'

'Everything you get is because of me.' Abbu presses against her harder. His lips are by her ear now. 'You got that, you stupid bitch?'

Ammi sobs.

'I said, "You got that?"!' He twists her arm so hard she falls to her knees.

That's it. Enough. I can't let this happen.

'STOP!' I shout, jumping out from our hiding place. I rush over to Ammi.

213

Abbu jumps at my voice. He lets go of Ammi and twists his body wildly. His arm connects with my body, making me stumble backwards. I crash into the stove, knocking the pan of boiling hot chai.

It spills over my forearm, burning my flesh.

I scream.

33

I've never felt pain like this before. Scorching, searing, blinding jolts are running up my arm, all the way through my body. All I can do is scream.

'Oh my God, Amani!' Abbu says.

He grabs my upper arm and leads me over to the sink. 'Quick, put some water on it.' He turns the tap and pulls my forearm under the stream. The cold water on the burn stings like hell for a second before it starts to soothe. Ammi rushes over.

'Amani, are you OK?' Ammi and Huda ask at the same time.

'Huda? What are you doing here?' Abbu asks, only now noticing her standing behind us.

Huda opens and closes her mouth, trying to figure out what to say.

'Wait, why are you both here? Shouldn't you be in school?'

I let out a little groan, partly to steer the conversation away from Huda, and partly because, holy shit, being burned really, *really* hurts. The cold water's starting to get too cold on my skin, so there's two types of pain to struggle with now. I pull my arm away and the air hits it, causing the stinging to start up again.

'It really hurts,' I whimper. Tears have sprung to my eyes, and there's a huge red blotch on my forearm.

'Go sit down at the table,' Ammi says. 'You need to keep putting cool water over it for a bit. I'll bring a big bowl over.'

I spare a glance at Huda as Abbu silently leads me to the dining room. She's just standing there, staring at my arm, her face frozen in shock. She's seen. She's seen the worst of our family. The worst of Abbu. I've gone all these years hiding it from her, hiding it from everyone, and now somehow she's found out accidentally, while looking for Pringles. This is a nightmare. She got so huffy last time, when she just *heard* the shouting – what is she going to be like now?

Ammi comes over with a huge bowl of water. She sits next to me, holds my arm over the bowl, and starts scooping the cool water over it with a cup. The water's warmer than the water from the sink, and this feels less painful.

'Is that better?' she asks. I nod.

'Moyna, I'm so sorry,' Abbu starts pleading, hovering over me. 'I didn't see you there. I swear, I didn't mean to . . .'

His words are empty. I've heard them so many times before, said to Ammi. The desperation in his voice is new though, and it tugs at me. It's stupid, but I feel bad for getting in his way.

I look down at my arm. Thankfully, it doesn't seem that bad. I think only a small portion of the boiling liquid caught my skin. It could have been much worse. Or maybe I'm just thinking that because the water is easing the pain.

'Maybe she should go to the hospital?' Huda says.

We all turn towards her, no doubt the same fear striking in all our hearts.

'No,' I say, at the same time Abbu says, 'There's no need for that.'

216

We're both thinking the same thing. The hospital will ask too many questions. We all know how things work around here. Huda, though . . . Huda could break all that apart.

'Honestly, it's not even that bad,' I tell her, trying to put a bit of lightness into my voice so she'll back off. She needs to back off. How do I get her to back off?

'It may seem strange, but keeping it wrapped up in this will help,' Ammi says, beginning to wrap my arm in cling film. 'It's OK, Huda, I know how to take care of her. I do first aid at work.'

'How often do people have boiling chai thrown over them in Morrisons?' Huda spits.

We all snap our heads up at that.

'I didn't *throw* it over her,' Abbu says fiercely. 'It was an accident and she knocked against the pan.' He glares at Huda for a second before returning his gaze to me, face loosening. 'I'm so sorry, Amani. Are you OK?'

'It was an accident,' I repeat, looking earnestly at Huda so she knows it really was. 'I'm sorry for coming up behind you unexpectedly, Abbu.'

'Wait, you're apologising to him?' Huda is aghast. 'That's not –'

'I think it's time you went home,' he interjects forcefully. He stares Huda down.

Huda, of course, stubborn cow that she is, doesn't seem intimidated at all.

'Actually, Amani and I were going to go upstairs to study.' She stares *him* down. Oh God, why does she have to be like this? Can she not read the situation? Abbu's already in a terrible mood – her egging him on isn't going to help; surely that's obvious. If she stays here, talking back to him, it's just going to get worse. I know it seems like worse isn't even possible right now, but I'm not prepared to test that theory.

'It's fine, Huda,' I tell her. 'Maybe you *should* go home. I'm . . . I'll be OK.'

She turns her gaze to me now, mouth slightly open, as if she really expected me to go against my dad for her. Her brow furrows and I'm scared that she's going to say something else to antagonise Abbu, and also terrified that she's going to tell someone about what she saw here today. Last time she heard the fight between Ammi and Abbu, I swore her to secrecy, but I can't really force her to promise right now, while my parents are both still watching on.

'Huda, please . . .' I say, trying to force some hidden meaning into my voice. We've been best friends for years; she should be able to pick up on what I'm desperate to convey. 'Just go home.'

Abbu and I wait, frozen, to see what Huda's next move will be. Ammi's still focusing on my arm. The tension of it all hurts way worse than the burn.

Please please please . . . I'm saying in my head.

Huda finally hears me. She scowls and storms out of the kitchen. A few moments later, I hear the front door slam.

34

I barely slept last night. I kept replaying the scene over and over in my head. The way Abbu had Ammi bent over the counter, her arm twisted behind her. The growl in his voice as he said those horrible things to her. The pain of the boiling chai on my skin. It plays in my mind now too, as I sit on my bed, letting Ammi check my wound. We didn't speak about what happened yesterday, of course. Abbu apologised a lot, and then I hid in my room. Part of me was waiting for Ammi to come in, for us to be alone like we are right now. But she didn't. She just sat downstairs with *him* while I cried myself to sleep.

'Is that too tight?' Ammi asks as she wraps fresh cling film around my arm.

'Why aren't you angry?' I blurt.

She looks up, confused. 'Why would I be angry at you?'

'At *him*, not me,' I say through gritted teeth.

Her head snaps back down. Her hands move quicker now, carefully wrapping my wound.

'It was an *accident*, Amani. Your father . . . he apologised . . .' she almost whispers.

'It wouldn't have happened *at all* if he hadn't been . . . hurting you.'

'Amani, please. Not now. You've got school –'

'We *never* talk about it, Ammi. We need to. You need to see –'

'Amani, stop!' She looks up at me. Her face is hard, but her eyes betray her – they're already red. 'We are not discussing this. It was an *accident*. You shouldn't have been there. He . . . It's better to just let it happen. You shouldn't have interfered.'

'But, Ammi –'

She gets up off the bed quickly. 'Enough, Amani,' she says firmly. 'Go downstairs and have breakfast. I'm going to shower.'

And then she leaves. Just like that. I hear the bathroom door shut shortly after.

I get dressed and pack my schoolbag, seething with anger. At Ammi and her refusal to address what's happening; at Abbu; and weirdly, at myself. Ammi was right – this wouldn't have happened if I hadn't butted in, hadn't skived yesterday. I could have just carried on living in denial. And then I wouldn't have to worry about Huda knowing either.

When I cross the landing, I can hear Ammi sobbing behind the bathroom door. My heart constricts, and I want to run in and console her, but she'd just brush me off, push me away. Pretend she wasn't crying in the first place. I leave her to it and go downstairs. There's a waft of cinnamon in the air. An undertone of Nutella too, which makes my mouth water. I hear movement in the kitchen – the sound of a pan setting down on the stove.

Pancakes. Of course. The Morning After Ritual. Abbu's go-to method of apologising. I hadn't expected this. I thought it was reserved for the worst nights with Ammi.

I drop my school bag by the stairs and walk into the kitchen to find Abbu standing behind Ismail, helping him flip a pancake, a smile spread over both their faces. But it leaves me cold. I'm immediately hit with a flash from yesterday. Abbu standing here, Ammi pressed up against the counter, crying out in pain.

Abbu turns around and looks right at me. I find my hand impulsively reaching over to my injured arm. His eyes follow.

'How are you feeling?' he asks. 'Is it hurting? Do you need a new dressing?'

I shake my head. 'It's fine. Ammi wrapped it up well.'

'Maani, look!' Ismail exclaims. He tries flipping the pancake, but it falls on the counter.

'Goddammit,' he curses.

'Ismail!' I chide. That's the first time I've heard him say anything like that.

He looks up at me. 'Sorry,' he mutters. He steps off the stool that Abbu's placed by the stove, snatches his dropped pancake and goes to the dining-room table, where his breakfast lies half eaten.

Abbu doesn't say anything to him, which annoys me. He's never the bad guy around Ismail.

'Maybe you should wear a long-sleeved shirt?' he suggests, still staring at my arm, which admittedly looks strange wrapped in cling film.

That's what he has to say to me? After everything? Ammi's upstairs sobbing and he's focusing on making sure no one finds out the truth.

'I'll wear my blazer,' I say as I brush past him to a plate of pancakes. I take the food into the dining room and sit next to Ismail. Abbu follows me in. I can't figure out how to act around him. He's apologetic, I can see that. I got that last night. What happened *was* an accident. Despite everything, despite the way he is with Ammi, he didn't mean to hurt me, I know that. But . . . but I still can't help but blame him. If he was just . . . normal, this wouldn't have happened. None of this would have happened.

Abbu sits down at the table with us. I look down at my plate instead of at him. The pancakes look delicious, but I don't feel like eating them, knowing he's made them just for show.

'Did you get your biology result yet?' he asks.

'Nope,' I say curtly.

'Oh,' he says softly. 'It's been a while. Maybe you should ask your teacher? I could call up the school –'

'There's no need,' I say, finally looking up at him. 'It's only been a week. The teachers are busy.'

He nods, falling silent, picking at his breakfast. Him bringing up school has got something boiling inside me. I've spent all these years doing what he's told me to do, ignoring what *I* want. But now I realise Abbu is never going to change. He's never going to become a better person. He's never going to treat Ammi how she deserves to be treated. He's never going to let our family go on as normal families should. Nothing *I* can do will make him better. So why am I trying so hard to please him? Why am I forcing myself to fit into the mould of what he thinks a Perfect Daughter should be? Why am I giving up everything, while he just sits there selfishly?

It's not fair. It's not right.

'Are you finished eating?' he asks me after a few minutes of awkward silence. 'I'm going to drive you both to school today.'

Ismail cheers, his mouth full of pancake.

'I can walk,' I say.

'Don't be silly,' Abbu replies. 'I had an event today but called in sick so we can spend some quality time together. Remember how us three always used to go out? I thought we could do something after school.'

Ismail cheers again. 'Can we go to the cinema?' he asks. 'Ooh, and to the park? The duck pond?'

Abbu laughs. 'Sure, we can do all that. And Amani? What do you want to do?'

I can't even bear to look at him. Can't endure this fake display he's putting on. Is this how Ammi feels when he tries to make it up to her? God, I remember thinking it was real, the other day when he bought her that bread maker, and gave a fake apology. I'm such an idiot. He's not sorry. He's just trying to cover his back. Make sure no one sees my burn and asks questions.

'Count me out,' I say. 'I walk to school with Huda. And we're studying together tonight.'

'You spend an awful lot of time with that girl,' Abbu says, crossing his arms.

I focus my attention on my untouched pancake, pick at it. 'Well, she *is* my best friend.'

'I don't think she's a good influence,' he says matter-of-factly.

My anger boils over. 'What?' I splutter. 'You barely know her.'

'I know enough,' he says in a dark voice. The voice I would

223

never dare talk back to. 'And you walk with her *every* day. Today, I'm taking you.'

'Can we pick Huda up on the way?'

He huffs. 'Are you joined at the hip or something?' His voice is rising again. 'What – you can't wait to see her at school?'

'Can we pick up Kai too?' Ismail asks. 'He's my new best friend.'

'Oh yeah?' I ask. 'What happened to Rahul?'

'He was an idiot. We broke up.'

'Ismail!' I chide again. 'Where did you learn all these bad words from all of a sudden?'

Ismail ducks his head and shoves the rest of his breakfast in his mouth before I tell him off again. Abbu, of course, just sits there in silence. God forbid he do some actual parenting. My hand goes towards my sore arm again.

'Can you write me a note for PE?' I ask Abbu.

It takes a second for him to react, but then he starts nodding. 'Of course. I'll do it for a few weeks.' He walks into the living room. 'Why don't you get your lunches ready? I'll do this, and then we can leave.'

I'm about to ask about Huda once again, but I don't want to push him. He's getting me out of PE for the foreseeable, so that's something. Huda, though. I haven't heard a word from her since yesterday. I sent her a bunch of texts, but she hasn't replied. I've been trying to think of something I can do to keep her onside, to make sure she knows yesterday was an accident. I keep reliving the scene in my head: Abbu towering over Ammi, Huda's grasp on my hand getting tighter as things got worse.

Huda knows.

She knows my full, ugly truth now. I can't hide it from her any more. She's a part of this. I just need to talk to her. I need to play the best-friend card, remind her of her promise not to say anything. I need to make sure she hasn't told someone already.

35

I look out for Huda on the way to school, but I don't see her. The drive itself is super awkward after Ismail's dropped off and his childish chatter disappears. Abbu and I aren't used to spending time one-on-one. He tries to get me to think of things we can do tonight, or this weekend. I give little input, but that's fine with him, since he loves the sound of his own voice. I cradle my arm against me, scared that I'm going to accidentally roll my sleeve up, or be forced to take my blazer off in class. I come up with the excuse in my mind that *I* was the one making chai and accidentally spilled it on myself. I'd seen the thing about using cling film for light burns on the internet so did it myself. That should cover all the bases if anyone asks.

Abbu pulls up outside the gates. I want to just get out and walk off, but I know he needs to dismiss me first.

'I love you, you know that, right?' he asks quietly.

I nod.

He pauses before continuing. 'And you know that yesterday . . . won't ever happen again, right?'

I want to ask him which bit. Whether he can promise the same about Ammi too, but I know it won't make a difference.

I know he'll just lie, and a part of me is actually too scared to ask, too scared of his reaction. A part of me is scared to be in this car alone with him.

'The bell's about to ring,' I tell him. 'I need to go.'

'OK. I'll see you tonight.'

I open the door and step out.

'Love you,' he says again.

I close the door on him, pretending I didn't hear.

I don't see Huda before registration. We don't have class together until second period, so I spend the first hour of school tuning out Monsieur Strachan talking about French verbs and focus instead on what I'm going to say to Huda when we meet in maths. Anxiety has been bubbling in my stomach all morning; she's going to be so mad. It's going to be hard to talk her round, but I'm determined. Determined but terrified. She could so easily ignore everything I have to say and tell someone about Abbu, about yesterday. If that happens, I'll say she's lying, make up something about her being jealous, but that would be it – the end of our friendship.

I'm nervous as hell as I walk to maths. I haven't seen Huda in the crowd yet, and part of me is hoping that she's not in school today, so I can avoid having to talk to her, having to sit next to her. But then I get into the classroom and there she is, sitting in her seat, my chair free next to her. Our eyes meet as I walk up. Neither of us smiles or makes any gesture of greeting. The words tumble in my head: what should I say to her, how do I even open up this conversation? How can I convince her?

'Hey,' I say as I sit down.

'Hi,' she says back.

At least she's talking to me, I guess. She's not mad enough to be giving me the silent treatment, so I guess that bodes well for the conversation we're going to have.

But not here. Not now.

Mr Hawthorne walks into the room and starts droning on about probability. I don't take any of it in. I'm trying to prepare what I'll say to Huda. I'm so stressed about it, I start sweating. It's a pretty hot day and the blinds are up, the sun shining right in on us. Almost everyone in the room has taken their blazer off. But I can't, obviously. I fidget in my chair, flapping the underside of my blazer to get some air. Huda gives me a quizzical stare, before realisation dawns on her face. She looks down at my arm and I automatically move it, letting it hang down on the side that Huda can't see.

After an hour of torture – both in terms of trying to learn maths, and the heat – the bell finally rings for break. I feel sick as the sound rings out, knowing what has to happen. I can't avoid it any more.

'Can we . . . talk?' I ask Huda as we get up from our seats.

'Ooh, having a bitch fight, are we?' Cleo asks, suddenly popping up behind us. She's got that trademark smirk on her face, the one that says she's about to cause trouble. She's obviously back to her old self.

'No,' Huda replies. 'We were just wondering where that smell of shit was coming from, but now it all makes sense.' She leans in to Cleo and sniffs.

Cleo's face immediately turns sour. Her cheeks redden and she stomps off.

Yet again Huda has the perfect comeback. I can't laugh today though.

Huda and I walk out of the maths block in silence. We pass a group of boys playing football on the field. I notice Ezra's there, which confuses me because I thought he'd still be in isolation for the assembly presentation incident. He turns his head and we lock eyes. He scowls, and I immediately look down and continue walking. Cleo's sitting on the grass too, with some girls I've never seen her hanging with before, but luckily they're around the corner from our bench. I sit down in my usual place, and Huda sits next to me. Everything about this moment, on the surface, is the same as it would be every day. And yet the silence says everything. Huda, who is usually blabbering away by now, hasn't said a word. I guess it's up to me to start things off. But I can't just jump into it, can I? I have to sort of . . . soften her up. I have to make it seem like I'm not just here to get her to keep my secret again.

'Um . . . How are things at home?' I ask cautiously. 'Any more progress on the Perfect Daughter plan?'

'Well, they spent this morning gushing over Nafisah's baby blanket so they can give it to their kid when it's born, so I'm gonna say no,' she replies curtly.

'That's not . . . that's not necessarily a *bad* thing,' I tell her. 'I mean, that doesn't affect you.'

'Yeah, exactly. None of it does. I could just not be there, and nothing would be different. They practically ignored me all morning, cooing over this tatty yellow cloth.'

I sigh. 'Huda, I get how you're feeling. But I don't think things are going to get better until you get that they're allowed to be excited. They're allowed to want to pass on their childhood items to their baby. That doesn't mean they care any less about you.'

'You're full of shit, you know that?' Huda spits. She turns her body so she's straddling the bench, facing me.

'Me?' I squeak. 'I'm just saying –'

'You spout all this advice, acting like you're so wise and knowledgeable, and yet you're so . . . you're so blind when it comes to your own situation.'

Well, that escalated quickly. 'I'm not . . . *blind* to anything,' I mutter. It's the opposite, I want to tell her. I see *everything*. I *hear* everything. I'm *aware* of everything. That's the problem. Maybe I should show her the video I've been putting together – the compilation of all the videos I've taken of myself on the Bad Nights to acknowledge what's happening.

Huda laughs harshly. 'Shall we swap roles?' she asks. 'Shall I give *you* some advice?' She doesn't wait for me to answer before continuing. 'Amani, you *have* to speak out now. You have to tell someone what's going on. You –'

'I told you I can't!' I interject forcefully. 'And you promised you wouldn't either.'

'Things were different when I made that promise,' she says. She grabs me by the wrist and gently moves my blazer sleeve up. She spends a few seconds staring at the bandage I wrapped over the cling film so no one would think it weird if they saw it. My mind is calling out for me to pull my arm back, to hide it from her again. If she doesn't see it, it's not there. 'It's getting worse, can't you see? How can you continue to ignore it after what happened yesterday?'

230

'That was an accident,' I say, yanking my arm away. A twinge of pain shoots up my arm. 'It wasn't his fault.'

'And what about what he was doing to your mum just before that? Was that an *accident* too?'

My face heats up.

'I don't understand why you keep protecting him. Nothing is going to get better if you stay quiet.'

'You think I haven't looked into it?' I say angrily. 'You think I haven't thought about telling someone, getting my mum to tell someone? They'll split my family up, Huda. I read a case study about it – how if they think . . . someone . . . is going to hurt the children, they take them away. They'll see my arm and jump to conclusions. It's the last thing I want, Huda, for my family to be broken up. You *must* understand that, considering everything –'

'I get that part, I do,' she says. 'But it wouldn't be . . . forever. They'd bring you all back together once your dad's locked up.'

'You want him to go to *jail*?!'

'Well, yeah. It's what he deserves.'

'What the fuck, Huda! He's my *dad*. Yes, he isn't always the best person, but he doesn't deserve to be in prison. I can't believe you said that.'

'And I can't believe you're being so pathetic about this.'

'Oh, I'm pathetic now, am I? For wanting to keep my family together? You're such a hypocrite. That's literally all you've been trying to do for the past few weeks.'

'I'm not the one living with an abuser.'

I suck in a breath. I can't believe she went there. I came over here to attempt to reason with her, but she is . . . unbelievable. There's no point even trying.

'Are you going to go back on your promise?' I ask her sternly. 'If you've ever cared for me, you won't tell anyone. I'll never forgive you, Huda, I'm telling you.'

She sighs, looks down at the graffiti on the part of the bench between her legs and rubs her thumb over a badly drawn heart, but doesn't say anything.

'Huda . . .' I prod.

'Fine, fine,' she relents. 'I won't say anything. I don't go back on my promises, you know that.'

My entire body relaxes. It's going to be OK. Huda may have said, and may believe, some hurtful things, but at least she'll keep quiet.

'But if I'm not going to say anything, you need to,' she adds.

I look up at her.

'Amani, you can't keep going on like this. It's OK to ask for help. There's so many people to help you. Teachers, counsellors . . . hell, the police. I'll come with you, please, let's –'

'Have you not been listening to a word I've said?!' I half shout. 'My family is going to be *ruined* if this comes out, Huda. My mum will be, like, ousted from her family, from our community. No one's going to take her side. They'll tell her to stay with him and put up with it, and she'll have no other choice. And it'll be worse after that, Huda. You think he won't get worse if everyone finds out and nothing happens? He'll just get more . . . brazen.'

'Isn't that what's already happening?' Huda asks. 'He hurt *you*, Amani.'

'It was an accident!' I shout. One of the boys playing football actually looks over, and I have to look down at the heart on the bench too.

'Amani,' Huda says quietly, 'if you won't speak out for yourself, then at least do it for your mum. It's not fair to leave her to suffer as she is. Not when you can help.'

'Just stop!' I say, getting up off the bench. She's got me so angry that my body is shaking. I can't sit there and listen to her any more. 'You have *no* idea what it's like to be in my position, or in my mum's position. So stop pretending you do. Get off your fucking high horse, Huda. It seems so simple and easy to you because you're not the one going through it. It's not up to you to tell me what to do, what's *best* for my family. You don't get a fucking say.'

'Amani, you *know* I'm saying the right thing,' she pleads.

'No, the only thing I know is that you're being a really shitty best friend right now.'

'And I think you're being a shitty daughter.'

I laugh harshly. 'Weren't you the one asking me to teach *you* how to be the Perfect Daughter?'

'Obviously I chose the wrong teacher. Even *I* know what you're doing is wrong.'

'Oh yeah, because you know everything, don't you?' I say. 'Huda the genius. Not just top grades at school, but in life lessons too! You should start up a business, y'know? Telling people how they should live their life. It seems to be what you like doing best.'

'I don't care about anyone else's life, Amani. I care about yours.'

'Funny way of showing it,' I sneer. 'If you cared about me at all, you'd understand that speaking out isn't an option. You'd let this go.'

'Let it go?' she scoffs, standing up too. 'You want me to just ignore the fact that your dad's an abusive piece of crap? He hurts your mum, he hurt you, and one day he's going to hurt Ismail too.'

I feel the heat rising up in my body. I'm filled with anger, and there's a flash in my head of what I want to do right now.

I want to punch Huda.

The realisation, the vivid image in my mind of me hitting her, shocks me. I can't . . . I can't let myself become this.

I can't follow in Abbu's footsteps.

Huda's staring at me, waiting for me to reply, trying to make me understand. But I can't be here. I grab my bag and run off towards my next class, cutting across the field. I spot Cleo whispering to her new friends while looking at me, and an image of me stomping over to confront them builds in my mind. I don't, of course.

36

It's lunchtime and Huda's avoiding me. Which is fine, because I was totally avoiding her first. I keep looking around the canteen to see if she's going to walk in late and come over to our usual table, but I know Huda. She just needs a bit of time to herself. I'm still angry at her for everything she said earlier, but the urge to lash out has thankfully disappeared. It really scared me for a second, made me consider whether Abbu's bad habits are genetic. The last thing I want to be is like him. I've reasoned with myself that it wasn't like his anger at all. Abbu gets angry when things don't go his way, he gets angry because he's not given the power he thinks he deserves.

I'm nothing like him.

If I keep saying it, maybe I'll convince myself it's true.

Huda will be back soon. I know it. This is the biggest fight we've ever had, but Huda and I can't be apart for long. We just need to let our anger die down and then things will be fine. For the time being, I'll have to make do. We don't have any more lessons together until tomorrow, so it's just getting through today. And I'm doing that by replacing Huda with Maggie. She's sitting next to me, munching her crisps. We've both brought Doritos for lunch. If that doesn't mean we're destined to be friends, I don't know what does.

'Did you hear about Stacey's mum?' Maggie asks me, scrolling on her phone with her Dorito-free hand. 'The school called social services on her after the whole blog thing.'

'What, really?!'

'Yeah!' Maggie's voice goes higher when she sees that I'm interested. 'They had to report it because of safeguarding or whatever. I heard from Juwairiyya that a social worker turned up at Stacey's house to check everything out. Stacey thought they were gonna take her into care.'

'Oh my God! So what happened?'

Maggie shrugs, and deflates a little. 'Nothing. They just talked to Stacey and her mum.' Maggie leans in close to me. 'Turns out that on that parents' evening, it was the anniversary of Stacey's dad's death. Think she just had a few drinks to not be sad. Probably shouldn't have come out in public, but y'know.'

'Oh God, that's awful,' I say softly.

'Yeah, I get it though. My mum wasn't in a good way for a while after my sister died. She still gets a bit down when, like, it's an anniversary or her birthday or something.'

I didn't know Maggie's sister had died. I'm a terrible friend. She told me about her media studies coursework the other day – the film about her sister – and I was so wrapped up in myself that I didn't even bother to ask about it. I feel like I should ask something now, but the blasé way she mentioned her sister makes me sort of afraid to.

'Poor Stacey,' I say instead. 'The blog's getting out of order, don't you think? That whole thing must have been really hard for her and her family.'

'It's all just bants, innit?' Maggie says, going back to her phone. 'It's not like whoever's behind it knew this would happen.'

I cock my eyebrow, even though Maggie isn't looking at me. 'You spill someone's secrets, there's *gonna be* a fallout. Especially with something as out of order as this. Even if Stacey's mum *was* an alcoholic, that's literally no one's business. There's certainly no need to spread it.'

'Oh, c'mon, Amani, lighten up. It's just a prank. I'm sure they'll soon go back to who's cheating on who, and who shat their pants.'

I hold in a groan. Why is everyone like this? Why does no one see how out of order these blogs are? How out of order it is to spread other people's private business.

'So . . . you had a sister?' I ask, trying to change the subject, making an effort to be a good friend. Not one that judges; one that asks and pays attention.

Maggie turns to me and smiles. It's a different one than I've seen on her before. A softer one. 'Yeah,' she says. 'Her name was Isla. She died five years ago. Car crash.'

'Oh wow, I'm so sorry.' It's a knee-jerk response. One I wince at, but it would feel rude if I didn't say it.

'It's OK,' she says. 'I'm over it. Mostly. You just get used to it and move on, innit?' *"It's what she would have wanted,"'* she continues in a mocking tone. 'So many people say that to me, as if they knew her. She wouldn't have wanted that actually. She would have wanted us all to be miserable forever, to think about her forever. She was a self-obsessed git, was our Isla.'

I burst out laughing. Maggie's eyes widen, probably shocked at my rudeness. 'Oh my God, I'm so sorry,' I say, immediately stopping.

'No, don't be sorry!' she says, smiling now. 'I hate it when people get all sentimental when I talk about her. She'd prefer laughter, trust me.'

'So what's your video about? Like, a tribute or something?'

'Nah, much better than that,' Maggie says, sitting up straight. 'I don't like that whole thing where you can only say good things about people after they die. Isla was a . . . she could be a bitch. But she was also hilarious. There's so much funny footage of her. I'm going to make a video that would embarrass the shit out of her. Wanna see what I've got so far?'

'Yes!' I say, craning my head over Maggie's phone. I watch as she flicks through her camera roll. And I'm watching as an email alert pops up.

A new blog post.

BLITHE ACADEMY BURN BLOG

Backpack may have said to stop the pranks,
but this isn't a prank.
It's a service.
(You're welcome)

And today's subject . . .
someone who runs under the radar.
Someone who's been doing so for years.

They say it's the quiet ones who have the biggest
secrets.
And that's certainly true of our pal Amani Akhtar.

'Why is she so quiet?' I hear you ask.
It's because she's terrified.
Of her father
(Mr CatBeard himself),
who likes to beat his wife.

And not just his wife . . .

Has anyone noticed the bandage on Amani's arm?
Wonder what that's hiding?

Today, the Blithe Academy Burn Blog
reports on a
burn victim.

37

This can't be happening.

It can't.

How did they . . . ?

Who . . . ?

Oh my God, I think I'm going to be sick.

A wave of anxiety floods through me. My heart starts thudding so hard I can feel it in my ears. My face, my body, everything heats up and I start sweating. The burn on my arm is pulsing, acting as a sort of siren for incoming trauma.

Everyone knows.

My biggest secret has been revealed to the entire world. This is exactly what I've been terrified of since the blog started. Maggie turns her attention from the screen we were both reading to look at me. We lock eyes. There's pity, confusion, concern, maybe a hint of condescension written all over her face.

I can't stand this.

I can't take it.

I can't.

'Amani . . .' Maggie starts.

I jolt up from my seat. 'I need to go to the loo,' I manage to get out. I know she knows it's an excuse. But right now I don't care. I don't care what she thinks. I just need to get away. I need to get away from the eyes that are all about to focus on me, from the whispers. I need to get away from the laughs and comments that are about to be thrown in my direction. I just need out.

I grab my bag and leg it out of the canteen and into the food-tech building, where the loos are usually empty. It's only when I push open the door and run in that I realise tears are streaming down my face. I rush over to the sinks, resting my palms down and bending over the basin. I'm going to be sick.

Oh God, everything is falling apart. Everything is ruined.

Why? Why is this happening to me? I've never done anything to hurt anyone. Why am I being punished like this? If this gets back to my parents, there's going to be . . . it's going to be terrible. Everything is going to be terrible.

Something pops into my head then – Maggie's comment about Stacey's mum and how social services got involved because of the blog. Oh God. What if they come for Ismail? What if they're making Ammi pack up his things right now? It'll all be my fault. Whoever's behind this blog clearly has it in for me. I'm the reason this is happening. My family's going to break apart because of me.

I look at myself in the mirror. My face is all wet and sticky. I look pathetic.

An idea comes to me.

I just have to convince everyone the post is fake. It's this blog's word against mine. They have no proof. I have to tell social services it's all a lie. That someone has it in for me. All of the rumours spread by the blog have been personal. The one about Stacey just spent the whole time calling her a bitch.

But who could it be? I can't help but wonder. Who is responsible for my whole life crashing down? The only person that knows is Huda, and she's promised not to say anything. I believe her. She wouldn't go back on a promise. Huda says she's been let down by too many people in her life, and that she'd never do the same to anyone.

Over my gulping sobs, I hear the door open and a voice. 'You OK?'

Maggie must have followed me. I quickly wipe my face with my sleeve, wincing as pressure is accidentally put on the burn. I sniff back my tears and snot, try to make myself look less of a wreck. I wipe away all I can before turning to the door.

'Thanks, Maggie, I'm fine,' I say.

Except it's not Maggie.

It's Huda.

38

Huda's standing with the door closed behind her so it's just the two of us trapped inside this small room. I try to examine her expression, but my tears have made everything blurry. I swipe at my eyes.

'Did you tell someone?' I shout. 'You *promised*. You fucking promised!'

'I didn't . . . *say* anything to anyone . : .' she mutters.

'How did the blog person find out then?' I ask.

And then it hits me. We had a conversation about it at break. Out in the open. Right next to the field. Cleo and her friends were sitting just around the corner from us. They were all whispering as I walked off.

'Oh my God – do you think someone was listening to us earlier, when we were at the bench?'

I can just picture it now: Cleo getting one of her minions to army-crawl over to where we were sitting, out of sight, but close enough to hear every word.

'Oh my God,' I repeat, mostly to myself. I'm screwed. If it *is* Cleo, she's not going to let this go. She's going to make things worse and worse until I can't take it any more. UGH! This must be revenge for the comments Huda makes to her.

Cleo's been fine with me since her blog got revealed. But if Huda's the one who caused this, she's the one who can fix it too. She's the only one I know who can put Cleo in her place.

'Huda, please, you have to help me. It must have been Cleo who did this. You know how much she hates me. She must have overheard us earlier and told whoever's doing the blog. Huda, you have to help me. You're the only one who can stop her. Huda, *please*.'

Huda doesn't say anything. She just stands there, looking down at her feet, fiddling with her bag strap.

'We have to convince everyone the blog is lying!' I say. I'm gabbling now. 'It was wrong about Stacey's mum – did you hear? She's not an alcoholic or anything. It was just . . . whoever's writing the blogs is only doing it to people they hate. We can stop them, Huda. We can work together and stop them. We have to make everyone else turn against the blog. If we convince them it's a lie –'

'It's *not* a lie though, is it?' Huda says fiercely.

I'm taken aback by her anger. I would have thought she'd be on my side. I thought she'd be the *one* person who would understand how devastated I am, just how bad this is.

'What do you mean?' I ask. 'You agreed to help me keep this secret.'

'No, I didn't. I said *you* needed to speak out, but you refused, called me a bitch and walked off. I agreed not to *say* anything.'

I stare at her, gobsmacked.

'And I kept my promise. I didn't *say* anything,' she says. 'I typed it.'

39

'It was . . . you?' I say, my heart thudding. 'With the blog? This whole time?'

She doesn't reply for a few seconds and I start to think I've misunderstood. It can't be Huda. It just can't.

She groans and then comes over to the sinks, next to me. 'It wasn't meant to go like this, OK? I only did this . . . for you. All of it. For you.'

'For *me*?' I ask. 'Don't you dare say this was for me. I would never have asked you to do anything like this.'

'But that's the thing,' Huda says, getting energised now. 'You didn't have to. That's what friendship is. I knew you wouldn't tell anyone about your dad. I knew if you had your way, you'd just keep this inside and things would get worse and worse until someone . . . someone got really hurt.'

I glower at her. 'Someone did get hurt. Me. I can't believe you . . . you . . . so, what? All of this. All the blog posts, they were you? Or just this one?'

Huda nods slowly. 'It's always been me. It started off . . . as an idea for the prank war, but I hadn't figured it out. And then Cleo . . . fucking Cleo just wouldn't leave you alone. I've always hated her, but when I realised how much she was picking on you, how upset it made you, it pissed me off so much, I had to do something.'

I stare at her. 'So you told everyone my biggest secret, literally destroyed my life and split apart my family . . . to get back at Cleo?'

'No! Of course not.' She gives a frustrated groan. 'It *started* off just to get back at her. To show that people can, and should, stand up to her. And then . . . then it went so well and everyone was so into it that I *had* to carry it on. I thought I'd use it to get back at some other dickheads. Cleo's coven for starters. I didn't realise how . . . *fun* it would be. I enjoyed seeing how everyone reacted to the blogs, hearing people talking about it. It's stupid, I know, but it made me feel . . . powerful. Like I was making a difference. Making people pay for being pricks.'

She pauses, as if waiting for me to clap, or thank her for her service, but I'm just confused as to why she's giving me this spiel. 'So at what point did you decide you'd ruin *my* life?' I ask. 'And how much *fun* did you have doing it?' A wave of sadness runs through my body; the last few words come out with a quiver.

'I've already told you yours was different!' she protests. 'That wasn't for fun, or out of spite. Amani, I did this *for* you. It all came to me after Stacey's blog. I felt . . . I felt bad after that one. I mean, she's a bitch, and she deserved it. But when I heard the school called social services, I realised I'd gone too far. I didn't mean for things to get so serious. I was going to stop, I promise. But then I realised maybe serious was good. Maybe this was the answer. Maybe this was the way I could help you! Your dad . . . he *hurt* you, Maani. That . . . that burn . . .

watching that happen, it was the last straw for me. I couldn't just sit back and let this carry on. I'd be the worst best friend in the world if I did.'

'You *are* the worst best friend in the world!' I shout. 'How does the whole school knowing my family's business help in *any* way? You say you started this blog for *me*, to protect me from Cleo's bullying. But you don't think people are going to make fun of me for *this*? People have been singing "Stacy's Mom" to Stacey and staggering about, pretending to be drunk around her, ever since her blog came out – you think it's going to be any different for me? What gives you the right to –'

The bell for the end of lunch rings, making us jump. I wait for Huda to leave, to go to class, but she doesn't move. And neither do I. I'm not letting her win this argument.

'I stand by what I did,' she says. 'Now it's out there, you can't ignore it. Your mum can't ignore it. Maybe this will be the push she needs to speak out.'

'Or maybe this will be the push my dad needs to actually fucking kill her. Did you even consider that?'

I can see the words hit home; her eyes widen and she lets out a small gasp. I decide to take it a step further. I'm not even paying attention to what I'm saying, I just want to hurt her as much as I'm hurting.

'You're a fucking shitbag of a person, y'know that? It's no wonder that Ali and Nafisah don't love you enough. You're a stirring bitch who doesn't *deserve* to be loved. D'you know how many people would give *anything* to have parents as loving as yours? Parents who care, who are normal? You're so lucky, Huda, and you don't even notice your privilege. You just use

248

it to have *power* over everyone else. How does that make you any better than my dad? Enjoy this while it lasts, Huda. I hope you can live with what you've done.'

I pick up my bag, swipe at my face with my sleeve one last time, and stomp out of the loos before Huda has a chance to say anything – not that I'd fucking listen to that bitch.

She's ruined my life.

40

By the time I storm out of the food-tech building, everyone is in class, thankfully. I speed off down the empty path, keeping my head low. I need to get home. I need to get away from all the people here who are waiting to make fun of me, who are waiting for me to break down in front of them. It feels like my entire world is crashing down, and for some people here, that's the most entertaining thing ever. I realise now why Cleo disappeared from school when her blog post went live. The desire to burrow away and hide is overwhelming.

'Amani?' someone calls behind me. A familiar voice. I make the mistake of turning around – a reflex. Dammit.

It's Mrs Farook, my PSHCE tutor. I run my timetable in my head to make sure it's not her class I'm supposed to be in right now, and luckily it's not. I can just pretend I'm late to class or going to the loo. I stop walking and wait for her to catch up, because I'm not a monster, and she's one of my favourite teachers. I duck my head, pretending to look in my bag for something, and secretly wipe my eyes.

'Amani, are you OK?' she says.

I lift my head up, plastering on a fake smile. 'I'm fine, miss. I'm just running late.'

'I was actually hoping to have a chat with you in private.'

Panic bubbles in my chest. If she keeps me talking for much longer, I'm going to dissolve into tears, I know it. Huda's opened the dam, and I've only just managed to close it, temporarily. If Mrs Farook prods, everything's going to come flooding out again.

'I'm really late, miss. Mr Juckes is going to give me detention if I don't get there soon.' I avoid eye contact with her, turning my head this way and that, trying to plan an escape route.

'It's OK, I'll sort it out with Mr Juckes.'

I look up at her. Her eyes are soft and kind, her smile just there. She's one of the few teachers that everyone likes. No one has a bad thing to say about Mrs Farook. Which means, when she asks you for something, you literally *can't* say no without seeming like a bitch. I look at her, then at the path behind her, the one that leads directly to the secret exit through some bushes. I'm so close, but she's looking at me so intently that all I can do is nod, and say, 'OK.'

Mrs Farook takes me into the room the counsellor normally uses. There's a sofa against one wall, which she points at for me to sit on. I do. She takes the chair opposite and puts the folder she's been carrying down on the tiny table between us, next to the box of tissues.

'Listen, Amani. I know you students think us teachers are dinosaurs who don't know how to use the internet, and that we don't see what you guys are doing on there, but the school has a responsibility towards you. We have to monitor what people are looking at, to make sure it's not anything bad.

And . . . well, I'm sure you've seen all that's been going on lately, with the . . . the blog posts.'

Oh God. She knows. She's seen.

'Yeah, I can see from your face you know what I need to talk to you about. I just want to make it clear that you're not in any trouble here, OK? This is a safe space, and you can trust me. I'm the school's Designated Safeguarding Lead, so it's my duty to look out for you and make sure you're safe. At school and elsewhere.'

I'm paralysed. This is literally the worst thing that could have happened. I thought it couldn't get any worse than my best friend betraying me, but now . . . Mrs Farook has that look of pity in her eyes. Her gaze moves to my arm. Luckily I'm still wearing my blazer.

'It's my job to follow up any accusations that have been made. That's all this is. Please know that you can talk to me about *anything*. I have your best interests at heart, and I'm trained for all kinds of situations. I've *dealt* with all kind of situations. I'm here to help, Amani, with *anything* that's going on at home –'

'It's all lies!' I blurt. 'The blog, everything it says. It's lies. It's all been part of the prank war. You know that happens every year, right? I swear, it's not true. You heard about Stacey Lineham, right? The blog lied about her mother, and then everyone created a fuss for nothing. That's what's happening here too.'

Mrs Farook bites her lip and shakes her head a little. 'Yes, well, that was unfortunate, what happened with Stacey. But we had to follow that up, Amani. You can see that, right? We *have* to follow things like that – and like this – up. Otherwise we wouldn't be doing our job.'

'Is that what you're going to do here?' I ask. 'Are you going to call social services?'

I try to keep the panic out of my voice. I know the key to a good lie is confidence. I've had to tell so many lies about this in the past that you'd think I'd be a pro by now, but this . . . this whole situation has rattled me. It's new, it's unpredictable. I have to keep on track if I want things to go my way.

'At the moment I'm just hoping we can have a little chat about home, what things are like, how you're feeling and so on.'

OK, good. There's still time. I have to convince her everything it said in the blog is bullshit. I can convince her. My whole life, my family's life, depends on what I say in here.

'My home life is fine,' I tell her, trying to calm my voice. 'Great, I mean. My dad . . . he's amazing. He's on TV, did you know? *Creature Clinic*. I don't know if you've seen it. It's about animals and, like, getting kids to understand them. He really loves what he does. The kids on the show love him too. He gets loads of fan mail. I'm planning to become a vet – maybe not on TV, but I've learned so much from Dad. He's a great role model. And . . . he loves my mum. Like, *really* loves her. Just the other morning he surprised her with this fancy bread maker she's been wanting for months. Woke up early to gift-wrap it and everything. It was so cute. My mum was so happy. She's been baking bread for us all ever since. He does that a lot – buys her nice things. He makes her breakfast in bed. That's not something that someone who . . . who does what the blog says would do, is it? He's a great dad. A good husband. And the thing about the burn? That's a lie too. I mean, not a lie, but . . . it was my fault. I was making tea and spilled the water on my arm. You can ask my parents, they were there. It was totally my fault.' I run out of breath and have to pause. My heart's pounding so hard she must be able to hear it. But I need to convince her, I have to.

'Amani, do you want some water?' Mrs Farook asks, reaching out to put her hand on me. She puts pressure on my arm, not knowing that's where the burn is, and I do all I can not to wince. 'You're . . . you seem to be sweating quite a lot. Do you want to take your blazer off?'

I shake my head. 'No, no. I'm fine. I just . . . I'm upset. I just . . . I don't like that someone's spreading this vicious lie about my family. It's making me really upset.'

'Oh, Amani, here, take a tissue if you need it.' She pushes the box towards me and I take one out of politeness. Maybe I could use it as a prop to make my story more convincing. I wipe the corners of my eyes and let out a little sniff. I've had my head bowed down the whole time, but part of me really wants to look at her, look right into her eyes and see if she's buying this.

'I'm sorry this is making you upset. And trust me, we're going to find who's behind that blog. They *will* be punished.'

Should I grass on Huda? I could get her in so much trouble. Mr Bach was talking about suspending people for pranks. Maybe she'd even get expelled – barred from taking her exams. That would serve her right.

'Can you think of anyone who could be doing it?' Mrs Farook asks. 'Anyone who would want to hurt you?'

I want to tell her so bad. It would be so easy. And yet, I can't. If I take Huda down, she'll definitely tell everyone what she saw first-hand. And then it'll be my word against hers, and I'm betting the school would believe Top Student Huda over me.

I just duck my head and shrug. 'It doesn't matter though, right? Whoever's doing it is lying – that's all that matters. Can I go?'

Mrs Farook puts her hand on my arm lightly again. 'Almost done here, I promise, Amani.'

I fiddle with the bottom of my tie – pick on a thread that's come loose.

'I've been having a look at your records,' she says, picking up the folder on the table. 'There's been a bit of a dip in your grades this term. Mr Cavanaugh's noted that your mocks and practice exams haven't gone well. And you're planning to take all three sciences for A level, is that right?'

Oh God. Why won't this end? Why won't she just let me go? I can feel the dam I've built inside myself collapsing. The tears are gonna come.

'It's . . . it's just . . . it's the stress of school building up. That's all it is. The pressure of practice exams, mocks, predicted grades. All the teachers keep saying how important GCSEs are, that they decide our future and whatever. It's just the stress of that, I swear. It's nothing . . . else. Nothing outside of school.'

I pause and look at her, right in the eyes. I can't tell whether she believes me, so I do that thing you do in exams where if you don't know the answer, you just blurt out lots of surrounding facts.

'Home is actually . . . the best part of my life at the moment,' I say. 'I have a little brother I adore. He and I, we . . . make films together! Just silly things with his toys. But it's a nice hobby we have. Mum joins in too. She paints the backgrounds and makes props. She's so good at art. And Dad . . . well, he's our biggest cheerleader. I show him the films and he's always so proud. It's just . . . It's nice to go home from a tough class to them. It's just . . . a nice environment, y'know? My parents are really supportive of everything I do.'

There's a sick bubbling in my stomach now. It's not just nerves any more. I feel terrible about all the lies I'm spouting. It's fine when you tell the occasional fib to divert attention, but when it all comes spewing out like that, it makes me feel physically sick.

But this is important. This is to keep my family together. I need to convince her, by any means necessary.

'That's good to hear,' Mrs Farook says. She smiles at me, and I think it might be a real, honest smile. The lies might be hurting, but they're also working. 'What about at school? Do you feel like you have a support network here? Good friends?'

My mouth opens to gush about Huda. But then I remember what she's done, and the pain runs through my body all over again. The bubbling of the lies is joined by the bubbling of my anger. I can't let that come out in my tone, and if I mention Huda, Mrs Farook will totally cotton on.

'I've got a really great best friend,' I tell her. 'I don't think you've ever taught her? Maggie Chan. She's in my form. We sit next to each other at registration, and have a few classes together. She likes making films too. We go round each other's houses a lot. She's . . . she's really great. Real funny, and a great . . . support.'

Mrs Farook smiles again. I relax a little; her smile has that effect. I'm guessing she hasn't noticed that Huda is basically the only person I hang around with at school. I start to get antsy. It feels as if she's been interrogating me forever. I think I've given her the right answers, or at least good enough answers. I don't see how she could take anything I've told her and turn it into a reason to go to social services.

'So . . . can I go now?' I ask. 'Is this over? Can we just . . . move on?'

'Sorry, Amani, just a few more questions.' She shuffles through the papers in her folder.

I fiddle with the thread on my tie again. There's a nervous tingling running all through me. This can't be normal. If she believed me, she would have let me go as soon as I said everything was fine. Maybe there's no convincing her. Maybe they've made their minds up already, like they did with Stacey and her mum. Maybe . . . maybe keeping me here is all a scheme.

My phone starts ringing, the noise making me literally jump to my feet. I've been poised to get up this whole time, and the noise makes my body spring into action.

'Amani! Is everything OK?' Mrs Farook looks up at me.

I slide out my phone from my blazer pocket. '*Missed call: HOME.*' They've already done it. Social services are already there. Mrs Farook brought me here to distract me, so I couldn't go and warn Ammi what was happening. Oh my God. I can't believe this is happening.

'Amani?' Mrs Farook says again.

'I have to go,' I mumble, before grabbing my bag and making a run for it.

41

I'm breathless by the time I turn into the alleyway to take the secret way home. I practically sprinted out of school because I was convinced Mrs Farook would follow me out, like literally run out after me. I know leaving the meeting like that was a bad move, but there's no way I couldn't. I call home again, but it's engaged. I try Ammi's mobile, but it goes to voicemail. I'm too scared to call Abbu. He's going to be so mad. God, what if Ammi's in trouble and that call to me was her cry for help?

I try her mobile again. Try the landline. No change.

I run through the alleyway, all the way home. I'm expecting there to be police cars outside our house when I round the corner, but there's just both my parents' cars in the driveway, like normal. Although there is a random fancy purple car parked on the road. Fancy enough to belong to someone who works for social services.

I stand on the doorstep for a few seconds, steeling myself. I listen for Abbu's voice, a screaming match between him and someone accusing him of . . . that. But it's quiet. Maybe he's on his best behaviour. I unlock the door and slip into the house. It's . . . normal. The TV is on in the living room, and I can smell Ammi cooking in the kitchen. The living-room door opens, and Abbu appears. I examine his expression, looking for anger, for him to tell me this is all my fault, but there's just confusion written there.

'Amani? What are you doing back from school so early?' he asks.

I peer behind him, into the living room. It's empty. I breathe a sigh of relief. They're not here. The school hasn't called them. Maybe my answers *did* satisfy Mrs Farook. Now my answer needs to satisfy Abbu. I've already lied my arse off today, so what's one more?

'Um, it was . . . It's a revision afternoon. No classes.'

'Oh, right,' he says. 'Well, go upstairs and revise then. Your Auntie Kameela and your cousins are coming round for dinner, so get as much done as you can before they arrive. I'm sorry we couldn't go out, like we had planned.' He pauses for a second, watching me. 'How's . . . ? How's your arm? Did anyone see it?'

'Everything's fine,' I lie. All that running has made it throb even more.

Abbu nods and returns to the living room.

I pop my head into the kitchen. Ammi's stirring one of the many pots on the stove. She doesn't even notice when I open the door, she's that engrossed.

'Salaam, Ammi,' I say.

She jumps a little, then turns to me. Her expression changes from frustrated concentration to pleasant and almost happy. 'Amani, you're back early.' She turns to stir a pan.

'Revision afternoon,' I explain, though I don't think she's really bothered. 'Um . . . did you call me earlier? I had a missed call from home, then tried calling back but no one picked up.'

'Huh?' she says distractedly. 'Oh yes, sorry, I accidentally called your number instead of Kameela's. Your auntie and cousins are coming for dinner. Can you give the upstairs a once-over with the hoover?'

'Sure.'

Everything's normal here. Nothing is different. Neither of them has any idea about the blog, about our worst nightmare coming true. I wonder whether to tell Ammi, to warn her about any repercussions. I watch her as she cooks, preparing for her sister's arrival. We never have people over to the house. Ammi's probably already stressed to the max, so I shouldn't add to that. Especially not after that talk with Mrs Farook. I've convinced her, I know I have. There's no point worrying Ammi even more over something that isn't going to happen. So instead I grab the hoover from the cupboard and take it upstairs.

Abbu is on his absolute best behaviour at dinner. He's being so charming and considerate, I almost can't believe it's him. If anyone saw him like this, they would never in a million years believe the rumour . . . the truth . . . that Huda's spreading around. Ammi seems happier than I've seen her in a while too. Ismail's having fun, finally having kids his own age here at home. Me? I'm on edge. I can't eat anything without feeling sick. Even though it's been hours, there's still a part of me that's terrified someone is about to storm through the doors. Scared that at any moment social services will turn up, point their fingers at Abbu and accuse him of . . . all that stuff. Then he'll be humiliated, and both Ammi and Auntie Kameela will blame me for everything. It doesn't help that my phone has been going crazy. Texts and DMs and tweets. Everyone's talking about me, saying horrible things. The meme of Abbu has gone viral within our school circle again, but this time people have edited it into more . . . crude versions. I don't look at all of them, but I'm too scared to block everything. I'll admit, a teeny tiny part of me is waiting for Huda to get in contact. For her to admit she's gone too far, like she knows she did with Stacey's mum, to say she's sorry and offer to help fix the mess she's caused. She'd know just what to do, how to stop everyone from talking shit, probably even how to sweet-talk social services – she's had so many dealings with them that she's probably an expert in how they work, how they think.

Auntie Kameela gossips all through dinner. About anyone and everyone. I tune out most of it, but my ears perk up when she mentions Aisha, the woman who left her abusive husband.

'She finally went back,' Auntie Kameela says. 'After her mother stopped eating and drinking and begged her to return, to save their reputation.'

No one says anything.

'It's only right, na?' Auntie Kameela continues, oblivious. 'What marriage *doesn't* have these kinds of problems?'

I notice Abbu giving Ammi a secret, stern look. Ammi isn't facing him, but I can tell from the rigidity in her posture that she's aware.

'Hopefully Raffi forgives her for breaking apart their family. If he can forgive her, then inshallah they'll get through it. What was she even thinking, trying that?'

I want to give Auntie Kameela a kick under the table. Everything she's saying . . . it's Ammi. Ammi, if she had the courage to leave. This is how they'd talk about her. How her *own sister* would talk about her. Everyone would slag Ammi off until she'd feel there was no other option than to go back to Abbu. Just like Aisha.

We move into the living room after dinner. Abbu sits watching TV as Ammi and Auntie Kameela chat quietly. I'm tempted to make an excuse about revision and go off to my room. It has been such a long, weird day, and I'm worried about how tomorrow is going to go. But I want to be a good daughter. I make tea for everyone and even bring in biscuits. Ismail runs up to Ammi and yanks a chocolate biscuit right out of her hand.

'Ismail! Don't snatch!' Ammi says. 'I would've given you one if you'd just asked.'

Ismail doesn't reply, just shoves half the biscuit in his mouth.

My five-year-old cousin, Idrees, comes up to Ammi. 'Please could I have a biscuit, please?' he asks, in a rather adorable voice.

Ammi smiles and passes him a biscuit.

'Thank you, khala,' he says, again adorably, before walking off.

'Such good manners,' Ammi says.

Ismail returns, still chewing, and holds his hand out for another biscuit.

'What do you say?' Ammi prompts.

'I want a biscuit.'

'What's the magic word?' Auntie Kameela joins in.

Ismail looks from her to Ammi. Then gives Abbu a glance. He considers it for a second before lunging for the open tin that's sitting on the table next to Ammi. He manages to grab a fistful of biscuits, knocking over Auntie Kameela's cup of tea in the process. Auntie Kameela jumps up with a squeal, and Ismail takes the chance to slip out of the room with his snacks. I hear his and Idrees's small feet running up the stairs.

Abbu tuts. He looks over disapprovingly. But at Ammi, not Ismail.

'Oh my God, sorry!' Ammi says, righting the cup and starting to wipe Auntie Kameela's clothes and the table.

My heart thuds. This is normally where Abbu would chime in. He'd tell Ammi she spoils Ismail, and that he only acts this way because she lets him, encourages him. That he's like this because of her. They had this exact argument a few days ago when Ismail defied Ammi's 'no snacks before dinner' rule. But today . . . today Abbu says nothing. Even weirder, he pulls out a couple of tissues and goes over to help Ammi clean up. It's so bizarre to me, and probably to Ammi, but not to Auntie Kameela. It wouldn't be bizarre to strangers. To anyone official.

If Abbu keeps this up, no one will believe anything bad about him. It'll be fine. He just needs to keep on like this. And I just need to keep telling people it was all a sick rumour. If we work together, we can continue to keep this under wraps. Despite Huda's best efforts to ruin my family, I won't let her.

42

I wake up to a phone screen filled with texts and DMs from my classmates. Most of them are kind messages, but my brain can only focus on the abuse, on the people laughing and making crude jokes. Still nothing from Huda though. I can't believe she hasn't even *tried* to reach out. She just throws a grenade into my life and swans off. Typical Huda, not caring about anyone besides herself. I spent ages focusing on her stupid Perfect Daughter plan, and when I need *her* help, she runs off in the opposite direction. Maybe I should skive today. It would be so much easier than facing up to everyone. Cleo got away with taking half a week off after her blog came out. I'm gonna need more time than that. Maybe I can just stay off until exams start. Maybe I can skip exams altogether. Surely this counts as extenuating circumstances.

I wrap my duvet around me. Maybe if I stay in bed long enough, Ammi will just assume I've already left. I try to force myself back to sleep, but my body betrays me – I roll around for a while, waiting for sleep to return, waiting for Ammi to go to drop Ismail off at school. Abbu mentioned he was going out this morning, so when Ammi leaves, I can hide away for a bit.

'Amani?' Ammi's voice comes from the landing. She knocks

and then pops her head round the door. 'You're still in bed?' she exclaims. 'You're going to be late! Hurry up! I'll drive you both. Get ready, now!'

So much for the skiving plan.

Walking into registration is just as bad as I imagined it would be. Everyone turns to look at me. A hush spreads. I duck my head and shuffle towards my seat. Whispers start up, trail after me. I instinctively cover my forearm with my other hand. I changed to a skin-toned bandage today, thinking it would be almost camouflaged if someone saw, but it feels like the wound is a siren, calling people to pay attention to me, even though it's hidden under my blazer. There's quiet laughter all around me, the sound of which makes my ears burn with shame. This was such a big mistake. I should have begged Ammi to let me skive. I could have faked cramps or the flu.

I finally get to my desk, where Maggie's already slouched over the table. It's weirdly comforting to see something that's the same. At least Maggie is constant. Although, the way I ran away from her yesterday after the blog came out, I wouldn't be surprised if she's gone weird on me too.

'Hey,' I say to her as I sit down, trying to keep my voice normal. The trick to moving forward is to try and pretend it's not getting to me. That's how someone would react if the rumour spread about them *was* a lie.

Maggie raises her head off the desk, sits up with a yawn. Her usual greeting. I smile.

'Hey, Amani, how's your dad?' Cleo shouts from the back of the classroom. 'Beaten up any women recently?'

I make the mistake of half turning towards the noise, before my face starts burning up.

Don't react, Amani. Don't react.

I wait for Miss Hoover to do something, to tell Cleo off, but she's too busy writing at her desk. I guess I just have to get used to it. Just ignore her, ignore them all. I can do it. Well, I can't, but I have literally no other option.

'As if having actual diarrhoea wasn't bad enough, now you've got the verbal sort too?' Maggie retorts effortlessly.

Another wave of giggles spreads across the room, but aimed at Cleo instead of me. It should make me feel good, but the sound of snarky giggling will never not fill me with anxiety, thanks to Cleo and her coven.

The focus shifts to Cleo after that. One of the boys at the back starts making fart noises and blaming it on her. I guess her secret was more entertaining than mine.

'Thanks,' I say softly.

'No worries,' Maggie replies, slouching back down with a yawn. 'I know it's all lies, don't worry. They'll get bored soon and shut up.'

You'd think I'd be used to this sick feeling at the pit of my stomach by now, but surprisingly I'm overwhelmed by it when she says this. I just put my head on the desk and do a Maggie until the bell rings.

The rest of the day passes in the same way. In almost every lesson, people make comments that make me want to cry. It reaches fever pitch during English and I have to excuse myself to the loo. I sit in the stall and bawl my eyes out, clean up my face as best as I can and then return quietly to class. I don't see Huda at all. I don't know if she's skived today or whether she's just doing a really good job of avoiding me. Either way, it makes me mad. She's probably basking in the misery she's caused. How are there no repercussions for her actions? It's not fucking fair. The overwhelming anger is rising inside me again.

I want payback.

I want her to see what she's done.

I want her to see everyone making fun of me, to feel how humiliated I feel.

I want her to lose as much as I've lost.

I want her to be as miserable as I am.

I want to ruin her life, just like she's ruined mine.

And I spot the perfect opportunity to do just that as I'm walking to class after lunch (spent thankfully being distracted by Maggie in a corner of the canteen – I even showed her some of my YouTube videos). I spot Mrs Farook walking across the quad. I saw her earlier too, but I ducked behind a bush because I was terrified that she'd have a go at me for running out of our meeting yesterday. But half the day has passed now and she hasn't called me in, so I'm thinking my answers satisfied her, and that everything's going to be fine. For me, anyway. I can't say the same for Huda. That bitch is going down.

'Mrs Farook!' I call when I'm a few metres away from her.

She turns and gives me a warm smile. 'Hi, Amani. How are you?'

I search for an undertone to her voice, one that might suggest she's still suspicious, but I can't find anything.

'I wanted to talk to you,' I blurt. My heart's pounding. I need to get it out before I think twice. No one would blame me for grassing on Huda. After what she's done, her getting punished for doing the blog is right. She knew what she was getting into. She deserves it. I have to keep telling myself that. She's ruined my life, so she deserves to be punished.

'Ah, we were just on our way to find you,' a voice says.

I turn to find Miss Kirtley, the receptionist, and next to her is . . .

'Mum?!'

Ammi and I lock eyes, and fear strikes my chest. I look between her and Mrs Farook. Ammi's face is stoic, expressionless, but there's panic in her eyes.

'I'll leave you here,' Miss Kirtley says to Ammi before walking off.

'Ah, hello, Mrs Akhtar. Thank you for coming in at such short notice.'

'It's no problem,' Ammi says.

'What's going on?' I ask.

'It's nothing to worry about,' Mrs Farook reassures me. 'I've asked your mum in for a little chat. Nothing serious. Please don't stress.'

DON'T STRESS?

How can I not stress when she's brought Ammi in to face her with Huda's stupid blog?

Fuck.

'Please, Mrs Akhtar, come with me. Amani, you'd better get to class.'

'Wait!' I say without thinking. I need to stop this, need to make sure she doesn't get Ammi alone before I speak to her,

269

before I warn her. I should have told her everything last night. God, why wasn't I just upfront with her? Maybe together we could have prepped for this. I need to speak to Ammi before Mrs Farook does.

'Mum, can I talk to you about something? It's important.' With my desperate eyes I try to communicate what's going on.

Ammi opens her mouth to reply, but Mrs Farook cuts her off. 'Amani, you can speak to your mother later. After school. Now go to class, before I write you up for detention.'

That's it.

It's over.

I can't stop it.

All I can do is watch as Mrs Farook leads Ammi off towards the same room she interrogated me in yesterday. Ammi doesn't even turn around so I can mouth a warning to her. They just walk off, chatting. Ammi has no idea. She's going to be so mad. This is all my fault. I'm the one who let this secret loose, who put our family in jeopardy. Yes, Huda was the one who spread the word, but I let the cracks show enough for her to see in the first place. We've gone so many years with no one finding out. I should have kept Huda at a distance, should have insisted we always hang out at hers. It's all on me. Our whole family is going to get broken apart because of me. Social services will probably put me and Ismail in care. And Ammi . . . how is she going to cope with all the gossiping aunties?

Although . . .

There's a tiny idea growing in my head. Mrs Farook said she's trained to deal with stuff like this. What if . . . ? What if she knows a way to handle it? Like, *properly* handle it. If she's the safeguarding lead, she must have dealt with things like this before, right? I can't be the first student this has happened to. What if . . . Ammi tells Mrs Farook the truth? The *real* truth. Things that even I don't know. If Ammi told her . . . maybe Mrs Farook would know what to do, how to save our family. That's basically her job, right? She's one of the kindest teachers; she would totally help. What if . . . Ammi uses this opportunity to put a stop to it? To put a stop to Abbu. Maybe . . . maybe we could even leave. Mrs Farook could help with that. She'd find a way to make sure that we don't get split up, that Ismail doesn't get taken away. She'd know how to keep us safe. Away from Abbu. My heart jolts at just the thought of it.

43

I'm waiting for Ammi.

But obviously I have to hide because I'm supposed to be in biology right now. So I'm loitering by her car. Specifically, crouching down on the ground next to the passenger door so I can grab her as soon as she gets here. Not weird at all. This is the only way I can do it though. There's no way I can go until the end of the day to hear what Mrs Farook said. God, Ammi is going to be so blindsided. I hope she's OK.

There's a loud click and I almost scream from the suddenness of it, but then I hear footsteps close by and realise it's Ammi, unlocking the car. I peek up over the edge of the window to make sure it's her. My legs are cramping from crouching, and I will her to walk faster. When she finally reaches the car, I open the passenger door at the same time she opens hers. I slip in as quick as I can and slouch in the seat.

'Amani, oh my God you scared me!' she says, still standing outside, hand on her chest.

'Get in, quick,' I hiss, like one of those TV spies.

'What are you doing? Why aren't you in class?' Ammi hisses back as she gets into the car. She slouches down slightly too.

'I'm so sorry, Ammi. I didn't mean to . . . It wasn't my

fault . . . I tried to stop it . . . What happened just now . . . Mrs Farook, everything. I didn't know it was going to go this far. It's all gone mental, Ammi.'

She turns to face me. There's thunder on her face.

'And exactly *what* has been going on?' she asks, pinning me with her stare. 'I've just had your teacher in there asking me . . . all sorts.'

I sigh. 'It was all . . . all Huda. After what happened the other day at ours, she got . . . I dunno . . . scared or whatever. She thought she was doing the right thing by telling everyone. God knows where she got that idea. What did Mrs Farook . . . ? What did she ask you?'

'She brought me in to discuss your slipping grades. Which we need to have a proper conversation about, by the way.' She stares pointedly at me. 'But we didn't talk much about that. She told me about the blog, what . . . what it said about you . . . about us. She told me they have to look into the accusations, and asked me if there was any truth to them.'

'And . . . and what did *you* say?' My heart is hammering, waiting for her answer like it's the only thing I've ever waited for in my life. I watch her face, watch for any signs. Her eyes aren't red and puffy, so there haven't been any tears . . . yet.

'I said no, of course,' she replies finally. She looks at me as if I'm crazy for expecting otherwise. She's acting like the whole thing *is* a lie. She's pretending. In front of *me*. As if I don't hear their fights almost every night, as if I haven't witnessed Abbu's anger in person on multiple occasions now. As if I don't have a ten-minute-long compilation video of my face from the Bad Nights. Her answer makes me angry.

She's thrown away perhaps the only chance we'll ever have to make things better.

'Ammi, you could have . . . you could have told her the truth and *ended* all of this! The school is already suspicious because of the blog. You could have taken the help. Mrs Farook said she's trained to deal with things like this. She's probably helped someone like you before. She'll know what to do. She could –'

'Amani, you have to promise you won't go to any of your teachers about this. We don't need their help, you hear me? This is a . . . private family matter. I don't want you talking to *anyone* about it.'

'They're trying to help,' I tell her. My body is full of nervous energy now. I was so convinced. *So* convinced she was going to tell them, that Mrs Farook was going to get the truth out of her, that *something* was going to change. I just can't understand why Ammi wouldn't take that chance.

'How is poking their nose into our private life trying to help?' she asks.

'It's better than us all just burying our heads in the sand,' I say, trying to put on a grown-up voice, one that Ammi might respond to, might listen to.

She glares at me again. 'You're a child, Amani. You have *no idea* about any of this. You think you know everything, but you're so young . . . You don't . . . you don't get it. We can't . . . *I* can't say anything. To anyone. This is something that's supposed to stay within our home. This is something . . . Amani, please trust me on this. No one can find out.'

'Huda already knows,' I mumble. 'She was there the other day, remember? When Abbu almost broke your arm, twisting it behind your back because you wouldn't tell him what he wanted to hear?'

'Amani, please . . . just . . . don't, OK?' Ammi lets out a big sigh. 'As for Huda . . . can you please ask her to keep her mouth shut? Let people think she's spreading lies. We're just lucky Mrs Farook believed us.'

'What do you mean? How do you know?'

'She said she had to forward it on to some MASH team, to show they've looked into it. But she seemed satisfied by what we said. She thought your grades were a red flag, but I told her you just weren't studying enough, and that would change. I told her the burn . . . I told her you did that yourself while making tea, and since I'm trained in first aid we managed it at home. Does that match your story?'

I nod silently.

Ammi breathes a sigh of relief. 'I think . . . I think we're in the clear.'

'Except for when we get home, and this all starts again?'

'Amani, stop. This is your father we're talking about. How can you *want* people to say bad things about him?'

'Because he's a bad person!' I finally explode. 'You're so under his thumb you don't see it. You don't see that he's never going to change. He's never going to stop. You don't see how much of an effect this is having on all of us. Did you notice how you jumped just then when all I did was *open the car door*? How can you want to go on putting up with this? You can stop it, right here, right now. Look, we can go back in and find Mrs Farook again. She's really nice. I –'

'Amani, we've had this conversation before. It's just not that

275

easy. There's so many things to think about. First, where are we going to stay? How are we going to live? My job isn't enough to support us all. Your father pays all the bills, earns all the money. Everything is in his name. Even if I got a better-paid job, who'd look after Ismail? And more than the practicalities, what are people going to say? This isn't . . . this isn't something you act upon. You just . . . you have to just put up with it. Carry on.'

'That's bullshit!'

'Amani! Language!'

'I'm sorry, but it really is. You can't just . . . you can't just stay in an abusive relationship because you're worried what other people will say. Our relatives aren't the ones living this. They'll move on to the next scandal soon enough. But you . . . Ammi, if you don't leave . . . You can't put up with this the rest of your life. It's not fair to you, it's not fair to *us*.'

'Do you have any idea what will happen if you or I went to one of your teachers and told them about this? Told them the whole truth? They'd probably take you and Ismail into care, especially after the burn. Your father – he would just deny everything. You've seen how he can twist things, how he behaves when we're around other people. You think they'd believe me over him, with his confidence? He's an actor, Amani. He'll talk his way out of it. Even if he didn't, these types of cases never end well. And it's not like your grandparents would take us in. We'd have no money, nowhere to live; we have no choice but to stay with your abbu. And you know things would be much worse if this actually came out . . . Amani –' she sighs, looks me right in the eyes – 'you think you're the only one who's imagined this future? A future where we can all just be . . . normal, happy. I've been imagining this other future for *years*. I've been over every single scenario in my head, and it *never* ends well. We've got it good at the moment. Your father is . . . He's a decent man when we don't anger him. We just have to learn his ways. You've seen how he is when there's no drama going on, when we just . . . stick to his rules. We can live a good life like this. Please, Amani, for me. Just . . . leave this alone.'

I don't say anything. I don't know what I could even say. She's weeping now, and I can feel the first few tears sliding down my cheeks too. I had no idea she was carrying all this inside her. I'm so stupid. Of course she's thought about all this. It's not like she enjoys what he does to her. If Ammi says we're stuck, then I guess we're stuck.

'Now, are you finally going to let this go?' she asks quietly. She sits up, turns to face the front, wipes her eyes. 'And while you're at it, I think you need to have a word with Huda. Stop her from spreading any more of these vicious rumours. Doesn't this count as cyberbullying? You should tell Mrs Farook about *that* instead. That's the real crime here.' She pauses for a few seconds. 'I'm surprised at Huda though. You two have been friends for so long. I can't believe she would do something like this.'

My instinct is to defend her. I've always defended Huda. But there's no defending this.

'Anyway,' Ammi says, putting her seat belt on, 'I assume you're not going back to class, so I might as well take you home.'

I wordlessly put on my seat belt too, feeling more despondent than ever.

* * *

Abbu's there when we get home, and it only occurs to me then that I have no excuse to be back from school this early. Sure enough, that's the first question out of his mouth.

'Why are you both home so early?' he asks. He's directing it mostly at Ammi, though. I run her schedule through my head and only now realise that she's supposed to be at work this afternoon. I try to think up an excuse that would exonerate both of us. An emergency of some kind. I quickly grab my stomach and put on a pathetic face.

'I wasn't . . . I wasn't feeling well,' I mumble.

'Stop it,' Ammi hisses at me.

I look up at her, shocked. That was the perfect lie to cover us both. She went to pick up her sick child; Abbu can't have a problem with that. And since he hates her job so much, he'd probably be pleased she skipped. Ammi frowns at me before taking a breath and looking at Abbu, who just seems confused.

'The school called me in,' she explains carefully. 'They wanted to discuss Amani's grades. They've been slipping recently. Quite badly, I might add.'

What? Why is she telling him?! I feel my ears heat up because I know he's going to be pissed about this. I expect her to finish there and let him get on with his shouting, but she surprises me by continuing.

'The school thought this dip in her performance could be something to do with . . . her home situation. There's been some stupid rumour going around the school, and on the internet, spread by Huda, that . . . that there's something untoward going on at home. They asked if you were abusing me.'

278

Oh. My. God. What is she doing?

I look at Dad.

His jaw drops.

Fuck.

44

I can't believe it. She's just blurted it out. It's not like he was pressuring her; Abbu would probably have accepted my story about feeling ill. Or she could have stopped at being asked in to talk about my bad grades. I would have happily taken the heat for that, rather than tell him the truth: that Huda's spilled our home life all over the internet.

'They asked you *what*?!' he exclaims. His eyes are wide, his body rigid.

I brace myself for an explosion.

'It was all so stupid,' Ammi says nonchalantly. 'Huda spread some vicious rumour about us to the whole school. She was bullying Amani. And the school obviously had to follow their safeguarding procedures and make sure there was no truth to it.' She pauses, and Abbu waits. He's staring at her as intensely as I did when she came back from her chat with Mrs Farook. The stare that says he doesn't know what her answer was in the meeting, the one that says he's hoping to God it goes his way, but he's also scared it won't.

'Of course I reassured them that it was all lies,' she says finally. She stares back at Abbu, and only now do I notice the slight shaking of her hands. She notices me noticing and occupies herself taking off her jacket and shoes.

'Of course,' Abbu replies slowly. 'So what . . . what exactly did they ask?'

She shakes her head a little as she takes off her hijab. 'They repeated the things Huda's said and asked me if there was any truth to it. I told them we were all very happy, and that nothing was going on. I think that Huda's jealous of your life, Amani. I know it must be tough, growing up in care like she did. But that's really no excuse to take a wrecking ball to our home, to our family. I don't want you spending time with her any more. And *please* do not invite her into our house again. She is not welcome here.' She looks at me, glares at me. It hurts hearing Ammi saying all these horrible things about Huda. I get that what she did was wrong, but that's no reason to attack her like this, to bring her background, her upbringing, into it.

Abbu turns to look at me. They're both deflecting onto me rather than looking at the big picture – that the school were suspicious, that they looked into it, are maybe *still* looking into it. But right now, their anger is directed at Huda, and therefore me.

'Is this true?' he asks. 'Huda's been spreading these lies?'

I want to point out it's *not* lies. All she's been spreading is the truth. In a stupid manner, but it's the truth. How dare he try to pin all the blame on her, when *he's* the one in the wrong? He's the one who's been beating his wife, terrorising his family for years. But of course, I can't say any of that. All I can do is follow Ammi's lead.

'We had a . . . a fight, and I think this was her way of getting back at me. I'm sorry, Abbu. I'm sorry she's done this.'

'People these days,' he huffs. I look into his eyes and . . . I swear there's a little bit of fear. He . . . he's scared. Scared the truth is going to come out. Scared everyone will find out what kind of man he really is. And if he's scared . . . that means . . . maybe, maybe, the answer to all our problems really *is* for everyone to find out. I guess that boat has sailed now though. We were offered one opportunity, and we didn't take it.

'You let people into your house, feed them, treat them like your own, and *this* is how they pay you back? I can't . . . I'm just shocked. I thought you were a better judge of character, Amani.' He turns to Ammi and smiles. 'At least you managed to put the school right. Who knows what could have happened if this went any further.' He reaches out, puts his arm around her and . . . pulls her in for a hug.

He's hugging her?!

I don't think I've ever seen my parents hug. I've been brought up to believe that intimacy and affection are things to be done privately. It's why I always look away when Ali and Nafisah hug, or kiss each other on the cheek. But now, when it's my parents hugging for the first time I've seen in my life, I can't help but gawp. I'm looking so closely that I can see the surprise on Ammi's face. I notice the way her whole body tenses, and she hesitates before returning the hug. Maybe it's not just in public that Abbu doesn't show affection.

He pulls away, and he's still smiling. 'I knew you'd be able to handle yourself in a situation like that,' he tells Ammi. 'The teachers, they . . . said nothing more is going to happen, right? They're punishing Huda for spreading the lies?'

Ammi nods quickly. 'They said they have to file a report,

282

just to show, officially, they've done the right thing. They . . . promised there'd be punishment.'

She doesn't say that the school don't know it was Huda. I don't know why she's keeping that part from him, but I go along with it. It's such a precarious situation, I'm scared of putting a foot wrong. I don't want her pressuring me to tell on Huda. As much as I feel like I *want* to tell on her, to get her in trouble and ruin her life like she's done to me, I know I never could.

'OK, good,' Abbu says, nodding lightly. 'Let's hope this doesn't get out beyond the school. You know what a fuss people in our community would create if they heard.'

'It won't,' I butt in. 'Everyone's probably . . . forgotten about it already. There've been . . . a few rumours like this. There'll probably be another one tomorrow, and everyone will be obsessed with that instead.' I find myself needing to reassure him that it's over. If he goes digging or thinks something bad might be happening . . . it'll just get worse.

It hits me then. Why Ammi blurted out the truth as soon as she got home. She knew it would be a million times worse if he found out some other way. She could have lied as much as she wanted, but if the school contacted Abbu directly, or he heard about it on the grapevine, he'd be madder than ever at Ammi. She chose the lesser evil.

'That's good,' Abbu repeats, almost absent-mindedly. 'I mean . . . good that they'll forget. It's a shame this sort of thing happens on such a regular basis. Teenagers these days, they need to learn how to be nice to other people. Kindness is a lost art form, it seems. Eh, Shirin?'

She jolts back to attention, looks at him and nods. He smiles at her again, and I almost expect him to pat her on the head for being a good little girl.

'I was thinking, actually,' he says. 'Shirin, you know how you were saying you wanted to take on some extra hours at work?'

Ammi nods slowly. 'Um. Yes? You said it . . . it wouldn't work, that . . . that it would affect the kids.'

'Oh, nonsense,' he says. 'As long as it's during school hours, I don't see why not.' He's smiling even wider now, full-on beaming almost. But not in a natural way. It's eerie.

'Oh . . . Are you sure?' she asks.

'Yes, I'm sure. When I get this job I interviewed for the other day, I'll have more of a steady schedule, so you can do more hours. Oh, and you wanted to do an art course too, right? Let's find you an even *better* one than that community-centre one you were thinking about. It will be expensive, I know, but you're worth it. I'll pay, of course.'

I didn't even know Ammi was looking for more hours at work, but I guess it makes sense. Less time in the house. I know that feeling all too well, with the amount of time I spend at Huda's. It only really hits me now.

I've lost my best friend.

Despite what she did, she really was . . . my person. She was the one I'd always run to when things got too bad at home. Without her, without her house to escape to whenever I need a break . . . where am I going to go? I'm going to have to just put up with it. Put up with the tension between my parents. Put up with my constant anxiety that a fight is about to break out.

But . . .

But maybe not.

Now that Abbu's almost been caught, now that he knows he's not completely untouchable, maybe . . . maybe things really *will* change here. I mean, he's just agreed to something he was adamantly against earlier. Maybe this scare will zap some sense into him?

Or . . .

Maybe not.

I mean, I have been burned like this before.

45

The notice board reads 10. Almost single figures now. My heart starts beating super fast, and a wave of anxiety washes over me. There's so little time left of school, left before study leave. Before . . . I'm stuck at home. All. The. Time. The weekend was *so* awkward. Abbu was being overly nice to Ammi – they even went out for dinner together, leaving me to babysit. I spent most of yesterday in my room, finalising my media studies coursework. Watching it back, it seems so stupid. So pointless. Of all the things I could have created, I made a stupid trailer for a horror film. I should have gone deeper, like Maggie with the video of her sister. I should have done something better. I tried working on some YouTube videos too – I feel less pressured to make them 'good' because they're mainly just for me and Ismail – but it still felt like everything was terrible.

It's been four days since Huda released the blog about me. Four days since the entire year started gossiping about me. Four days since I've spoken to Huda. I feel so lost without her by my side. Something funny will happen and I'll go to text her, and then remember how angry I am. Then I get angrier, because it's been four fucking days and she hasn't even reached out. Not even just a 'sorry'. I've seen her around school, and she's been sitting in her usual seat in class, but I can't bring myself to go and sit next to her, or even go up and talk to her. She's in the wrong, so she should make the first move. Though I am tempted to tell her how much trouble she's caused. How the school interrogated Ammi. But maybe she would get a thrill from knowing she had that effect.

I so wish I had the guts to grass on her. Life would be so much easier if I could be as much of a heartless cow as she is. Get her suspended. Or worse. I wish I could be that evil. But maybe it's a good thing I'm not; it proves Abbu's cruelty isn't genetic.

School is still hell. I thought all of the blog stuff would have blown over by now, but people are still making stupid comments, maybe because there hasn't been another blog post since. Not Cleo though. It's weird – after everything, all those years of bullying me, she seems to finally be over it. She doesn't make any comments as I walk into registration, even though we accidentally make eye contact. I guess she got fed up of the attention it drew to her. It also looks like the Burn Blog really did break up her coven. The three of them still sit at separate tables.

What's new, though, is Maggie. She's basically become Huda's replacement. She sometimes talks back to people for me (though never with the same quality of comebacks as Huda used to). I sit with her at lunch too now, and even in the classes Huda is in. She's asked a bunch of times why we're fighting, but I've just given her lame excuses.

'God, things are getting so boring round here,' Maggie moans, slouching down in her chair after answering her name on the register. 'It's been forever since anything happened. Why can't there be another blog post already? Or a prank? Someone

287

needs to liven things up around here. Ooh, maybe I should start something.' She sits up in her chair, eyes bright.

I laugh. 'Like what?'

'I dunno. Something cool. We should do something better than anything that's happened so far.'

'What's this "we" business? I never agreed to anything.'

'Oh, you will,' Maggie says. 'Remember what Mr Voake said? We have to "make our mark on the world".'

I laugh. 'He meant with film, not pranks!' The bell rings for first period. 'C'mon,' I say. 'Maybe media studies will *inspire* you.'

Just being in the media studies room brings me peace, makes me forget everything else. Our last few lessons have been free periods for us to finish our final projects. Mine's technically done, but something's been bugging me ever since Maggie showed me her film – the one about her sister who died. It moved me so much I cried. That's what media should do, I think. Make you feel something deeply. I definitely can't say that about my project. I wonder if I should do something deeper. Something more personal. For a moment I consider submitting my Bad Nights compilation, but the thought of writing a reflective commentary on it makes me want to be sick.

'How about "A Day in the Life"?' Maggie asks me as we sit at the computers. She's been trying to help me think of new project ideas all lesson.

'My life isn't interesting enough for that.'

'YouTubers do it all the time, and they live boring-ass lives. Yours would at least have me in it. This face will guarantee you a good mark.' She flutters her eyelashes.

I laugh. 'How about I follow *you* around? "A Day in the Life of Maggie Chan".'

'It would feature a lot of sleeping,' she says, slouching in her chair and scrolling down the page of some gossip article she's reading.

I scan through the stuff I've filmed already, trying to find a way to repurpose it into something meaningful. 'It has to be something unique,' I mutter. 'Something that only I could make.'

'Why don't you do something about the Burn Blog?' Maggie asks.

'What?' I turn to her, but her eyes are still glued to the article.

'Like, what it felt like to be attacked like that. How the lies made your life hell. Have the emotional stuff but also bring in the mystery of whodunnit. I'd so watch that.'

I mull over her words. My gut reaction is obviously NO WAY – I'm hardly going to spread the stuff the blog was saying even more. But then I think about my Bad Night videos – how filming them helps me deal with what happens at home. I could take myself out of it completely, fictionalise it, and focus on the concept of someone anonymous doing this. The impact it's having . . .

'Right, gang,' Mr Voake says, clapping his hands once and disrupting my thoughts. 'Everyone listen up.'

I turn my seat around. Maggie just cranes her neck.

'Since it's almost our last lesson together, I thought I'd talk to you individually about your coursework, how you're feeling about it, and just have a chat about things. I'm gonna call you up to my desk one by one. The rest of you, I'm trusting you to work quietly while I'm doing this. Oh! And I also have a little gift for you all. You'll have to wait for your turn at my desk to see what it is though.' He wiggles his eyebrows comically.

While other people go up one by one, Maggie and I stay at our computers, her shopping for new Doc Martens, me brainstorming. I get so obsessed with the idea of doing my coursework on the Burn Blog that Mr Voake has to call me twice before I look up. He smiles and gestures me over to his desk.

'Ah, Amani, how are you?' he asks as I sit down. His table is cluttered with papers and various USB sticks with little labels on.

'I'm good, sir,' I reply. I don't know what to expect from this chat, but I'm weirdly not nervous or scared. I would be if it were any other teacher and any other subject. But Mr Voake's media studies class is almost like my safe space. The only place I *really* feel comfortable, and like I belong.

'Good, good,' he says. 'And how's your coursework coming along? I like what I've seen so far.'

If it were any other teacher, I'd lie and say it was fine.

'Actually . . . I'm thinking of changing my project.'

His eyebrows rise. 'Oh?'

'I just . . . I want to make something that makes people *feel* something. I want it to have an impact.'

'And your apocalypse trailer didn't make you feel anything?'

I shake my head. 'The videos I make . . . they're usually just a distraction. I never really do anything deep. But . . . I *like* deep things. I like watching emotional documentaries, exploring tragic stories.'

'So, do you have another idea?'

'I do. I need a bit of time to think about it, but could we have a chat once I've got a solid plan?'

'Of course. It's late in the day to be changing though. Do you think you'll be able to create something in the time you've got left?'

I nod enthusiastically. 'Oh yeah, for sure. Once I've got the idea down, I can work quick. I become a woman possessed when I'm passionate about something.'

He laughs. 'That's good to hear. I have every faith in you, Amani. I know you can do it. You're one of my best students. Don't tell the others though.'

I smile, and blush a little.

'Anyway, I got you a little something. As a "good luck/well done" gift. It's not much, but I hope you'll like it.'

He hands me a small white envelope. I slot my finger under the flap and run it along. I pull out a piece of card. It's black and glossy, with decorative gold writing. The top header reads RSVP. I scan the words: 'I, Steve Voake, accept my invitation to Amani Akhtar's film premiere.'

I look up at him, confused. 'What film premiere?' I ask.

He laughs a little. 'For the future,' he says. 'I'm getting my RSVP in early. I know you'll go on to do great things, Amani. You're very talented, and I have no doubt that you'll succeed in this field. So this is me, saving my spot at your first film premiere. I'm going to be there in the front row, cheering you on, telling everyone how I taught you about continuity.'

I look down at the card again and feel my eyes filling up with tears. 'Oh my God, this is the sweetest thing,' I mutter, trying to stave off a sob.

I can't believe it. It's hands down the best gift I've ever been given. So thoughtful and considerate and personal.

'I'm glad you like it!' Mr Voake says.

'I . . . I love it. Thank you, sir. It's . . . it's so kind.'

'I mean it though, Amani. I believe in you. I wish you would believe in yourself.'

I make the mistake of looking up at him. He's looking right at me, with an almost sad expression on his face. It makes me feel so exposed.

'You sure I can't tempt you to take media studies next year?' he asks.

I smile back at him, but only a quick flash. I can't maintain a real one. It's such a sore subject.

'It's not too late, y'know?' he says, leaning back in his chair. 'I know you'd do well. Class won't be the same without you.'

'That's . . . nice of you to say, sir. But I've missed the deadline.' I didn't mean to say that. I meant to say that my future is fixed. That Abbu would go crazy if I even suggested taking media studies. If I diverted from the carefully prepared life plan he's made for me, to do something I enjoy and am good at.

'If it's something you really wanted to do, we can make exceptions,' Mr Voake says. 'There's still space in my class for next year, and like I say, it won't be the same without you. Something to think about.' He smiles at me one last time, and that's my cue to leave.

I walk back to my computer, clutching the RSVP in my hand. I am so overwhelmed right now. Mr Voake's words, his faith in me, it's . . . it's so new to me. His words have opened up a door I'd been keeping locked in my mind.

It's not too late to change.

It's not too late to do what *I* want to do.

46

As it gets closer to study leave, people have been paying less attention in classes. As if they've checked out already. But every class fills me with dread. Well, every science class anyway. Today Mr Cavanaugh makes us work in pairs to create revision cards on certain topics. He's going to put them together and make a full set for everyone. I'm working with Stacey Lineham. I haven't spoken to her since the blog about her mum went out. I can't make eye contact with her, knowing it was Huda who did it. Should I tell her?

Mr Cavanaugh hands out the index cards then retreats to his desk. Looks like even the teachers have checked out.

Stacey and I sit in awkward silence, while everyone else gets to work or just chats.

'You think everyone's talking about us?' she asks.

'Huh?' I ask, turning to look at her.

'The two Burn Blog girls. People have been making comments at me non-stop. Can they resist the both of us being together? How *will* they cope?'

I laugh. 'Nah, they've got better things to talk about,' I say. 'Like mitosis.'

She smiles at me, then quickly drops her gaze.

Awkward.

'Listen, Amani,' she says quietly, softly, 'I've been meaning to catch you for the last few days. I thought maybe you'd want someone to talk to. Someone who's been through the same thing.'

'Oh . . .' I say. I don't know how to respond.

'It's shit, isn't it?' she asks when I don't reply. 'Everyone talking about your parents, making fun of them, when they've literally never met them.'

I look down at my textbook, wishing for this conversation to be over.

'That blog made such a mess of my life,' she continues. 'They called social services on my mum, did you know? Of course you know. Nothing stays a secret in this school. Not when it's such *juicy gossip*. Anyway, they interrogated my poor mum. She's already . . . She was . . . she was sad, OK? She misses my dad and she was sad. So she had a few drinks on the anniversary of his death. I'm so pissed that someone would take that – something private – and turn it into something for everyone to gossip about.'

'I know,' I say. 'It's such . . . it's such bullshit. All of it. It's messed up how much people are enjoying this.'

'Ugh, I was one of those people though! When it first came out, I was so into it. I enjoyed Cleo's humiliation, did exactly what everyone is doing to me. I hate myself for that.' She shakes her head a little. 'That piece-of-shit blog exists just to tear people down, make everyone take things the wrong way.'

I try to think of what to say, but inwardly I'm praying for her to move the conversation on, so she can't ask whether there's any truth to my secret. I pull out an index card and write 'Mitosis is . . .', hoping she'll get the hint.

'Anyway, you just gotta hang in there,' she says, pulling her textbook towards her. 'There'll be another poor victim soon, and you'll be old news. Well, old*er* news. I'm still getting the odd comment. But it's not as bad as it was. You just gotta wait for the next one.' She starts flicking through her book, thankfully ending the conversation.

But something she said sticks with me. I wonder whether Huda is going to carry this on. She said she started the blog to get back at people she hates, to get revenge for things like some comment Stacey made literally five years ago. And even though Huda said she regretted what happened with that, I wonder whether she regrets it enough to stop. Or whether she has more people on her hit list.

Stacey and I focus on making the revision cards. It's weird. We've sat next to each other all term, yet we've barely spoken to each other. Though I cringed at the conversation we just had about the blog, it makes me think of Maggie's idea for my media studies project.

'Hey, so, I wanted to ask for your help with something . . .' I tell Stacey about wanting to do my coursework on the Burn Blog, to show people how much mayhem it caused. I ask her if she'd be willing to talk about the emotional trauma it caused for her family, but make sure to emphasise that she won't have to do anything she's not comfortable with.

'That sounds amazing!' she says in response. 'I get to be the *star* of a film? Hell yes!'

We spend the rest of the lesson planning the video while

pretending to work on the revision cards. I don't know why Huda hates Stacey so much; she's actually lovely. As we walk out of school together, we swap numbers.

Abbu's not there when I get home. Ammi says he's out doing work stuff. I don't ask for details, don't even point out that he doesn't technically *have* a job since he quit *Creature Clinic*. Part of me wonders if he really did quit, or if he was fired. I'm on a high from everything that happened at school, and I don't want that to be ruined. Since it's just us three at home, Ismail begs Ammi to play Monopoly. He doesn't understand the rules very well, but he loves being the banker, being in charge of the money. I normally don't let him because he cheats, but today I don't argue and just set the board up.

'You're in a good mood,' Ammi says to me a few turns in.

I smile at her. I want to tell her about my coursework idea, but she would no doubt warn me off it, tell me to go with something safer. I rationalise that only Mr Voake will watch it. Oh, and the external examiners. And Stacey, probably. It'll be fine. It'll be good for me to get my feelings out on video.

'Just a nice YouTube comment,' I tell Ammi instead, looking down at my phone, where I've got the comments section for my latest video loaded up.

'You know you need to be careful with doing those videos, right?' she says quietly, as she moves her piece. 'If your father ever found out . . .'

'I know, I know,' I say quickly. 'Don't worry, it's not under my real name. And I only work on stuff when he's out, or when I know he's busy.'

She frowns at me.

I babble desperately. 'I know you said . . . that it's best to stop, but, Ammi, I . . . I can't. It's like the only thing that makes me –'

She reaches across the sofa and touches me on the wrist. 'No, moyna, it's OK. If you . . . if you enjoy it that much, keep doing it. Don't stop because of . . . because of him. I don't want him to suck the passion out of you too. Just . . . careful, yeah?'

I nod. 'You . . . you can do the same too, y'know?' I say enthusiastically. 'Now that Abbu's arranging that art course, you can . . . you can do what makes you happy too.'

She gives me a smile, which in turn makes me smile. It's nice to see her excited about something. I'm about to ask her more about the course, but Ismail cuts me off.

'Maani, it's your go!' he says. 'Ammi's in jail.' His voice is filled with glee.

Half an hour later I'm bankrupt, thanks to Ismail's made-up rules. I sit there on my phone while Ammi tries to gather enough money to unmortgage her properties. My battery's about to die so I rifle through my school bag for my portable charger. Tucked into the side pocket, I find the RSVP card from Mr Voake. Just looking at it makes me smile. I can't get over what a thoughtful gift it was. I also can't get his words out of my head.

Before I know it, I'm googling 'how late can you change your A-level choices?' A weird feeling starts up in my stomach as I read about people who changed their choices just before exams, and some who changed them a week into A levels. A butterfly-like feeling. Excitement. The possibility of changing my choice, of studying the subject I really want to study, doing what I really want to do, is making me feel so excited I honestly feel a bit sick.

I have to do it, right?

I need *something* in my life that isn't just misery. Ammi's even given me her blessing. Kind of. Abbu doesn't even have to know. I could just . . . pretend I'm still doing all the sciences. I could maybe keep biology and chemistry and *only* change physics to media studies. Physics isn't essential for becoming a vet. I could so get away with it.

A car pulls up outside. Ammi's head whips round, and we both see Abbu getting out of the car.

'Ismail, pack this up right now,' she says hurriedly. She sweeps all the houses and pieces off the board and throws them into the box.

'No!' Ismail cries. 'I was winning!'

Ammi frantically collects up the cards and shoves them into the box too, not in their designated slots, which I know she hates. She keeps flicking her gaze back to the window.

'Ismail, you already won!' I say, trying to stop his impending meltdown. 'Well done, you made Ammi bankrupt too. You know what winners get, don't you?'

'A prize?' he asks.

'Yes! And today's prize is . . . ice cream! C'mon, I'll get you some.' I leave Ammi hiding the game box away under the sofa and take Ismail to the kitchen. The front door opens.

'Everything OK?' Abbu asks as he walks in. He smiles at Ammi. A proper smile.

Ever since Ammi's conversation with Mrs Farook, Abbu has actually been in a good mood. Not just OK, not just passing for normal. But, like, over-the-top good. Much better than his usual good days. It's been both weird and brilliant. I genuinely think this is the beginning of change. The thing that he feared most has happened – the truth is out there. In a tiny form that Ammi made sure no one is really going to pay attention to, but it's out. And he knows that now that it's out like this, it could travel into the ears of the wrong people. And that's brought about the change in him that me and Ammi have been waiting for. He's actually changing for good. Permanently. I believe it. And, if that's happening, maybe he'll be more understanding about me? Maybe I could finally tell him I don't want to follow his career path, that I have literally zero interest in becoming a vet.

A little bud of hope blooms within me.

So much has been changing recently. I think . . . I honestly believe that Abbu would be open to this. If I could just gather up the courage to talk to him. To tell him that I want to drop the sciences and take media studies . . . If I show him some of the videos I've made. (He's never even seen one – when he found out about them, he was too mad to even bother watching one. I really think he might like them.) If I tell him how passionate I am about film-making, tell him that even Mr Voake thinks I'm talented . . . It could . . . it could happen. I wouldn't have to live like this any more.

I could change my future.

I could be in charge of it.

47

When I come down for breakfast, I find Abbu sitting at the head of the dining table, with Ammi and Ismail on either side. Before I can turn to leave, he calls me over to sit and eat with them. He says it so sharply I know I can't refuse. I pour myself some Shreddies and sit there eating in silence.

'Keep the phone line free today,' he says to Ammi. 'I'm due to hear back about that job. They didn't say whether they'd email or which number they'd call, so best to not use the phone.'

'OK,' she replies.

'It's just a formality,' he continues. 'I got strong feelings from the interviewer that the job is mine. Let's just hope their background check wasn't . . . too thorough.'

This makes me look up. Surely he can't be . . . referring to the Bad Nights?

'I know she's your friend, Amani. Well, ex-friend, I hope. But if Huda ends up being the reason I don't get this job, I will be furious.'

Ammi and I exchange a look. We both know that if he doesn't get this job, there'll be hell to pay.

Abbu stares at me, waiting for an answer, so I respond. 'I'm sure they won't look that deep,' I say. 'The blog was only sent to people in my year. No one else would care about seeing it.'

'And if they *did* find it,' Ammi jumps in quickly, 'they'd know it's just a pack of lies, right?' She looks at me intently, so I have to nod.

'I just can't believe she'd do something so stupid.' Abbu shakes his head and forks his scrambled eggs. 'Does she have no respect? Well, I guess not, with the way she's been brought up. There's something about her parents – her foster parents, I mean – that's never sat right with me.'

I stare at him, gobsmacked. I know he wants to trash-talk Huda, but now he's slagging off Ali and Nafisah too?

'They're so . . . inappropriate,' he expands, with a dismissive wave of his hand. 'Kissing, hugging, in *public*. It's just wrong. Some things should stay private.'

Like the bruises all over Ammi's body. Like how we're all so fucking terrified of Abbu. Like how sometimes I wish he was dead.

'Ismail, hurry up and eat your Weetabix. You're going to be late for school,' Ammi says, thankfully ending his monologue.

'I don't want Weetabix!' Ismail moans, pushing his almost full bowl away. 'I want pancakes!'

Ammi tuts, reaching over and sliding the bowl back towards him. 'We have to leave in ten minutes. Eat your breakfast. Or I'll have to feed you it like a baby.'

'No!' Ismail says, leaning back in his chair and folding his arms. 'I don't want it!'

'Ismail!' Ammi chides. 'This is the same breakfast you have every day – why is it suddenly not good enough?'

'It's disgusting!' Ismail says. 'I want what Abbu has.'

'That's a grown-up breakfast. You need energy to keep you going through the day – that's what Weetabix is for. C'mon, just eat it. Do you want some more hot milk?'

'I want a big-man breakfast!'

Abbu laughs. Actually laughs. He ruffles Ismail's hair. 'You can have a big-man breakfast when you're a big man, son.'

'I am!' Ismail says, sitting up in his chair. 'Look how much I growed. I'm a big man now. I need a big-man breakfast.'

He wants to be just like Abbu, and the thought of that makes me want to puke my Shreddies all over the table.

'How about I put some fruit in it?' Ammi asks. She's clearly exasperated but knows Ismail's in a mood that won't be tamed easily.

'No! Fruit is for girls. I hate it!'

Abbu laughs again, which makes me want to scream.

'I want the same as Abbu!' Ismail crosses his arms, huffs and sits back in his chair, pursing his lips.

'Just make him some eggs, Shirin,' Abbu says, scrolling on his phone. 'It won't take long.'

Ammi and I share a look. Her expression tells me she's just as worried as I am. Ismail is getting worse by the day. I can't even tell when the switch happened. He was such a sweet kid, and now for some reason he's turned into a brat. I need to stop this. I need him to realise that Abbu is *not* a good role model. His behaviour shouldn't be copied. But how do you tell that to a five-year-old?

I leave the room wordlessly, putting my bowl in the sink as Ammi cracks an egg into a pan.

In assembly Mr Bach gives us a lecture about the Burn Blog. He goes on and on about how harmful rumours are, how the school has a duty of care towards us and so will investigate everything thoroughly. I slouch down in my seat, the tips of my ears burning. I can feel people looking at me, trying to see my arm. The wound's healed enough that I've stopped putting the bandage on it, but I don't dare take my blazer off at school.

'The site has been blocked, and as always, we will be monitoring your internet activity on school computers and Wi-Fi,' Mr Bach says. 'Just know that we *will* find the person or people behind this blog. And they *will* be dealt with. If anyone has any information, I urge you to come and talk to me.'

I turn my head and find Huda already looking right at me. There's a weird expression on her face. Not anger, not happiness, not even the high-and-mighty look she had when releasing the blog post. She looks . . . sad. It's the only way I can explain it. I've only seen her this sad once before – when she was asking for help with her Perfect Daughter plan. Is it weird that I feel almost *bad* that I haven't asked her how she's feeling lately? I know she's probably having a tough time with her carers and the baby, and as her best friend I should really check in, even if I'm mad.

But no. She doesn't deserve that. She hasn't even *tried* to make contact with me since she wrecked my life. There's no way I'm going crawling to her. I have Maggie now. She sits next to me in assembly, alternating between whispering, 'I wish that projector thing would happen again,' and resting her head on my shoulder to sleep.

I sit with Maggie and her friends at lunch, as I've been doing for the past few days. They're nice people, and we've already made plans to go to the cinema as a group during study leave. We're halfway through our lunches when whispers start up around us. I immediately assume they're about me, about the blog post, so I shrink down in my seat, adjusting my headscarf – a nervous habit.

'Did you hear that?' Juwairiyya, one of Maggie's friends, asks excitedly, looking at a couple of boys who are rushing out of the canteen, laughing.

We all look at her.

'Something's going down over by the humanities block! Sounds like a prank war thing!' She starts hurriedly packing up her stuff. Everyone else does the same. I want to stay sitting here, finish off my Doritos. I don't want any part in this prank war. It's doing my head in. I try to stand my ground, but Maggie tugs on my arm so much that I literally have no choice but to go.

As we approach the humanities block, we can see a crowd outside the doors. Maggie speeds up; I almost trip over. We arrive at the back of a deep circle of students – mostly Year Elevens. Maggie and I crane our necks, but we can't see anything.

'I think Backpack's in the middle!' Maggie says, after jumping to get a look at the centre.

A girl in front of us turns around, a huge grin on her face. 'He's caught them!' she says with a weird glee. 'He's caught the ones doing the pranks!'

This lights a fire inside Maggie; she doubles her efforts to get into the middle and manages to drag us a little bit further in – it involves stepping on a few feet, and lots of people swearing at us, but we finally get to a spot where we can just about see Mr Bach standing facing someone. I can't quite make out who, no matter how much I crane my neck. Mr Bach's voice booms over the crowd though.

'. . . Disgusting behaviour. I warned you all about what would happen if this continued. Do you have ANY IDEA how much damage you've caused?'

'What did they do?' I ask Maggie, even though I know she doesn't know.

She ignores me. Her phone is out now, filming, as are a lot of other people in the circle.

'Right, LISTEN UP!' Mr Bach booms. 'Everyone to the hall. NOW.' There's so much anger in his voice, people get scared and start shuffling. 'Anyone not in the hall within five minutes will be suspended!' he adds.

People scatter immediately.

I've never seen the hall so packed. There's no chairs out, because of the haste, but Maggie and I have luckily managed to find a spot on the floor. Students from all years are standing around the edges of the hall, spilling out of the open doors.

'I wonder what happened,' Maggie says. 'What could have made Backpack mad enough to bring *everyone* here?'

The gossip mills had been churning all the way to the hall, and someone told us that the person Mr Bach was shouting at was Ezra. I don't know why he'd keep going with the pranks, given that he's already been caught and put in isolation for a few days. Although someone else said his parents are getting a divorce, and that's why he's been acting out. Who knows? You don't see me making life hell for the teachers, and look at how *my* parents are.

Mr Bach doesn't even come into the hall in the end. No one spots Ezra either. Everyone's too busy gossiping about what his punishment is gonna be, trying to figure out what prank it was that he actually pulled, or was trying to pull (I've heard so many different stories, I don't know what to believe), to notice Ms Powrie walk onto the stage. She's not a teacher to be ignored though, and within seconds she's yelling, 'SILENCE!' Everyone falls silent immediately.

'There's been an *incident* involving the school's water supply,' she says. 'And legally we're not allowed to keep you on campus any more. Everyone is to return home. Or just leave the site. We don't really care where you go, as long as it's not here.'

No one laughs. Because even though it's funny, Ms Powrie gets super annoyed if you laugh at anything she says.

'There are teachers posted at all the doors, with a letter for each of you to take home, explaining the situation. Make sure to take one on your way out.' She leaves the stage and voices erupt all over the hall.

'Oh my God!!' Maggie squeals. 'What did Ezra do to the *water*? How do you even get access to that sort of thing?'

'EVERYONE. OUT!' Ms Powrie roars again.

This time it has the desired effect and everyone scatters.

'I'm gonna go find out what happened,' Maggie says as we leave the hall. 'Wanna come?'

'Nah,' I reply. 'Think I'm just gonna go home and watch Netflix.' I don't tell her that I'm trying to keep away from the gossip, that I'm fed up of it. But I can see that Maggie is all hopped up on the excitement of everything. And, deep down, I really *do* want to know what Ezra did to make them close the entire school.

'Text me when you find out, yeah?' I say to her, just before she bounds off after the group of girls we sit with at lunch. As they disappear around the corner, I spot a familiar figure.

Huda.

She's walking along, alone. As if she can sense me, she looks up and our eyes meet. It's the second time we've had a moment like this today. I expect her to drop her gaze and walk off, but instead . . . she heads my way. I look around, thinking she *must* be going to someone else, but nope, it's only me here. The closer she gets to me, the more I feel anger rising up.

'Hey, Maani,' she says when we're a metre apart.

I don't respond. I don't know what to say. I don't know why she's here. I hate that I just want to hug her right now. To hold her tight and make everything go back to the way it was.

'You OK?' she asks. There's hesitation in her voice.

And then I get it. I get why she's here. Why she's here *now*.

'You worried I'm gonna grass on you?' I ask her. After that assembly, she's got to be terrified of being found out. Of being expelled before her exams. That's the only reason she's here. She doesn't care how I am.

'What? No, of course not.'

'Because I'm such a pushover, right?' I ask. 'I'd never stand up and say anything.'

'That's not what I said. I'd never say that about you.'

'But you might *type it*, right?' I ask with a sneer.

307

'Amani, no. Look, I just . . . I want to apologise.'

I pause, my insults dying in my mouth. 'What?'

She takes a breath, looks around awkwardly. 'I just . . . I'm sorry. For everything. I shouldn't have done it. It was stupid, I wasn't thinking.'

It's what I've been waiting to hear from her, but somehow it doesn't feel like enough.

'I miss you,' she continues. 'I miss sitting next to you in class. I miss hanging out with you, miss teasing you about your terrible taste in snacks.'

This is where I'm supposed to tell her I miss her too, because I do. But somehow something else comes out. 'It's taken you *five days* to tell me this?'

Huda's eyes widen in surprise, and weirdly that makes me feel good – I'm showing her I'm not the weak little pushover she thinks I am.

'Do you know what's happened in those five days?' I ask. 'Do you know how much chaos your stupid little *mistake* caused?' I take a breath, waiting for her to butt in so I can cut her off and feel good, but she doesn't even try – just stands there staring. 'The school called my mum in, Huda. They interrogated her, put her on the spot. They've . . . they were going to call social services. They were going to split my family up, Huda. I was terrified.'

'Shit, Amani. I feel terrible.'

'So you should!' The anger's rising within me again. I've been wanting to get this out, to say this to her ever since that stupid blog went out. When we had that first fight, I was in shock, too emotional. But now . . .

'You said that you didn't regret it – that you thought you were doing the *right thing*. I tried to see where you were coming from, I really did. But I can't. Because no best friend would ever do what you did. No *decent* person would ever do that – feed off other people's misery. You've made things worse, Huda. So much worse.'

She doesn't reply, just looks at me with a downturned mouth and tears in her eyes. It makes me madder than ever. I groan in frustration.

'Just do everyone a favour and fuck off, Huda. Honestly, the only good thing about this past week has been *not* having you in my life,' I spit. 'Maybe you *were* right. Maybe it did do *some* good.'

I don't give her a chance to reply. Just walk off towards the gate. As soon as she's out of my sight, the adrenaline inside me disappears, and I feel like shit.

48

Neither of my parents are home when I get there. It's only one o'clock, so they're both probably still at work. I really need to start paying more attention to Abbu's schedule – it's been all over the place recently. I guess it'll settle down if he gets this job he's interviewed for. God, I hope he gets the job.

I walk in, dump my bag and shoes and go into the living room. I'm still reeling from the fight with Huda. I both wish I'd said more and wish I hadn't said so much. It's weird, the house being so quiet. I could do so much. Watch TV, bake a cake, clean the house . . . revise? I think I really do just want to lie in bed and watch *Brooklyn Nine-Nine* though. I walk into the living room and check the pile of post that's stacked on the table. I hear a car door slam. Followed closely by another. I crane my head and look out of the window, to our driveway, where both of my parents' cars have suddenly appeared. Fear strikes in my heart and I duck down, even though I'm not doing anything wrong by being here. I even have a letter to prove – oh shit. Guess who forgot to pick up the letter on her way out of school! Shit shit shit! I literally can't believe this. Without that letter, I can't guarantee my parents will believe my excuse. After Ammi got called in to

310

discuss my grades, they've both been on at me to focus on schoolwork. If they find me here, and Abbu's in a bad mood, then it's all going to go to hell. I should have just gone straight upstairs. They can't see me here. They can't. I could risk running upstairs, but I might not make it to my room before the front door opens.

The front door opens.

I panic and wriggle behind the sofa, kneeling on the floor and curling myself into as tight a ball as I can. I'm hoping they'll go into the kitchen and close the door. That way I can sneak up the stairs quietly without being seen.

'I was just asking why you seem so happy, with the whistling and everything,' I hear Abbu say as they walk in through the front door. 'There's no need to be defensive.'

'Do I need a reason to be in a good mood?' Ammi asks, with a nervous laugh. I hear her drop her keys into the bowl we keep by the door.

'I'm just taking an interest,' he says. His voice has an edge to it.

'It was nothing special,' she expands. 'Just a good day at work. Friendly customers, not too busy.'

'Aren't you going to ask how *my* day was?' Abbu asks after a few seconds' pause.

Ammi responds immediately. 'I was *just* about to ask about your day.' There's a tightness in her voice that I recognise all too well.

Please not here. Not now. Please don't start something, Abbu.

They both walk into the living room. Damn, there goes my hope of sneaking upstairs.

'Did you talk to your manager about getting those extra hours?' he asks, ignoring Ammi completely.

'I did,' she replies carefully. 'I was going to talk to you about it tonight. They've offered me an extra day in the week, and a few extra hours on my other shifts. They gave me a printed rota – I can show you later.'

'Why later? Why not now?' he asks.

'I just thought you might . . . have better things to do.'

'Or . . . or you're hiding things from me.'

'What? What would I be hiding from you?'

'Exactly. That's what I'm asking.'

It's torture kneeling behind the sofa, having to listen to this. I try telling myself that they're just talking. It's not going to escalate. Abbu's been good recently. We haven't had a Bad Night since Ammi spoke to Mrs Farook. The streak is going to continue. They'll get past this, they will.

'Why don't I just look for myself, if you won't tell me what you're hiding?' Abbu says. I hear his footsteps and then rustling.

'I'm not hiding anything from you, I promise!' Ammi says. 'Please . . . please don't go through my bag!'

'Why not? If you're not hiding anything from me.'

She pauses for a second; she knows not to fight him. 'I proved that I don't hide things from you the other day, didn't I? I told you what happened at Amani's school.'

Abbu doesn't reply. I can hear him on the other side of the room, rifling through Ammi's bag and then unfolding some paper. 'What's this then?' he asks.

'That's . . . a job application,' Ammi says carefully. 'My

manager thinks I could be a supervisor. Now that I'll be doing more hours. It's a decent pay rise. I just need to fill –'

'What's wrong with your current position?' Abbu's voice is at the highest level of danger. I feel myself tensing up even more.

'Nothing. It's just a few more responsibilities. It'll be good on –'

'What about your *responsibilities* at home?'

'I can do both.'

Abbu's quiet for a few seconds and I'm praying it's all over.

'You can't apply for this job,' he says forcefully.

'But . . . it's not any different than what I'm doing now. Now that I'm getting more hours.'

'You can't get those extra hours either.'

'But . . . but you said!'

'That was before!' he shouts. Violent shouting. Bad Night shouting. 'That was before those idiots rejected me for the job. You can't get extra hours now. You need to be at home.'

Abbu didn't get the job? Shit.

'Surely this means I *need* the extra hours,' Ammi says carefully. 'If I'm going to be the only –'

The sound of the slap reverberates around the room, and I wince. I screw my eyes shut and pray. *Please please please let this be over soon.*

'I know what you're doing,' Abbu growls.

My heart spikes, thinking he's noticed me. I peek around the edge of the sofa and he's still looking at Ammi, the application form in his hand. Ammi's hand is over her cheek. I retreat again.

'You're planning to leave, aren't you?' he says.

'What?!' she squeaks.

'The pay rise . . . You wanting to keep your own bank account . . . You're trying to get enough money to leave me, aren't you?'

'What? No! That's not –' She squeals instead of finishing her sentence. Abbu's probably got her by the wrist now.

'You think I'm an idiot?' he hisses. 'I know what you're doing and you're not going to get away with it. Tell me the truth – did you say something to those teachers?'

Ammi whimpers. 'No, I swear. I swear, I haven't said anything to anyone. I'm not planning anything.' She lets out another little squeal, but this one of relief. Her words have satisfied him.

'You know you wouldn't be able to cope on your own, right?' he says. 'Your stupid little supermarket job won't support two kids. You'd be homeless without me. You'd be broke.'

Ammi doesn't say anything.

'So you go for this job, save up your money and leave, and that's the life ahead of you. A life of *nothing*. You are *nothing* without me. You got that?'

'Yes,' she whispers so faintly I barely hear.

'Good. Remember that. Now, about that form . . .'

The sound of paper being torn into pieces rips through the room.

'I think it would be best if you quit your job altogether.'

'What?! But –'

'But nothing. This isn't up for discussion. You can't be selfish when you've got a family to think of. You're handing in your notice tomorrow.'

This is normally the time during the fight that Ammi succumbs, goes all meek and agrees to whatever Abbu wants,

314

because that's the only way to make it end. But I know how much that job means to her, and I can tell she's not going to take this lying down.

'That's not your decision to make,' she says quietly but firmly.

'*What* did you just say?' he growls.

Oh God. I wrap my arms tighter around myself.

'My job doesn't affect anything at home. I make sure of it,' Ammi says. 'I cook, I clean, I look after the kids. I even . . . I even dealt with Amani's school. You can't tell me I'm doing anything wrong. I won't go after the supervisor position, I'll even give up that art course you signed me up for, but you can't take my job away from me.'

'I can do whatever the fuck I want,' Abbu says.

Ammi lets out a pained noise; I can't tell exactly what he's doing to her, but it sounds horrible.

'Stop it! Please! You're hurting me,' she pleads.

There's a sound of a scuffle, and I hear the table scrape against the floor.

'DID YOU JUST FUCKING PUSH ME?!' Abbu bellows.

'I didn't mean –' She doesn't even manage to get her words out before the first blow comes. She lets out a cry, but that only seems to spur him on.

'Think you can fucking push me around?' He punches her so hard it sounds like he's winded her. 'I could have fucking fallen over, hit my head. I COULD HAVE DIED!'

Ammi's breath splutters as she continues to try to reason with him. A few seconds later I hear her body fall to the floor.

'Please, don't!' she cries, desperation lacing her hoarse voice.

But it doesn't work. It never works.

The first kick comes.

Then the second.

Then the third.

'DON'T.' *Kick.* 'FUCKING.' *Kick.* 'TALK.' *Kick.* 'BACK.' *Kick.* 'TO.' *Kick.* 'ME.' *Kick.*

I can't be here any more. I can't stand it. Their usual arguments are never this bad. Even the dinner where he spilled food over her was nothing compared to this. I've never been close enough to hear the sound of his foot against her stomach, how her sobs sound up close. I've never felt more helpless than I do right now.

I need to get away. I need to leave right now.

I peer around the edge of the sofa to check whether I could make a break for it without being noticed, but somehow I become transfixed watching them. Part of me is telling myself to say something, to stop this RIGHT NOW, but the bigger part of me is screaming at me to run, to get as far away from this scene as I can, to keep burying my head in the sand. I'm the worst daughter ever. I know I should jump up and stop him, that if I said something, just showed myself, he'd back down.

He's looking down at Ammi, who's curled up in a ball, letting him do whatever he wants to her. She moves her arm slightly, and I see her face. There's a cut on her head, already bleeding.

She's looking right at me.

I suck in a breath.

Her eyes widen. I'm somehow paralysed.

'RUN!' she mouths at me.

I should do it, I know. But her expression . . . the fear in *her* eyes. I can't leave her like this; I'd never forgive myself. I need to be brave. I need to be brave for her. I can stop this. I've done it before. I need to stop it NOW. I look up at Abbu; there's an animal look on his face – it scares me to my soul. At dinner the other day, he looked as if he was enjoying it. Now it's just pure anger. I know me just *saying* something isn't going to be enough to make it go away. I need to *do* something.

He raises his foot again, but before he can kick her, before I even know what's happening, I'm charging at him.

'STOP!' I roar as my hands connect with his back. I push him hard enough for him to stumble. But he doesn't fall. He whips his head around and there's that look again, the one of pure rage – eyes wide, teeth bared.

His eyes don't really focus on me. Before I know it, he's got his fingers digging into my upper arm.

'GET OUT OF HERE!' he shouts. He digs his fingers so deep I gasp in pain, and then . . . and then he shoves me.

But I spring back. I reset my balance as he turns back to Ammi, who's struggling to get up off the floor. I grab his arm again, try to do it as hard as he did with me.

'Abbu, please, stop!' I beg. Why isn't he listening? Why isn't he stopping? I had the power last time. Me being there helped last time.

'Amani!' he shouts. He turns to face me, and I don't even get to see if his expression has changed before he slaps me. The force of the blow makes me lose my balance again and I stumble back, falling on the sofa.

He *hit* me.

Abbu slapped me.

49

'GET AWAY FROM HER!' Ammi's voice suddenly rises above everything. Next thing I know, she's in front of me, shielding me from Abbu, who's standing there, panting, glaring at her.

'You fucki—' he starts. He looks as if he's about to lunge at her, but Ammi raises her hand. She holds her hand palm out towards him – the same gesture she uses on Ismail to get him to stop running. It works on Abbu too. I stand up, right behind Ammi. She uses her other hand as a barrier between me and Abbu, protecting me.

'You touch her again, and you'll regret it,' she says with a confidence I've never heard from her. She's never stood up to him like this.

'You fucking bitch!' He lunges at her again.

I scream, and cower. Ammi shoves the table towards him and it connects with his leg, wiping him out. There's a crash as he falls to the floor with a grunt.

'Amani, quick!' Ammi says. She grabs my hand and pulls me along. I don't know what's happening, or what to say, so I just let myself be pulled. It's like I'm not even in my body any more, not in charge of my movements.

Ammi pulls me towards the front door, then turns her head to look back at Abbu.

'Shit!' she says. 'He's coming.'

Ammi swore.

I've never heard her swear before.

'YOU FUCKING BITCHES!' Abbu screams from the living room. The sound of his feet is thunder.

'Amani, quick!' Ammi says. We're too far away from the front door. But not from the downstairs bathroom. She quickly shoves me inside, pulls the door behind us and locks it.

Within seconds, Abbu is pounding on the door so hard I'm sure he's going to actually break through. He's yelling non-stop – I can barely register the actual words over the pounding in my ears.

'Oh God,' I say without meaning to. 'Oh God, oh God, oh God.'

I look to Ammi, hoping she's got some sort of plan, but she's just staring, eyes wide, face streaked with melting mascara.

'Ammi . . .' I say. I grab her hand and squeeze it. It's the first thing that comes to mind. I don't realise how badly I'm shaking until our hands meet.

'YOU DUMB BITCH, GET OUT HERE RIGHT FUCKING NOW.'

More terrifying bangs on the door.

'He's going to break it!' I squeak. 'He's going to get in here. Ammi, what do we do?'

I look at her, hoping she has a plan.

'Do you have your phone on you?' she asks me quickly.

I nod, and fumble in my blazer pocket. I unlock it and hand it to her.

She taps on the screen with a trembling hand. She brings the phone to her ear. 'P-police, please,' she says in response to a voice on the other end.

50

Ammi quickly gives our address, and the call handler assures her that help is on the way. They keep Ammi on the phone, talking to her over the noise of Abbu banging on the door and shouting threats, and everything spills out: how this has been going on for years, how Abbu wants to control her, stop her from working, how he . . . how he hit me. Ammi's crying and shaking, curled up in the corner of the bathroom, between the wall and the sink. I kneel in front of her, not knowing what to do, how to help. I feel so useless. Abbu's voice is as loud as ever, his blows haven't got weaker, even though we've been in here for, like, ten minutes.

'Please hurry!' Ammi says down the phone again. 'The back door's unlocked. They can come through there. Just *please* . . .' She sobs.

I tear off some toilet tissue and wipe her face. She makes eye contact with me, and there's so much vulnerability in her expression – she looks like Ismail after a Bad Night. I hold the tissue up to her nose and she blows. We both flinch when there's a different loud thudding outside. But not on the bathroom door; somewhere further in the background.

'I think they're here,' Ammi whispers into the phone.

There's a commotion outside. Voices, lots of them, deep and growly, and then, above them all, Abbu.

'WHAT THE FUCK?' he shouts. 'I HAVEN'T ASSAULTED ANYONE! THAT LYING FUCKING BITCH!'

There's another thud at the door; Ammi and I yelp. The call handler says something to her, but we can't tear our eyes away from the door. The last blow sounded like something had splintered. More shuffling. More deep voices. More of Abbu yelling. His voice sounds like it's moving further away though.

There's silence. Eerie, scary silence. Even the call handler has stopped speaking.

Then two gentle knocks on the door. Ammi and I yelp again.

'It's the police,' a voice says. 'It's safe. You can come out now.'

I look at Ammi – her face is wet and sticky. There's a bruise already blooming on her cheek, and a bleeding cut on her head. Her eyes are wide, bewildered. She looks right at me.

'We're safe, Ammi. It's over.'

51

Ammi's in the living room talking to the police. She's . . . she's actually doing it. She's done it. She's told someone. Someone official now knows the horrible truth of our family. And Abbu's not here to deny or twist the truth, or to scare her out of speaking up. The police have taken him away. Arrested him for assault.

Abbu's been arrested.

Abbu hit me.

He would have done worse, maybe, if Ammi hadn't stepped in.

This whole afternoon has been so surreal. I still can't believe Ammi's talking to the *police* about Abbu. They're going to talk to me next. I wanted to sit with Ammi while she spoke to them, but she said there were things she had to say that she didn't want me to hear. My hand keeps inching towards the door handle. The truth is, I'm scared. I'm scared this is going to be a repeat of Ammi's meeting with Mrs Farook. That she will lie and insist everything's fine. That she'll protect Abbu once again. I'm scared this isn't the end at all. That I'm getting my hopes up for nothing. But then I have to remind myself that Ammi called the police herself. She's doing this on *her* terms now. And I have to respect that.

There's a knock at the front door, and the sound makes me

jump. My mind immediately races to the idea that it might be Abbu. That he's escaped the police and come back to finish Ammi and me off. But of course, if that were true, there's no way he'd be knocking.

Through the frosted glass, I see a woman wearing a blue headscarf, turban-style, and a smaller figure next to her.

'Salaam, Nafisah,' I say, opening the door. 'Thanks for picking Ismail up.'

She launches herself at me, pulling me into a hug. Her belly is so big it makes the hug awkward, but still lovely. I close my eyes and relax a little.

'Oh my poor baby, what's happening, are you OK? Why is there a police car outside?' She pulls away too soon, holds me by the upper arms and inspects me, just like a typical auntie.

'Where's Abbu?' Ismail asks grumpily.

I look down at his face, just so thankful that he wasn't here today. That he didn't witness what I just witnessed. I try to wrap him in a hug, but he pushes me away.

'Where's Abbu?' he asks again. 'He was supposed to pick me up. He *always* picks me up on Tuesdays!'

I look at Nafisah, and she frowns. I only gave her a very brief explanation when I called her earlier, because I didn't think I could tell her everything over the phone. With Ismail, though, I don't think I could ever tell him the truth. The full truth anyway. So instead, like I always do, I try to distract him.

'Hey,' I say, bending over so we're eye to eye. 'How do you feel about helping me make another –'

'I want Abbu!' Ismail screams. He throws his bag down on the ground and it hits me on my toes.

I jump up, yelping in pain. 'Ismail!' I say. 'That really hurt!'

He doesn't say anything, just stands there with the grumpiest look on his face. He huffs and crosses his arms, looking down.

Nafisah looks from me to him. She squats down to his level and gives him a poke in the side. 'How about you and I bake some cakes? Eh? Chocolate ones?' she asks him.

'No!' Ismail replies, actually stomping his foot. 'I WANT ABBU!'

'Ismail, baby, c'mon . . .' Nafisah tries.

'I hate you, you bitch!' Ismail yells in her face.

I'm too shocked to respond. Even Nafisah is stunned. We just stare with our mouths open as Ismail runs upstairs and into his room.

'I'm so sorry,' I tell Nafisah. 'I really don't know what's happening with him.'

'Don't be silly, not your fault.' She groans as she gets up. I reach out and help her. 'Oh, thanks, sweetie. God, I can't wait for this baby to come out so I can move like a normal person again.'

'Not long now, eh?' I ask.

'Four *long* weeks,' she says.

I'm about to say how she should enjoy this time while she can, but she stops me with a pointed stare. 'You wanna catch me up now?'

I pause. What do I tell her? She's seen the police car outside, she knows Abbu's not around, I don't know how much longer I can keep the truth from her. And, come to think of it, Ammi probably *needs* her best friend right now. Someone outside of the family she can talk to.

'Let's get some tea,' I say, leading her to the kitchen.

52

Nafisah tries ringing Huda to come and help look after Ismail, but she doesn't pick up, which I'm glad for. Though I sort of *do* wish she was here right now. She's always been the person I'd go to in a crisis, and it feels weird to be going through all this without her even knowing. I stick on *Frozen 2* upstairs on my laptop and Ismail sits watching it with a pile of snacks. It feels like I'm rewarding him for bad behaviour, but none of this is his fault, and honestly, it's probably the only way to keep him occupied. The police finish speaking to Ammi and she comes out of the living room, puffy-faced and sniffling. I hug her right away; she yelps – maybe in surprise, maybe from pain.

'Are you OK?' I whisper in her ear.

'Yes, moyna, I'm . . . I'm OK.'

'I'm so proud of you,' I blurt.

She laughs a little as she pulls away. 'I think I'm the one who's supposed to say that.'

'Works both ways,' I tell her.

'They want to speak to you now,' she says after a second of silence. 'They've said I can sit with you. Just a few questions. If you don't want to, then –'

'No, it's fine. I can do this.' I take her hand and squeeze.

We sit side by side on the sofa as DC Burns asks me to go over what happened today, to describe how life's been at home. It feels weird . . . I'm hesitant to say anything. After all, that's been the motto for years: never tell anyone anything, pretend it's not happening, just get on with it. But now, this woman is asking, and Ammi is holding my hand, encouraging me to go on. It's like my entire world has been turned upside down in the past few hours.

But I do it. I tell them everything.

The police finally leave a few hours later. Nafisah, Ammi and I do our prayers together. I say an extra prayer thanking God for saving us today, asking Him to protect us all. We're all exhausted – Ammi in particular. She said she didn't want to go to the hospital to get checked out, but I see her wince every time she moves. Nafisah gets up from her prayer mat and goes to the loo. Ammi and I stay sitting on ours in silence. It's an awkward silence. A silence filled with things we should say, things we need to say. On any other day, we'd pretend the awkwardness didn't exist. But it's not an ordinary day.

'Are you OK?' I pluck up the courage to ask. 'Like, *really* OK?'

She turns to me; her face is sad, tired, bruised. 'I don't know,' she says quietly.

That does it. The dam inside me breaks, all the guilt comes pouring out.

'I'm so sorry, Ammi. I should have . . . I should have stepped in earlier, before he got so angry. Or maybe I shouldn't have stepped in at all? I know you said it's best to let him just get on with it. But . . . I was so scared, Ammi. There was this . . . look on his face. I've never been that scared of him. Of anything. I was just . . . I was frozen. I should have done something earlier. Something better.'

'No, no, don't be sorry,' she says, reaching over and squeezing my hand. '*I'm* sorry you had to witness that. I'm sorry you've had to put up with this for so long . . .' She takes a breath. 'I'm so sorry he hurt you. I should have done better. I should have protected you. I –'

'What? No. No no no. You need to stop blaming yourself, Ammi. None of this is on you. It's on Abbu. I've realised . . .' I take a breath. 'I'm sorry I've put it all on you. I kept asking why *you* don't leave, why *you* put up with it. When in reality *none* of this is on you. I should have been asking *him* these questions. Should've been asking why he can't stop being such a . . . monster.'

She takes a sniffly breath. 'Well, I just hope . . . that it's over now. Today was the last straw, Amani. All these years . . . I told myself it was best for you and Ismail, that children are better off with both parents in their life. But to think he could . . . *hurt* you. I'll never forgive myself for letting things go this far.'

'It was all *him*, Ammi. Not you. You didn't make him like this. You couldn't have changed him. And anyway, it's not on you to change him. It's not your responsibility. I'm just . . . I'm glad he's gone. I hope he never comes back.'

'He won't,' she says firmly. 'The police helped me to file an injunction. It's going to stop him coming to the house, or near us wherever we are. At least until we get things sorted out.'

Nafisah clears her throat from the doorway. 'I wasn't listening, I promise,' she says quickly when Ammi and I look over. 'Well, OK, I heard that last bit. I just wanted to say that you all should come and stay with us for a few days. It might make you feel a bit safer. He doesn't know where our house is, does he, Amani?'

I shake my head. Huda's family moved about a year ago, and Abbu's never dropped me off or picked me up from there.

'Are you sure, Nafisah?' Ammi asks. 'We'll be all right here, with the injunction and everything.'

'Don't be silly, what are best friends for?' Nafisah says. 'Huda's going to be *thrilled*, eh, Amani?'

Oh God, I'm going to be living with Huda? Only this morning, we had a huge argument; I said some super horrible things. Things I didn't even really mean. I was just angry. She tried to apologise, and I bit her head off.

And now we're going to be living together.

During the drive to Huda's house, I try to come up with things to say to her. Ismail's chattering away excitedly next to me about how he's going to play Monopoly with Huda every day. He made sure I brought my camera equipment so we can make more videos together. The excitement of the move finally got him to stop whining about Abbu, so Ammi and I don't even try to get him to shut up now. I'd have thought his voice would be a great distraction, but I'm fixating on what I'll say to Huda, and how she'll react. When Nafisah tells her we're going to be sleeping in the same house – Huda and I in the same room, probably – will she get angry? Will she shout? Say that she doesn't want to share her space with a bitch like me?

We pull up, and it's too late to think about it. Time to go live it. I take a deep breath and help Ammi unload the car.

'Huda?' Nafisah calls as soon as she opens the front door. 'Why have you been ignoring my calls? I've got a surprise for you!' She says it all sing-songy, as if this is something Huda is going to like. Little does Nafisah know.

I follow Nafisah up the stairs with our bags. Panic builds in my stomach with every step.

'Huda?' Nafisah calls again. She knocks on Huda's door and then enters.

Deep breath. I can do this. Well, I have no choice. I step in too.

The room's empty.

Nafisah and I look around. The wardrobe doors are open, the hangers inside mostly bare. Huda's laptop, which she keeps on her desk at all times, is gone, as are the photo frames that are normally there.

'What's going on?' Nafisah asks, looking around, as if Huda's about to pop out suddenly. She walks towards the bed, where there's a bright green Post-it note stuck on the white pillow. I follow and read the note over her shoulder.

Nafisah, Ali,
I know I should explain, but all I can say is sorry.
Huda

'What?' Nafisah says. Her head whips up. She looks at me, then at the empty wardrobes. 'Has she . . . has she run away?'

My heart constricts. Run away? Would Huda really take such a huge step?

'Oh God, where could she have gone? Has something happened? Is everything OK at school?' Nafisah starts babbling, the panic rising in her voice.

I should tell Nafisah that Huda and I aren't on speaking terms right now, that I have no idea what's going on in her life, that the last time we spoke I shouted at her. But I can see how upset Nafisah is – her frown lines and her creased watery eyes. I can't add to her stress. It's not safe, with the baby.

'Why don't you come and sit down?' I say, leading her to the bed. 'I'm sure everything's fine. You know how Huda is. She's probably just out doing something, hanging out with someone. Look, I'll call her.' I try her phone. It just rings and rings.

'She's taken her *clothes*, Amani. That's not normal. I know she's not the type to constantly update me on where she is and when she'll be back, and that's fine. We give her her freedom, but this . . . with the note and the missing clothes. What else could it mean?'

'Maybe . . . maybe she went to . . . do laundry?' I suggest. 'And the note was . . . um . . . sorry for not doing it earlier?'

Nafisah just gives me a look.

'Look, Nafisah, it'll be fine. This is Huda we're talking about. She's going to be OK.'

'Was she . . . upset or anything? Anything going on that would make her want to . . . to run away? You know her better than anyone, Amani.'

I should tell her. I should tell her about the Perfect Daughter plan. About how Huda's feeling threatened by the baby, about how worried she is that Nafisah and Ali won't want her around after it's born. I should tell Nafisah about the blog, about how

331

Huda and I have fallen out. It's the best way to find Huda, to give Nafisah all the information. But it's also the one thing that Huda would want me NOT to do. I know she betrayed me by spilling my secret because she thought it was the best thing to do, but I won't make that mistake.

'Nafisah, I'm sure we're worrying about nothing. I'll go out and look for her. You stay here. Where's Ali?'

'I called him before we left your house; he was at work, but he's on his way home now.'

'OK, good,' I say, getting up off the bed. 'You stay here with Ammi. I'll go and look for Huda. I'm sure she'll come home soon, laughing at us all for freaking out over nothing.'

'I hope so,' Nafisah whispers. 'I couldn't bear for anything to happen to her.'

I wish I could capture it on film – Nafisah's face filled with worry, the love in her voice as she talks about Huda. It's something I wish Huda could see, could understand.

'I'll find her, I promise,' I say.

53

I go to school first. I scurry around, checking all the loos, the canteen, and the bench we always sit at. I bump into a man in a hi-vis jacket who asks me what the hell I'm doing and don't I know the school is closed. I run away without answering. After that, I try our usual hang-out places. There aren't many, since nowadays we just go to her house, but I think back to where we used to go when we were younger, in the vague hope that maybe she's gone there. There's a park we visited every sunny day the first few summers of secondary school. It was a tiny, crappy park. The swings got wrapped around the top bar almost every week, the spring horses were too small for us to actually get on without falling off, so we spent all our time on the roundabout. It had seats that our butts barely fit into, but we'd sit there for hours, spinning it slowly with our feet. We'd just sit there and talk. About anything, everything.

Being at the park brings back those memories. But it doesn't bring back Huda. There's no one here. The sky is starting to get darker now. It's going to get harder to find her. Nafisah is more likely to panic. She's already had to call the police, and Huda's social worker, because of fostering protocol. *Think think think, Amani.* Where could Huda be? I made a promise to bring her back, and goddammit I'm going to keep that promise. I go over to the roundabout and take one of the seats. Well, try to. My butt doesn't even fit in there now, so I sit on the arm rest. I reach my leg out and kick off, letting the roundabout spin slowly.

Huda, where *are* you?

What's happened to make you do this?

As I spin, I think about all the good memories that happened here. That time Huda set up a treasure hunt for my thirteenth birthday, making me dig through dirt to find a friendship bracelet she'd bought, the time we created a mini Olympics using the park equipment and Huda even made medals out of tin foil.

I don't even notice when I start crying.

I've missed Huda a lot.

I try to put myself in her mindset, to figure out what could have made her run away. Could it have been our fight? I did say some truly awful things to her. She wanted to apologise, and I pushed her away. I remember she looked so upset in assembly, and then she reached out to me. She's going through some stuff, it seems like, and she came to me, like I would have done to her, and I shouted at her and stormed off. God, I'm such a terrible person. It's my fault she's run away, and so I have to be the one to bring her back. No matter what.

I think about the situation like I would plan a detective film. The trick is to examine the clues that are obvious first. Clues: Huda has taken some of her clothes. She's left a note saying '*I know I should explain, but all I can say is sorry*'. I could look into what the '*sorry*' means, but since I haven't exactly paid much attention to her life lately, I probably wouldn't be able to guess without talking to her carers, and they're already worried, plus I can't ask them questions without telling them about the Perfect Daughter plan. Any other clues? Not that I can think of.

I close my eyes as I spin. I try to picture Huda, wherever she is right now. She's probably got a backpack for her clothes – she wouldn't want to lug around a suitcase. I don't think she has any other close friends she could go and crash with. Would she go to a hotel or something? Nah, she wouldn't want to waste her money if she's planning to fend for herself.

Ugh. This is so frustrating. I just wish there was a way I could know exactly where she is. Some way I could pinpoint her location right away.

Oh my God!

That's it!

I sit up on the roundabout, almost sliding off as I do.

I know how to find Huda.

I take out my phone.

54

It was Huda who first suggested we set up 'Find my Friend' on each other's phones. She painted an imaginary situation where I'd been kidnapped by Asian aunties trying to marry me off to someone back home and she needed to come to save me. But as I spot her sitting on the bench on the empty train platform, I don't think she remembers that day, or that I have access to her location.

The barriers are open, so I walk through and up to her. She's hunched over her phone, looking at her photos, scrolling through, pausing on one, then scrolling again. The photos are of all the people in her life – Ali, Nafisah, me. I even spot one of the two of us with Ismail.

'Where you off to then?' I ask her.

She startles, almost dropping her phone as she looks up at me. 'Amani . . . how did you . . . ?'

'Next time you try to do a runner, turn your location sharing off,' I say as I take a seat next to her.

'I'm not . . . I'm not doing a *runner* . . .' she mutters.

'Just going out to do some laundry then?' I ask, nudging the backpack on the floor with my foot.

'Why are you even here?' she asks, moving the bag under

the seat. 'Why do you even care where I go, what I do? You hate me.'

'I don't . . . *hate* you, Huda . . . I could never. You just . . . you hurt me.'

'I hurt everyone,' she says, tears now stinging her words. 'That's all I do, hurt people, make things worse. It's better for everyone if I leave.'

'Shouldn't *we* get to decide what's better for us?' I ask. 'Nafisah's at home going crazy, worrying where you are.'

Huda turns her head to me. 'Really?' She looks sad. 'That's not . . . that isn't what I wanted. I thought she'd be better off without me.'

'Literally *why* would you think that?'

'Like I said, I'm a terrible person. Just look at how I messed your life up. It's not long before I do the same to everyone else.'

'What's the plan then?' I ask her. 'Where you off to?'

She shrugs. 'I was waiting for the late trains so I can sneak on without paying. I'm gonna take the next one.'

I look up at the electronic schedule board. 'The next train terminates here,' I tell her, trying to stifle my laughter.

'God, whatever. There's no need to make fun. So I don't know what I'm doing. Nothing new there, right? You don't need to take the piss.' She starts crying then, sobbing and covering her face with her hands.

'Whoa, whoa, calm down. I'm not making fun. Just . . . just talk to me, Huda. What's going on?'

'What's going on? What's going on is that I've driven everyone away. First you . . . with the blog. I . . . I'm sorry

337

about that, Amani. I honestly, truly am. And not just because I want us to be friends again. I realise now that I was wrong, that I never should have done that. It wasn't my place to tell everyone that. Not after promising you I wouldn't. I fucked up.'

I say nothing. I don't know *what* to say. My instinct is to say I forgive her, tell her whatever it takes to make her come back home. But I'm still not over what she did. I *do* feel bad though, for the fight earlier, for saying all those horrible things. I'm about to tell her that when she cuts me off.

'I was being selfish,' she says. 'I thought that putting the truth about your dad out into the world would . . . would save you. I wanted to protect you. I thought *I* could be the one to save you, to save your family. I thought if I could get that right, be the hero . . . I thought . . .' She sighs. 'I thought that Ali and Nafisah would see I'm a good person, that I can do good things. I thought they'd decide that I was worth keeping in their lives. I . . . I honestly thought I was doing the right thing.'

'I know that,' I tell her. 'I can actually . . . I can sympathise with that. I kept . . . I kept pushing Ammi to tell someone about Abbu, to speak out. I kept putting it all on her, and that wasn't fair. I should have known she'd speak out when she was ready. I should have given her that power. Well, I guess she did have it in the end.'

'Wait, what do you mean?'

'Oh God,' I laugh a little. 'So much has happened, Huda. Today's been ridiculous. But we can talk about that later, when you're back *home*.'

I stand up, but she doesn't.

'I can't, Amani. I can't go back. I can't take back all the bad stuff –'

I sit back down, reach over and pinch her arm.

'Ow! What are you doing?'

'Stop being so pathetic,' I tell her. 'So you did some bad things. And now you're feeling bad. That's normal, Huda. Now you apologise and hope everyone forgives you. That's how life works. You don't run away over something so stupid, OK? Let's go.'

She stares at me for a second before breaking out into a smile. 'God, I've missed you,' she says.

'Me too,' I say, knocking her shoulder with mine. 'Now, c'mon, let's go home.'

She shakes her head. 'It's not just you I've pissed off though. Things with Ali and Nafisah are . . . they're never going to be perfect. There's too much going on there.'

'Who needs perfect?' I ask. 'Huda, you've been trying so hard to become this "perfect" version of yourself that you haven't even stopped to think that Ali and Nafisah might actually love you just the way you are. They don't need you to be weirdly polite, or cook amazing food, or know how to build a changing table. They just want you to be you. You've been with them for almost five years now, and you've all been happy. This baby isn't going to change that.'

She goes to butt in, but I stop her with my hand. 'Things will change, of course they will. Babies do that. But it's not like they're going to completely forget you, throw you out like mouldy pizza or whatever. I felt like this just before Ismail was born, that he'd disrupt everything, make everything terrible, but . . . but oh my God I love that kid more than anything.'

'But it's not –'

I stop her with a hand again. 'I'm not done.'

She closes her mouth and watches me. There's a look of awe on her face. I've never been this firm with her.

'You keep saying that you released the blog about me because you thought that it was better out in the open, that you wanted me and Ammi to speak out about it. Well, aren't you being the biggest hypocrite? You do realise that everything could be fixed if you'd just *talk* to Ali and Nafisah. You *know* they'd hate to hear you're feeling like this. They're good people, Huda. You know they are. And I know that you love them, that you love living with them. Why would you give that up without even fighting for it?'

'Can I speak now?' She asks after a moment's silence.

'You may.'

'Um . . . actually, I don't know what to say.'

'You say, "Yes, fantastic Amani, my best friend in the entire world. You are so right. Also beautiful. Let's go home."'

She laughs. 'I've really, *really* missed you.'

'Annnnnddd I'm right, right?'

She sighs. 'Yeah, probably. It's just scary shit. The thought of . . . opening up to them. Of admitting what I'm feeling. Because it makes me sound like a brat, doesn't it?'

'No, of course it doesn't. Honestly, Huda, what you're feeling is so totally normal. Especially considering your childhood. They'll understand, I promise. And if they don't, you can come live with me!'

340

'The train now arriving at platform two terminates here,' crackles over the tannoy. Huda and I both look across as a train pulls in, the doors open and people start trickling out.

'So, what's it gonna be?' I ask her. 'Are you gonna take this train to nowhere? Or come back with me?'

55

We make a detour to the park on the way home. When I told Huda that was one of the places I looked for her, she insisted on going there right away. I tried to make her call Nafisah first, to tell her we'd be there soon, but Huda wimped out and texted instead. I let her off, because I'm still not convinced she won't run off again if things get too scary.

The park's empty when we get there. Huda feels the same hit of nostalgia I had. It makes me smile that she remembers it as much as I do. She heads straight for the roundabout, but she doesn't fit in the seat either, so she perches on the raised platform in the middle, while I take my seat from earlier, on the armrest, and kick the ground to spin us. It's like being transported back in time.

As we slowly go round, I tell her about everything that happened today. I describe how it felt to see Ammi in pain so close up, how awful it was listening to her cries for help while being too scared to do anything. I tell her about the animal look on Abbu's face, and how I don't think I'll forget that any time soon. There's a feeling of dread and anxiety in the pit of my stomach just thinking about that scene.

'But it's over now,' I say, trying to push away the memory.

'He's been arrested. Hopefully they'll push through Ammi's injunction quickly so he can't come near us even if they let him out. I don't think he'd test the law like that, like, risk being caught. I think he'll stay away.'

'Wow, shit, and you . . . you're OK with that? I mean, you used to say you thought he could change. That he *was* changing.'

I laugh. A bitter, hollow laugh. 'OK with it? None of this is in any way OK. But given the circumstances, I'm glad he's gone. That Ammi's safe. That *we're* safe. I can't believe I was so stupid. This has been going on for *years*, Huda, and I still thought he could change. He just kept doing the same thing over and over, never once trying to change. Even when he apologised to Ammi, he'd always follow it up with something that would blame her. "I'm sorry I hit you, but you just make me so angry." It was always such a bullshit apology, looking back on it.'

'Is that what you think of *my* apology tonight?' Huda asks with a nervous laugh.

'No way,' I reply. 'For one thing, you cried. I know you're serious when you cry.'

She laughs. 'Shit though, Maani, this is . . . this is *big*. It's gonna change everything. He's still your dad, y'know?'

'I hate him, Huda. Literally *hate* him. He's ruined our lives for way too long. I know I'm supposed to be all sentimental because he's my dad, and yeah sure, there'll probably be times I miss him, but God, I'm so angry at him. I'm so . . . I'm *scared* of him. Is it, like, completely terrible of me to feel relieved and happy about the fact he's been arrested?'

'Fuck no,' she replies. 'Remember what Mrs Farook used

to say? "Feelings are feelings, they're not right or wrong." You can feel whatever the fuck you want. Don't feel bad for that.'

I laugh. 'I'm so glad you're back. That we're friends again. I know it sounds cheesy, but I don't care. I know I can talk to Ammi about this now, but it's also . . . it's good to have you to talk to too.'

'You know you can tell me anything.'

We spin in silence for a few seconds. Something inside me is bubbling up. I stop the roundabout with my foot.

'Can I . . . ? Can I show you something?' I ask, sitting up. My head's spinning, and I know hers will be too, but I need to show her now, or else I'll never have the guts.

'Sure.' She sits up, and as I expected, laughs a little at the dizziness.

'You said . . . you said that you released that Burn Blog post so everyone could know the truth, right? About my dad?'

She nods.

'Well . . . considering *everything* that's happened, I wanted . . . I wanted to show you the *actual* truth. I can *tell* you, of course, but I want you to *see* what it's like . . . living with that.' I get out my phone. My palms are already sweating. I never thought I'd show anyone this video. But it feels right. Huda is my person. I can show her this.

'I started filming this years ago,' I tell her as I hand it over, video already loaded. 'Just little clips every time he was . . . when there was stuff going on. I guess I just wanted to . . . acknowledge it? And this is how I chose to do it. This . . . this is my truth.'

I watch Huda as the compilation of all my Bad Nights clips plays out. Me staring at the camera, crying, as Abbu yells at Ammi in the background, as he slaps her, kicks her. There's videos of me and Ismail together, videos of me sobbing uncontrollably, videos of me having been woken by the shouting. The burn on my arm makes an appearance too. Huda's the first person to ever see this, to see me. I hadn't realised before that while all this was happening *to* Ammi, it was affecting me too.

'Amani . . .' Huda breathes when the video comes to an end. There's tears all down her face, her eyes all watery and puffy when she looks at me.

'I just . . . I wanted you to know. I wanted you to see the truth. The *real* truth.'

'Maani, these clips . . .' Huda sniffs. 'They're . . . wow!'

I laugh a little. 'I always said I wanted my videos to make people *feel* something. I guess I've achieved that.'

Huda looks up at me in surprise. 'You've put this up on your channel?!'

'God, no! I made this just for myself. You're the only other person who's seen it. Not everything has to go on the internet, Huda!' I laugh.

She splutters, and apologises. But her comment has ignited something inside me. Something I hadn't allowed myself to consider – until now.

'Maybe . . . maybe someday though? Like, way in the future, when it feels less . . . raw. Maybe someday my video will be able to help someone else going through this? Help them feel seen? Let them know it gets better? I dunno.'

Huda doesn't say anything, just stares down at the phone, where my frozen, teary face looks out at us. I start to wonder whether maybe she thinks it's a terrible idea, totally inappropriate. But then suddenly she throws her arms around me and pulls me close. She's sniffly and snotty, and I'm about to make a joke about her ruining my headscarf, but she cuts me off.

'You're amazing,' she whispers.

Her words bring tears to my eyes and a smile to my face. I'm so lucky to have her in my life. I squeeze her as tight as I can.

And it's perfect.

Just me and my best friend, sitting in a park full of memories, hugging, crying, baring the deepest, darkest parts of ourselves to each other and knowing that, no matter what, the other will accept us as we are.

After all, what are best friends for?

56

We walk back to Huda's house in near silence. Not because it's awkward, but because Huda has started to feel nervous. I link arms with her so she doesn't feel alone, and also so she doesn't run.

'It'll be fine, I promise,' I tell her as we walk up her drive. 'Just be honest with them, about everything. Even how you pick your nose and wipe it on the sofa.'

I wait for her to laugh, but she doesn't. She's transfixed, watching the door. I'm about to give her another pep talk when the door opens in front of us. Nafisah is standing at the doorway. Her face fills with relief when she sees Huda. She pulls her into the house.

'Oh my God, I'm so glad you're OK!' she says, hugging Huda tight. Huda's expression goes from anxious to shocked to a faint little smile.

'I'm . . . I'm so sorry,' Huda says, her voice muffled by the hug. Nafisah shows no signs of letting her go.

'Huda?' Ali calls from somewhere in the back. He almost runs to the front door. 'Oh, thank God!'

Ammi appears in the background too; I go over and give her a less tight hug, wary of her injuries.

'You brought her back then?' she asks, as we watch Nafisah

gush over Huda while Ali goes to update the police and Huda's social worker.

'She was just being silly. She does that a lot.'

'No wonder you two are best friends then,' Ammi says, poking me in the side. I look her in the face, expecting to see happiness plastered all over her, now that Abbu's gone, and there *is* a smile there, but it's not . . . it's not her proper smile – not the one she gets when she's finished a painting she's proud of, or when Ismail says something cute. It's forced.

'How are you, Ammi?' I ask.

'I'm fine. Just . . . just tired, I guess. It's been a long day.'

'You know you can talk to me, right?' I say. 'About . . . about anything?'

She laughs a little. 'Aren't I supposed to say that to you?'

I nod. 'You have. And I will. Talk to you, I mean. I just wanted you to know you can do the same.'

She smiles. A proper smile this time. 'Thank you, moyna.' I can see her gaze float over my head. I turn to look too. Huda's standing there, awkwardly shuffling on the spot.

'Sorry,' Huda says. 'I just . . . Maani, Nafisah and Ali want to have *a talk* in the dining room.'

'You just need to be honest with them,' I tell Huda. 'Don't filter your feelings.'

'Would you . . . Can you come with me? I really want you to be there. You . . . you make me brave. You don't have to say anything. I just . . . I feel more confident when you're there.'

I look from Huda to Ammi. She smiles and nods at me.

And so I go.

* * *

Huda sits at the head of the dining table, with Ali and Nafisah on either side. I decide to hover in the corner of the room, by the window. I'd feel weird sitting at the table. I encourage Huda to just blurt out everything that's on her mind, and that's exactly what she does.

'I love you guys, like, seriously proper love you. You're the best carers I've ever had, and I've loved all the time I've spent here. Nafisah, I love how thoughtful you are, how you send me photos of news headlines you think I'll find funny, how you always go over-the-top proud parent when you come to award evenings, even when it's embarrassing as fuck.'

'Ahem.' Ali clears his throat. 'Embarrassing dad here too, y'know.'

Huda laughs. 'You *are* the most embarrassing dad ever. Your cheesy jokes, oh my God, they're the worst. But I love you for it. I love that you don't let people's opinions change who you are. I love how we sit together and do the commentary on TV shows together. I just . . . I love you both, so much . . .'

'So then . . . why?' Nafisah asks desperately. 'Why did you run away?'

'I just . . . I loved it so much, I didn't want it to end.'

'That makes no sense,' Ali says. 'You didn't want it to end so you tried to run away? Which would . . . make it end?'

Nafisah slaps his arm impatiently. 'Why would it end, Huda? What was going through your head?'

Huda takes a deep breath and looks over at me. I smile at her and nod a little.

'I heard you talking,' Huda says quietly. 'Years ago. Before

349

you took me in. I heard you telling the social worker that you couldn't have kids. I assumed that's why you were fostering. I thought I would be sort of like . . . like a replacement kid. It's stupid, I know. But then, when you got pregnant . . . I just . . . I started getting scared. I'm still scared, I guess. About there not being space for me here once the baby comes. Once *your* baby comes. I've been trying to . . . to change myself into, like, a better daughter, someone you'd *want* to keep around, even with the baby, but I don't think . . . I dunno, it feels wrong – trying so hard, knowing that I'm going to ruin everything at some point in the future anyway. And then, I dunno. It just felt inevitable, that things would end, so I thought I'd end it on my terms instead, so that it wasn't *you* who rejected *me*. I just . . . I feel like I'm in the way a lot. Like you've got each other, and now the baby, and it's all so perfect. And then there's me, butting in from the side.'

Huda goes quiet and part of me is dying to reach out to her, to let her know how proud I am that she managed to get it all out. To tell her how well she did. Like I'm a third proud parent.

Nafisah reaches out and takes Huda's hand. 'Oh, honey, we don't feel like that about you at *all*, do we, Ali?'

'God, no,' Ali says. 'We love you, Huda, just as you are. You don't need to change yourself, in fact we'd prefer it if you didn't. We kinda like the weird little person you are.'

'And as for the baby,' Nafisah says. 'There is no way that it could *replace* you. When we look into the future, we see *both* of you there. We want you to be a part of this baby's life. We want it to learn your sense of humour, your kindness, your mad Scrabble skills. We want your influence to rub off. As far as we're concerned, you are this baby's sister. No foster, no step. Just *sister*.'

Huda's head snaps up, and my own chest constricts so hard I feel the urge to cry. 'Really?'

'Yes, silly!' Ali says. 'We need someone who will protect the baby like only a big sister can, stick up for them when they need it, sneak them chocolates when we've said no more, and, of course, change their smelly nappies.'

Huda laughs, wipes the tears from her cheeks.

'No matter what happens in the future,' Ali says in a more sincere tone, 'you'll always be part of this family, part of our lives. You're not getting away from us that easily.'

'We mean it,' Nafisah adds. 'Even if . . . even if you decided you didn't want to be with us any more, or if some sort of circumstances tore us apart, you'd still be our daughter, Huda. You're always going to be our daughter. You're part of this family, and nothing can change that.'

Huda bursts into actual sobs then, which releases my tears too. I feel the urge to go over to her, but Nafisah beats me to it. She moves her chair right next to Huda and they hug.

'What can we do?' Nafisah asks quietly. 'To make you believe this. To make you believe how much you mean to us.'

'Shall I hire a skywriter?' Ali asks. 'I could get them to write "HUDA, WE LOVE YOU, BUT PLEASE STOP LEAVING THE TOOTHPASTE LID OFF."'

Huda chuckles a little, turns her head while still in Nafisah's hug. She looks at Ali.

'I don't . . . I don't know,' she admits. 'I can see you mean it. And I believe you, I do. But it's just . . . sometimes the bad thoughts, the doubts, they creep back in.' She shrugs a little.

'So we'll just keep reminding you,' Ali says matter-of-factly. 'We'll prove it to you over and over again until the doubts leave forever. Sound good?'

'That sounds . . . great,' Huda says. She sniffs away her tears. 'I love you guys.'

'Not half as much as we love you,' Nafisah says. She wraps her arms tighter around Huda, who reaches a hand out to Ali. He takes it and squeezes, with a smile. I take this as my cue to leave. I slip out of the room just as Huda asks, 'Can you still get me a skywriter though?'

Looks like they're well and truly back to normal.

57

It's strange having a full table at breakfast. Ammi and Nafisah cook pancakes, which makes Ismail extremely happy. Everyone talks, and laughs, and I can't help but think this is what a real family feels like. What a *happy* family feels like. Maybe we're on our way to this too now.

The school emailed to say the water issue was fixed, so we have to go back today. Nafisah is insisting we stay with them for a few more days, even though, with the injunction coming, we're fine to go home, without the fear of Abbu showing up. I think Ammi was grateful for the offer; I know I was.

Ammi and I clear up from breakfast together. I've made a resolution to help her with house stuff a bit more. She needs to know we're a team, that united we can face anything. She didn't bring her make-up with her, so the purple bruise on her forehead is clearly visible.

'You're not going to work today, right?' I ask, as I put the plates in the dishwasher.

'No,' she replies, pouring out the last few drops of coffee from her mug before putting that in the dishwasher too. 'Nafisah's got the day off too, so we're just going to Netflix and chill.'

I snort. 'Oh my God, Ammi! I don't think you quite know what that means.'

She looks confused, and I burst out laughing.

Suddenly, she takes my hand and pulls me into a hug. 'It's nice seeing you this happy,' she says. 'I hadn't realised, but I haven't seen you like this in a while.'

I feel the tears rise immediately and hug her lightly, worried about hurting her.

'I love you,' I whisper.

'I love you too,' she says.

Suddenly there's something wrapping itself around our legs. Ammi and I look down to find Ismail's run in to join the hug.

'I LOVE YOU TOO!' he yells. Sugar high.

Ammi laughs. 'Just us three now,' she says. 'We can do this, right?' She looks at me, uncertainty on her face, and I give her a smile before bending over and wrapping my arms around them both. 'Family hug!' I say, as Ammi bends slightly too, with a wince.

'Where's Abbu?' Ismail asks, buried underneath my arms. 'Shouldn't he be in the family hug too?'

A weight drops into my stomach. It's like Ismail's poured ice-cold water on the beautiful warm moment we were having. Even the mention of Abbu ruins everything. I straighten up, turn to Ammi, and can see my own panicked expression mirrored on her face.

'Your dad's . . . gone away for a bit,' Ammi says slowly. 'It's just us three for now. We're gonna have lots of fun, aren't we, Maani?' There's a slight crack to her voice, gaps I need to fill.

I nod frantically, putting on an over-the-top smile. '*So* much

354

fun. You were excited yesterday, weren't you? About playing Monopoly, and making more videos? We can do that *all the time* now. Sound good?'

He considers it, his face stuck on sad. 'But I like playing Monopoly with just Abbu. He makes car noises when he moves his piece. And he fake cries when he's in jail. It's so funny.'

'We can do that,' I say quickly. 'And you can be the banker every time.'

He turns from me to Ammi. 'Will he still pick me up from school on Tuesdays? He always gets me an ice cream with a flake and sprinkles from the ice-cream van.'

Ammi and I exchange looks again. Her face is downcast, her eyes beginning to water; she's struggling to find the words. I need to step up, convince her we can do this. It took so much strength for her to do what she did yesterday, and I know she's going to doubt herself at times. I need to prove to her that we can get through this.

'How about I pick you up on Tuesdays instead?' I ask Ismail, forcing a smile into my voice. 'I'll even let you get chocolate sauce.'

His eyes light up. 'Really? Abbu never lets me get sauce. He says it makes his car too sticky.'

'Well, I don't drive, so that doesn't matter.'

He considers it for a second and I'm scared it won't be enough, that he'll keep asking questions I won't know how to answer.

'We can sort out ice-cream orders later,' Ammi says suddenly, cutting off our conversation. The crack has disappeared from her voice, replaced with the same forced lightness I'm putting out. 'We have to *get* you to school first. C'mon – go and grab your bag. Amani and Huda will drop you off.'

Ismail thankfully lets it go. He runs out of the kitchen and up the stairs. I notice Ammi's on the verge of tears, on the verge of collapse. We both know this is going to happen again and again, that we can't just erase Abbu from Ismail's mind. Ammi and I know what a monster Abbu is, and though Ismail knows about the abuse, he still sees some good in Abbu. He's used to us as a family of four. It's going to be tough convincing him we're better off now.

'We can do this, Ammi,' I say, taking her hand and squeezing. 'This is the right thing – for all of us. We're strong enough to get through this. As for Ismail, distraction is probably the best way forward for now.'

Ammi takes a deep breath then shakes her head lightly, with a smile. 'Honestly, when did you become the parent in this family?'

58

Huda and I walk through the school gates together, like old times. After everything that's happened over the last twenty-four hours, it's weird to be back to the normality of school. We walk into the quad, and I expect to feel anger rise within me when I see the notice board, but nothing comes.

'God, I can't believe there's only eight days left,' Huda says, staring at the number. 'Have you done much revision? I feel like I haven't done anything.'

'You're smart enough to coast though. You don't even have to try.'

'Bitter, much?' Huda laughs. 'Anyway, we can pull an all-nighter today, studying our butts off, *roomie*.'

'It'll be weird not to have to come for lessons any more, won't it?' I ask, looking around campus. I spot Mr Voake walking out of the staffroom.

'I'll be right back,' I tell Huda before jogging off towards him.

'Sir! Wait up!' I call.

He turns and smiles at me. 'Morning, Amani. Everything OK?'

'Sir, I was hoping . . . well, wondering, I guess – did you mean what you said the other day? That you could make an exception, if I . . . if I wanted to change my A-level choices?'

His face lights up. 'Are you considering taking media studies?'

I nod. 'Not just considering. I've made my mind up. I want to drop all my current choices and take media studies, English language and film studies. I want to do something film-related at uni and make films when I'm older.'

'That's great!' Mr Voake says. 'You seem really happy about the decision, so I guess I don't need to ask if you're sure?'

I laugh.

'OK then. You'll need to have a talk with the head of sixth about this – just to check your grades are OK for you to take the others. I can get you started on media studies though. There's a form you have to fill in. I'll bring one to class.'

'Awesome, thank you, sir. And . . . thank you so much for your gift. It meant a lot.'

He smiles. 'I'm really glad, Amani. I'll see you later.'

I skip back to Huda. It feels weird for life to be going so well. When the good times come I've usually had an underlying fear that things are going to collapse again. And there's a tinge of that now, but mostly . . . I'm happy. I'm *truly* happy, for what feels like the first time in my life.

'What's with the Cheshire Cat grin?' Huda asks.

'I just sorted out my future plans.'

'You asked Mr Voake to marry you? I know you like him, but gross.'

I shove her arm. 'Shut up. I've changed my A-level choices. Say goodbye to Amani the vet.'

Huda stops in her tracks and stares at me. 'What, really? I thought you were super into that?'

I shake my head. 'My *dad* was super into that. He didn't really give me any other option. But now . . . now I've got them. I can do anything. And what I want to do is make films.'

'That's awesome, Amani. Really. Although, wow – how did I not get that you weren't into the vet thing? Do you know how much time I spent looking stuff up so that we could talk about it?'

'Seriously? That's so sweet. Wait, maybe you can take my science exams then? I'm pretty sure I'm gonna fail.'

'We can add that to our super-fun study plans tonight, *roomie*.'

'Only if there's jelly babies.'

'There's that grin again,' Huda says. 'Stop picturing Mr Voake naked.'

'Oh my God, shut up!' I whack her arm again, looking around to make sure no one heard her.

She laughs. 'Seriously though, it's nice seeing you this happy.'

I smile and feel a warmth inside me. 'It feels good to *be* this happy.'

'I guess . . . everything worked out in the end?'

'Yeah, I guess it did.' I look at her and she's raising her eyebrow at me. I roll my eyes. 'I'm not thanking you for posting that blog though. That was still way out of line.'

'Ah, yeah . . . sorry. Again.'

'Good. You should be. Now say it another thousand times, and I *might* fully forgive you.'

Huda clears her throat and drops to her knee, as if she's about to propose. 'I, Huda Farquhar, hereby promise to spend the rest of my life making it up to you, Amani Akhtar!' she announces at full volume.

'Oh my God, stop!' I laugh, trying to pull her up. 'Cleo's already spreading rumours about us – there's no need to add to it!'

'Fuck rumours,' Huda says, standing up and wiping her trousers.

Fuck rumours, indeed.

'What're your plans for the Burn Blog, anyway?' I ask. 'And also, how the hell did you even find out all that stuff?'

She shrugs. 'I'm an excellent eavesdropper. I think my hijab makes me invisible; no one seems to notice me standing there when they start talking to other people about their deepest, darkest secrets.'

'An excellent snoop, more like. So, are you gonna do any more posts?'

'Well, I do have a few more secrets tucked inside my hijab . . .'

I give her a pointed stare, and she rolls her eyes with a laugh. 'Don't worry. I'm over it,' she says.

'Good to hear. Oh, that reminds me actually. Can I run my new media studies coursework idea by you?'

'Sure.'

I tell Huda about my idea to make a documentary about the Burn Blog and the effects it had. She makes a face when I tell her Stacey's agreed to be interviewed, but I slap her on the arm and tell her Stacey's probably sorry for what she said all those years ago, and that maybe Huda should give her a second chance, considering the repercussions of the Burn Blog. She just rolls her eyes and says she'll think about it.

'That actually sounds like a really good idea,' Huda says after I've finished describing the idea to her. 'As long as you don't tell people it was me, obviously. I know we're on a truth kick, but that would be taking it a bit too far.'

We both laugh.

I leave Huda and walk off to registration. I'm on a high. I'm so distracted by the positive energy flowing through me that I don't notice Cleo in front of me until I bash right into her. Looks like she's running late too. We both groan and take a step back, rubbing our foreheads where they collided.

'Fucking watch out!' she shouts. Her eyes are slits, her face a bright shade of red.

'Sorry,' I say immediately.

'Guess it's genetic then?' she says, pure spite in her voice. 'Taking after your violent dad, Amani?' Her voice is loud and assured, the way it used to be when she'd pick on me pre-Burn Blog. It confuses me, because she's been so subdued since that happened. Barely said a word to me, let alone this loudly, this cruelly.

But then it hits me. She's only being like this because it's just us in the corridor. There's no one around to speak back to her, to put her in her place. Because we both know that I would never normally dare say anything back.

But we're living in the new normal now. It feels as if all the bad stuff in my life has finally gone away. It's only fair that Cleo should too.

'You know what, Cleo? My life is literally none of your business,' I say. My voice comes out more confident than

I've ever heard it. 'I know you have this *need* to feed off people's misery, but I'm not going to let you do that to me any more. Do you remember what it felt like when everyone read that blog about you? The fact that you had to take days off school to get away from it, because you knew how bad it would be here? *That's* how you make people feel. You're just a bully, Cleo.'

Her mouth opens a little, but in surprise, not to spit out more abuse. I've done it. I've finally got her to stop. I know this isn't the end of it, that Cleo's not going to stop being a bitch just because of something I said. But hopefully this means she knows I'm not going to take it any more. I step around her, as she stands there silently, and walk into registration without looking to see if she follows me.

'Hey!' I say to Maggie as I take my seat next to her.

She grunts a little, slouched over her desk, scrolling through her phone that's hidden behind her bag.

'What're you looking at?' I ask.

She sits up in her chair. 'I was just checking out this film festival that's happening in London this weekend. Hope and I are gonna go. Do you wanna come with?'

'Really?' I say. 'I get to meet your girlfriend?'

Maggie smiles shyly; it's so unlike her, and also so damn cute. 'Yeah, well, she finally met my parents last week, so now I get to show her off to my friends.'

'Awww, love's turned you soppy.' I elbow her in the side, and she shoves my arm back with a laugh.

'Is that a yes then?' she asks.

'Yes! What kinda films are they showing at this festival?'

I lean over to look at Maggie's phone as she shows me the poster. An email alert pops up on the screen.

'Ooh, look!' Maggie says, her voice all animated. 'It's another blog post!'

BLITHE ACADEMY BURN BLOG

Hello all.
Me again.

Still not going to reveal who 'me' is,
but today's post *is* a little different.

When I started this blog, I was angry.
I still am, tbh.
But things have changed.

I realised something . . .
I'm not perfect.
No one is.

I judged people on this blog,
Revealed secrets that weren't mine to tell.
I hurt people,
made their lives hell.
And I just want to say,

I'm truly sorry.

We live in a society
that thrives on tearing people down,
making us feel like we're not worthy unless
there's someone below us.
And I want to combat that.

As well as saying sorry, I want to lift people up.
I want to show them that they *are*
worthy.

So that's what this blog is going to be about from now
on.
Focusing on the good.

See you soon.

59

Halfway through third period, there's a knock on the door. It's Miss Kirtley, the receptionist. She smiles at the class before approaching Mr Hawthorne, who's sitting at his desk. They have a whispered conversation and then he stands up.

'Right, everyone, orders from above to go to the hall right away. Pack up your stuff and follow me and Miss Kirtley.'

Everyone starts rustling, getting their stuff.

'Oh my God, do you think someone figured out I'm doing the blog?' Huda hisses. 'Backpack said they'd punish anyone who even looks at it. Are they calling everyone in to, like, make an example of me? Fuck, what if I get expelled?'

'Whoa, calm down. No one knows it's you. If they did, trust me, you'd know by now. Cleo, at least, would be all up in your face.'

Huda looks around in a panic. Her gaze stops on Cleo, who's staring right back at her.

'Or . . . maybe she's taking a different tactic,' I whisper. My heart sinks. Shit.

'Come on, everyone, move!' Mr Hawthorne instructs.

We all traipse out of the classroom and over to the hall with the rest of our year. I squeeze Huda's hand as we sit down.

'It'll be fine,' I tell her. 'Deny everything. They can't prove it.'

I know I'm saying the right words, but inside I'm also freaking out. Mr Bach said they were monitoring internet usage. Maybe they've caught Huda that way.

Mr Bach takes the stage and everyone falls quiet. 'I know you're all wondering why we've pulled you out of lessons,' he says. 'Well, I just wanted to take this moment to say what a pleasure it's been being your headteacher for the last three years. You've driven me crazy, but it's been an . . . experience. Your exams are coming up very soon, and I want you to know that my door is always open if any of you need to come and chat. It's a stressful time, so please take care of yourselves. With all that said and done . . . the time has come to start study leave. You're free! No returning to class today, the teachers will escort you off campus. Your exam timetables are all online, and you should have received a paper copy – if not, see your form tutors. There will be revision classes scheduled for next week, and your tutors will be contactable by email for feedback on work. But other than that, good luck to you all.'

There's a huge cheer throughout the room.

'It's . . . it's over . . .' I say to Huda as we merge with the crowd shuffling out of the hall. I can't quite believe it. The end of an era.

'I know, it's amazing!' Huda squeals. 'I *told* you they'd chuck us out before the actual date.' She gestures towards the notice board, which stands proud, still showing eight days.

I stare at it for a second and laugh inwardly. This stupid board has been a thorn in my side for weeks, counting down to my doom. I remember the anger I used to feel seeing it, the pit of dread that would open up. But now . . . that's gone. Now I'm ready. Not for exams, not for GCSEs, but for the future. I can actually think about my future without wanting to be sick. That's new.

The teachers kick us off campus, but the whole year just goes to the field opposite and we spend an hour taking group photos, signing each other's shirts and saying tearful goodbyes.

'Ready to start *the rest of your life*?' I ask Huda, mimicking Mr Bach as we start walking home.

'Oh God, gross. I don't want to think about that yet.'

'Wasn't that part of the Perfect Daughter plan, to figure out what you wanted to do with your life?'

She shrugs. 'I think I only came up with that from seeing how set you were on the vet thing. I thought *everyone* was like that. It made me panic that I have literally no clue what to do with my life. After talking to Ali and Nafisah, I realised that whole plan was stupid. There was no way I'd be able to keep all that up. Do you know how hard it is to make biryani the way Nafisah likes it? They love me the way I am anyway, so fuck that shit. Anyway, we're only sixteen. Ali said he didn't decide to become a paralegal until he was, like, twenty-two. We've got time. Don't know why the school wants to make us panic about it all now.'

'Hear, hear,' I tell her. 'I think we'll have a fun time trying to figure out where your . . . um, *talents* are best suited.'

She shoves me. 'Hey, I have *plenty* of talents, I'll have you know.'

'Oh sure, maybe you can write gossip columns in trashy magazines.'

'Ha ha.' She pauses for a second before continuing. 'For real though, things only just seem to be settling down for me, y'know? Like, my whole life, I was wondering what would come next, whether the placement I was in would last, and for how long. What the next people would be like, whether I'd get my own room, that kind of thing. But now . . . I'm finally starting to feel like I belong somewhere, y'know? It's a good feeling. I don't *need* to worry about the future any more, because it's not so scary.'

'I totally know what you mean,' I say, feeling a little shiver of excitement at the prospect of doing the A levels *I* want to do.

Huda's phone beeps and she pulls it out.

'Another Burn Blog post?' I tease, craning my neck to see her screen.

'Holy crap! Nafisah's having the baby!'

'What?' I ask. 'But she's not . . . she's only eight months, isn't she? Is something wrong?'

'I don't know,' Huda says quietly. 'Ali just texted to say they're at the hospital. Fuck. Something must be wrong. Oh God, what if I caused this?' She looks at me, wide-eyed. 'What if I made her stress so much that it's hurt the baby?'

60

Huda rushes off to get a bus to the hospital, while I walk back to hers. I spend the journey praying that Nafisah is OK, that the baby is OK. The idea that something could happen to either of them terrifies me. That family deserves something good; Huda deserves something good, after everything she's been through.

When I get to Huda's, I have to ring the bell. It feels like forever before I see movement on the other side of the door. The glass is frosted, but I can see the blurry version of Ammi pop her head out of the living room. She doesn't approach though, and I think maybe she can't see me, so I give a little wave. Finally she comes up to the door, but opens it just a minuscule amount, leaving the chain on. She peers through the gap and I see her face transform from fear to relief when she sees it's me.

'Ammi, are you OK?' I ask, slipping in as soon as the chain's off.

'Yes, yes, everything's fine,' she says. Her voice is shaking though, and I realise she's home alone and must be terrified. She pulls me into a hug before I can say anything else. 'I don't hug you enough,' she says with her cheek against my shoulder. 'I'm gonna change that from now on.'

I melt into her hug, still keeping it loose so as not to hurt her, realising she just wants to let the moment pass. 'That sounds like a good plan.'

'So you're on study leave now, eh?' she asks when we finally pull apart. 'Did Huda tell you Nafisah's gone into labour?'

'Yeah, is everything OK? She's not . . . she still had time, didn't she? Is something wrong?' I follow Ammi down the hall.

'Sometimes these things just happen,' she says. 'She's thirty-six weeks, so it's not that scary. Inshallah everything will be all right.' We walk into the living room, where Ammi has started blowing up balloons.

'I know Nafisah and the baby probably won't be back today,' she says. 'But I thought it would be nice to liven the place up. I was working on the mural in the nursery earlier but got a bit tired. Hopefully I can finish it by the time they come home. I thought I'd decorate downstairs a little for Ali and Huda. Do you want to help?'

'Sure.'

Ammi and I fall into a rhythm; she blows up more balloons and I hang them up. Ali and Nafisah aren't into gender stereotyping, so the balloons are all different colours. Ammi gets up from the sofa to hand me a neon-orange one, and accidentally knocks into the table. She hisses in pain, and a second later a glass smashes on the floor. Ammi lets out a little scream and falls back onto the sofa, wrapping her arms around her head in a protective manner. I can make out a look of pure terror on her face. Shit. Shit shit shit.

I quickly climb down from the ladder and rush over to her. 'Ammi, Ammi, hey, it's OK. It was just a glass. I can clean

371

it up. It's OK. You're OK,' I babble, not knowing what to say, what to do.

She moves her hands and looks up at me, and there are tears streaming down her face.

I kneel on the floor next to her and take her hand. 'I'm here, OK? You're safe. It's just . . . it's just us.'

She breathes deeply and smiles a wobbly smile. 'Sorry, I think I'm just a bit . . . jumpy.' She pauses for a minute, just breathing heavily. I give her space to recover.

'I . . . need to tell you something,' she says eventually. 'The police called earlier.'

'Oh.' My heart sinks. 'What . . . what did they say?'

'They've released him on bail. But . . . there are rules. He can't come near us. We're safe, don't worry. The injunction should go through soon, so he'll have to stay away permanently.'

'Where . . . ? Where is he going to stay, do you know?'

She ducks her head, looking down at her trembling hands, twisting her wedding ring, and I immediately feel like crap. 'God, sorry, I shouldn't have asked. Forget –'

'No, no, don't be silly,' she says. She squeezes my hand. 'Amani, I want you to know you can ask me anything. You can talk to me about anything. It's such a . . . a weird time. I know everything that's happened affects you too. But . . . I want to keep you in the loop. You're old enough, mature enough, to have dealt with . . . with everything, so it's only right that you know what's going on. You can ask me anything, OK?'

I nod, feeling tears creep up in my eyes.

'He's listed his address as his brother's house in Birmingham. At least we know he'll be far away.'

I nod, satisfied. We're safe.

'Is he . . . ? Is he still going to be a part of our lives?' I think back to this morning, how keen Ismail was to bring Abbu in on our family hug.

'Do you *want* him to be a part of your life?' she asks slowly.

I look at her, right into her eyes. 'No,' I tell her. 'I hate him for what he's done. I hate him for the way he is. I'll never be able to forgive him for any of that, for what happened yesterday. But . . . you saw how Ismail was this morning. He knows what Abbu can be like, but he looks up to him too. I think it's going to be hard to cut him out completely.'

She nods. 'I don't know how we're going to get around that. Or how we're going to move forward. But we'll take each day as it comes. There's so much to think about, but we'll figure it out as we go.'

'That sounds good,' I say, putting my hand over hers and squeezing. 'I'm glad you're getting the injunction. I just want you to be safe.'

'Thank you, moyna,' she says, pulling me in for another hug. It's awkward, since I'm on the floor and she's on the sofa, but nice nonetheless.

'I'm going to look for a therapist for you and one for Ismail,' she says as she pulls away with a wince. 'I think it would be good for you both to have someone to talk to.'

I smile at her. 'Make sure you find someone for yourself too.'

'The police have put me in touch with some support groups and charities. I'll give them a call tomorrow. But for now –' she unrolls a long silver banner saying 'Congratulations!' – 'let's get this up.'

61

Huda is officially a big sister! Nafisah gave birth to a healthy baby girl. Well, I say healthy – they're keeping her in for a few days as a precaution, since she was early. Ammi and I pack some balloons in the car and go to the hospital. Our little chat earlier raised a lot of emotions. I think the baby's come at just the right time – it's given her something else to think about.

I text Huda for an update, but she hasn't messaged me since she left for the hospital. I'm starting to get worried. Maybe she freaked out and did another runner after seeing Ali and Nafisah with the baby. But Ali would have told us . . . unless he was too preoccupied with the baby. It's all I can think about as we get in the lift, as we walk down the corridor to the maternity ward. Did Huda even come to the hospital? Or did she run off again? Why isn't she answering her phone?

I'm scared enough that I consider telling Ammi about my worries, but then the next thing I know, we're walking into a side room. The balloons obscure my view for a few seconds, but when I push them aside, I see why Huda's not been answering my calls. She's sitting in a big blue chair next to Nafisah's bed, the baby in her arms, a look of adoration on her face. I've never seen that expression on her.

'Congratulations!' Ammi says as she walks over to give Nafisah a hug.

'Thanks, Shirin. How you holding up?' Nafisah asks.

Ammi and Nafisah get into a conversation as I walk on over to Huda.

'Well, hey there, big sister,' I say.

She looks up and a grin spreads over her face. 'Look how cute she is, Maani.' I look down at the little bundle in her arms. She's tiny and red.

'Everything OK with her?' I ask.

'Just a touch of jaundice,' Huda says, looking back down at her and stroking her cheek. 'They'll shine some special light on her and it should go in a few days. Nafisah says it's nothing to worry about.'

'It's a good look on you,' I tell her. 'The big-sister act.'

'It's so weird,' Huda says quietly, still looking down at the baby. 'Just . . . from the moment I saw her . . . I know it's cheesy as fuck, but . . . she's just so . . .' Huda looks up at me now. 'She's my sister, Maani. She just . . . *feels* like my sister. I already love her so fucking much. I didn't realise it would be like this.'

'That's great! But good big sisters don't swear in front of their siblings,' I say with a laugh, trying to hide the tears that are threatening to come out, watching how happy Huda is. 'Trust me, I know. I'm the *best* big sister.'

Huda laughs. 'You *were*. Now I'm taking the crown.'

'Oh, that's an idea!' I get my phone out of my pocket and load up the camera. 'I'm gonna make a film about this. You trying to become the Perfect Big Sister. Let me get a shot of this first meeting.' Huda laughs as I point my phone at her. 'Anything you want to say to your little sister?'

Huda looks down at the baby. 'Hi there, little sister. Welcome to the world. It's really nice to meet you. I'm going to look after you. You and me against the world.' She looks up at the camera with a grin. 'When you watch, and understand, this film, sometime in the future, please can you tell Amani that I'm a *much* better sister than her?'

'We'll see about that,' I say, laughing.

'Oh, Amani, good, you're already filming!' Ali says from behind me.

I turn and focus the camera on him. 'How does it feel to be a dad then, Ali?'

'I've been a dad for almost five years already, duh, Amani,' he says, winking at Huda.

Huda beams. I catch it on film.

'OK, I need you to record this for me, yeah?' he says excitedly. He turns to Nafisah's hospital bag that's on the bed and starts rummaging through it.

'You want me to record you looking through a bag instead of the baby?'

'I do have a nice butt,' Ali says. 'Make sure you zoom in on that.'

'Oh, gross!' Huda says. 'The baby's only a few hours old and you're already embarrassing her.'

Ali turns around to face us, holding a small bundle of black material in his hand. He's got the biggest grin on his face. 'Shirin, can you take the baby for a second?'

'Oh, yes, please!' Ammi doesn't need asking twice.

Huda hugs the baby closer to her. 'Noooo! Five more minutes!'

'I need to give you something,' Ali says. 'You'll need your hands for this.' He wiggles his eyebrows and waves around the rolled-up black item.

'Ugh, fine,' Huda says. She gets off the chair and hands Ammi the baby. I catch a few seconds of joy on her face before turning back to Ali. I step back so I can get him and Huda in the frame.

'Right, you ready?' Ali asks. He's so excited, it's adorable. He hands Huda the black cloth. She takes it and unravels it. It's a T-shirt.

'Oh my God!' she says, her entire face lighting up.

'What is it?' I ask impatiently. 'Show the camera!'

Huda turns the T-shirt around, the grin still plastered on her face. The shirt is black, with a drawing of four stick figures – two adults, one child and one baby. There's an arrow and the words 'BIG SISTER' in big, bold letters pointing to the child.

'We bought matching ones,' Ali says. 'Mine says "Dad". We're gonna wear them and get professional photos done. It's gonna be so cheesy.'

'Put it on! Put it on!' Nafisah says from the bed.

Huda laughs and slips the T-shirt on over her school shirt. She sticks her arms out and does a twirl for the camera.

'Suits you perfectly,' Ali says softly. He smiles at Huda, who just grins back at him. 'Now, we could do with some snacks. Go and show that top off.'

Huda can't stop staring at her reflection in the lift. She even smiles back at people who notice her top and give her a smile. It's adorable.

'Sorry,' she says to me as we get out on the ground floor. 'I've been so wrapped up with the baby, I haven't even asked how your mum is.'

'She's putting on a brave face, pretending to be strong for me and Ismail. But I think she's terrified.'

'And you?'

I shrug. 'It just . . . feels weird. Everything's changed so much. I'm scared about how we're going to cope, like money-wise and everything. I feel like those worries are blocking out the relief, and that annoys me. I should be happy, right?'

'Feelings are feelings, they're not right or wrong, remember?' Huda says. 'Your life's been turned upside down in, like, the space of a day. It's natural to have conflicting thoughts. But honestly, try not to worry too much. Things will work out. Your mum's got that promotion at work. And you know Nafisah and Ali will help you guys out however they can. I guess it's just about taking things one step at a time.'

'Look at you, all wise and mature,' I say. 'That's literally what Ammi said earlier.'

'What can I say?' She shrugs, looking down at her top. 'Becoming a big sister has changed me.'

'It has!' I agree. 'You've been smiling *way* too much. It's like Huda 2.0.'

She jabs me with her elbow as we walk into WHSmith. 'I mean . . . I know that things aren't going to magically become perfect – for either of us. But the only way is forward, right? The only thing we can do is to keep going. Keep trying.'

'Yeah,' I say softly. 'And when things get too scary, at least we'll have each other.'

'For sure!' Huda says. She turns to me with a smirk. 'Unless you start a new Burn Blog, then you're on your own.'

RESOURCES

If you have been affected by any of the issues raised in this book, please consider reaching out to the organisations listed below.

Childline
A private and confidential service for young people up to age nineteen. Counsellors available to talk about anything.
Call free on 0800 1111
or talk online at www.childline.org.uk

The Hideout
Help and information for children and young people experiencing or witnessing domestic abuse at home.
www.thehideout.org.uk

Refuge
Help for women and children who have experienced or are experiencing domestic abuse, including information on what to do if you're worried about someone else.
Call free on 0808 2000 247
www.nationaldahelpline.org.uk

Become
Help and advice for young people in care, or care leavers.
Call free on 0800 023 2033
or email advice@becomecharity.org.uk

ACKNOWLEDGEMENTS

They say Book 2 is one of the hardest books you'll have to write, and dear God are they right. This book has been a journey and a half, and for sure it would not be what it is without an incredible cast of people who put up with me and helped me out along the way.

First and foremost, my brilliant editor, Emma Matthewson, who pulled apart this idea in its initial state and made me really think about the story I was trying to tell, made me realise what the heart of this book was. Thank you so much for your unflinching belief in me. It bewilders and motivates me on a daily basis. I'm so privileged to be able to work with you.

Hellie Ogden, my brilliant agent, for being there to calm me down from all the 'I CAN'T DO THIS ANY MORE' moments (and believe me, there were a LOT). Also to Rebecca Carter, who helped get this book moving when I was at rock bottom.

Mega love to all the team at Hot Key Books, in particular Talya Baker, who will always, *always* go above and beyond to help out, and writes the best copy-edit notes, that I actually look forward to receiving. Thank you for all you do. Also shout-out to Sophie McDonnell for the most amazing cover I could have asked for, Emma Quick for all the brilliant TikToks, PR guru Molly Holt, and Jane Hammett for her eagle-eyed proofreading.

Aisha Bushby, who has been by my side every step of this publishing journey, and is always there to listen to my worries and constant moaning. Thank you for being my go-to soundboard and helping me figure out so much of this book, and let's be honest, so much of my life, in gen. I love you.

Lucy Powrie, who gifted me a Dale Winton cut-out and made me the happiest gal ever. Thank you for being the bestest pal and always being available for ghost hugs and embarrassing photo stickers. Thank you for validating my struggle with this book, and always checking in. Love you lots. (Also hi to your mum and Daisy!)

Nizrana Farook, for being an absolute gem. I don't think I've ever met a more pure person. Thank you for letting me vent always, for reading terrible drafts of this book and for being my 'Asian/Muslim opinion', since I'm such a coconut.

Hanky Tooke for all the motivational messages interspersed with loud wailing and email-summoning chants, and obvs the fun videos of your cat being a dick.

Big up the MAWYP gang for being amazing cheerleaders, and the Stroops groupchat for just being there – in particular Rachel Huxley, who was this book's first reader, and is just generally the sweetest. (And yes, she did give me permission to call her a bitch in the book.)

Thank you to Katya Balen for all the photos of your beautiful derp of a dog and your annoyingly rational replies to my daily freak-outs, and to Sarah Juckes for sharing my penchant for darkness and allowing me to be my full morbid

384

self. To Holly Jackson, for listening to my pitch for this book and recommending me *Pretty Little Liars*, which I became immediately obsessed with; Joseph Elliot, for all your help on the ins and outs of being a children's TV presenter (please have a cat attack your chin and live out this book's funniest scene in reality); and Struan Murray for your chemistry expertise, which I then completely wrote out of the book (because of personal spite? Who knows?).

Thank you to Lesley-Anne for always being around for a chat, whether about life or, more likely, *Frozen*. To Danielle Jawando for sharing writing misery with me, and Sara Barnard for always providing distraction TikToks and harsh realities about being a writer. To Gabriel Dylan for regaling me with funny school rumours that were too dirty to actually be used in this book, and for informing me about school safeguarding procedures. Much thanks to Rosie Farrell also for her safeguarding knowledge. Huge thanks to Dr Sarah Jennings for your medical expertise (and general cuteness), and to Kim Burns for your police knowledge.

A ginormous thank you to Callen Martin for your amazing sensitivity read on this book, for answering all my 'This is the last question – I SWEAR's, and for all the work you do to ensure accurate portrayals of children in care. I tip my hat to you, sir. Any mistakes left in the text are entirely mine.

Thank you also to Annie Shafi from My Foster Family and Abdurrahman Sayed from Foster Care Link for your time and knowledge.

My biggest thank you goes to the lovely ladies who were kind enough to share their experiences of domestic violence with me (and thank you to Mariam Khan for being the bridge between us). I am grateful beyond words for your openness and trust. In particular, thank you to Mariyam Khan for your sensitivity read and live DM reactions. Your support of this novel means more than I can ever say. Thank you for sharing your truth with me, and making me cry with your notes. I was looking for a sensitivity reader and ended up with an amazing friend.

Lastly, thank you to everyone who read and said nice things about my first novel. Your support kept me going through debut year and motivated me so much through writing this one. Sorry if it sucks. All the blue heart emojis.

About the Author

Yasmin Rahman is a British Muslim born and raised in Hertfordshire. Her first novel, ALL THE THINGS WE NEVER SAID, was the runner-up YA book in the inaugural Diversity Book Awards. She has MAs in Creative Writing and Writing for Young People. Her short story 'Fortune Favours the Bold' was published in the Stripes anthology *A Change is Gonna Come* in 2017, with the *Bookseller* awarding the contributors a YA Book Prize Special Achievement Award for commitment to making YA publishing more inclusive.

When she's not writing, Yasmin makes bookish fan art; her designs are sold worldwide on behalf of John Green. THIS IS MY TRUTH is her second novel.

ALSO BY YASMIN RAHMAN

YA Runner-up of the
Diverse Book Awards 2020

Read on for an extract . . .

1. MEHREEN

4th April

Bismillah hir-Rahman nir-Rahim . . .
In the name of Allah, the most gracious, the most merciful . . .

I take a deep breath and step onto the prayer mat, ready to start the dawn prayers. As I mutter verses from the Quran under my breath, I lose myself in the rhythm, letting the Arabic flow through me, cleansing me from head to toe. Mum is kneeling on the mat next to mine. As she turns her head to the left, I see she's got a slight smile on her face, a visual expression of the serenity that encapsulates her when she prays. The same sense of serenity I yearn for every time I pray.

My religion has always meant a lot to me. People make fun of how much it dictates my life, but it's the only thing that's kept me going so far. Sometimes, when the Chaos in my brain is so loud that it feels like my head is about to crack open, I *have* actually found some comfort in prayer. Not like a ray of sunshine floating down or anything, but it . . . it soothes me, drowns out the incessant voices in my head – for a while, anyway. I can't really explain it. I guess I'm just a no-questions-asked believer. I believe in God, I believe in heaven, I believe that the afterlife is what we should be preparing for, that it's the only place I'll find true peace.

Mum finishes her prayers and leaves the room, but I stay kneeling on the mat. It's said that dawn is the best time to ask for things, so I start a little personal prayer.

Allah,

I feel like there's something wrong with me: something completely and utterly unfixable. I just want to live a life where I don't keep being overwhelmed by sadness. Where I don't suddenly feel like someone has punched me in the gut and I can't breathe, can't think, can't see – when my head is so crammed with worry that I can't even focus on what I'm doing, who I'm with, or even whether I'm breathing. I'm fed up of feeling like this, of being continuously battered by what I call 'the Chaos'. I want my brain to slow down, to just . . . be normal. I need something to live for, Allah, because right now the only thing keeping me here is you. And I'm starting to feel like that's not enough.

As usual, I find myself so overcome with tears that I can't continue. I curl up on the prayer mat in the foetal position, squeezing my eyes shut, clenching all my muscles, trying to push away the darkness.

'Mehreen! Come down and eat!' My mother's voice is at the pitch that tells me this isn't the first time she's called. When I stand up, my body is stiff and the sun is blazing through the curtains. I wipe my face and compose myself before making my way downstairs.

In the kitchen, Mum is at her position by the sink, furiously scrubbing a pan and talking about some drama involving her family back in Bangladesh, while Dad sits at the head of the table, tapping away on his phone, paying no attention to her whatsoever. The Angry Birds theme tune hums quietly around the room. Imran is leaning against the counter near the toaster, also on his phone. I slip into the room, fix myself some cereal and sit down at the other end of the table.

No one looks up.

No one says anything.

They don't even notice when you're in the room.
THEY'RE BETTER OFF WITHOUT YOU.
They don't care about you.

I spoon some Shreddies into my mouth, feeling the hard ridges of the cereal poke and prod my cheeks and gums. I chew extra hard, trying to cover up the Chaos that's starting to seep through. The Angry Birds theme changes to the melody of having lost a life; Dad grunts, then lets the phone clatter to the table. Imran laughs as he butters his toast. I watch from the far end of the room as Mum dries her hands and touches Imran on the back to squeeze past him to the cupboard. She pulls out a plate and silently hands it to him. He sighs and drops the toast onto the plate before taking a seat next to Dad, who's picked up his phone again.

'Want me to do it?' Imran asks with his mouth full.

'Almost got it,' Dad mumbles. The lost-a-life tune plays a few seconds later. 'Dammit!'

Imran laughs, snatches the phone and starts tapping away.

Watching the three of them is like watching a totally normal family interacting. It's nothing momentous, what they're doing, but it's the little things that make a family a *proper* family.

Look how happy they are on their own.
THEY'RE BETTER OFF WITHOUT YOU.
No one would even notice if you were dead.

Mum's started chopping some vegetables on the counter. I drop my bowl in the sink, roll up my sleeves and grab the sponge.

'What're those marks on your wrist?' she asks, turning her head to look at me, the knife poised mid-slice. Her eyes are firmly fixed on my wrist.

There's a jolt in my chest. The heart I thought had become stagnant starts up again. Jumps straight into my throat.

This is it.

The moment I've been both dreading and hoping for.

I shake my arm to loosen my sleeve so that it rolls down and covers the scars, but it only slips down a little. My heart is thudding so hard I can feel it against my top.

I stare at her intently, hoping that she'll finally *see* me, that this pressure, this pain, will finally go. When I was a kid, Mum used to be able to fix everything with a few words and a kiss; I've been secretly longing for her to do the same with whatever's happening in my head. But when she does finally make eye contact, nothing happens. There's no love on her face, no concern. Her brow is creased, her posture stiff.

'Did you get them from your bangles?' she asks, her eyes only lingering on my face for a second before returning to her chore. 'I told you to stop wearing such cheap jewellery.'

Of course she doesn't see. She doesn't realise because things like this don't exist for her. In her world, there's only sunshine and butterflies. No one ever hurts. No one ever feels the need to not exist. Everything is *perfect*.

'It wasn't a bangle,' I whisper, shaking the excess water off my bowl before placing it on the drying rack. I shove my sleeves down.

'Bangle, bracelet, same thing,' she says, chopping in Morse code. 'Why don't you use all that time you spend in your room to find a job instead? That way you could afford things that don't ruin your body.'

I stare at the knife as it moves up and down between her fingers, willing it to slip, wishing it were my skin beneath it.

'Who'd want to hire her?' Imran laughs from the table, his eyes still glued to Dad's phone. 'It's not like she's actually good at anything. Besides being a loser.'

He's right; you're such a loser.
No one will ever love you.
LOSER. LOSER. LOSER. LOSER.
They're better off without you.

I get that urge rushing through my body, that tight constriction in the middle of my chest, my wrists beginning to itch. There's already an image in my head of the trail of red, the sense of relief I'll achieve. I wrap my fingers around my wrist and squeeze.

Dad's phone lets out an upbeat melody and he whoops, patting Imran on the shoulder as he takes his phone to start the next level. Imran sits back in his chair, looking smug. His gaze moves to me, but before he can even start his next insult, I'm out of the room, up the stairs, slamming my bedroom door.

None of them care about you.
CUT. CUT. CUT. CUT.
YOU'LL FEEL BETTER.
They don't want you around.
CUT. CUT. CUT. CUT. CUT. CUT. CUT. CUT. CUT.

The need to cut is a physical thing. My wrists pulse, my heart races, my nails dig into my palms to try to quell the rage within me. But that's never enough. I'm not strong enough to resist. Weak and pathetic, that's me all over. Every time I do it, I hate myself, literally *hate* myself for doing that to my body. But once the thought enters my mind, there's no other way to get rid of it. So I kneel on the floor and take out the craft knife that's hiding under my mattress, like the loser I am.

You're so stupid. **WORTHLESS.**
No one would even realise if you weren't here.
LOSER. **CUT. CUT. CUT. CUT. CUT. CUT. CUT.** **JUST END IT ALL.**

When I'm done and have tidied everything up, I log on to my laptop, feeling completely spent. Cutting usually makes the Chaos quieten down for a bit; it's one of the only times I can actually think clearly.

I load up the website I haven't been able to get out of my head since I stumbled across it a few weeks ago. MementoMori.com – a website with a simple message on the homepage.

Fill out a questionnaire to be matched with a suicide partner and have a pact tailored to your needs.

[. . .]

2. CARA

You'd think Mum would just go shopping without me, or leave me outside with the dogs on their leads. (I told her I could make a sign that says 'Hungry Disabled Orphan' and make a few quid, but she just rolled her eyes.) For some reason though, she forces me to go in every time, which means I have to be around other people. And I fucking hate other people.

I feel like a bloke being dragged clothes shopping by his girlfriend, having to wait outside the dressing room in that little space saved for men. Unfortunately there's no space reserved for people in wheelchairs. Most of the time there's barely enough room for me to go up the aisles. More than once I've knocked over a whole bunch of clothes, the fabric becoming trapped in my chair as I tried to escape.

'I need to grab that biology textbook for you,' Mum says as we leave yet another shop. 'We're starting digestion after the Easter hols, and I need to brush up on it myself before trying to teach you it.'

I say nothing.

'I saw this experiment idea on one of those home-schooling forums. We just need to get some baking soda and . . .'

I stop listening. Her yapping gets really fucking annoying

after a while. She thinks that by talking to me all the time she'll make me . . . not depressed or something. It's why she's always dragging me out, as if misery is stuck inside our house.

The sky is so dark it looks like it's about to start pissing it down again. I'm surprised Mum isn't already holding an umbrella over me. I keep my eyes straight ahead as I move towards the crossing. I can tell everyone who passes by is eyeballing me, whether it's a quick maybe-she-didn't-notice-me look or the braver I'll-stare-as-long-and-hard-as-I-want-to look that mostly comes from old women or little kids too young to be embarrassed. At the traffic lights, I reach out to push the button for the crossing, but a chubby woman with a dog gets there first.

'I'll get that for ya, darlin',' she says, practically shoving me out of the way.

She looks right at me as she presses the button, her eyes skimming over my face, over my wheelchair, settling on my body as she tries to diagnose me, tries to piece together my story.

I turn away, wishing she'd disappear, that her yappy fluff-ball would eat her up or at least bite her on the ankle so she'll stop giving me the pity face. She stands silently and I know she's waiting for me to thank her. For me to act like the damsel in distress I so obviously am.

I've mostly learned to tune people out. Learned not to bother putting up a fight. Stopped trying to make them see that while I might not be able to use my legs any more, I still have a functioning brain. That I'm still a person.

Or maybe I'm not. Maybe I'm only half a human now. (Paraplegic humour, get it?)

I ignore the woman and look straight ahead, wishing I had the courage to move forward right now, straight into the middle of the busy road.

But that wouldn't work; what kind of monster doesn't do an emergency stop for a cripple?

The woman's hovering so close I can smell the vinegar-laden chips she just ate. Her dog sniffs at my ankle, then the right wheel. He lifts his leg.

'Michael, no!' She tugs on the lead and jerks the dog back before he actually manages to piss. He whimpers. 'I'm so sorry!' she says. To Mum, not me. 'He's just a bit . . . over-friendly sometimes.'

'Oh, it's no problem,' Mum says. 'He's a cutie. What breed?'

Vinegar Lady launches into a full-blown conversation about her rat of a dog who's now sniffing at my feet again. I zone out, just listening to the slosh of the tyres on the wet road, the clatter as they go over grates. Wondering what it'd sound like if a car rammed into my chair.

Then Vinegar Lady is whispering, and I know she's talking about me. My disability. You'd think she'd be more subtle, especially since I'm right in fucking front of her. Of course Mum doesn't hesitate to give out the gory details.

'. . . car accident ten months ago . . .'

I try to block it out, block her voice out, block the whole world out, focus just on the pedestrian-crossing light. Why the hell hasn't it turned green yet?

'. . . paralysed from the waist down . . .'

The dog coughs or sneezes or farts by my feet and I look down at it. He's still sniffing around, nudging my loose shoelace with his nose. I tell my feet to give him a little kick, but of course they don't listen. He raises his leg again and starts pissing all over my white Converse.

I shoot forward, away from the pissing dog, away from my mother who can't stop talking about me as if I'm invisible, away from the stranger who thinks she has a right to know everything about me.

I'm on the road now and my heart's hammering, the adrenaline pumping. Cars roar around me and I know one's coming,

closer

closer

closer.

Brakes screech. I wait for Mum to shout, to come running after me, but none of that happens. Am I already gone?

I look to the right and the car is still. The people inside it are still.

It's silent.

And then . . .

BEEPbeepBEEPbeepBEEP.

The pedestrian light has turned green.

When we get home, Mum unloads the shopping while I throw my shoes away. She has to make three trips because she refuses to use the handles on my wheelchair to hang stuff, like I keep suggesting. I told her she could even put stuff on my lap and use me as a trolley, but she just rolled her eyes again. Not one for disability humour, my mother. My therapist, Dr Sterp, says jokes are a coping mechanism a lot of paraplegics adopt. I almost told him that a better coping mechanism would be death.

Almost.

I'm not an idiot; I know he'd tell Mum right away if I said anything suspicious. Lately our sessions have been filled with him talking about all these *inspirational* wheelchair users and me replying with light-bulb jokes.

'What about Jess Stretton?' he'll say. 'Won gold at archery at the Paralympics when she was your age.'

'How many actors does it take to change a light bulb?' I'll ask.

'She even has an MBE,' he'll say, ignoring me.

'One,' I'll say, ignoring him right back. 'They don't like to share the limelight.'

And so on until I run out of jokes or he runs out of examples.

There's no point trying to tell him that maybe I'm not as good a person as these celebrities. Maybe I'm not destined for great things. Maybe that accident should've been the end of me. He wouldn't understand. No one does.

[. . .]

3. OLIVIA

There's a new photo on the mantelpiece.
It sits directly centre;

the smaller frames   pushed to each side so
there's nothing in the vicinity   of this new addition.

In the photo, Mother's hair is down and curled. Her style of
choice for special occasions: dinner parties,

galas,

dates.

Her smile S T R E T C H E S across the picture.
Her head on *his* shoulder.
His arm wrapped around her.
His fingers digging into her arm.
His mouth forming an easy smile.
I pick up the frame. Run my fingers over the sharp corners.

I want to SLAM it to the ground. To hear the glass

C   A   K
R   C

against the wooden floor, see the tiny pieces splinter

far   and   wide.

I want to take out the photo and *riiiiiiiiiiiiiiiiiip* it to shreds. Set them on fire and **burn** that smile off his face.

'It's beautiful, isn't it?' Mother asks from the doorway.

I place the frame back on the mantelpiece, ensuring it's placed perfectly

> centre
> and
> straight.

'Just lovely,' I tell her.

We sit down for supper. The smell of lobster permeates the room as Maria brings the plates in. It's a special occasion, according to Mother.

He sits at the

H

E

A

D

of the table, <u>*in Daddy's seat.*</u>

I've already had three glasses of champagne. It's a *special occasion* after all.

I'm still not drunk enough.

I can still see straight,
          see the way she l
                    e
                         a
                              n
                                   s into him when he
talks, the way she pushes her food around on the plate, no
doubt still stinging from the comment he made about her
weight last week.

He kisses her on the neck.

I pour another glass.

She giggles. Shoots a glance my way. Reminds him that they've
got company.

Company.

I've lived here my whole life and *I'm* the company.

He looks over at me.

I   my head, focusing on the mush on my plate.
   duck

He suggests she tell me the news.

My head **SNAPS** up.

The champagne hits. Makes my head *spin*.

I force myself to look over at her.

                    Fuzzy-faced,

                              oblivious

                                   Mother.

I ask her what news he's talking about.

To her credit, she looks mildly uncomfortable, fiddling with
her pearl necklace.

He reaches over and squeezes her fingers, that **disgusting**
smile

S P R E A D I N G

across his face.

He encourages her to go on.

She straightens her back.

Clears her throat.

She tells me that they've been dating for a while now.

As if I didn't know.

As if I wasn't aware of the

preposterous

amount of time they've been spending together,

the amount of time *he's* spent in my presence.

She says it's time they **took the next step**.

No.   **No.**

No.   **No.**

No.   **No.**

I look up at her.

Pleading.

Begging.

Wishing.

She proudly tells me the lease on his flat is up.

They've rented a van to bring his stuff over.

Next week.

He looks at me.

Smirks.

Winks.

We're going to be roomies, he tells me.

The glass

S H A T T E R S

                                             in my hand.
Champagne goes everywhere.
                              It's a special occasion after all.
The glass
               CUTS
                          into my fingers.
                          into my palm.
          The sound of cracking glass slices through the silence.
          'Oh, Olivia!' Mother chides. 'That's a crystal flute!'
          'You really should be more careful, Liv,' he says.
LIV.   **He calls me Liv.**
Maria rushes over dutifully, dustpan and brush in hand.
She tries to smile at me as she clears away the mess, but all
I can focus on is the shard of glass in my hand.
     I want to place it against my throat and drag it along
                    s   l   o   w   l   y
To feel my skin slice open.

                                        Y
                                   A
                              R
                         P
To watch the blood   S   P   R   A   Y
                         P
                              R
                                   A
                                        Y   over everything.

[. . .]

HOT KEY BOOKS

Thank you for choosing a Hot Key book.

If you want to know more about our authors and what we publish, you can find us online.

You can start at our website

www.hotkeybooks.com

And you can also find us on:

We hope to see you soon!